To the Readers of Rye

Hereafter

Terri Bruce

◆ **Mictlan Press** ◆

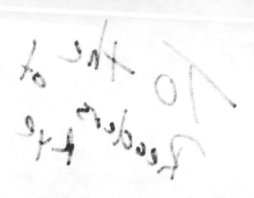

Hereafter (Afterlife #1)
Copyright © 2012, 2014 Terri Bruce

Cover artwork by Shelby Robinson
Cover model Chelsea Howard
Cover design by Michael Ezaky and Jennifer Stolzer

Digital ISBN: 978-0-9913036-1-8
Print ISBN: 978-0-9913036-0-1

Printed in the United States of America
Second Edition

For my Uncle Nelson,
who would be thrilled to have a writer in the family,

and for my mother,
who would not be surprised.

ACKNOWLEDGEMENTS

This book would not have been possible without the support of my friends and family — thank you for sticking with me all these years and cheering me on during this last, mad dash to the finish. We made it!

First and foremost, thank you to my husband and my sister — my heart and soul, respectively. This is your book as much as mine. To my father, who read to me when I was a child, and to my mother, who always bought me as many books as I wanted. To the bestest friend on all the planet — Heather Barrett — who read those first serialized novels I wrote in high school and didn't laugh (at least, not to my face). To the Portsmouth, New Hampshire Public Library for supporting writers and the Portsmouth Library's Writers' Group, especially my mentor Charles Grosky, may he rest in peace — thank you for all the buffeting about adverbs, passive voice, and all of the other travesties new writers commit against the English language. And, finally, thank you to the wonderful women of Broad Universe for their friendship and support — Broads really are the best!

Special thanks for this revised edition go to my editor, Janet Hitchcock at *The Proof is in the Reading*, and of course, the fabulous Shelby Robinson for the amazing artwork that graces this book's cover. Last, but not least, thank you to Anna Erishkigal, Jean Oram, Jennifer Lopez, Kelly Harmon, and the innumerable other authors who held my hand and walked me through the steps necessary to get *Hereafter* back out into the world. I can never thank you all enough.

One

Irene opened her eyes.

Confused, she looked around. Strong sunlight glinted on water, blinding her.

Where the hell am I?

She was standing on the side of a road—by a brown, marshy river. Cars rushed by on the causeway behind her.

No, really, where the hell am I? And more importantly, how did I get here?

Irene racked her brain. For a moment, she drew a blank. Then memory rushed in.

She remembered meeting Alexia and LaRayne at the first bar—a yuppie, after-hours tapas place. There had been a parade of free drinks from cute financial analysts and investment bankers. No question, peach margaritas had played a prominent role.

She remembered the second bar—a euro-trash, wannabe-techno club. Alexia, recently single and on the prowl, had wanted to go dancing. The light reflecting off the beads on LaRayne's flapper-style sheath had looked like flashes of lightning under the strobe lights. Irene was pretty certain Long Island iced teas had made an appearance.

The third bar was a little fuzzier. A serious bar for serious drinkers—more of a roadhouse really, complete with broken jukebox. Possibly…tequila shots.

Then last call and stumbling out of the bar, laughing. Something had been funny.

A short line of taxis bunched together near the door like a school of tropical fish. LaRayne and Alexia had angled toward them, buoyed and jostled by the handful of stumbling drunks and the permanently pickled emptying out of the bar, while Irene continued more or less straight.

"What are we gonna do now?" she asked.

"Are you nuts?" Alexia shouted. "Some of us have to work tomorrow!"

LaRayne added, "Yeah, Monday is a school night for some of us."

They looked like a moving letter A, leaning on each other's shoulders as they walked, their legs moving away at a slight angle from their bodies. With their heads so close together, it was hard to distinguish LaRayne's dark cornrows from the cascade of Alexia's chemically-induced violet-red hair.

"What are you macaroons talking about? I have to get up in the morning, same as you!"

Alexia and LaRayne hooted with laugher, clutching each other to stay upright. "I think you mean *maroon*," Alexia shrieked through gasps of laughter.

"I think you both mean *moron*," LaRayne howled, tears running down her face.

Irene had laughed, too. It was funny. Everything was funny.

As the girls headed for the taxis, Irene kept moving toward the street.

"Yo! Where are you going?" LaRayne called.

Irene didn't stop. "My car."

"Yo, loser. You parked over here, on the other side."

She could hear the howl of the girls' laughter over her own.

"Oh, yeah."

She changed trajectory in a wide, sloppy arc, still plumbing the depths of her handbag for keys.

"You are so wasted!" Alexia screeched over peals of laughter. Irene stumbled past them as they hung onto a taxi's open door. The driver sat in glassy-eyed boredom, waiting for them to get in. "You better ride with us."

"Yo, dim wit. How the hell am I supposed to get to work in the morning without my car?"

That set them all off again. Then LaRayne had shoved Alexia into the cab. "Let's go. I got like four hours until I gotta get up." LaRayne gave Irene one last, sympathetic look over the top of the cab. "You sure you won't come with?" She waited a second, and then she also disappeared into the cab.

Irene remembered all of this. Less clear was what followed: fumbling to unlock the car door; getting in and starting the car; driving away; realizing she had left the driver-side door open and stopping to close it.

She remembered a harvest moon — swollen and heavy — low in the sky. The moon had been straight ahead as the road stretched out before her. Its burnt umber glow had seemed to expand until it blotted out everything else, and the dark line of the road had led straight into its heart. She remembered thinking that it was as if she was driving directly into it.

Then…a yawning pit in the middle of her memory. The next thing she remembered was the world changing. Light had disappeared. Buildings and streets and streetlights had vanished. In their place had been a foaming, swirling mass of green-blue light — light with texture and weight. It moved around the car, crowding it, covering it, filling it. She stared at it, fascinated by its beauty.

It had taken a moment for her to understand.

It wasn't light.

It was water.

Water was pouring in the open window of the car.

There was sinking.

She remembered the sinking.

Then…nothing.

Now she stood on the side of the road, staring at a river as cars rushed by, and it was morning. Her silver BMW was beside her, clean and dry.

She took in her surroundings and instantly recognized where she was. She should—she drove this road twice a day on her way to and from work. She would have had to drive it last night, as well.

I must have fallen asleep at the wheel. I must have dreamed it all.

If that was true, then what had happened after that? Had she slept in her car on the side of the road all night? She didn't remember waking up or getting out of the car. However, she was still wearing her clubbing outfit: a thigh-length, candy-apple red cocktail dress with spaghetti straps and sliver sling backs with four-inch stiletto heels.

She sighed and ran a hand through her hair. Last night pins had held the mahogany-colored strands in a chic updo, but now half of it hung down to her shoulders, loose and tangled. She pulled the rest of the pins out and ran her fingers through it, restoring her usual stylishly tousled look.

She'd had some wild nights before but had never blacked out. Must be another one of those perks of getting older—thirty-six and no longer able to hold her liquor. LaRayne and Alexia would pee themselves laughing when they heard this story.

Irene glanced at her watch and did a double take. "Shit!" Was it really two p.m.? Yes, that was the little hand and that was the big hand and it was indeed two o'clock. She groaned. She was up the creek as far as work was concerned.

Irene rubbed her temple. Surprisingly, her head didn't hurt. She actually felt fine. Stressed, but fine.

What a mess. She wasn't really keen to explain to everyone what had happened. She could just imagine the conversation with her mother:

"Yes, Mom. That's right. I was so shit-faced I passed out in my car on the way home. What does shit-faced mean? It means I drank myself silly. Yes, that's right. I was drunk. Mmm hmmm. That's right. I missed work because I spent the better part of the day sleeping it off. Yes, I was sleeping off a drunk.

No. No, we weren't celebrating anything. No, it wasn't a special occasion. No, I didn't get engaged to anyone. Yes. That's right. You didn't raise me that way. Uh huh. I know, Mom."

She sighed again. Well it was obviously too late to go to work. By the time she got home, showered, changed, and went to the office, it would be time to leave. At least she could use the drive home to think of a good excuse. She had killed off an imaginary uncle for cover last month. The month before had been the story of an emergency hospitalization due to food poisoning. She ran through the list of stories she had used in the last six months to cover over-indulgences—flat tire, the flu, sick mother. Nuts. It looked like alien abduction was the only thing left.

She opened the car door and slipped behind the wheel. At least the keys were still in the ignition.

How did I end up standing by the side of the road?

The engine purred to life. She had been unconsciously holding her breath and now she blew it out in a loud, fast rush. Well, whatever had happened last night, at least she still had the means to get home.

With a quick look over her shoulder, she eased onto the road. Steadying the wheel with one hand, she groped around on the seat beside her with the other. Through random flailing and the occasional removal of her eyes from the road, she managed not only to find her purse but to open it and fish out her cell phone. She held the phone up in front of her and, with one eye on the road and one on the phone, tried to dial Alexia's number. The screen remained stubbornly dark, despite random jabbing of buttons.

No juice.

Frustrated, she snapped the phone shut. She flicked her eyes to the seat beside her just long enough to ensure the tossed phone landed safely. As she lifted her eyes back to the road, the angle of the sun changed, blinding her. She lowered the visor. Well, at least it was a nice day. The Indian summer that had made it possible for her to wear a little nothing of a dress without a sweater or coat in Boston in mid-September seemed to be holding. She frowned. Usually the nights cooled down, though. She was dressed in a short, thin, rayon dress. If she had slept in her car, she would have gotten cold and woken up, wouldn't she?

Date rape scenarios flashed through her mind. All the news stories she had ever heard of strangers slipping women "roofies" melded together in a panic-inducing collage.

Maybe someone had *dumped* her by the side of the road.

A sudden, unexpected movement ahead of her shoved these thoughts aside. Instinct made her slam on the brakes before she was even sure what was happening. The sight of a gray-green Buick cutting in front of her registered and she leaned on the horn while swerving around the slower moving vehicle. She lifted her hand from the horn only long enough to gesture emphatically as she passed the offending driver. The woman, perhaps in her sixties, stared resolutely ahead, refusing to acknowledge her.

"Learn to drive!" Irene yelled, even though the windows were up in both cars. She breathed out hard through her nose as she heard ex-boyfriend-Aaron's voice in her head, *"You know they can't hear you, right?"*

She settled back and focused on the drive home. The nondescript triple-deckers and seedy strip malls of the run-down, blue collar city of Lynn passed in a blur; she crossed into the historic and decidedly nicer Salem and the view improved. Irene continued north for a few more blocks, passing the beautiful Federal-style mansions that populated the historic district, and then turned off the main street into a neighborhood of modest but well-maintained 1950s era Cape Cod-style homes.

As her driveway came into view, Irene felt both relief and dread. She still felt disoriented and vaguely out-of-sorts, and she hadn't figured out what she was going to say to her boss, Donna.

She mentally shrugged as she turned off the engine. "Oh, well. Fuck it."

Shower first, then the firing squad.

She climbed out of the car and surveyed the yard for any signs of the neighbor's dog. "Kitty," the hairy little rat, had made her life hell since Jamaica had adopted him a year ago. The Jack Russell terrier raised ankle biting to an art form. He had learned how to jump like a pogo-stick, which gave him enough height to clear the chain-link fence that both encircled and divided the white duplex's back yard.

Kitty was usually napping in the grass around the time Irene arrived home each night. The moment she pulled into the driveway, he would jerk to his feet and start yapping for all he was worth as he bounced higher and higher. Every night it was a race to see if Irene could scramble through her front door before Kitty gained the height to clear the fence. If only she could find a way to poison the wretched little thing without Jamaica finding out.

She was in luck. The yard was empty. It was still early afternoon and Jamaica wasn't home yet. Which meant Kitty was locked safely in the house.

"What the...?" She almost fell over the large stack of mail that lay in wait for her behind the front door. In fact, she had to step sideways into the front hall to get around it. She gave the door an absent-minded shove to close it as she surveyed the mess. This appeared to be a week's worth of mail. Was the mailman on a bender again?

With a sigh, she waded through the debris, not really sure what to make of it. She'd deal with it later—just as she'd deal with her boss.

She stopped in the bright, airy foyer to drop her keys onto the console table and leaned down to pull off her shoes, balancing with one hand against the wall.

She pulled off each shoe in turn and tossed it onto the hardwood floor and then followed the short, narrow hall straight back to the kitchen.

Irene tossed her purse onto the table, unbuckled her watch and necklace, and tossed them on top. She got a glass from the cupboard and mixed herself a gin and tonic. She glanced at the blinking light on the answering machine and did a double take. *Fourteen messages?* How could she possibly have fourteen messages since last night?

She checked the caller I.D. Sure enough, dozens of missed calls. Alexia. Work. LaRayne. Alexia. Work. Work. Work. Alexia. Her mother.

She hit play.

"I hope your headache is as big as mine," Alexia said the first time, in the subdued voice of one with a throbbing hangover.

The first message from her boss contained irritation. "Irene, it's past ten. Wondering if you're coming in today."

LaRayne's message was simply, "You are the devil."

"Yo! What the fuck? Where are you?" There was no real anger in Alexia's second message, just mock indignation. "Been trying work and the cell all day. Please do *not* tell me you called in sick. I dragged *my* ass out of bed this morning. Not cool!"

Her boss's tone had changed to concern by her third message. "Irene, I hope everything is okay. I'm really worried since I haven't heard from you. Please call me as soon as you can."

Confusion almost hid the regular absent-minded vagueness in her mother's frail voice. "Irene? This is your mother. Somebody from your work called asking if you were okay. Well...call me, I guess."

The last message was also from her mother. "Irene...I do wish you'd call." Her mother sounded both worried and annoyed.

Unease prickled under Irene's skin. She took a long swallow of her drink. She had planned to take a nice, long bath, but she should probably check on her mother first. She headed back down the hall, intending to go upstairs and change her clothes, but the sight of mail cascading through the mail slot brought her to a halt.

"What the...?"

The mailman had clearly already been by once today. What was he doing back again? Setting her drink absently on the hall table, she slipped and slid her way through the pond of mail to the front door and wrenched it open. The front stair was empty. She stepped out and looked around. The mailman was casually making his way down the street.

"Hey!" she shouted, but he continued unabated. She started down the steps and then realized her feet were bare. She turned to go back into the house but paused, mid-step. Something seemed out of place. She scanned the driveway, Jamaica's yard, the street. Then she looked up. The sun was shining brightly overhead, as if it was mid-day, even though it must be late afternoon. She was no Galileo, but even she knew that at this time of year the sun should be much nearer to the horizon.

She ran back into the house, searching for a clock. She started toward the living room, remembered the microwave had a clock, and changed directions toward the kitchen.

She stared at the unwavering blue numbers, glowing iridescently against the black of the microwave with rising panic.

Eleven o'clock? How could that be? It was two o'clock when I woke up in the car.

She paused — no, that wasn't right. She hadn't woken up *in* her car. She had woken up *beside* it.

That couldn't be, either. Maybe she had pulled over to be sick. Maybe she had thrown up and then passed out right there on the side of the heavily trafficked main drag that was pretty much the only way into Boston from here.

How had no one seen her or stopped to help or call the police?

The date rape scenario flashed through her mind again.

Her heart began to pound. She tried to quash the rising panic. *Get a grip*, she told herself.

She went through the house, looking for her watch. She found it on the kitchen table.

Two o'clock, it insisted.

She shook it and then held it up to her ear.

Nothing.

"Crap," she said aloud, her shoulders drooping with relief. The watch was broken.

She probably would have had enough time to get to work after all. She pursed her lips in frustration, feeling stupid. "Double crap."

A niggling bubble of doubt floated to the surface. *What about all the voicemails?* Donna had called three times and her mother twice, all before eleven a.m.? That didn't sound right. Plus, there was the mail.

She shook her head. No. No way. This had to be a joke.

It had to be

She left the kitchen and sprinted up the stairs to the bedroom. Carelessly, her movements frenzied, she pulled clothes out of drawers and changed her clubbing dress for a T-shirt and a pair of jeans. She shoved her feet into a pair of flip-flops and fled for the front door. She only just managed to remember her house keys before closing the door behind her. She walk-jogged the four blocks to her mother's house with grim determination, keeping all speculation and worry tightly suppressed.

When the mustard-yellow aluminum siding of her childhood home came into view, she suddenly felt foolish and thought about turning around and marching straight home. What, exactly, had frightened her? What was so scary about a lot of voicemails and a big stack of mail?

She worried her lip with her teeth for a second. Well, since she was here, she might as well check on her mother.

Irene skirted the front of the house, heading for the back door. Some leftover teenage resentment made her avoid the hated front door to this day. She remembered her angry flood of tears when she'd seen it and the matching shutters the day her father had brought them home. She had been twelve.

"Why can't we have white? Brown and yellow? Together? It looks like dog poo."

"That's enough out of you. Why don't you go to your room until you cool off," her father had said in that gentle, unruffled, authoritarian way of his. Disguised as a suggestion, it was, nonetheless, a command. She'd flopped down on her bed in a sulk that had lasted for a week, until it had faded away to join the stock of smoldering resentments she had cherished throughout her adolescent years.

Irene glanced absently at the yard. The last of her fear evaporated, replaced by long-standing exasperation. The grass needed mowing. She sighed.

Ever since Irene's father had died ten years ago, her mother had not been able to keep up with the yard or the maintenance on the house — or, for that matter, day-to-day requirements, like paying the bills on time. Weeds sprouted up through cracks in the asphalt driveway and the paint around one of the Cape's dormers was peeling badly. Irene had concerns about the condition of the roof, too.

People had started to notice the neglect. Nice Mr. MacKenzie next door had taken to trimming the grass whenever an aura of abandonment pervaded her mother's house and that helped — at least, with all things lawn related.

It wasn't enough, though, and her mother wouldn't let Irene hire someone to help. "Oh don't fuss so, Irene. I'm fine," her mother said every time Irene brought it up. What she really meant was she wanted Irene to do it. Irene didn't understand the logic — it was better that it didn't get done than to have a stranger do it? She suspected her mother thought Irene had a lot of free time on her hands, time she was greedily keeping to herself.

What else did the woman want? Irene had given up her apartment in Boston because it had been too hard to make the daily trips back and forth that were necessary in order to take care of everything that had fallen on her to do. There was only one Irene to go around and not enough hours in the day to do everything.

Irene pulled out her back door key, but as usual, it wasn't necessary. Lately, her mother had taken to forgetting, among all the other things, to lock the back door. It sprang open when Irene twisted the knob. She sighed again and stepped into the house, rapping on the door as she entered. "Mom?"

Irene crossed through the kitchen that time forgot: teal-blue kitchen, Barbie-pink bathroom, and all the modern conveniences and kaleidoscope colors of the post-war era.

Irene found her mother in the living room, as expected. However, she was on the phone instead of watching TV. Something serious must have happened. It was time for "the soaps" and someone had to be dying for her mother to miss "her shows," as she called them. Good God, had someone died? That would account for all the phone calls.

Irene rapped on the living room doorframe to get her mother's attention.

"Hey," she said in a subdued voice, not wanting to interrupt the phone call. Her mother didn't seem to notice. Irene stepped forward and stood right in front of her.

Deborah looked at her lap, twisting the phone cord between nervous fingers. "No, nobody's heard from her."

Irene reached out and tapped her mother's shoulder. "Mom?"

No acknowledgement.

"Well, Irene can be thoughtless…"

"Hey! I'm standing right here."

"…but she would never go away without telling me," Deborah continued, as if Irene hadn't spoken.

"Mom?" Irene's voice faltered. "Mom?" She leaned down so she was eye level with her mother. Still, her mother didn't look at her.

"Mom? Give me the phone." Irene reached out and tugged the phone out of her mother's hand. Deborah made a wild grab and pulled it back.

"Hello? Are you still there? Oh, I'm so sorry. I just dropped the phone. It just slid right out of my hand."

"What? No, Mom, that was me!" Irene clamped a tight lid on her rising fear and confusion. She needed to call Aunt Betty. Something had clearly happened to her mother. A stroke, maybe? An aneurysm? Something. No, not Aunt Betty — nine-one-one.

Wait, does this constitute an emergency? Her mother wasn't bleeding or unconscious.

Irene gave herself a mental shake. She wasn't thinking clearly. She could drive her mother to the emergency room—Salem Hospital was just down the road.

"Okay, Mom, stay here. I'm going to go get my car and I'll be right back. I'm going to get you to a doctor."

She ran across the living room, flung open the front door, and raced down the stairs. Her flip-flops slapped the sidewalk as she pounded down the street.

Two

Irene's heart raced. She was running blind, without any other thought than to get her mother to the emergency room. Suddenly, as if out of nowhere, a boy appeared in her path. She veered around him, intending to continue on, but something about him made her skid to a halt. She turned around to look at him and realized he was staring at her, his face a mask of astonishment, his mouth hanging open.

"Hey kid, watch where you're going," she said, more confused than annoyed.

He was maybe fourteen and nearly as tall as her, at that "beanpole" stage, as her grandmother had called it—the tall and scrawny look of one growing too fast. The little bit of his face visible under a curtain of straw-colored hair was pointed and sharp—cheekbones, chin, and nose. His hair, cut in an asymmetrical bob that left it longer in the front than the back, was parted on the side and hung in his face, concealing his left eye. Somehow, the way one washed-out hazel eye was visible and the other hidden reminded her of Pete, the dog from the *Little Rascals*.

She realized he hadn't moved a muscle and was still staring at her gape-mouthed.

"Did you hear me?" she asked.

He gave a little shake of his head, as if he was doing a double take. The motion caused the curtain of hair hanging over his eyes to sway. "Yeeesss," he said in a slow, cautious, drawn-out way.

"Why are you staring at me?"

"Well, it's just, because...you know. You're..." He trailed off.

Irene narrowed her eyes. "I'm what?"

The boy turned beet red and took a step back, giving a hard gulp that made Irene fear he had swallowed his tongue. "Well...dead," he stuttered.

Irene looked around sharply, scanning in both directions. She expected to see kids jumping out at her with squirt guns. It sounded like the kind of thing they'd do. They would soak her and shout, "Ha ha, got you! You're dead."

Only there was nowhere to jump out from. There weren't any trees or parked cars here, only Mr. MacKenzie's lawn, cut with Stepford-like precision, in one direction and the Robella's confusion of flowers, which had progressed from neat raised beds to tangled jungle over the years, in the other.

Irene turned back to the boy and looked him up and down with a critical eye. He didn't look like a troublemaker—he was dressed neatly in khakis, a long-sleeved T-shirt, and sneakers. The exposed wrists and ankles—the telltale signs of a boy growing too fast for his clothes—and the dusting of freckles across his nose helped to cement an air of vulnerability and sincerity. She pursed her lips.

"Okay, you know what, smart ass? I'm having a bit of a personal emergency at the moment—my mother is having a stroke or something. You might want to remember that next time you decide to try and play a joke on someone." She turned away, ready to move on, but his voice, vibrating with hurt, stopped her.

"It's not a joke. You've got the...the...aura, like the book said. That means you're dead."

"I what?" Irene's voice rose in disbelief. Reflexively, she looked down at herself. There did seem to be a faint flicker around her, a pearly blue-white, sparkling like faded opals. Her heart began to beat faster. She spun around.

"What the...? Did you put something on me?"

He blinked at her, surprise opening up his face, and his mouth formed an *O* again. "So you don't know that you're dead? Huh."

"I'm *not* dead!" she cried, throwing up her hands again. "Stop saying that."

Some of his surprise seemed to have worn off and now he studied Irene with relaxed interest, seeming to assess her much the same way she was assessing him. He balanced on one leg and scratched the back of it with the sneakered-toe of his other foot. "I'm really sorry," he said, and he really did sound sorry.

For some reason, his sympathy frightened her more than anything else. She backed away, shaking her head in disbelief. Then she whirled away from him and fled, racing for home.

Behind her, she heard the sound of sneakers slapping pavement. She looked over her shoulder and saw the boy, at an unhurried pony-trot, following her.

She slowed as she approached her driveway. The boy came to a halt beside her.

"Stop following me," she said, unafraid but exasperated, as if speaking to a stray dog. Somehow the scrawny, pale, interested boy was about as frightening as toothpaste.

"Car accident, huh? That sucks."

She stared at him. He was studying her house and yard with the same rapt fascination with which he had regarded her.

"What? What are you talking about?" However, as she glanced at her car, she could see that it had the same pearly blue glow that seemed to surround her.

The boy shook his head. "I'm sorry," he said again.

"I'm not dead!" she shouted in exasperation, but her heart was thumping uncertainly.

Then how did you end up on the side of the road? a small voice inside her head asked.

He frowned at her. "You didn't kill yourself did you?" he asked doubtfully. "I heard how you can kill yourself by sticking a hose from the tailpipe into the car —"

"Of course I didn't kill myself. Jesus!" She shot him a look of deep disgust. "And I'm not dead." Despite her words, the sinking feeling in the pit of her stomach worsened as she looked at her hands and arms again, confirming that the weird glow was still there.

Something dark in the grass of Jamaica's yard caught her eye. Kitty was lying with his head cushioned on his front paws, a droopy, depressed look on his face. Jamaica must be home.

Squaring her shoulders and shooting the boy another look of reproach, she marched up Jamaica's front walk. "I'll prove it," she said, more to herself than to him.

Kitty's ears perked up and he jumped to his feet, watching Irene. He gave a small, inquisitive growl and thumped his tail again. Irene mounted the steps and rang the bell. Kitty followed her movements with interest. As the doorbell chimed, he let out a short bark and his tail began to wag furiously.

A sound behind her made her turn her head. The boy had followed her up the stairs.

"Why are you following me?"

He shrugged. "I dunno. You seem kinda…lost. Like you might need some help."

"Well I don't, so go away. Shoo!"

He retreated to the sidewalk. Irene rang the bell again.

"Coming!" Jamaica called from inside.

The boy was still there, watching her.

"What are you doing?" she asked.

"I want to see what happens." His tone intimated that he was expecting it to be something, if not exactly bad, at least interesting and possibly quite amusing.

Irene sputtered incoherently. The door opened, interrupting anything she might say.

Jamaica frowned and then leaned past Irene to look in both directions, calling out, "Hello?"

Irene waved a hand in front of Jamaica's narrow, angular face. "Jamaica! Can you hear me? Hello?"

Kitty barked again and turned in a small circle, quivering with excitement.

Jamaica stepped back, as if preparing to shut the door. Irene heard her mutter, "Odd" under her breath. Without thinking, Irene put a hand to the door to stop Jamaica from closing it.

"I don't think you should do that," she heard the boy say.

Jamaica frowned at the stuck door. She pushed harder, trying to force it past the resistance. Irene stood firm, holding the door with both hands. "Jamaica," she pleaded, "come on, you have to be able to hear me."

Jamaica pulled the door open again and Irene's heart leaped, but Jamaica only peered at the front of the door, looked down at the threshold, and then tried to shut it again. Irene pushed back even harder, trying to wedge the door open enough to slip into the house. As soon as she put a foot over the threshold, Kitty let loose with a rapid-fire burst of high-pitched, staccato yapping like machine-gun fire. He launched himself at the fence, barking furiously.

Jamaica yanked the door open. "Kitty, stop that! Stop it!" She bolted down the stairs. "Kitty! Naughty! No!"

Kitty ignored her, keeping his eyes on Irene and barking non-stop.

Irene used the distraction to slip into the house. A few seconds later, the boy followed.

"What are you doing?" Irene cried. "You're trespassing!"

"So are you," he said hotly.

"She's *my* neighbor."

"I don't think that makes any —" he started to say but Jamaica returned, holding Kitty with a finger and thumb clamped around the dog's mouth like a muzzle. She didn't seem to notice either Irene or the boy. As Jamaica shut the door with her foot, Kitty whimpered and stretched out a tiny paw to Irene.

"What a bad boy you are today," Jamaica scolded indulgently, dropping Kitty to the floor.

Irene backed away, expecting Kitty to lunge for her ankles. Instead, he seemed puzzled. He plunked down on his haunches and stared at Irene, emitting bewildered whimpers and turning his head to cast Jamaica intermittent, inquisitive looks.

"What?" Jamaica asked. "No, you can't have a treat. You're a bad boy."

With the boy trailing behind, Irene followed Jamaica down the hall to the kitchen. Something was cooking on the stove in a large pot and Jamaica went to stir it.

Irene glanced around, trying to find some way of getting Jamaica's attention. She grabbed a pen from the counter and used it to scrawl the words "Jamaica, it's Irene. I need your help" on a nearby pad of paper.

The boy let out a squawk of alarm. "I *really* don't think you should do that."

"No one asked you," she retorted.

His ears turned pink and he ducked his head, causing the curtain of blond hair to fall across his face.

Irene waited until Jamaica was rummaging in the refrigerator to slip the note onto the counter near the stove. Then she held her breath.

A moment later, she watched in exasperation as the paper, propelled by the breeze of Jamaica's movements, fluttered unnoticed to the floor. Irene gritted her teeth, retrieved the note, and set it back on the counter. This time, Jamaica set a package of raw meat on top of the paper, effectively ruining it. A few minutes later, the note, plastered to the bottom of the now empty meat packaging, went into the trash.

Irene scrawled the same message on another piece of paper and held it in front of herself at chin level. She stood behind Jamaica, waiting for her to turn away from the counter where she was now chopping vegetables.

"You don't give up easily, do you?" The boy was watching Irene's efforts with a look somewhere between incredulous and amused.

"Quitters never win," she replied.

"I thought that was cheaters."

"Whatever. It works for both."

It seemed like Jamaica was never going to turn around. She lifted her head a couple of times, as if catching something out of the corner of her eye, but then went back to what she was doing.

Finally Jamaica did turn around, holding the cutting board loaded with cut food in one hand and the knife in the other. She walked to the stove and, using the knife as a scraper, began sliding the meat and vegetables from the cutting board into the pot. Suddenly she stiffened and whipped around, as if sensing someone behind her. She let out an ear-piercing shriek.

Some instinct made Irene take a step back and then duck. At the same instant, the boy cried out in alarm and scrambled backwards. Vegetables, meat, cutting board, and even the knife flew through the air like a volley of arrows, passing through the spot where Irene had stood only a moment before, and pelted the cabinets behind her.

"Holy shit!" Irene bolted for the door. She ran down the front steps and then raced next door to the safety of her own home. The boy was right behind her and followed her into the house before she could stop him. She slammed the door shut behind them and leaned against it, trying to catch her breath. Every few seconds she pulled back the curtain and peeked out the sidelight to see if Jamaica had followed her. However, outside all was still. No one was in sight.

The boy appeared to be dumbstruck. He stared at her, his eyes were wide and his mouth hanging open.

"So...that was kinda crazy," he said finally.

"I didn't see you doing anything to help," she said angrily. "Now start talking. What is going on?"

His expression changed to one of nervousness. He shifted uneasily from foot to foot. "Look, I gotta go..."

"Oh no you don't." She grabbed him by the arm. "In here." She dragged him across the hall and thrust him into the living room.

"Hey! HEY!" The boy flailed his stick-thin arms in protest. "This is accosting a minor. You can't do that."

Irene let him go, suppressing a smile as she did so. "I'm pretty sure there's no such crime as accosting a minor. Now talk. Who are you?"

The boy pushed his hair out of his eyes and peered around the room. "Jonah, Jonah Johnson. I live a few blocks from here." He turned in place, taking in everything. "I like your couch."

"So why do you keep saying that I'm dead?"

He looked at her, one eyebrow raised. "You're glowing and no one can see or hear you. That sounds like a ghost to me."

"A ghost?" She didn't like the sound of that, but he seemed sincere. It would certainly explain everything that had been happening to her. She looked him up and down again, almost ready to believe him. "Wait a minute...you don't glow. Are you a ghost?"

He suddenly looked furtive, his eyes dropping to the floor. "No."

"Then how come you can see me?"

"Er...well, that's kinda complicated..."

"Ha! That's what I thought," she said triumphantly. "Nice try, kid. You're obviously some kind of delinquent. I don't know if this is just for kicks or what, but I'm calling the police." She headed for the kitchen.

"Hey," he cried, trailing after her. "I'm an honor student!"

"That doesn't mean you're not a delinquent."

"Huh," she heard him say, "I wonder if they have police in the land of the dead." His voice deepened in an imitation of a television announcer: "Cops Undead: Miami." Then it rose back to his normal pitch. "That would be cool!"

Irene crossed into the kitchen and picked up the phone. "We'll see how much of a smart ass you are when they're threatening to throw you in juvie hall."

"For what? I didn't do anything."

"Then start talking."

"I told you…"

Irene paused in the middle of dialing the phone, waiting for him to finish the sentence. The silence stretched out. She turned around. The hall was empty.

"Jonah?" Irene moved back down the hall peering into the other rooms and calling his name. "Jonah? This isn't funny." It only took a minute to realize that he was nowhere to be found. She was alone. The boy was gone.

Three

The gin and tonic she had mixed earlier was still on the hall table. She grabbed it and drained the glass in one long swallow.

"Okay, think, Irene." The sound of her voice was reassuring in the silence. With the boy gone, the house suddenly seemed incredibly empty. "Think. There has got to be a logical explanation for all of this." She thought about that last sentence. "Okay, a logical reason other than being dead."

A boy who disappears into thin air...the inability of anyone to see or hear me...waking up on the side of the road.

She bit her lip, contemplating options. Other than the whole "being dead" thing, she couldn't think of a single thing that would explain what was happening to her.

What if she was dead? What then?

No, she refused to believe that. There had to be something else going on. There was no way she could be dead.

Think! she told herself. She needed help. How was she going to get it?

She could always go back and leave a note for Jamaica to find—by the bed or in the living room, perhaps—but what would be the point? The whole idea had been stupid from the beginning. What did she actually want Jamaica to do? How was Jamaica—or anyone she might try to contact—

supposed to fix whatever was wrong with her if she herself didn't know what the problem was or how to fix it?

A heavy, dull ache began gnawing at the pit of her stomach. She went to the kitchen and mixed another drink, pausing to take a swig of gin straight from the bottle for good measure before putting it away. The greasy, scalding burn of the straight gin was like a dash of cold water to the face and momentarily subdued the rising panic.

She downed half the glass in one gulp and began to feel like she was in control again. She set the glass down and looked at her hands and arms and then at her torso and legs. The glow extended all around her body. She noticed the occasional odd flash of light when she moved suddenly, like sunlight reflecting on a mirror.

Could I really be dead?

She put a hand to her chest. How could she be dead when she could feel her heart beating, her chest rising and falling as she breathed, her skin growing clammy from fear?

Besides, when you died, wasn't there supposed to be a white light and a tunnel, then Heaven? She racked her brain, trying to remember everything she knew about life after death. What was it the boy had said — something about this being "the land of the dead" and that she was a ghost?

What about him, then? He'd said he wasn't a ghost but clearly Jamaica hadn't been able to see him, and he had just disappeared into thin air. Maybe he was the one who was dead and didn't know it. Maybe he was the cause of all of this.

What about the mail and all the voicemails, the little voice asked. Irene shook her head as if she could physically dislodge the thought.

She wasn't sure what to do next. The house was quiet and still. She felt the thick, gathered pause pushing around her. Irene shivered. She crossed her upper arms, trying to smooth away the sudden goose bumps. How could she get goose bumps if she was dead?

She grabbed her drink again. Just at that moment, the phone rang, causing her to jump. Her drink crashed to the floor. She stared at the phone stupidly, and then, recognizing LaRayne's phone number on the caller I.D., she grabbed the receiver.

"LaRayne?"

"Irene?"

"Yes, it's me!" Relief flooded through her. LaRayne could hear her!

There was a pause and then LaRayne said, "Hello?"

"LaRayne? Can you hear me?"

"Hello? Irene?"

Relief fizzled away. Disappointment washed over her, so strong her knees buckled and she grabbed the counter for support.

The line went dead. LaRayne had hung up.

Slowly, Irene replaced the receiver, numb with shock.

The phone rang again. Irene let the answering machine pick up this time.

"Hey, Irene. It's LaRayne...I've left you some messages...well...you know...call or whatever."

Irene cleaned up the spilled drink, sweeping the broken glass into a dustpan and dumping it in the trash, and then mixed herself another. She wandered back to the hall and then back to the kitchen and finally to the living room where she dropped heavily onto the couch. She sipped her drink, not really tasting it. Then she spied her laptop across the room on a chair. She fetched it, firing it up with mounting excitement.

Email. Yes, that's it – email. I'll email everyone and tell them what happened, she thought through a fog of mounting hysteria.

Even as she thought it, dully watching the computer scroll through start-up screens, the "drunk emailing" incident of a few years ago—which had led to then-boyfriend Chase becoming ex-boyfriend Chase—came to mind. The part of her that was still thinking rationally pointed out that maybe it wasn't such a good idea to email anyone until she knew for certain what exactly was going on.

You still don't know what you want anyone to do, she thought. Call a doctor? Perform an exorcism? What, exactly, was the remedy here?

She stared blankly at the computer screen. After thinking hard for a moment, she launched the Internet browser and typed "life after death" into the search field. Excellent! Now she was getting somewhere.

The next thing she knew, she was blinking awake. Daylight streamed through the windows. She sat up, disoriented. Then the previous day's events came flooding back.

Searching the Internet had been a gigantic waste of time, revealing hundreds of websites on near-death experiences, none of which resembled, in the least, her current reality. The only thing she had learned was that almost universally everyone saw a white light, a tunnel, and even angels — except her. That seemed like an indicator that she maybe wasn't dead after all.

She groaned in frustration. She was no closer to finding an answer, and she had no idea what to do next.

She stood up, her muscles, cramped after a night on the couch, protesting. She groaned again, this time from pain. She stretched muzzily, still not quite awake. On autopilot, she shuffled upstairs and brushed her teeth. She avoided looking in the mirror — she wasn't really interested in its perspective on the situation. She wasn't given to histrionics, but if she looked in it and didn't see a reflection she would be forced to freak out.

She climbed into the shower. She stood under the water, letting it run over her for a long time, her mind heavy and blank. She had no idea what to do next. Everything seemed so…uncertain.

As she rubbed shampoo soothingly through her hair, a thought came to her.

I can't be the only dead person around. Not that I'm dead, she amended, *but if I am…there must be others.*

She finished her shower in a rush, jumped out, and hastily threw on some clothes — barely pausing to dry off. She stopped just long enough to run a comb through her hair then sprinted for the front door where she slipped and slid through the lake of mail in the hall before emerging outside.

Irene hesitated at the end of the walkway, unsure which way to go. She knew the neighborhood well — after all, she had grown up here — but she'd never gone ghost hunting before.

She thought for a moment and then struck out in the opposite direction of her mother's house, reasoning that she hadn't noticed any ghost along that route yesterday. Her stomach swirled with a mixture of excitement and anxiety.

As she walked, she could see jarring deviations from her childhood memories. The Bassetts had erected a swing set in their yard. The Gunds had cut down the giant maple tree. She couldn't remember how many times Mrs. Gund had chased her and Becky out of that tree with a broom. Fresh sawdust ringed the massive stump, which looked raw and out of place, and laid bare the bay window, protruding from the front of the house like a wart.

The Woodburys had painted their house green. Irene raised a hand in greeting as she passed Mrs. Woodbury watering her lawn. Mrs. Woodbury didn't wave back. Irene let her hand fall, her buoyant mood suddenly evaporating.

A few blocks later, her spirits lifted again when she saw, approaching from the opposite direction, a distinguished-looking man wearing an old-fashioned three-piece suit — the jacket reaching nearly to his knees — complete with waistcoat, pocket watch, and top hat. A faint blue glow surrounded him, and when she waved, he inclined his head ever so slightly to acknowledge her. He didn't stop, however, and as he passed, the sound of his ebony walking stick striking the pavement at regular intervals faded into the distance.

Everyone else on the street took no notice of her.

Irene made a loop around the neighborhood, eventually circling back to her mother's house. Across the street, her old babysitter, Mrs. Boine—whom Irene, as a girl, had delighted in torturing by purposely mispronouncing her name so that it sounded like "bone" —was sitting on her patio, shaded by a palatial table umbrella. Her ample figure was clad in a vivid muumuu—what she always referred to as a "housecoat" —of shockingly bright shades of purple and pink. Her short, straight, iron-gray hair looked the same as it had when Irene was a kid.

Irene raised a hand in automatic greeting. To her surprise, Mrs. Boine waved back. Irene's heart lurched then broke into a gallop. She darted across the street.

"Mrs. Boine?"

"Well, hello there, Irene! How are you, dear?" Mrs. Boine's eyes, watery and blue behind her eyeglasses, lit up with delight. She had a flyswatter across her lap, like a scepter, and, with the Robin's egg blue of the tiny bungalow behind her and the assorted children's toys scattered around the yard like pebbles, she reminded Irene of the staged portraits of English royalty.

"You can see me?" Irene clutched the waist-high slats of the white picket fence with both hands.

"As clear as day. Same as you can see me." Mrs. Boine said this as if it was the most ordinary thing in the world.

Irene went limp as the tension drained out of her. "Oh thank God!" She sagged against the fence, holding onto it for support.

"You're not going...to...believe..." Irene trailed off. "Mrs. Boine, would it sound crazy if I said that it...well, it looked like you were sort of...glowing?"

Mrs. Boine burst forth with a thin, high-pitched peal of laughter. Irene tried to swallow the lump of mounting dread that had risen to the back of her throat. "Mrs. Boine? Can I ask...are you...dead?"

The old lady laughed again. "Well, I've been dead every day for the last two years, so I suppose I still am."

Irene's hands clenched on the fence, the wood digging into her hands. "What? When did that happen? Mom never said anything."

The old lady waved a hand in the air. "Oh, well, a lot of fuss and bother about nothing."

Irene felt a twinge of dismay. *How could I not know?*

Behind her, she heard the muffler of a passing car rattle as the car hit a large pothole.

"Damnation!" the old woman cried. "Will they ever fix that?" Then she seemed to recollect herself and added, "Excuse my French." She waved her hand again, this time beckoning Irene forward. "Why don't you come on in and take a load off. Visit for a while. I'd love a bit of company."

Not sure what else to do, Irene accepted the offer. She stepped through the gate and started forward. "Oh, close the gate, dear. It drives my daughter crazy when it's left open. She always blames the girls."

Irene latched the gate and then took a seat. She settled herself on the edge of a brown and maroon striped cushion and braced her arms, hands on knees. She wanted to ask a million questions at once and wasn't sure where to start.

"I can't say I'm surprised to see you here," Mrs. Boine said companionably. "I knew something was going on. The police were at your mother's house a few days ago, but since I didn't see an ambulance or nothing, I knew it wasn't anything to do with her."

Irene blinked. "A few days ago? What do you mean?"

Mrs. Boine clucked in sympathy. "Oh well, it's a shock at first." She patted Irene's knee. "So what happened? Not drugs, I hope."

"No, of course not!" Irene had forgotten that Mrs. Boine had a flare for the lurid. "Nothing happened. I was out with my girlfriends just last night."

Mrs. Boine patted Irene's knee again. "It isn't anything to be ashamed of, Irene. It's got to happen to us all sooner or later."

Irene felt numb, not sure how to feel about Mrs. Boine's words. She watched impassively as a car slowly trundled down the narrow street, swerving unsuccessfully to avoid the pothole. A scraping sound accompanied the rattling of the muffler.

Mrs. Boine twitched with irritation. "Damnation!"

29

Irene sighed. "I don't understand. Suppose we are dead. Isn't there supposed to be a tunnel or a white light or something? You know, angels and harps and all that? Where's Heaven?"

Mrs. Boine held up her hands in self-defense. "Hold on, hold on. Goodness gracious, Irene. You always did get so worked up about things."

"I'm not worked up!" Irene cried.

Mrs. Boine reached out and patted Irene's hand. "There, there," she said, as if Irene were six. Irene felt a long-ago teenage need to grind her teeth, stamp her feet, and slam doors welling up within her.

"Don't I always tell you that things will work out? And don't they always manage to find a way to?"

Irene bit back the scathing retort that sprang to her lips. With as much self-control as she could muster, she said instead, "Okay, fine, you're right. I'm not panicking. See? I'm fine."

Mrs. Boine smiled in delight. "That's my girl. Such a trooper. Didn't even cry when your dad died. Oh, I remember that day like it was yesterday. Such a sad day. You were so brave, supporting your mum and all—"

Irene had no interest in revisiting that particular memory, so she cut in, saying, "Okay, so tell me this: where are all the dead people? Shouldn't this place be wall to wall dead people?"

At that moment, the front door of Mrs. Boine's house opened and two little girls in long pigtails pelted down the stairs, leaving the door hanging ajar.

"Grandma, Grandma," they cried, tumbling across the lawn, "push us! Push us!"

"Oh, they want their buggies," Mrs. Boine said, her face going soft with fond indulgence.

Each girl threw herself onto a three-wheeled toy—the preschooler version of a tricycle—and continued to cry for Mrs. Boine like a chorus of baby birds at feeding time.

"Okay, I'm coming." The old woman heaved herself out of her chair.

Before she could reach the children, though, the silhouette of a woman appeared in the open front door of the house. "Girls? What are you doing? Get in here."

"Grandma's going to push us!" the girls cried in unison.

"You know you're not allowed in the yard when I'm not there. Get in here this instant!"

The girls reluctantly complied, climbing off the "buggies" and dragging themselves back to the house, whining, begging, and pleading the entire way. The front door closed with a decided snap.

With a heavy grunt, Mrs. Boine reseated herself. Irene gave her an inquiring look. The old lady beamed. "My grandbabies."

"They can see you?"

"See? No, but they know I'm here."

"How do you know they know you're here?"

Mrs. Boine didn't seem in the least bothered by the incredulity in Irene's voice. "They talk to me and leave me little presents. See here..." She drew a wilted dandelion from her pocket and held it up for Irene's inspection, beaming as if it were a lump of gold. "I tuck them in and sing them to sleep every night. Oh, they know I'm here alright."

"What about your daughter?"

Mrs. Boine set the flower down and then waved a dismissive hand, her smile disappearing under a heavy-browed frown. "Oh, Gloria was always too stubborn by half. Thinks the girls have too much *imagination*." She said the word as if it were something catching. "It's a damn shame how the living only see what they want to see, but that's life, I suppose."

Mr. MacKenzie appeared in his yard, closely inspecting his lawn and seeming not to like what he saw. Mrs. Boine raised a hand in greeting. "Yooo-hooo!" she called. Mr. MacKenzie didn't notice.

Mrs. Boine dropped her hand with a wistful sigh. "That man," she said with a regretful shake of her head, as if she deeply pitied Mr. MacKenzie.

Irene was still thinking of Mrs. Boine's daughter. "Well, can't you just write Gloria a note or something? Provide irrefutable proof that you're still here?"

Mrs. Boine looked at Irene over the rim of her glasses. "Let me give you some advice, dear. Don't upset the living and they won't upset you."

Irene shook her head. "There has to be a way to make people believe that we're here. I can't believe that I'm just...stuck. That I...I just have to hang around...*forever*...doing nothing."

Mrs. Boine gave Irene another disapproving look. "There's plenty to be doin'. Who's gonna watch over your mother now that you're gone?"

"My mother is just going to have to learn to take care of herself for once," Irene snapped without thinking and then instantly wished she could take back the words.

Mrs. Boine's face twisted in an affronted pucker. "Oh, well...if you don't have anything to keep you here, then I suppose you'll be going off to the city to live again...or going off to look for your angels and harps and whatnots."

"Well, if there's somewhere else to go, why *wouldn't* we leave? Why would anyone hang around here?"

Mrs. Boine looked at Irene as if she'd lost her mind. "Why would I leave? I've got everything I want right here. This house has been my home for fifty years, and now Gloria and the girls live here. I would never dream of leaving."

There didn't seem to be anything else to say. Mrs. Boine seemed very certain that both of them were dead. She also seemed very certain that hanging around as a ghost was perfectly natural.

Irene climbed to her feet. Mrs. Boine looked surprised. "You're not going, are you?"

"Yeah, I have...stuff...to do," Irene finished lamely, realizing that she didn't actually have anything to do.

"Well, don't be a stranger, Irene."

A car bounced down the street. Irene heard Mrs. Boine swear as she closed the gate behind her.

Four

Well, she had managed to confirm that she wasn't the only person stuck in this limbo-like state, but she wasn't sure where that left her.

She passed a faded young woman — surrounded by a blue glow — standing on the sidewalk, a frozen tableau of wistfulness as she gazed at an old yellow colonial. She looked like an old photograph bleached by the sun, so worn and pale she was nearly translucent. She wore a slim, empire-waisted dress and her colorless hair, cascading in unbound curls, fell to her waist. She turned her wide, faded, green eyes to Irene.

"They won't let me in," she said. The woman spoke with such sadness Irene felt her own heart constrict with pity. She dropped her eyes and hurried on, feeling embarrassed and ill at ease all of a sudden.

She had a sudden image of spending her days taking unseen care of her mother until Deborah also died and joined Irene in the afterlife. Irene shuddered at the thought.

If she was to believe Mrs. Boine, this was it. There was no bright light, no pearly gates, no harps and halos. Of all the possible outcomes of dying that she had been led to believe — including the belief that there was no life after death — none of them had been quite this...ordinary. Certainly, no one had ever said Irene would have to spend all of eternity with her mother for company.

She became conscious of the fact that she had stopped walking and was standing before a plain white house with forest green shutters—the kind of modest, run-of-the-mill house she had so desperately wanted as a kid. It didn't look familiar. She studied the neat exterior, trying to figure out what had made her stop. She noticed the name on the mailbox—Johnson.

Johnson. Johnson. Why does that seem familiar?

She remembered the tall, scrawny boy from the day before. Hadn't he said his name was Johnson and that he lived in the neighborhood? She felt a flutter of uncertainty. He'd been a weird, annoying kid, true, but on the other hand, he did seem to know what was going on. More importantly, he could see her.

She bit her lip. It was really galling to think her ability to figure out what came next rested entirely in the hands of a fourteen-year-old, but no other resources were coming to mind.

"Come on, Irene," she told herself. "Put on your big girl pants. Other people manage to get through death on their own."

Still, she hesitated. What could it hurt to pick the kid's brain?

She headed up the walk to the front door. A tawny yellow cat—the color of old gold—lay stretched out, sunning itself in the front yard. As she approached, the cat opened a lazy eye and regarded her with suspicion. Never a fan of cats, she stuck out her tongue as she walked past. The cat closed its eye and went back to sleep.

Her ex-boyfriend, Geoffrey, had once told her that she had "cat eyes." She didn't know what he'd meant. She'd thought maybe he meant the color or the shape, but since she had wide, expressive brown eyes—rather than slanted, enigmatic green ones—it hadn't really made sense. Later, she had learned he hated cats—thought them untrustworthy—and if they hadn't already been broken up, that would have done it.

As expected, the front door was locked.

Shouldn't I be able to walk through doors and walls, now? she thought as she walked around to the back door, which was also locked. She bit her lip, thinking hard. She could always break a window, but that seemed extreme.

An open first-floor window saved her from having to commit a random act of vandalism. It took some effort to get the screen off since it opened from inside the house. She had to bend back one corner so she could squeeze a hand in and slide the metal clips holding it in place off the screws. She tossed the screen to the ground, pushed open the window, and boosted herself up over the sill. As she wiggled inside and slid to the floor in an undignified heap, she was torn between laughing and crying at the absurdity of the situation. She stood up and dusted herself off.

She was in the living room. Irene surveyed it with interest. Whoever had decorated it — she assumed Jonah's mother — favored pastels and floral fabrics but sensible, affordable furniture. The overall impression was of a blue-collar French-country chic.

A noise startled her and she turned to see a dowdy, middle-aged woman carrying a basket of laundry past the room. The woman had paused and was searching the area where Irene was standing with surprised eyes. Then, seemingly satisfied, she turned and continued on her way.

Irene let out her breath. The woman had seen her — just for an instant, but she *had* seen her, Irene was sure. A couple of times she'd thought Jamaica had seen her, too, out of the corner of her eye. Perhaps Mrs. Boine had been right — the living could see the dead but chose not to.

Curious, Irene followed the woman — who she assumed was Jonah's mother — up the stairs to the second floor. Photos lined the wall all the way up, and Irene stopped to look at them. Overall, it looked like an ordinary happy family. Everyone was smiling, though Jonah always seemed on the periphery of each photograph, as if he was trying to sidle out of the shot. There appeared to be a sister, perhaps sixteen, who was very pretty and a bit of a vamp. In every photo she was striking a theatrically seductive or flirtatious pose.

Irene suddenly realized she was snooping in someone else's home and felt a prickle of discomfort. Now she understood why the afterlife was always described as being "elsewhere"—up in the sky or deep underground—and why people tried so hard to mark ghostly noises and moving objects up to seismic activity, tricks of the light, or UFOs. How would you ever feel comfortable again knowing there were invisible people about? It was bad enough to think that God was watching you everywhere you went—even in the bathroom—but what about complete strangers? Even worse, people you knew! Irene shivered. She definitely did not want Grammie trailing her to bars and watching her random hook-ups.

She hurried upstairs, anxious to find Jonah and leave.

The woman was in a large bedroom to her left—Irene took this to be the master bedroom. Straight ahead was a bathroom. To her right stood two closed doors, one with a large, pink sign that said "Caitlin's Room" circled by hearts; the other must be Jonah's.

Irene rapped softly on the door, hoping the mother didn't hear. When no one answered, she pushed the door open and stepped inside to take a look.

"Huh."

The room was fairly neat for a teenage boy. There were no piles of dirty clothes, trash, or dirty dishes. There were, however, piles of intermingled textbooks and paper covering the desk, the end of the bed, and sections of the floor that, on closer inspection, turned out to be book reports, neat rows of math calculations, and lists of vocabulary words. A jumble of model parts—perhaps a space station or perhaps a castle, it was hard to tell—covered the surface of a small table in the far corner. A poster—almost as tall as Jonah himself—of a purple and red dragon adorned one wall. The other walls, painted a quiet shade of beige, were blank.

Something nagged at Irene. It seemed pretty clear that Jonah was a regular, living, breathing boy. So how could he see her when no one else could, and why hadn't Jamaica been able to see him?

The answer probably had something to do with the books crammed into a tall wooden bookcase. The shelves were so full the whole thing looked ready to burst. *A History of Death: Burial Customs and Funeral Rites, from the Ancient World to Modern Times. The Enchantments of Judaism: Rites of Transformation from Birth Through Death. Death for Beginners. Hindu Death Rites. Death Ritual in Late Imperial and Modern China.* Good grief—there was definitely a theme here. Two additional sets of shelves were also crammed full of similar books.

The one thing missing here was Jonah himself. Irene sighed and then picked up the small white-board hanging from the doorknob by a string. With the attached marker she wrote: "I need your help. Irene Dunphy." She thought for a moment and then added her address. She looked around for a place to put the white-board where he would see it, but his mother would not. Finally, she replaced it on the doorknob, hoping he'd see the message written on it.

She made her way back downstairs, skirting Jonah's mother who was carrying another load of laundry upstairs, and let herself out the front door as quietly as she could.

As she continued down the street, she saw an elderly man—living—walking a miniature poodle. *What would I normally be doing at this time of day?* she wondered. She guessed that it was around three o'clock.

Three o'clock on a Tuesday...she'd be going to Starbucks for a latte.

Then she would head back to her desk and power on through the work of designing and managing a major retailer's e-commerce strategy until six or seven p.m. Then to the gym for two hours, and finally, out—either on a date or with friends for dinner and drinks. Well, she wouldn't be doing any of that anymore.

There had to be more dead people around here somewhere. It was impossible that a city as old and full of history as Salem could only produce three ghosts—well, four if she counted herself.

She decided to head downtown—the old town hall, historic Derby Wharf, the Witch House, and the old Federal style ship captain homes of Chestnut Street all seemed likely places to find dead people.

However, three hours later, a street by street search of the historic district and the downtown had turned up only one ghost—a young man in an old-fashioned, knee-length vest, knee breeches with white stockings, and a strip of white linen tied round his neck who asked, "Have you seen Mr. Corey?" as he hurried past.

As she walked through the Essex Street pedestrian mall, a sign advertising ghost tours and a museum of "supernatural curiosities" caught her eye.

This ought to be interesting, she thought as she slipped through the door. Twenty-minutes later she left, torn between amusement and exasperation. The museum had just been a schmaltzy wax history museum meant for tourists. It didn't contain anything about the actual afterlife.

Her feet hurt, and she was officially out of ideas. The only thing she could think to do at this point was to go home and wait for the boy to show up.

Five

The next thing Irene knew, someone was shaking her. Her eyes flew open.

"Hey, wake up!"

Irene bolted upright, blinking hard. Jonah stepped back to avoid having his nose broken by her head.

She had come home and had a drink...or two. Annoyed by the mail in the hall when she had walked in, she had scooped it all up, with no grace or care. She'd heard the crackle of paper colliding and the sound of cellophane being bent and mangled as she gathered it all into one big pile in her arms. Without looking at any of it, she had dumped it in the trash. After all, what was the point? As if she was going to pay the bills, and there wasn't really any reason to follow fashion trends and celebrity gossip anymore. However, this simple act had left her feeling restless and bored and, to be honest, more alone than ever.

She had taken her drink to the living room where she had turned on the TV. She'd tried watching some Judge Judy, but everyone's problems had seemed so small and unimportant. On a trip to the kitchen she'd spied a half-read novel, forgotten in a stack of old magazines, and fished it out, intending to finally finish it. She must have fallen asleep reading it. Now the amber rays of light driving horizontally through the windows indicated that it was after five o'clock.

"Oh thank God!" Irene said, throwing her arms around Jonah.

"Er, get off?" He tried to disentangle himself from Irene's embrace. Irene let go just as abruptly, pushing Jonah away to hold him at arm's length.

"You disappeared!"

"When?" he asked, bewildered.

"Last time I saw you; you just vanished! Where did you go? You freaked me out."

"Study Hall was over. I had to get to class."

"Class?" Irene let Jonah go and sat back, examining him more closely. "It didn't occur to me that you actually go to school and stuff."

"Uh, yeah. 'Course I do."

"So you *really* aren't dead?"

"Er, not technically?" It sounded like a question, rather than an answer, and Jonah suddenly had a guilty air about him.

"What does that mean, 'not technically'? If you're not dead, then how come you can see me?"

"Well, like I said, it's kinda complicated..." he said evasively.

"What do you mean?"

"You say that a lot."

Irene's expression turned threatening.

"Okay, okay." Jonah held up his hands. "It's just that it's going to sound weird. I...I kinda found this book. It's all about, like, what happens when you die and stuff."

"And?" She shook him a little, prodding him to continue.

Jonah shrugged and looked down at the floor, scuffing one foot against the other. "Well, there's a spell in it that lets you visit the land of the dead," he said in an embarrassed rush.

"A spell?" Irene's eyes narrowed with suspicion. "What, you mean like magic? Are you on drugs?"

Jonah scowled, turned a delicate shade of rose-petal pink and he looked away,. intent on scuffing one toe along the bottom edge of the couch. "It's instructions for a transcendental meditation, a kind of astral projection, really." He shrugged. "It's like magic, and spell just sounds cooler."

"Is any of that even English?"

Jonah frowned at her. "You don't get out much, do you?"

"I think what you mean is, I don't stay *in* much. Is this some kind of geek thing, like Dungeons and Dragons?"

"No! It just means I can separate my spirit from my body and when I do, I can see dead people."

She stared at him, at a loss for words. Finally, she said, "You can...separate your...spirit...from...your body? Yeah, okay, pull the other one, kid."

Jonah looked blank. "Other what?"

"My leg!" She stood up so suddenly she nearly knocked him over. "You're pulling my leg."

"No, I'm not," he said earnestly. He looked hurt. She stared hard at him, trying to figure out if he was for real or not.

"Look, I really don't think I'm dead." She put a hand to her chest. "I can feel my heart beating. I'm breathing. I took a shower..."

Jonah put a hand to his own chest. "Yeah," he said, clearly feeling all the same signs of life that she did. "I don't know. Maybe it's like when a chicken gets its head cut off but keeps running around for a while."

Under her hand, her heart gave an odd, galloping lurch. "What, like I'm on borrowed time and then the juice is just going to run out and that'll be it?"

Jonah looked alarmed, seemingly recognizing that he had just taken a giant misstep. "No," he said hastily. "No, I meant, maybe it's more like a memory...like your brain thinks you're still alive and so it *thinks* your heart is beating and stuff."

Irene thought this over for a moment, not convinced. Then she sighed and ran a hand through her hair. "I need a drink. Do you want something?"

Jonah's eyebrows shot up to his hairline. "I'm thirteen!"

"I meant like a soda."

"Oh. Yeah, okay."

Irene went to the kitchen. She returned, holding a highball for herself and a can of Coke for him. Jonah had arranged himself on the edge of a white suede overstuffed chair and sat hunched over, hands clasped between his knees. She handed him the soda and then flopped back onto the couch.

She took a sip of her drink and thought for a moment, trying to make sense of everything he'd been saying. "So you're not actually dead?"

"Er..." Jonah paused in the act of carefully lapping overflowing soda from the top of the can. He tried to divide his attention between answering Irene and preventing the soda from spilling over. "No."

"So...what? You do this trans-meditation thing for...fun?"

"Uh...yeah?"

"And you found this...*spell*...in a book?"

"Yes."

Irene got up and paced back and forth, edgy and restless. The entire conversation seemed so surreal, so strange. "And you said you just happened to find this book lying around somewhere?"

"Yeah, in the school library. It was just there."

"You found this book in a school library?" Irene asked, incredulous once more. "I don't...okay, I'll bite. How the hell did it get there?"

Jonah jerked in his seat as if he'd been stung. His face turned fuchsia. "How the hell should I know?"

"Watch your mouth."

Jonah looked murderous, as if he wanted to say something heated, but he compressed his lips into a thin line and said instead, "Look, did you want something?"

"Yeah, I want to know what's going on! Suddenly only two people in the world can see me — one of which is you — both of whom say I'm dead. Except, I'm *not* dead!"

Jonah's anger melted away and now he looked sad, his pale green-blue eyes wide with sympathy. "I'm really sorry." He looked down and became intent on spreading a bead of soda around the top of the can.

It was the sympathy that did it. Her anger deflated and she flopped down on the couch, her legs suddenly as weak as jelly.

"How?" she cried. "Wouldn't I know if I was dead? Wouldn't I remember dying?"

"You don't remember?"

"No! Nothing. Just waking up on the side of the road. You said something about a car accident, but I don't remember it."

Unbidden, the memory of floating in the beautiful blue-green light resurfaced, dancing before her eyes. She felt the crushing weight on her chest again and a wave of panic washed over her. She shook her head to dispel the images and took another long drink, draining her glass.

"You didn't wake up in the cemetery?" he asked.

She stood up. "I need another drink. Do you want anything?"

She saw him glance surreptitiously at her glass. Then he shook his head. She went to the kitchen, mixed a rum and coke, and then returned to the living room. She began pacing once more.

"Okay, fine. Let's say for the sake of argument that I am dead. What's your book say about what's happening to me? Where am I supposed to go? What am I supposed to do?"

"Uh, well, I don't know. It's mostly in some other language. I can't read most of it."

"So what you're saying is you don't actually know anything?"

Jonah bristled. "Hey, I know a lot of stuff. A lot more than most people!"

"Like, for instance...?"

"Okay, well, I know the word for Heaven in twenty-six languages. Heban, Heofan, Himil, Tian, Loka, Elysium, Yalu —"

Irene threw up her hands. "Great. Very helpful. That was just the information I was waiting for. Now it all makes sense."

A red flush crept up Jonah's neck. "You know, you're really sarcastic."

Irene's shoulders sagged and she let her head fall back so she could stare at the ceiling while she counted to ten. In a more reasonable tone of voice she said, "Any description of where Heaven is or how to get there?"

"What makes you so sure you're going to Heaven?" The words rushed out and he clearly regretted them as soon as he said them. He ducked behind his hair and focused intently on the top of his soda can again.

Irene stared at him. Frostily, she said, "Why would you think I wasn't?"

"I just meant," Jonah mumbled, "that Heaven usually comes later. First, the dead have to go through judgment or a sort of waiting room—"

"Nice save," she said dryly.

The bit of Jonah's ears visible through his hair turned maroon but he continued, "...like the Asphodal Meadows, Hel, Misvan Gatu—"

"Wait...Hell?" Her heart thumped uncertainly.

"Er, with one 'l.' That's the Norse version of purgatory."

She contemplated this for a moment. Then she sat down, willing herself to be calm and logical about the situation. "So you're saying I'm in purgatory? Well, how long does that last?"

"No. Actual purgatory also happens after you've been judged. It's one of the three possible outcomes of judgment, along with Heaven and Hell."

"That would be the double-l version of Hell?"

Jonah nodded, though he clearly thought she was being sarcastic again. "Anyway, it's where the people who haven't been very bad, but who haven't been very good either, go until they're good enough to enter Heaven."

"Okay, whatever," she answered. "The point is, I'm not seeing any kind of hall of judgment or anything. So what am I supposed to do?"

"Well, you have to get to the land of the dead first. You know, Hades, Mictlan, Olam Haba—"

"That is *really* annoying!"

"Sor-ree," Jonah replied. "You asked."

"Okay, wait. What do you mean I have to get to the land of the dead? Isn't this the land of the dead?"

Jonah shrugged. "I think this is still the land of the living."

"What do you mean, 'you think'?"

"Well it's not like I've done this before."

Irene blinked. "What do you mean by that?"

Jonah shrugged and slurped his soda, avoiding Irene's eyes.

"Jonah?"

Irene watched with amusement as the tips of his ears turned pink again. It was kind of funny the way they went from white to red and back again like a mood ring.

At that moment, the phone rang. They both froze, the strident ringing growing more insistent. The machine picked up and the muffled sound of her mother's voice floated in from the kitchen. In the background, the refrigerator cycled on, the mechanical hum unnaturally loud against their silence.

They remained frozen until the shrill beeping of the answering machine alerting Irene to the fact that she had a new message began to sound.

Jonah shifted in his seat and then answered the question Irene had posed before the phone rang. "Well..." he said, "technically, you're the first dead person that I've met."

"I..." Irene cut herself off and snapped her mouth shut. She breathed out slowly through her nose, once more needing to count to ten before continuing. "I thought you knew all about this?"

"I do!" he protested. "I know everything there is to know about the afterlife. I've read every book there is."

Irene snorted. "Yeah, I saw them in your room. It was kind of creepy."

"Speaking of creepy...how did you get into my house?"

"Me? How about you? How did you get in here by the way?"

"The front door was unlocked," he said heatedly, slapping the can of soda down on the table, "and you invited me." A small geyser of dark liquid shot out of the can, puddling on the beautiful maple surface.

"Oh crap! I'm sorry," he cried, using the edge of his T-shirt to frantically wipe at the liquid.

Irene jumped to her feet. "Christ! Be careful! That stains you know." She ran for paper towels and returned a second later with a handful.

"I said I was sorry," Jonah muttered as Irene brushed him aside to mop up the spill.

"Whatever."

As she wiped up the mess, her mind returned to what Jonah had been saying earlier about the land of the dead and the different types of possible afterlives. If it was true, then there was an afterlife—an actual Great Beyond—somewhere out there. She just had to find it. She left the room to dispose of the paper towels and wash her hands, her mind working furiously.

She returned to the living room, her lips pursed in deep thought. "Okay, so say I wanted to get to…the land of the dead. I don't suppose you know where the tunnel is?"

Jonah frowned. "Tunnel? What do you mean?"

"You know…when you die you see a white light guiding you to a tunnel, right?"

Jonah's frown deepened and he shook his head. "No, it always starts by crossing a river—over a bridge or by boat. I've never seen anything about a tunnel."

Irene quirked an eyebrow. "Are you kidding? It's always a tunnel. You know, in the movies 'follow the light, Timmie!' That kind of thing? Tell me this sounds familiar."

"Huh." Jonah seemed puzzled. "Yeah, that's weird…" He frowned up at the ceiling, as if thinking hard. "I know what you mean but none of the stuff I've read says anything about that."

"Well maybe you've been reading the wrong stuff."

Jonah gave her an exasperated look. "Hardly. I've read *everything* there is."

"Yeah, I saw the books in your room. It's a little creepy."

"You said that already."

"Yeah, well it's worth repeating. It was *really* creepy."

Jonah turned pink. "I needed the information for a report for school."

"A report? On what?"

"Burial rituals of the ancient world. It was for history."

"That's when you found your magic book?"

Jonah nodded. Irene studied him through narrowed eyes. Jonah saw her scrutiny and shrugged. "I just found the stuff interesting is all. It's actually pretty cool. Like, did you know that most cultures bury objects with their dead that they think they'll need in the afterlife, like money and swords and food and stuff, and — "

"Jonah! Focus. Tunnel. Location."

He scowled again, but then, just as quickly, his look turned thoughtful. "Okay, well, maybe the tunnel or the bridge or whatever is in the cemetery? Because normally that's where you'd be, right? You'd die and get buried and so it would make sense for it to be right there, the first thing you see when you wake up."

Irene stood up. "Well, okay, Einstein, that's an easy enough theory to test out. Greenlawn is just up the road."

Jonah looked surprised. "What, now?" He looked out the window. "It's dark out."

"I thought this was just the kind of thing teenage boys loved," she said, a challenge in her voice.

He sighed and stood up. "You're like a two year old, you know that?"

She glared at him and then headed for the hall. She stuffed her feet into her sneakers and grabbed her keys from the table. She held the door open for him and then followed him outside.

It was cool but pleasant out, and a gentle breeze ruffled the leaves on the trees. As the days grew shorter, the nights were growing chillier. They were still almost two months from the first hard frost, but the gentle beginnings of fall were already in the air.

They set off toward Sargent Street, a wide, tree-lined avenue that would take them straight to the cemetery. Irene shivered and rubbed her hands over her arms. Jonah looked at her. "Do you want to go back and get a jacket?"

"No," she said. "I'm not actually cold. Just..." She wasn't sure what she was. She felt like she should be cold—should, in fact, be creeped out and afraid to the point of knee-shaking terror. She was caught in a limbo-like existence—not really dead but not really alive—and now she was visiting a cemetery—at night—looking for some kind of tunnel that would take her...where, exactly?

She didn't feel anything, though. She was just sort of numb, like none of this was real, and that bothered her, too. She didn't want to be scared, but she didn't want to be an emotionless automaton, either. Perhaps this was shock. Maybe she just needed time for it all to sink in.

They were walking parallel to the cemetery now, a dense copse of oak trees shielding the graves from view. Irene turned off the road and cut through the woods. A minute later, they stepped onto the neat grass lawn of the cemetery.

The graves stretched out before them, tidy, solemn, and still. A clear, bright moon shone high overhead, which was lucky as neither one of them had thought to bring a flashlight.

Irene remembered the last time she had been here—a bright and sunny day in June ten years ago when they had buried her father. The sun had seemed like an insult; shouldn't it be raining when you buried someone? As much as she hated a clichéd, syrupy scene, she had felt a sharp resentment at the ludicrous sunshine.

She paused to look out over the rows of tombstones. She had no idea where her father's grave was. They all looked alike, arranged as if they were troops in formation. She shivered. At some point, they were going to put her in a place like this—cold, orderly, suffocatingly uniform—and then they would forget about her. She swallowed and hastily pushed the thought aside. With luck, she wouldn't be around when that happened.

Jonah had kept walking and was wandering down a row of graves, looking at the headstones. She followed. "So, any ideas?" she asked.

He shrugged. "I guess we just look around." He pointed at a headstone. "Some of these are pretty interesting."

Irene made a non-committal noise.

"You know, it's really interesting how different the beliefs are about how to bury people," he continued. "The ancient Egyptians mummified people but Jewish people don't embalm their dead at all. Hindus and Buddhists cremate their dead, but the Baha'i forbid it."

They had reached the end of the row. They turned and walked back down the next one. "Did you know it took anywhere from fifty-three to more than two hundred days to mummify someone?" he asked.

"You know, I always thought it was weird that we put mummies in museums," she said. "Those were people. Just ordinary people and we've dug them up and put them on display. How would we like it if someone did that to us?"

Jonah looked surprised at this. He seemed to mull it over for a second; then his eyes softened with approval as he looked at her. "Huh."

They wandered up and down the rows reading headstones, which ranged in size from simple flat stones embedded in the ground to grand mausoleum vaults, from unadorned headstones to elaborate statues of weeping or praying angels, their stony heads bent in delicate and moving sorrow over the graves. Jonah threw out occasional bits of trivia about burial procedures in various cultures and time periods as they walked.

They paused to read the headstone of a man who had fought in the War of 1812. Was the man's ghost wandering around here somewhere, Irene wondered.

"Did you know that the Japanese cremate their dead and then the family picks through the ashes with chopsticks to take out the bones?" he asked in a fascinated tone, as they passed three teenagers — living — sitting against a headstone, smoking pot. The sweet, heavy smell of cannabis tickled her nose as they passed.

Some of the graves had additional decorations—fake flowers "planted" in front of the headstone, small flags marking veterans, and even small porcelain statues and figurines. Some bore signs of recent visitation—fresh flowers, small rocks or pennies set on the headstone, and on one, an unopened can of beer.

"What are the rocks for?" Irene asked as they passed a headstone with a neat, orderly row of beach rocks laid upon it.

Jonah shrugged. "It's just a custom, a way to show that someone visited. I don't think it has any significance." Then he added hastily, "Well, I mean, it's not part of any particular custom. It's just a thing people do."

Irene looked over the cemetery spreading out before her. Something bothered her about it. The graves seemed endless, and this was just one of several cemeteries in Salem alone. When you thought about the entirety of the dead population—over thousands of years—the number became incalculable. Where was there a place big enough for everyone to be together—for all of eternity? She couldn't imagine a place so vast. For some reason she had thought of the afterlife as being small—surely, smaller than the land of the living. After all, it had to fit inside the land of the living, didn't it? It had to exist, if not on earth, then at least within the realm of the known universe. She was no astrophysicist, but something seemed wrong with the mechanics of the whole thing. She began to feel uneasy. Could such a place really exist?

Jonah broke into her train of thought. "It's really late. I gotta get home." He sounded reluctant to go.

While they had searched only a small portion of the cemetery, it was pretty clear to Irene that they weren't going to find any kind of portal to the afterlife. Other than the group of pot-smoking teenagers, the place was still and silent. There were no other dead around. She imagined that if there was a tunnel, it would be easy to see, shining out like a beacon, visible from anywhere in the cemetery.

Irene shifted uncomfortably. "Well, what am I supposed to do next?"

"Can I just point out that you *are* a grownup? What do you usually do?"

"Live! Which I can't do anymore...because I'm dead."

His eyes widened with alarm. "You're not going to cry are you?"

"No," Irene snapped. "I'm not going to cry!"

Jonah looked torn. "I really have to go. *Now*. If my parents find my body, they'll freak!"

"Your what?"

Jonah rolled his eyes, sighed theatrically, and, as if talking to a four year old, said, "When I go into the trance, my spirit gets separated from my body. My body gets left behind at the place where I was when I went into the trance, which, right now, is my bedroom. It's like I'm in a coma, but it—I mean my body—is still alive and my spirit can return to it. Unlike a real dead person."

"I thought you said you hadn't done this before?"

"No, I said you were the first dead person I'd met. I've been visiting the land of the dead for months. I just never met any dead people before."

"I thought you said this wasn't the land of the dead?"

"Whatever! The point is, my parents are going to freak if they check on me before they go to bed. I have to get home. Okay?"

"But—"

He cut her off. "Look, I'll come back later...like tomorrow...with the book. Okay? Maybe there's something in it that can help you."

Irene reluctantly nodded. She couldn't do much else.

"Okay, fine, then I'm going..."

"You know, a gentleman would have offered to walk me home, made sure I got back safe," she said drily.

He seemed surprised by this, then chastised. "Yeah, alright." He shoved his hands into his pockets and looked at the ground.

She laughed. "I was joking. It's fine. Like you said, I'm a grown woman. Plus I guess I'm already dead..."

He gave a half-shrug. "No, it's okay."

They didn't talk on the way back. Once they were in front of her house, she said, "So I'll see you later?"

"Yeah." He kicked at the sidewalk. "Tomorrow." Then his gaze sharpened and his head came up as if he was listening to something in the distance. Then, as before, he was simply gone.

Six

She wanted coffee.

Irene had gone to bed in her clothes. She had drifted off to sleep reviewing the events of the last few days and wondering if things might have turned out differently if she had gone home with the cute but boring guy who had tried to pick her up at that last bar.

She spent a restless night, jerking awake every few hours from frightening dreams of blue-green water that turned into a white light that floated away like a soap bubble in the wind while she chased it, sobbing from an ache so profound and vast she thought it would break her apart.

Unfortunately, coffee was an impossibility since she didn't have a coffee maker. She grabbed the orange juice from the fridge. As she poured some into a glass she glanced at the clock. It was already late morning. Jonah must have gone to school. That meant she wasn't likely to see him for a while. She felt a touch of panic at the thought of trying to kill an entire day by herself. She threw a few splashes of vodka into the orange juice and then, glass in hand, padded into the living room. She settled on the couch and picked up the TV remote.

"Let's see what's happening in the land of the living today," she said. She watched a bit of the news, mostly out of habit, but found it annoying after a few minutes. "War, death, pestilence. Yeah, yeah, yeah." She tried to feel superior to be beyond such concerns, but failed. Somehow, it just made her feel alone—isolated and disconnected from everyone and everything. If there was no point in caring about what happened to the living, then what was she supposed to care about? Well, other than being dead, that is.

She continued flipping. A striking set of gold bangle bracelets with iridescent stones caught her eye on the shopping channel. She felt a stab of melancholy. They would have made a great Christmas present for LaRayne. Now she'd never buy another Christmas present ever.

She paused her channel surfing on a weekly crime drama. The main character was saying, "Based on when Christine last saw him and the coroner's report on how long he'd been dead, we estimate the time of death at between eight and ten p.m. Tuesday night..."

Irene frowned at her drink. Would they be able to tell that this glass had been dirtied after she'd died? Would they know that these clothes had been worn recently even though she'd been dead at the time? She looked around the room, trying to notice things she'd moved. Had people noticed that the lights had been on in the house last night? She bit her lip, hesitating, and then thought, *fuck it*. She wasn't going to sit in the dark to please anybody. Still, maybe it would be a good idea to take the mail out of the trash and replace it in the hall when she got up.

She clicked off the TV, feeling irritated and restless. She heard Jonah's voice echo in her head: *What do you usually do all day?*

Right now, she'd be at work.

She wondered if anyone was talking about her disappearance. If she believed Mrs. Boine then she had been dead for at least a few days. Suddenly, she had an irresistible urge to check her email.

While she waited for her laptop to start up, she slipped back out to the kitchen. She opened the fridge and leaned over to study its contents. She couldn't remember the last time she'd eaten. She felt an obligatory rumble from her stomach, but it seemed like it was complaining more from a feeling that it should rather than from actual need. So she grabbed the orange juice and mixed herself another screwdriver. Drink in hand, she sat down at the computer and logged in to her work email.

The list of unread emails spanned into the hundreds. She looked at the date of the most recent one and realized that it was more than a week since she had gone out with the girls.

A week?

She'd been dead a week already? How was that possible? If it was true, where had she been all that time?

She shoved that worry aside to join the growing stack of uneasy thoughts and unanswered questions bubbling in the back of her mind and scrolled through the unread emails, looking for any that might relate to her.

There weren't any.

Well. That was…disappointing.

It occurred to her that the world outside still continued on, uninterrupted. She had died, but the world had kept going. Had anyone even noticed that she was gone? Had her passing made any dent in the world? No one knew she was dead yet, but she had been gone long enough for people to realize something serious had happened and to suspect the worst. Her mother was handling everything with her usual vague interest, but at least she was still calling intermittently to check on her. So was LaRayne. Alexia's calls seemed to have petered out.

Irene's boss had noticed her absence, that was true, but Irene had to wonder—what had Donna felt? Worry? Loss? Sadness? Or merely annoyance that Irene's disappearance had created the chore of finding someone to replace her? What about her coworkers—did they feel worry at her disappearance or irritation they were now saddled with her work?

What about her neighbors? Had Jamaica noticed that Irene hadn't been home for some time with no advance warning? Irene usually asked her to collect the mail and look out for packages when she was away. Jamaica clearly hadn't been over to collect the mail—what did she think was going on? Was she worried? Concerned? Or had she not even noticed that her—well, if not friend, then at least close acquaintance of eight years—had been missing for a week?

Who else would notice that she was gone? Who would care? She tried to think who would go to her funeral. Other than LaRayne and Alexia—and Alexia refused to attend funerals because she thought they were in bad taste—and her coworkers, the bulk of the attendees would most likely be her mother's friends. She felt a pang as she realized how few friends she had, how few lives she was truly connected to.

She wondered what the people who did show up would say about her. Would the really miss her? Would they cry? Or would they just come out of obligation, because they were supposed to? She was reminded of the scene in Tom Sawyer where he watches his own funeral. Her lips quirked with amusement, but just as quickly she grew thoughtful again. What was that old saying—the only thing worse than being talked about was to not be talked about at all? She had a sudden desire to visit the office to see what kind of splash her death had made. She scooped up her car keys and headed for the door.

It wasn't until she was approaching a four-way stop that she suddenly realized driving might not be the smartest move. She assumed her car was as solid as she was and just as invisible, which meant the other drivers couldn't see it but could run into it. She sat at the stop sign, waiting for the car on the left and the car on the right to proceed through the intersection, but neither moved. They sat there, apparently each waiting for the other to go. After a minute, Irene hit the gas, hard. She zipped through the intersection, praying she made it before either of the other cars started to move. Safely on the other side, she looked in her rearview mirror to see the two cars proceeding through the intersection as if they had been waiting for her.

That's odd, she thought with a flicker of unease. *There's no way they could have seen me.* Yet, it seemed strange that they hadn't gone until after she did.

At the next intersection, as Irene stopped at the stop sign she glanced in her rearview and was alarmed to see a car approach from behind. Irene hit the gas and then, just as quickly, hit the brakes as a car zipped across the road in front of her.

She hunched her shoulders and shut her eyes, bracing for impact as the car behind drew up. She waited for the crash, but it never came. Cautiously, she opened one eye and looked in the rearview. The other car had stopped several feet behind her.

A third car had stopped behind the first, and the driver, apparently confused as to why the first driver had stopped so far from the intersection, now tooted his horn. The car behind Irene began to creep up, and Irene hit the gas without a second thought, wanting only to get while the getting was good.

The living see what they want to see, Mrs. Boine's voice echoed in her head.

Irene thought about all the times she had seen drivers leaving large gaps between themselves and the next car, especially in stop and go traffic, and she had often wondered why the other driver didn't move up. Or when cars would start to change lanes on the highway only to jerk back into their original lane for no discernible reason. Or people, standing in line, leaving large gaps between themselves and the next person. Or every time she had circled a packed parking lot looking for an empty space, and everyone seemed to be bypassing this one primo spot. She'd wondered why everyone else had passed it by, but then so would she.

She realized now it must be the dead. Subconsciously, the living could sense them, enough to avoid walking into them, sitting on them, or even running into them with cars. The living didn't want to see the dead, but, apparently, they did want to avoid them.

The pattern seemed to hold as she merged onto the highway. She held her breath, but it quickly became apparent that the other drivers sensed her presence, and she didn't have any problems beyond the usual bad drivers who didn't pay attention to anyone else on the road — living or dead.

Forty minutes later, Irene paused in front of the main entrance to the thirty-story office building where she had worked. She checked that no one was around before pulling open the door. She was surprised that the lobby looked the same. Somehow, she had expected it to be different. Her life had changed so much in the last few days it seemed strange to see everything else looking normal.

She had the same feeling of disappointment when she stepped out of the elevator. Everything looked exactly the way she remembered it: the receptionist's desk, curved in a welcoming grin of opaque green-blue glass, the sea of blue-gray cubicles, even that weird new carpet smell that always lingered in the air.

She wasn't sure what she had expected — her face, four feet high, staring out from giant "missing person" posters on the walls? Makeshift memorials of flowers and stuffed animals in front of her desk? A wake-like atmosphere of reverence and sorrow?

There was none of that. People were bustling back and forth. Phones were ringing. People were shouting back and forth over cubicle walls. Photocopiers were copying. In short, it was a normal workday, full of normal activity. She had that unsettled feeling again as once more she realized the world had simply gone on without her, that her life had been a temporary distraction — like a brook bending around a stray stick — rather than something permanent and immutable.

Irene strode briskly down the hall toward her office. The whole place was humming, as usual. Irene felt a fierce sense of pride wash over her — the aliveness of the place, the humming, rustling, rushing, bustling of it all, was what Irene had always loved about her work. She paused as she realized with surprise how much she had loved it. As much as she had skipped out due to hangovers, she genuinely liked her job.

She felt a tiny pang of regret. She'd worked hard, put in her hours and got the job done—and done well—but hadn't really put her heart into it, hadn't really taken things as seriously as she should have. She wished she could tell her boss, Donna, how much she'd like working for her.

Irene stopped in front of her office. The door was slightly ajar, and she could see that someone was there—*in her office*—sitting at her desk, with his feet up. Irene shoved open the door. "You little toad!" she hissed, red-hot anger gushing through her like molten lava. Not only did no one seem to care that she was missing, someone had already moved into her office—replaced her as if she had never even existed at all! She had seen the callousness when employees left: coworkers descended on the empty workspace, cannibalizing the supplies and equipment before the poor SOB was out the door, but she had thought that, somehow, she was different, that people wouldn't do that to her, that she mattered. To make matters worse, the betrayal came from her own executive assistant.

Eddie looked up as the door opened, dropping his feet to the floor and bolting upright.

"I know you can't hear me," Irene said, " but I just want you to know that you were a terrible assistant. You're a two-timing, back-stabbing, social-climbing good-for-nothing piece of shit!"

She was so angry she was shaking. How dare he sit in *her* office like he owned the place.

Eddie got up, poked his head out the door, checked both ways, and then re-shut the door. He settled himself back at the desk, feet up, and refolded the newspaper to a more convenient shape.

Okay, fine, so maybe she hadn't taken her job as seriously as she should have, but at least she had lived. She hadn't been married to her job, like some people. She'd known when to kick back, relax, and have a good time. That had to count for something.

She narrowed her eyes at Eddie. "You know what? I take that back. You're welcome to the office. In fact, I hope you live to be a hundred and have to spend *every day of your life* in it."

Irene threw open the door so hard it hit the wall, making the entire office shake. Behind her, she heard Eddie's feet hit the carpet as he bolted upright once more. "What the...?" he muttered.

Irene tossed her hair and strode into the hall. Without thinking, she was halfway to Donna's office when it occurred to her that the result was likely to be the same. No one cared that she was dead. Worse, it was as if she had never even existed.

So much for Frank Capra, she thought. Then rebellion rose up within her.

"No," she said. Then again, and louder, "No!" She refused to accept this. She *had* existed, damn it — and she damn well wasn't going to let people forget it.

It was lunchtime, and as usual, the place had cleared out. It was easy enough to snag a marker, some scotch tape, and a framed photo — of a recent office Christmas party — that prominently featured her from the many empty desks in the area. Then she walked to the photocopier. She didn't encounter anyone on the way. She felt a malicious twinge of disappointment. While she didn't really want people flinging things at her when they saw a marker and tape floating through the air, her mood was such that she wouldn't have minded sending people stampeding in terror.

"Now I understand poltergeists," she muttered. Frankly, their victims got what they deserved.

With a few minutes' work, she had a thick stack of serviceable legal-sized posters. Her face — cropped and enlarged from the photo — floated above the words, "IRENE DUNPHY IS WATCHING YOU," inked in heavy, dark letters. She chuckled in anticipation. She hung a few around the photocopier.

She made her way around the floor, stopping to tape up posters in various offices or leave them scattered in cubicles. At one point, she heard Eddie asking Leslie, the administrative assistant, if she knew where Juan or Bill were. "Something's wrong with my office door–it won't stay closed."

Irene bolted for the office, racing to get there and paper the walls with posters before Eddie returned. As she taped the last one in place, she laughed, relishing the thought of giving Eddie a fright. It would serve him right!

She stepped back to admire her handiwork and wished Alexia or LaRayne was here to see. Just as suddenly, though, the whole thing seemed pointless. It would get people talking, get her name back in front of them, but it wasn't going to get her job, her life, or her friends back. This wasn't going to make people miss her, or care that she was gone, or believe that she was still alive, stuck in limbo somewhere. If it was this easy to convince people of the existence of ghosts, then someone would have done it already. Her heart sank.

She tossed the rest of the posters on the closest desk and walked out without a look back, a black torpor settling over her. She drove home feeling numb. Was this really it? Was her life as she knew it really over?

The thought was too terrible, too big, so she stuffed it down deep, shutting her mind to everything related to death and dying.

You're going to be fine, she told herself, clinging to the thought like a life raft, repeating it over and over as she drove home.

She pulled into her driveway and turned off the engine. She sat for some time, staring at nothing. At last, she managed to find the strength to open the car door and get out. She looked up at the sky. The stars were out, twinkling against a smoky gray background. She wondered what time it was. As if in answer, a church bell began to ring in the distance.

As she walked to the front door, a shadow near the corner of the house seemed to shift and move, sliding away toward the back of the building.

She narrowed her eyes, trying to bring the darkness into focus. "Hello?" she called, slowing down, but the only thing there was house, grass, and bushes. She paused and then shrugged away the momentary unease.

61

Heavy and beautiful, the last peal of the distant bell trembled on the air and then faded away.

Eight o'clock.

If Jonah had come, she'd missed him. It was probably too late for him to come back again tonight, so she'd have to wait until tomorrow to get any answers on what she was supposed to do next.

She slipped into the house with a sigh.

Seven

Irene poured herself a glass of orange juice. It had been another restless night. Now the sun shone bright and full through the kitchen window. She stared absently into the fridge and drummed her fingernails on the side as she leaned against it with one hand. *Today is the first day of the rest of your afterlife,* she thought. *How do you want to spend it?*

After a few minutes, however, the beeping of the answering machine alerting her that she had messages was driving her crazy. She closed the refrigerator and went over to study the machine, trying to figure out how to turn down the volume. She finally solved the problem by hitting random buttons until she accidentally played the message her mother had left two days ago.

Great—now she'd retrieved her messages after she was dead. Crap. Well, okay, fine.

She yanked the phone cord out of the jack. Problem solved. She wandered into the hall to retrieve the mail, and then remembered she wasn't supposed to do that either. She returned to the kitchen to fish the rest of the mail out of the trash and then realized it would just be in the way if she put it back on the floor in front of the door.

Jesus, she couldn't do anything right! Who would have thought being dead was so hard?

Suddenly the house felt stifling. She went to the hall, grabbed her keys, and restlessly threw open the front door.

Once outside, however, she wasn't sure where she wanted to go.

A living, heavy-set, middle-aged woman was walking by and cast a startled look at the house — Irene realized it must have looked like the front door had opened of its own accord — and then continued on her way, looking confused. Irene gave the woman a dirty look, knowing the woman couldn't see her.

Irene looked around, surveying the street. A cat was walking down the far side. It stopped to look around, as if checking to make sure no one was looking, and then ducked under a hedge and disappeared from view.

As she stood on the top step, she replayed yesterday's visit to work in her mind and again felt the icy-hot mixture of anger and humiliation. Memories of Howard Schlim's death a couple of years ago danced into view. Howard was the tyrannical leader of a tiny fiefdom in the accounting department. Pedantic, bureaucratic, and self-important, he made life a living hell for anyone who needed to pay a vendor or asked for travel expenses. Donna had once flung a stack of papers at him and called him an officious twit after he had sent back a travel voucher for the third time. Donna never had gotten that travel reimbursement. Then he had dropped dead of a heart attack, and suddenly everyone missed Howard. The halls had filled with gentle sniffles of grief and the hushed reverence of fond reminisces. When Cheryl, one of Howard's most hen-pecked subordinates had tried to say, for the tenth time, that she just couldn't believe he was gone, Irene had cut in impatiently, "Howard was an A-Number-One asshole."

Cheryl had looked at her in silent disapproval, her pursed lips showing just how deeply her sensibilities had been offended. The she had said, in a quiet, no-nonsense voice, "Yeah, but you don't speak ill of the dead." And that had been that. Irene had bit her tongue, and people had openly and demonstratively mourned for two weeks the passing of a man they had all wanted to murder.

Was that it? Was that all she could expect? People would grieve her passing and speak well of her because they had to, because it was gauche to speak ill of the dead?

Come to think of it...why was it wrong to speak ill of the dead? Was it because deep down inside, people knew that the dead were listening? How hypocritical of the living to either forget or idealize the dead, just so long as they didn't have to see or hear from them again.

Well, fuck them. She'd just make some new friends on the other side.

A sudden thought gripped her. Hadn't Mrs. Boine intimated that the city was full of dead people? That was it! She'd go to Boston and make some new *dead* friends. In fact, the more she thought about it, the more excited she got. Now that she was dead — without the responsibilities of a job, a mortgage, or an aging mother — she was free! She could move back to the city and do what she wanted, when she wanted, with whoever she wanted. It would be like the good old days when she was in college, except without homework and tuition bills. The afterlife might just be awesome after all!

She turned and re-entered the house, leaving the front door open as she race-walked through rooms, looking for her purse. It was on the couch. She grabbed it and turned around to head back to the front door only to come face to face with Jonah. She let out a shriek.

He was dressed in a long-sleeved oxford shirt and tan chinos and had a large, heavy-looking backpack slung over one shoulder.

He reared back in alarm. "Jesus, take a pill!"

"You scared the crap out of me!"

He raised an eyebrow.

"Don't you knock?"

Jonah raised both eyebrows even higher. Without a word, he marched back to the front door, went out of the house, and closed the door behind him. Irene heard a sharp rap on the door.

"Nobody home," she called. She heard the front door open and close. "You can't come in — I didn't invite you!"

"That's vampires," he said, striding into the living room.

She frowned. "Where the hell have you been, anyway? You said you were coming right back...two days ago."

The scornful look on his face was replaced by sheepishness. "I meant to come back right away, but I fell asleep."

"What about yesterday?"

"I had school and stuff..."

"What, even at night?"

"If you must know, it was my birthday. My parents took me out and stuff."

"Your birthday?" Irene echoed. "What do you mean?"

"It's not that big a deal."

"Not that big a deal?"

"Will you stop repeating everything I say? Honestly, it's not that big a deal. So can we just drop it?"

"Yeah, but you just turned thirteen —"

"Fourteen."

"Fourteen...that's a big deal, right?"

"What's so great about fourteen? You're still not allowed to do anything," he said sulkily, dropping cross-armed onto the couch. "I can't drive. I can't get a job. I can't stay out past ten..."

"Okay, fine, I get the point." She gave him another sidelong glance and then said, "Speaking of school, aren't you supposed to be there right now?"

Jonah shrugged. "It's not like anyone notices when I'm not."

"Accosting a minor might not be a crime, but contributing to the delinquency of one is."

Jonah rolled his eyes. "The world won't end if I miss a day or two of school."

Irene picked up her purse again. "Okay, well, fine, whatever. You have good timing...let's go."

"Go? Go where?"

"To the city. You know...tunnel...afterlife."

Suspicion darkened his eyes. "I thought you wanted to look at the book?"

"Jonah, I can't even begin to describe how incredibly boring it has been sitting in this house for the last couple of days." Irene ushered him up off the couch and out to the hall. She held the front door open. "I need to get out, get some fresh air, stretch my legs."

He scuffed his feet as Irene urged him out the door. "Yeah, but—"

"Look, the tunnel can't be that hard to find...other people do it. So let's just go. If we get stuck, we can consult your magic book, okay?"

A faint look of alarm shimmered across Jonah's face. "Er, what do you mean *we*?"

Irene blinked in surprise. "Well, you and me. You're coming with me to look for the tunnel aren't you?"

"Me? Why would I go?"

"Because you're the supposed expert on the afterlife, with what appears to be the only user manual for it, so you *have* to go. Besides, this is your big hobby, right? What you do for fun? I thought you'd be excited to go with me."

"No way—that's kidnapping! I don't even know you!"

"Oh, what are you, scared? We're dead, Jonah. I don't think it gets any worse from here on out."

"*I'm* not dead. Besides, I have chores and school and stuff. My parents would freak."

"It's one afternoon in the city. I'm not asking you for a lifetime commitment."

He scowled at her. "You can't just order me around, you know."

She gave the door a shove, closing it with a heavy thud. "Fine. I'm not going to beg you to come with me. Just give me the book and then you can run on home."

He was shouting now, quivering in outrage. "No way! You can't just take it, it's mine!"

She crossed her arms over her chest. "Well, now, technically, I believe it belongs to the library, which makes it public property, and now I want it, so that makes it mine."

"You can't just do that, you know. Just 'cause I'm a kid doesn't mean you can take my stuff and make me do what you want."

"Oh, Jonah," Irene said sweetly. "It's not because you're a kid. It's because I'm bigger than you are. Now, you can either hand over the book or agree to go with me. Which is it going to be?"

Jonah muttered something under his breath and kicked the carpet.

"What was that?" she asked sharply.

"I said," Jonah repeated loudly, "you're not very nice."

Irene's smile was full of saccharine. "Thank you for noticing."

"God, what are you, two?"

She didn't bother dignifying that with a response, as it was clear that he was giving in. She opened the door again and ushered him through. As they went down the steps, she said, "While we're on the subject of that magic book...explain to me this disappearing thing that you do."

"Well..."

"The short version," she said. She unlocked the car but waited before opening the door to hear Jonah's explanation.

"I wake up."

"Okay, not that short."

Jonah sighed. "Really. That's it. When I wake up, I...I mean my spirit or whatever...goes back into my body."

"In English."

"Don't you watch movies and stuff? Jeez!"

"Not *stupid* movies, no."

Jonah's mouth screwed up like a prune. "Well, in some movies...*good* movies...the person's spirit gets separated from their body and they have to re-unite the two...you know, the ancient Egyptians thought people were made up of five different parts and when you died, different things happened to different parts...the 'ba' or spirit—"

"Yeah, okay, enough. What does that have to do with you?"

"That's what I'm telling you!" he cried, throwing up his hands. "Look, this isn't my body, right? This is just my...my spirit or whatever."

"Yeah, okay, I get it...out of body experience." .

"Yeah, and I get back into my body by coming out of the trance-thingy that lets me separate my spirit from my body in the first place."

"Okay, but how do you just 'wake up' whenever you want? I mean, one minute you're here and the next minute you're gone."

Jonah lit up. "Oh, well that's the really cool part. It's like hypnosis. You ever watch someone get hypnotized?"

"No."

"No?"

"It's all fake, you know."

"That's wrestling!" He harrumphed and then continued, "Well, if you did know about it, then you'd know there's usually a word or a sound—like snapping your fingers— that wakes the person up. I have something similar. There's a word I can say to wake myself up."

"It's not 'supercalifragilisticexpialidocious' is it?"

By the time she finished speaking, she was talking to herself—Jonah had disappeared.

Irene shook her head resignedly, walked back into the house, and sat down on the couch. About fifteen minutes later, she heard the front door open and close. Jonah walked in, a scowl on his face. "That wasn't funny."

"Actually, it kinda was."

"Can we go now?"

"Oh, now who's in a hurry?" she retorted, but she got up and led the way out of the house. Irene opened the car's driver side door, threw her purse in the back seat, and started to climb in.

Jonah stopped, his eyes goggling. "We're taking your car?"

"How else does one get to Boston?"

"There's the train..."

"How else does one get to the train station?"

"Yeah, but—"

"Just come on!"

Irene didn't wait for him to argue. She started the engine, put the car in reverse, and let it roll back an inch. Jonah remained rooted where he was. "Coming?" she asked and then slammed the driver's door closed.

Jonah sighed and dragged himself to the passenger side. "Well, I don't see what you need me for. You seem to have it all worked out."

"Oh, I'm sure you'll find a way to be useful."

Jonah gave her a disapproving frown. "I don't think you're taking this very seriously."

"Hey, I'm dead serious." She shot him a grin. "See what I did there? I made a funny."

"Did you?" he asked.

"Jeez, lighten up."

Emboldened by her previous day's success, Irene drove as she normally would, not worrying about the living. She turned onto the main street and headed west, toward the highway. Jonah sat stiffly beside her, ill at ease, and his eyes darted every which way as he watched the road, hardly blinking, one hand holding the door handle in a death grip.

It was mid-morning, which meant there was little traffic, and Irene had no problem avoiding the living cars on the road.

"So," she said, "tell me about this magic book of yours."

"Like what?"

"I don't know. Anything that might be helpful about finding the tunnel or tell me about the land of the dead or whatever. What should I expect if I go through the tunnel?"

Jonah relaxed slightly and settled back against the seat. "Uh...well, in most cultures it's believed that the dead person wakes up in a sort of waiting room or pre-land of the dead."

"Yeah, you said that before."

"Yeah, well some cultures believe that the dead person has to journey from the first place to the land of the dead, overcoming obstacles on the way. Like drinking from the river of forgetfulness and paying the ferryman to ferry you across the River Acheron."

"You mean the River Styx."

"No, that's a common mistake. It's actually the River Acheron."

She took her eyes off the road long enough to shoot him a dark look. "Yeah, okay, whatever, with you so far. Here's me, overcoming obstacles and traveling to the land of the dead. Got it."

Jonah twisted around to look at the backseat. "Which reminds me, you didn't pack anything."

"Pack?" Irene echoed. "I'm dead. What's there to pack?"

"Are you kidding?"

"No." She shot him a questioning look. "Are you?"

"Everybody always makes a big deal about the stuff that gets buried with the dead because they'll need it in the afterlife...the Egyptians, the Chinese, the ancient Romans and Celts..."

"Whatever happened to 'you can't take it with you?'"

Jonah grunted and slumped into his seat.

"Do you have even the tiniest sense of humor?"

Jonah grunted again. "I don't know; say something funny and we'll see."

"Ha. Ha."

They had reached the highway. As soon as Jonah realized what was about to happen, he squawked in alarm and grabbed the door with both hands. Irene floored the gas, racing to accelerate up the impossibly short on-ramp. The car slid sleekly into traffic and accelerated again as Irene swerved into the left lane, passed a slower moving car and then swerved back to the right again. Jonah gasped and gave her a sidelong look of disquiet, which she ignored.

"So, anything else about the afterlife?" she asked.

Jonah shifted slightly beside her, relaxing enough to take one hand off the door. The other, however, he kept firmly wrapped around the handle.

"I did a little more research into tunnels to the afterlife," he said. "It turns out Buddhists believe in a tunnel. A tunnel of light. Wise sages — they call them buddhas, meaning enlightened ones, which are people who have reached spiritual enlightenment, which they call Nirvana — guide the dead person to the tunnel."

Irene flashed Jonah a wry, bemused look. "I think I managed to follow that. I'm not sure you qualify as a wise sage, but okay. So then what happens?"

"Well, if the person chooses to enter the light, it means they have achieved spiritual enlightenment and they reach Nirvana. Which is like Heaven, I guess. The person casts off all vestiges of their earthly life and joins the great spiritual consciousness."

She was only half listening, but suddenly the words came into focus. Her frown deepened. "You said the person can choose to enter the light. So what happens if they don't go?" She couldn't believe a Mrs. Boine-like ghostly existence was really the only alternative.

Jonah shrugged.

"Okay, what? What's with the shrug? I know you do that when you don't want to say what you're really thinking."

Jonah shrugged again and then blushed. Then he twisted in his seat to face her, drawing in a deep breath. "Okay, it's like, sure, there's a choice, but why *wouldn't* you go into the light? Like, who would ever choose not to? It seems like a no-brainer."

"Well, you're thirteen —"

"I'm fourteen, and I'm not just a stupid kid, you know! You wouldn't have gotten this far without me."

"Okay, listen, buster, first of all, we haven't gotten anywhere yet. And second of all, I was already leaving for the city — without you — when you showed up this morning. So I could, too, have gotten this far without you."

"Buster? You sound like my mom."

Irene raised her voice, talking over the interruption. "Third of all, what I meant was that, if what you just said

72

is true about joining the spiritual consciousness or whatever, then going into the light means giving up everything you are. Losing your personality, your individuality, forgetting your friends, your family, everything. At thirteen...fourteen...you don't know who you are yet. You're still trying to figure it out, so it's not such a big deal for you to give all that up. I, on the other hand, do know who I am, and I like who I am. I don't want to be part of a...a collective—"

"Borg," Jonah said sagely.

"Bork?" Irene asked. "What are you, the Swedish chef?"

They exchanged puzzled glances.

"Okay, whatever," Irene said. "The point is, I want to be separate and independent. I want to be *me.*"

Jonah slumped against the seat, arms folded and head bowed in a sulk. However, he looked at Irene out of the corner of his eye, listening intently to every word. "Yeah, but it's Heaven—"

Irene stabbed the air with a finger. "No, Jonah. It's not Heaven. It's bliss. As in, 'ignorance is bliss.' You ever hear that saying before?" He nodded. "It means it's better not to know. Like, say, for instance, not knowing what a great life you had and how sad you are now that you don't have it anymore. You said it yourself before. The stories say that before they enter the afterlife, the dead have to drink from the river of forgetfulness. We have to *forget.* Sure, that means you won't be sad because you miss your friends or family, and you won't have any regrets about your life or sit around wishing you'd had more time. Because you won't remember *any* of it! You ever hear of a guy named Cerin? He has a famous quote, which goes, 'Please, dear God of happiness, show the radiance of your spectrum to our world, which here means to forget *everything.*' They try to hide it, dress up nicely, make you think Heaven and bliss are all the same thing but one is more of the good stuff you already have and the other is a lobotomy. They are two entirely different things."

Jonah looked surprised and mildly impressed. Then his forehead creased with thought. He seemed to be turning her words over in his mind. After a moment's contemplation, he finally said, with a faint tinge of suspicious hostility, "Who's Cerin?"

Irene laughed and relaxed against the seat as she changed lanes and passed a tractor trailer truck. Then she shrugged sheepishly. "So I took a philosophy class once. I thought I wanted to meet a sensitive guy." Jonah raised an eyebrow. She flashed him a crooked grin. "It's also a toast you make when you plan on getting totally shitfaced. It means you intend to get so drunk you can't even remember your own name." Jonah's face changed to a dry look that said this was more like what he expected from her, while clearly disapproving. Irene waved a hand in dismissal. "Forget it. The point is, Heaven may not be as great as it's been made out to be if the...Buddhists...or whatever...are right." She thumped against her seat. "On the other hand, staying here as a ghost doesn't strike me as terribly appealing either." She drew in a breath and then exhaled in frustration. "Arrrghhh!"

"Okay, well, the first thing is to actually find the tunnel. Maybe we're wrong. Maybe it's not that kind of tunnel."

Irene shot Jonah an exasperated look. "Well who made you so logical?"

Jonah turned his head but wasn't quite quick enough to prevent her from seeing his lips twitch with a self-satisfied smirk.

They were in Boston now and she switched lanes as their exit approached. She took the Storrow Drive exit, maneuvered through the heart-stoppingly complicated merge of adding and subtracting lanes as they crossed the interchange from one multi-laned, fast-moving road to another, and managed to exit to the city streets without incident.

Jonah, whose face had gone ashen during all of this, twisted in his seat, peering in various directions. "Where are we?"

Irene maneuvered through the tangled nest of narrow one-way streets at the heart of one of the city's oldest neighborhoods. The buildings here, old and small, was tightly packed and thrown into shadow by the surrounding skyscrapers of the downtown and financial districts.

Irene slowed down, hunting for somewhere to park. "We're in the North End. It's one of the oldest parts of Boston. As you pointed out, people have been dying for millions of years, right? So I figured, since it's so old, this would be a good place to find some other dead people."

"Dead people? I thought we were looking for the tunnel?"

"We are, but I'd also like to get some answers and see what the options are before I make a decision, okay? And that involves finding other dead people."

"Hello! How many dead people have you met here so far?"

Irene opened her mouth, but Jonah cut her off, "I don't count."

Irene shut her mouth, recalculated, and said, "Actually met? Well, just one, but—"

"Yeah, one. One dead person out of the millions and millions who have died in all of human history? You don't think that's weird?"

Irene's frown deepened. "Well…"

"Exactly. They all went somewhere and didn't come back. I don't think you're going to find a lot of dead people just hanging out."

"I saw three just the other day," she said hotly. "I'm noticing a lot of 'you' being used suddenly. I thought you were the one who loved all this afterlife stuff. Well, now, here's your chance to do some first-hand research."

Irene spied an empty parking spot, slid into the space at the end of the line of meters, and cut the engine.

"Uh, you know it says no parking," Jonah said as they climbed out of the car, with the cautious tone of one who knows he's sticking his hand into a hornet's nest.

Irene just smiled. "It's like Wonder Woman's jet."

"Huh?"

Irene walked away with a roll of her eyes. "Oh God, don't tell me you don't even read comic books? You are *the* weirdest kid."

Jonah's brow puckered for a moment. Then the confusion cleared. "Oh, you mean, like, it's invisible?"

Irene's smile widened. "Exactly. So how are they going to ticket me?"

"Yeah, but—" Jonah started but Irene cut him off.

"No buts. Now," she held out her arms indicating the directional choices before them, "which way?"

"We're really going to just wander around?"

She raised an eyebrow. "You could always go to school."

His eyes said he wanted to call her bluff, but he just shrugged. "Whatever."

"Okay, fine. Simon says..." Irene pointed in a random direction. "Left."

Eight

"My feet hurt."

Jonah stopped and waited for Irene to catch up. "This was your plan," he said.

"Look, there's a little park over there." She pointed limply, too hot and tired to raise her arm all the way. "Let's sit down, just for a minute, okay?"

They found a shaded spot under a rugged maple tree. Jonah dropped his backpack to the ground and settled down next to it. Irene dropped less gracefully into a heap across from him.

Their ghost slash tunnel hunting hadn't been going well. So far, all they had seen were two men leaning against the Old State House, each enjoying a cigarette. Dressed in the ubiquitous red coats and white pantaloons of British Revolutionary War soldiers, Irene had thought they were costumed re-enactment actors until she realized that the blue glow of the dead surrounded each of them. She'd been too flabbergasted and, frankly, too intimidated to try and approach them.

"Do you think they know the war is over?" she'd asked Jonah.

He looked at her quizzically. "Sure. Why not?"

Irene wasn't so sure. They seemed so...real. More accurately, they made far off history seem more real, more immediate, more tangible. She almost expected to smell gunpowder and hear cannon fire.

Later, Irene caught a glimpse of the backside of a ghost woman — this one in a tight-waisted, puffed-sleeve dress that had been fashionable around the turn of the last century — disappearing around a corner onto State Street. When they reached the corner, however, the woman had already melted away into the crowd.

Irene started to feel as if someone had thrown all of history into a blender and hit puree. Jonah thought it was great. She wasn't so sure. History had not been her strong suit in school, but she remembered enough to know that history tended to be rather bloody. She wasn't keen to run into angry Native Americans, angry Puritans, angry mill workers, angry Civil War soldiers, or members of any other group that might still be holding a grudge after hundreds of years.

Jonah smiled smugly as they relaxed on the grass. "Want to look at the book now?"

Irene ignored him. She tore off a blade of grass and began shredding it with her fingers. Jonah stretched out his legs, leaning back to brace himself on his forearms. He watched her for a moment, a faint crease marring his forehead.

"How's your mom?" he asked, his hazel eyes full of sympathy.

"Huh?" Irene hesitated, her eyes darting sideways to glance at his face. "How did you know about my mother?"

"You were coming from her house the day I met you, remember? You thought she was sick or something."

Irene frowned, surprised that he had remembered this minute detail from their first, chance encounter. She gave him a suspicious look. "Yeah, she's fine, I guess."

"You guess?"

"Well, I haven't been back. There didn't seem to be a lot of point. She can't see or hear me." Irene paused and grabbed a handful of grass, yanking it up by the roots. "Besides, it's not really like that with us...my mother and me, I mean. She's got her own little world and I have mine." Irene knocked back her hair with a sharp toss of her head. "It's different for you. With your mom, I mean. You're thirteen—"

"Fourteen."

"...fourteen...and you're a boy. Boys and their mothers is not the same as girls and their mothers."

Jonah pondered this for a moment, tracing the seam of a pant leg with an absent-minded finger. "Yeah, I get that I guess."

Irene tried to keep her tone light, but a note of bitterness colored her words. "Boys are always mommy's little angel. Girls...forget it. Then there's no pleasing the woman. My mother was very fond of saying, 'Dear God, what did I ever do to deserve a girl?'"

"Do you have brothers or sisters?"

"Me? No. Just me."

There was a thoughtful silence. Irene was coming to recognize these thick, ponderous silences as the sound of Jonah thinking deeply. She braced herself for one of his surprisingly clever, but generally annoying, insights.

"My sister is a pain, but it's good to have someone else around who gets it."

Irene nodded—God, what she wouldn't give right now to have someone else around who understood what she was going through.

"So in these stories you keep talking about...how do the dead people know where to go? You said it starts with a journey, but how do people know which direction to go?"

Jonah shrugged limply. "It's all different. Some cultures say the land of the dead lies to the east, some to the north, some to the south, some say it's over the mountains, some say it's in a cave, some say it's in the sky, and others say it's underground."

"Uh, okay, so really anywhere. Not helpful."

Jonah let out a squawk of protest.

Irene dusted the shredded grass remnants from her fingers, plucked another blade, and began the process again. "God, this sucks! I hate this! It's not supposed to be this difficult. The afterlife is just supposed to be there, right in front of you."

"Maybe it is. We haven't really looked that hard."

"We shouldn't *have* to look hard. That's my point. The white light and the tunnel have to be easy to find, right? I mean, everyone, even children and babies, has found it, so it has to be in plain sight and easy to get to." Irene paused, then added, "Unless I'm being punished for some reason," as a vision of blue-green water suddenly loomed before her.

"Why would you be punished?"

"I wouldn't!" Irene threw down the crumpled grass. "I didn't do anything wrong!" She forced herself to relax, taking in a deep breath and then releasing it slowly. More calmly, she said, "I did everything I was supposed to—I got an education, I got a good job, I had family, friends, a love life. I traveled, I kept up with the news, I listened to music, I met people. I don't know what more there is. What was the point of it all, if not that?"

Jonah stretched forward to retie a loose shoelace. "Well, is there anything you want to do that you didn't? Any regrets or wrongs you want to set right? Any unfinished business?"

"No!" Irene threw up her hands. "You know, I don't get that kind of stuff. You know, those sappy movies about the things that are supposedly so important in life. No, I didn't stop to notice the particular shade of green that trees are in the spring. You know why? Because I don't give a shit. They're trees. So the fuck what? No, I didn't get married or have kids, and you know what? I didn't because who gives a shit? There're other things in life, too."

Jonah's eyes were like saucers and he was leaning away from her, as if the force of her words was pushing him backwards. "Okay, okay!" he cried. "I get it."

"Yeah, well, if this is supposed to be like one of those Lifetime movie specials where I learn to value what was really important in life and all that bullshit, then the cosmic powers-that-be can stick it in their ear. What right do they have to tell me I didn't do things the right way or enjoy the right kind of things?"

"Uh...I think that's the point of the whole 'judging' thing."

"Yeah, well fuck them. Who are they to judge me?"

"The creators of the universe?"

"Yeah, well...fuck them."

"You keep saying that."

"Yeah, well—"

"Stop!" Jonah cried, cringing and putting his hands over his ears.

Irene flopped back onto the grass. "Okay, fine. You win. Time for the magic book."

"Look, I think we should go to the library."

Irene sat up again, scowling contemptuously. "The library?"

"Look...a lot of the book is in a foreign language. At the library we can sit down—on chairs. It's inside, it's comfortable...there aren't any bugs..." Jonah swatted an ant off his knee. "We can look at the book, we can use the Internet to translate the foreign parts, and we can do some more research, too, if we get stuck."

Irene sighed but climbed to her feet, dusted herself off, and then held out a hand to help Jonah up. "I suppose you know where the library is?"

He gaped at her in disbelief, as if her not knowing where the library was located was the most unbelievable thing he had ever heard, shook his head, and set off. They returned to the street, turned left at the next corner, and were waiting for the streetlight to change at the end of the next block when Irene heard someone say, "Read your palm?"

She turned and spied an impromptu parlor set up right there on the sidewalk. The man who had spoken—somewhat rumpled and careless looking—was slouched in a folding chair, a cigarette dangling from the corner of his mouth and dark sunglasses covering his eyes. In front of him a cheap card table, draped with a piece of red felt and displaying a deck of Tarot cards, propped up a sign that said "Tarot & Palm Readings—$5."

"You're a little late," Irene said.

The man tilted his head and looked at Irene over the top of his shades. "Oh, sorry. Didn't realize. My mistake."

A plump, middle-aged woman passing by stopped and looked at the palm reader. "Are you talking to me?"

"Sorry. Just talking to myself." When she looked doubtful, he flashed her a sexy grin. She started to grin back, seemed confused, and finally just turned and continued on her way.

Irene looked the guy over. He was actually rather good looking, in a scruffy, unkempt kind of way. She had intended to keep walking, but now she turned to face him, moving closer and smiling.

Jonah elbowed her and whispered, "Not blue."

Irene realized he was right. The palm reader wasn't dead, but he could see her. "Hey, can I ask you a question?" she said.

He shook his head. "No offense, but you're bad for business. I can't talk to you. So if you don't mind..." He jerked a thumb, indicating Irene should move along.

"Look, I just need some information—"

"Can't help." He jerked his thumb again. "You want the occult shop down the street."

A young couple, walking hand-in-hand, swerved away from the psychic with alarmed looks, stumbling off the sidewalk into the street.

"Look, you stopped me," Irene said. "I just..."

The guy had already put his head down, burying his nose in the cheap paperback in his hands.

Jonah touched her arm. "Come on."

Irene bristled and opened her mouth to speak, when a young woman sat down at the table. "Can I get a reading?" she asked.

Irene let Jonah steer her away, muttering, "That guy was kind of an ass," as they walked.

Jonah shook his head but didn't say anything.

"Well?" Irene demanded. "This is the part where you're supposed to agree with me."

"Well, it sounds like we found a lead," Jonah said.

Irene shook her head, both amused and exasperated by his pragmatic response. "Yeah, okay, Nancy Drew."

They continued down the street and then drew to a stop in front of a short, squat building sandwiched between two brownstones that seemed towering in comparison. Various neon signs offering Tarot and palm readings and other assorted spiritual advice decorated the entrance. A sign over the door proclaimed it to be *Madame Majicka's Shop of Mysteries.*

Irene was dumbfounded. "This can't be what he meant!"

Jonah looked the shop over, trying to find the flaw. "Why not?"

"It's a dump!"

"It's blue."

"It's still a dump," Irene said, pulling open the door.

"You're doing it again," Jonah said as he followed her into the store. "Why don't we at least go in and check it out before giving up?"

Once through the door, Irene rolled her eyes as she surveyed the neat—but tacky—little shop: the cheap, laminated counter circling the perimeter of the room, the stacks of books, candles, crystals, incense and the like, and the rack of pentagram necklaces by the cash register. "Oh yeah. Yep. Yep. Just like I thought. There's even a bead curtain. Yep, here comes the woman dressed like a gypsy."

The woman in question was coming through the curtain from a room in the back. The silk scarf tied over her dark, voluptuous hair, the large gold hoops on her ears, and the multitude of gold bangles on her arms did indeed give her a certain gypsyesque appearance. However, instead of the expected peasant top, layered gauzy skirt, and heavy make-up, her trim figure was dressed in a tailored pantsuit in a rich plum color, and she wore little make-up. The woman smiled broadly, revealing a row of perfect white teeth, startlingly bright against the Mediterranean tinge of her skin, and her dark eyes, rimmed with lashes so thick she didn't need eyeliner, were warm and welcoming. "Come in, come in! Don't stand there with the door open. Everything is twenty-five percent off today."

"Uh..." Irene said as Jonah pushed past her into the store.

"Whoa...cool!" Jonah bee-lined for a display of occult paraphernalia that included fake skulls and black candles — all glowing blue. Irene rolled her eyes again. "Jonah..." she said, trying to call him back, but it was a lost cause.

"So...are you looking for anything special or just browsing?"

"Are you the owner...Madame Majicka?" Irene stumbled over the name but managed to keep disdain out of her tone.

The woman smiled again. "Of course. How can I help you?"

"Well, I hope this doesn't sound strange, but I'm looking for the afterlife, a tunnel to the other side, other dead people, or anything like that."

"Oh? Well good for you," the woman said. Then she called to Jonah, who had picked up a packet of incense and was turning it over in his hands, "Oh you don't want that, dear. It doesn't do anything but give you a headache." She added, in an aside to Irene, "The college kids always come in looking for it though, so what can you do?"

"Uh, okay..." Irene floundered, feeling a little adrift. "So how about it?"

Madame Majicka blinked in surprise, or possibly confusion. "How about what?"

"The afterlife. A guy down the street said you could help me."

Madame Majicka's laughter trilled across the upper range of human hearing. "Well, I'm sorry to disappoint, really I am, but I just carry odds and ends that help seekers connect to the other side."

"Okay, well I'm trying to get to the other side."

Madame Majicka frowned thoughtfully. "Well, for you — seeing as you're dead — the other side would be this side...so, technically, you're already here."

"Yeah, I just left here," Irene said flatly.

"And now you're back." Madame Majicka brightened. "So that's worked out."

"I never left! I mean...I'm trying to go forward...not backwards."

"That seems very sensible. No sense spending time stuck in the past. Always look to the future, that's what I say...oh, take care with that, dear. It bites." Jonah had picked up a statue of what appeared to be a turtle. He cast Madame Majicka a questioning look and then apparently decided she was serious, because he set it down with a quick, careful movement.

Irene shook her head. "God, this must be how Alice felt."

"Who?" Jonah asked, crossing in front of her to examine the shelves on the other side of the store.

Irene threw up her hands. "The pair of you are completely nuts!"

"Can I offer you some tea? You seem like you're having a bad day."

"She's offering me tea," Irene said dryly to Jonah in a loud, theatrical voice.

Jonah, who was inspecting—Irene did a double take—what might very possibly be a collection of giant, dried insects, each as big as her hand, called back just as loudly, "I think you should have some."

Irene heard the bell over the door tingle. She turned to see who had entered, but no one was there.

Madame Majicka smiled apologetically. "Excuse me." The psychic then headed toward the back of the shop and disappeared through the bead curtain.

"Come on," Irene said, turning to look for Jonah. He was inspecting a jar of thick gray sludge. "I don't think she knows anything. That guy was just having a laugh at my expense."

Madame Majicka reappeared, shaking her head. "Tourists," she said tragically.

Irene pursed her lips. "Come on, Jonah. We're going."

"I think you should have that tea," Jonah said, turning over a book titled *Living with the Living*.

Madame Majicka brightened. "Oh yes, the tea...I almost forgot. So you're staying then?"

Irene drew in a deep breath. "Look, can you tell me how to find the tunnel to the afterlife...you know...the land of the dead...Hades...uh...Hel..."

"Duat...the Garden of the Rain God...Sheol —" Jonah added from the far side of the store.

"Yes, thank you," Irene said, cutting him off. "Anyway...do you know where I can find a tunnel to any one of those places?"

Madame Majicka gave Irene a slow, searching look. "Well, I do and I don't," she said, cautiously.

"What does that mean?"

"Well, my dear, that's both a little easy and a little difficult to explain."

"Are you going to keep doing that?"

"Well I might and I might not. It's entirely up to you."

"Okay, now you're just doing it on purpose."

Madame Majicka gestured to a tall, pub-style table flanked by tall stools. Both table and chairs were made of wood so ancient it had turned black and been worn as smooth and hard as iron. "Why don't you have a seat, my dear, while I get the tea?"

Irene threw back her head and screeched in frustration. "Look, I just want to get to the afterlife, that's all."

"In those clothes?" Madame Majicka frowned.

Irene looked down at her T-shirt and jeans. "What's wrong with my clothes?"

"Well, it's just that they're...they kinda show."

Irene noticed once more the occasional sharp, mirror-like flash whenever she moved.

Jonah had moved to a low coffee table in the middle of the room and was handling what appeared to be — there was another double-take — a collection of small waxed dolls that Irene had the nasty suspicion were meant for voodoo. "You'd better get that tea," he said without looking up.

Irene threw up her hands. "Okay, fine, tea."

"Wonderful! Here, I'll tell you what. This might help..." Madame Majicka swooped behind the counter and returned in a moment with a thin black book. "Why don't you take a look at this while I get the tea?" She handed the book to Irene who glanced down at the cover. Embossed in stark, white letters on the otherwise uninterrupted expanse of black were three words: *So You're Dead*

Irene raised an eyebrow. Madame Majicka nodded in encouragement then bustled off to the back of the store and disappeared behind a lace curtain, presumably to get them all tea.

Irene held the book for a second, hesitating. Then she flipped to the first page. It contained only three lines, printed in a large, plain font:

1. You're Dead.
2. No, really, you're dead.
3. But life goes on.

Irene's eyebrows arched upward in surprise. Was this a joke? She peeked around the store with suspicious eyes. She looked down again and then, gingerly, as if something might jump out at her, turned the page.

4. Being dead can be fun.
5. It depends on your attitude.
6. So look on the bright side.

"Oh really? There's a bright side?" she muttered. She looked around the store again. Jonah was still engrossed with the various displays. He had apparently set himself a goal of touching every single object in the place. Now he was handling what appeared to be some kind of dried and shriveled root vegetables.

7. Yes, there is a bright side.
8. You can only die once.
9. You're as old as you're ever going to get.

Irene's eyebrows shrugged in reluctant agreement. *Well, okay, you have a point.* She flipped the page.

10. Stop moping.
11. Get back into the swing of things.
12. Read the FAQ.

"That's it?" Irene turned the book over, looked at the back cover, and then looked at the front cover again. She turned the pages again and found some additional text printed on the inside of the back cover.

Q: Why haven't I crossed over?
A: Death isn't about a right and a wrong way to do things. It's about having options.

Q: Why can't the living see or hear me?
A: Metaphysics.

Q: Why do I look so young and healthy?
A: If you have to be dead, you might as well look good.

Q: Do I need to eat or sleep in the afterlife?
A: That's a personal decision that each person should make for his or herself.

Q: Does this prove that there is a God?
A: No.

Q: Does this prove that there isn't a God?
A: No.

Q: Is this Hell?
A: It depends on your point of view.

This time, that really was the end. Irene crossed the room, the thin volume wrapped in her arms, and hitched herself up onto one of the stools flanking the table. Jonah wandered over, looking at her in amusement, clearly enjoying himself. "Not a word," she threatened. He shrugged and shoved his hands into his pockets. She pushed the book across the table to him. He opened it and began reading intently.

Madame Majicka returned in a few moments with a tea tray piled high with cups, saucers, spoons, lemons, and other accoutrements and settled herself gracefully on a stool opposite Irene. For a time, there was only the sound of china clinking as Madame Majicka poured three cups of tea. Irene wiggled on her stool, feeling the hard, wooden surface bite into her backside. She pushed a filled teacup along the table toward Jonah. He ignored it. Instead, he leaned forward, resting his arms on the table.

Madame Majicka finished stirring her own tea and her smile turned expectant. She tapped the book with a finger. "Did this help, my dear?"

Irene pursed her lips. "No."

Jonah ducked his head, hiding a gurgle of laughter in his arms. Irene nudged him. "Don't encourage her," she muttered.

Madame Majicka was the very picture of stunned dismay. "Well, my dear, I am shocked to hear that."

"Really?" Irene said drily. "Look, I just want to get to the other side, okay?"

"Well, really, you'll forgive my saying so, but you hardly seem ready. You'll get eaten alive. You're much better off staying here."

"I'm dead," Irene said flatly.

Madame Majicka patted Irene's hand and said sadly, "That *is* unfortunate."

Beside her, Jonah choked on suppressed laughter. Irene kicked him under the table.

"Look, can you help me or not?"

Madame Majicka spread her hands in protest. "But, my dear, I don't know what it is you want."

Jonah dropped his head again but not quite fast enough to hide the sound of laughter. Irene jabbed him again with the toe of her shoe.

"Ow!" he protested, reaching down to rub his shin.

"Look, I just want some information on the afterlife, okay?"

"But, my dear!" Madame Majicka protested, gesturing to the book on the table. "I've told you everything I know."

"What, this?" Irene picked up the book and tossed it back on the table with disdain. "Oh come on, you must be able to tell me something...anything."

Madame Majicka shook her head, a look of deep regret etched on her face. "I really can't. I mean, how could I? I'm not dead."

Irene was taken aback. She looked Madame Majicka up and down and then she leaned closer, peering at the other woman. Jonah had raised his head from his arms and was listening closely.

"If you're not dead, then how come you can see me?"

Madame Majicka made a limp gesture of protest. "Well, my dear, who can explain why we're born the way we are? I'm sure there are things you're good at, too."

Jonah was laughing into his arm again. Irene doggedly kept on, despite all evidence that logic was as lost here as a snowball in a field of snow. "You seem to be alive." Irene reached out and tentatively poked Madame Majicka in the arm. "The store is blue, though."

"Only the front." The medium's tone suggested Irene had insulted her.

"Uh, okay, just the front," Irene replied. "What's that got to do with anything?"

Madame Majicka blinked. "I don't know. What does it?"

Irene threw up her hands. "I just meant, for instance, Jonah can see me, despite not being dead, because he has a magic spell. What's your excuse?"

"Just lucky, I guess," Madame Majicka responded.

Jonah touched Irene's arm to get her attention, leaned close, and said in a low tone, "She's a psychic."

"Yeah, I know."

"So, that's why."

"Oh." Irene turned this over. "But..."

Madame Majicka gave her a sympathetic look. "It says it right on the door."

"Yeah, but…psychics. Really?" Irene looked back and forth between Jonah and Madame Majicka. They both nodded. Irene exhaled hard, taken aback by the sudden realization that psychics were actually psychic.

"Okay, then tell me this: there are all these stories about the afterlife, right? So which ones are true?"

"Well, all of them," Madame Majicka said, as if she didn't quite understand the question.

"What do you mean?"

"I mean," Madame Majicka said gently but insistently, "all of them—the Milky Way is a collection of stars and galaxies, a river in the sky, and a universal consciousness. There is a single god and there are many gods. There are cities of the dead and lakes of fire and a blinding light and all your family is there. There's a bridge to the sky and a boat across a river and a hill separating you from the next village. You must both forget and remember. You will both eat the best of everything and have no need of food. You will be both naked and clothed. You will be a part of everything and apart from it. You will be omniscient and you will be insignificant."

Madame Majicka's voice became like a spell, weaving a world that shimmered before Irene's eyes. It hovered just beyond her sight, on the edge of her consciousness, like a streetscape seen through a rain-blurred window. She could feel and smell and taste it all, just beyond the range of her current senses. It was as if she was remembering a far off place she had visited long ago. Somehow, it all felt familiar.

Irene blinked and the vision dissolved. She felt an unaccountable wave of bitter and crushing loss break over her. She blinked again and was surprised to find her eyes were wet.

Jonah was listening with rapt attention and was gripping the edge of the table with both hands. He leaned forward, nearly panting with excitement.

"Yeah, but they're just stories…" Irene said helplessly. "I mean…the afterlife isn't really going to be like that…"

Madame Majicka picked up the teapot and poured another cup of tea. "Well, my dear, just because it's a story doesn't mean it isn't true."

"How could *all* of that be true?" Irene cried. "Everything you just said is completely contradictory!"

The psychic smiled. "Finding out is half the fun. More tea?" She held out a cup to Irene. Irene shook her head and pushed the tea away.

Jonah tugged on Irene's sleeve. "See? It's a quest. Just like I said."

"We're not pirates!"

Jonah sagged with exasperation. "Pirates? Man..." He shook his head. Then he perked up again. "Wow, this is the coolest thing that's ever happened to me. I'm so glad you kidnapped me. We're going to go through the tunnel and I'm going to get to meet Charon and Cerebus and –"

"First of all, *we* aren't doing anything until I know for certain what's on the other side because this is starting to sound a little complicated. Second of all, I'm not entirely sure this is a healthy past time for you."

Jonah squeaked in outrage, but the trill of the bell over the door prevented him from arguing further. "Excuse me," their host said, and once again she disappeared through the curtain.

After a minute, Jonah got up and went over to it. He stuck his head through and Irene heard him say, "Oh wow! There's like a whole other store on this side." His head reappeared and his eyes were shining. "For live people. It's like two stores stuck back to back."

"Uh...great – it's the Oreo of occult paraphernalia."

Jonah frowned disapprovingly. "God, don't you find anything interesting?"

"Yeah," Irene said dryly. "New shoes."

Jonah started to cast her a disgusted look, but then his expression changed to surprise and he scampered back to the table, where he engaged in actively looking nonchalant. Madame Majicka emerged through the lace curtain a second later. She resettled herself on her stool and gave Irene a warm smile.

Irene waited for Madame Majicka to say something, but the other woman just sat there, smiling at her with big-hearted affection.

"Okay, sooo...any ideas on how I prepare for what's on the other side, then?" Irene asked.

"My expertise only covers the land of the living. You'll have to find a guide, I'm afraid."

"A guide? What, like this?" Irene disdainfully flicked the slim black book.

Madame Majicka looked horrified. "Oh no, my dear, not a guide *book*. A guide."

With effort, Irene managed to suppress the urge to throttle Madame Majicka. "How do I find such a person?"

Madame Majicka shrugged and took a sip of tea. "Oh, just spread a little goodwill around. One will generally show up."

"You know, that's a fat lot of no help."

Madame Majicka smiled, unperturbed. "Well, really, I do wish I could be more help, but you can't get blood from a stone. Now, if you'd like a bloodstone, that I could help you with."

"No, thanks, I—"

Jonah frowned, suddenly thoughtful. "I think you should get one. Bloodstones are supposed to be able to help guide people."

"Okay, fine," Irene said desperately, agreeing just to get everyone to shut up. "I'll take one. How much?"

Madame Majicka beamed. "Only five dollars. Such a deal!"

Irene reached into her purse and pulled out her wallet. "I don't have any cash on me. Do you take cards?"

Madame Majicka looked horrified. "My dear, you can't use that!"

"Why not?"

"My dear, how many people have you ever heard of charging up their credit cards *after* they died? Well, really, it's just not done."

"Well, yeah, but...this is my money...my stuff."

"What belongs with the living stays with the living," the psychic said softly, "and what belongs with the dead stays with the dead."

"I don't..." Irene was bewildered. "Well then how do you expect me to pay?"

Madame Majicka just smiled sadly and shrugged helplessly. Irene slipped off her stool feeling flustered and disgruntled. She felt like a house had dropped on her. She had already caught on to the fact that she couldn't do things that made it appear she was still alive — like send emails or throw away mail — but the full ramifications were just now hitting her. She couldn't make phone calls — not that anyone could hear her anyway — withdraw money from the bank, or even rearrange anything in her own home. She was starting to feel a lot like a prisoner...or an unwanted house guest.

Madame Majicka picked up the teapot. "Are you sure you won't have some more tea?"

"No, I'm all full up on tea, thanks. Come on, Jonah, I think we're done here."

Irene marched to the door.

"Please come back any time," Madame Majicka called.

"Yeah, right," Irene scoffed in a low voice to Jonah as they exited the shop. "Over my dead body."

Jonah gave her a dry look.

"*Don't* say it," she warned as the door shut behind them.

Nine

They didn't say much as they continued on to the library. Jonah seemed to be lost in some sort of rapturous daydream, while Irene felt uneasy.

Once inside, Irene surveyed the walls of books, the dining room-sized wooden tables, and the scattering of people pouring over the tomes with a reverence she couldn't imagine for a church, let alone a book. She racked her brain to remember the last time she was in a library.

"You look lost. Do you need some help?"

Irene turned to look at the speaker — a women, who glowed blue. She was younger than Irene, perhaps in her mid-twenties, with a pixie face and wearing a stylish yet sensible sweater set with a matching pleated skirt of pale blue that evoked the 1950s.

Jonah said, "No," at the same time that Irene said, "Yes." Irene elbowed him with a quelling frown.

The other woman pushed a stray curl — one of the short, riotous mop that covered her head — behind her ear and stuck out her hand. "I'm Amy Gilp."

Irene took the proffered hand. "Irene Dunphy. Nice to meet you Amy Gill."

"It's Gilp. With a 'p.'"

"Gilp?" Irene repeated, not sure she had heard correctly.

"Close enough." The young woman smiled. "What brings you to the library?"

"We don't need any help," Jonah hissed to Irene.

Irene elbowed him again, wondering at his sudden hostility. To Amy she said, "Well, I'm just trying to figure out what I'm supposed to do now that I'm dead."

Amy nodded and made a sympathetic noise. "Recent, huh?"

"Yeah."

Amy smiled brightly. "Well, the good news is that being dead doesn't mean your life is over."

Irene's brow furrowed. "Uh...technically, I think it does — "

"It can be a little sad at first, but you'll get over it," Amy continued.

Something from Madame Majicka's book stirred in Irene's memory: *so get back into the swing of things.*

Well, that was why she was here wasn't it — to make some dead friends? Irene smiled. "Actually, that's exactly what I was hoping to do. I was hoping to find out what there is to do for fun, now that I'm dead."

Amy lit up. "Oh, you should totally come out with us some time. I could introduce you to some people."

"*Dead* people?" Irene asked.

"Well, of course. The living really aren't all that much fun. Well...fun to hang out with, I mean, when you're dead. When you're alive — "

Jonah was fidgeting, a growing scowl darkening his face. He cut in, saying, "Come on," as he grabbed Irene's wrist and tugged her away.

"Hey!" Irene protested, trying to dig in her heels, but the determined bent of Jonah's head brooked no argument.

"Oh, well I'll see you later," Amy called to her.

"No, wait!" Irene said, but Jonah had already pulled her around a corner and out of ear shot. She wrenched her hand out of his grip. "Will you stop?"

He thumped his backpack down on a nearby table. "I thought you wanted to find out about the tunnel and stuff, not spend all day talking to people," he said petulantly.

"Well, Einstein, I wanted to do both. By talking," she pantomimed talking with her hand, "to dead people…I might learn…something…about the…afterlife." She illustrated each phrase with exaggerated charades-like gestures.

Jonah glared at her and dropped into a chair. "Yeah, well, she was stupid."

Irene shook her head. "No wonder you don't have any friends."

"Who says I don't have any friends?"

Irene cocked an eyebrow. "Yeah, right. Because the popular kids all prefer to hang out with dead people."

"Oh yeah? Well…well, I bet you'll be happy to be hanging out with the one guy who has almost every book on Earth about the afterlife when I help you find the tunnel!" Jonah cried.

"Will you keep it down!" An older woman, fashionably arrayed in a red and black pantsuit accented by a handsome string of pearls, came around the corner, directing a quelling look at Jonah. The heavy, black-rimmed cat's-eye glasses and stiff bun that characterized crabby old women in every movie ever made since nineteen forty ruined the fashionable aura.

Blue, Irene realized as she looked closer. The woman crossed her arms over her chest. "This is a library," she said and Irene had a flashback to her fifth grade math teacher, smacking the board with the pointing stick after each word as she said, "There is *no* talking during class."

Irene stiffened, annoyed at the interruption. "Who are we bothering, exactly? We're dead. No one can see us. No one can hear us."

"Of course they can hear you," the other woman said. Jonah and Irene exchanged incredulous looks and then smothered chokes of laughter.

The woman went on, raising her voice to talk over their giggles. "Use of the library is a privilege, not a right. Do I make myself clear? I don't want to see any nonsense. No taking books off the shelves in front of the patrons. No carrying books past the patrons. No flipping pages in front of the patrons. Do not take books that patrons are looking at. Do not make photocopies in front of the patrons. No using writing implements in front of the patrons. In short, no distressing the patrons by doing anything that suggests that this library is haunted." She concluded her speech with a short, sharp nod of her head. Then, as an afterthought, she added, "And the deceased do not have lending rights. All materials are to be used here." She turned away with a jerk and stalked off.

Irene's eyes slid to Jonah. "Book Nazi," she mouthed to him. He giggled.

She hadn't finished giving Jonah a dressing-down for his tantrum, but now the moment had passed and it seemed pointless to bring it up. She pulled out a chair and sat down, and Jonah followed suit. He began to fish in his backpack for something. Irene heaved a sigh as she tried to force her mind to focus. She frowned as she tried to remember all the questions, all the concerns, all the niggling doubts about the afterlife swirling in the back of her mind.

"Madame Majicka said something about finding a guide. Does the book say anything about that?"

Jonah pursed his lips in deep thought as he continued to rummage. "Uh…well I know that the Aztecs buried a dog with their dead —"

"A dog?"

"Shhhh!" came a harsh, admonishing hiss from somewhere nearby.

Jonah nodded and lowered his voice. "Yeah, to be the dead person's guide in the afterlife."

"Okay, that's sick; I'm not killing a dog."

Jonah flushed. "You asked!"

Irene dismissed this comment with a wave of her hand. "Okay, so forget the guide. What about the tunnel? What does the book say about that?"

Jonah pulled a thick, black book from his bag. For a moment, Irene thought he had taken the *So You're Dead* book from the magic shop. As she looked more closely, though, she realized that this book was not just thicker, but that its cover was black and rough as tree bark, rather than smooth and supple like leather.

"God, it's ugly." She grabbed it from his resistant hands. "It doesn't even have a title or anything." She ran a finger over the random, meandering lines embossed on the cover, ignoring Jonah's mute glare of outrage.

She flicked the book open with a finger and then squinted at the page. The writing was multi-layered. The main text, in a small, black calligraphy-like font, was indeed completely foreign. The strange characters were interspersed with triangles, dots, and other symbols. Occasionally there were other pages—obviously inserted later—in different, sometimes more recognizable, languages. Some of these were even in English. On top of the main writing, in a multitude of implements and hands, were cross-outs, additions, underlines, and exclamation points. These later embellishments covered the main text and spilled into the margins, cramming every page with a crazy quilt of text, nearly obliterating the underlying words. Even the pages in English had this treatment.

"Jesus!" Irene said. "This thing is going to make me blind."

"You see what it's like," Jonah said, reaching across her to flip a thin, nearly translucent page, crinkled like old vellum. "Only some of it is in English. The rest is in some foreign language."

"Foreign language? This doesn't look like any language I've ever seen. It's like Sumerian or something."

Jonah leaned forward in excitement. "Can you read it?"

"Uh no. My MBA didn't come with a minor in dead languages I'm afraid."

"Then what makes you think it's Sumerian?"

Irene shot him an exasperated look. "That was just random, Jonah. I get the History Channel, too, you know."

He flushed with embarrassment. "Whatever," he muttered.

She pinned a paragraph with a fingertip. "Well, some of it I recognize. That's French or Spanish or something." As Jonah opened his mouth, she added, "No, I don't know any of those, either." She was quiet as she slowly turned the pages, scouring each one for anything familiar.

"God, this thing is just gibberish!" She slammed the book closed. Guiltily she looked around to see if the noise had startled anyone, but none of the living patrons seemed to have heard it. In a more reasonable tone of voice, she said, "How did you ever make any sense out of it?"

Jonah sighed and reached for the book. "Okay, look...it's like the book is a catalog of all the beliefs that people have about death. Like, look at this page. See the pictures? There's swords, and coins, and people...I think those are servants. This is all the stuff different cultures bury with their dead. See...here's a dog, even. So I bet the text on this page talks about the stuff that people need to take to the next life."

Irene stared at the book for a moment, turning Jonah's words over. "Yeah?"

"Yeah. See here," he flipped forward a few pages, "how the stuff that's in English says Judaism–one year, Zoroastrians–three days, and Egyptians–seventy days? I think that has to do with how long before the dead wake up in the afterlife. Then here..."—again he flipped pages—"Aztecs–nine, Hindus–fourteen, Chinese–nineteen, and stuff? That all has to do with how many levels of the afterlife there are according to different cultures."

Irene was impressed. "Wow, you figured all that out by yourself?"

Jonah's flush of embarrassment cascaded across his ears and down his neck. "Aww, don't get mushy on me."

Irene laughed. Then Jonah's words sunk in. "Wait...what do you mean 'levels' of the afterlife?"

Jonah shifted uncomfortably. "Er...yeah. About that...some—well, a lot—of cultures believe that there are different levels to the afterlife—"

"Wait a minute! Are you telling me—"

"Let me finish! So you know how there's the waiting room and then the actual afterlife? Well, some cultures think there's a whole bunch of different obstacles — in different lands — between the two and the dead have to cross these different lands to get to the afterlife."

She gave him a dry look. "Why?"

Jonah's face went blank. "Why?" he repeated. "What do you mean, 'why?'"

"Why do the dead *have* to do all this stuff? Says who? For what purpose?"

Jonah looked shocked. "Well...well...that's just the way it is."

"Yeah, well, fuck that."

"But...but..."

She shook her head. "As far as I can tell, no one is making me move on. I can choose to stay here if I want, right?"

Jonah stared at her for a moment, and then he finally said, nonchalantly turning his attention to flipping pages of the book, "Yeah, that's true. It probably is better just to stay here. The journey through all the different levels of the afterlife is just a way to judge which souls are worthy to enter Heaven, and you said you didn't want to deal with all that judging stuff."

The implication that she was afraid to be judged — or wasn't brave enough to complete the journey — infuriated her, and Irene slapped a hand down onto the middle of the book, her eyes narrowed to slits. Jonah looked up, meeting her eyes. "Listen, buster. No one tells me what to do. *If* I decide to go through the tunnel, no one, and I mean *no one*, is going to stop me from getting to where I want to be, got it?"

She wasn't sure, but she thought she saw a glimmer of a smile pass over his face, and she had the feeling he'd tricked her in some way. However, all he said was, "You're doing that fake mom thing again. It's kind of annoying."

She was about to make a sharp retort when two living girls approached their table. "How about this one?" one asked her companion. A wave of alarm washed over Irene — what if the girls tried to sit there? What if they sat *on* her?

To her relief, the second girl pointed to a different table. "How about there?"

The two girls moved off.

Must have sensed us, Irene thought, just like with the parking spaces. How many times had she done the same thing—wandered around a theater or cafeteria, passing up perfectly good seats because of some vague, unsettled feeling that it wasn't quite right?

Irene looked down and words caught her eye. She lifted her hand off the page. "Wait a sec...what does this say? Something about seventy days..."

Jonah looked at the page. "Yeah, this is the part where it catalogs how long people are dead before they wake up as ghosts. Most cultures don't think you wake up immediately in the afterlife. There needs to be time for a proper burial and all the necessary rituals and all that stuff."

"Are you telling me I've been dead for *two months?*"

Jonah hurriedly pointed to another area of the page. "No, look, see...here, it says 'seven days' and it's circled. I think that's really the right answer."

"So it really has been more than a week since I went out with my friends?"

Jonah squirmed in discomfort. "Yeah. Sorry."

"You're just chock full of interesting tidbits, aren't you?"

Jonah flushed scarlet, and Irene instantly regretted taking her frustration out on him. She felt her own cheeks warm. She looked down at the book, searching for a peace offering.

"Okay, so how did you know about the glowing? Where does it talk about that?"

"Ummm..." Jonah flipped some pages. "Here." He pointed to a small picture of a man with a halo of lines radiating away from him. Next to it, a penciled note said: *Distinguished by a pearlescent aura.*

"I had to look up pearlescent," Jonah admitted.

Irene took the book from him and studied the page with a frown. "Wait," she said. "What's this? *Cherchez la lumiere.* Something about a light...uh, I think it means to…to…to look for. Look for the light. Here it is in English…'*Follow the light.*' What does that mean?"

She tilted the book so Jonah could see the penciled inscription, scribbled in the margin, heavily underlined.

Jonah shrugged.

"Do you think it means the ghost-light?"

"Ghost light?"

"Yeah," Irene said impatiently. "You know, the 'pearlescent aura.' The light that lets you know someone's dead. Ghost-light."

Jonah shrugged again and accompanied it with a shake of his head.

"Follow it how?" Irene said, thinking out loud. "Like…find other dead people…or maybe there's a trail of dead people…or a strip of lights pointing the way — like on an airport runway, or maybe it's the tunnel itself? Don't they always tell people to follow the light in the movies?"

Jonah just kept shaking his head.

Irene's frustration boiled over. "Jesus, for someone who's supposed to be so smart, you're a fat lot of help."

"Sor-ree!" Jonah cried. "I don't know!"

"Well, isn't there anything in any of your other books about a tunnel to the afterlife?" She slammed the book shut, her foul mood growing worse by the moment.

"No!" Jonah shouted, looking furious. "I told you that already. Jeez, take a pill!"

"Shhhh," the ghostly librarian admonished, striding toward their table. "Keep it down. This is a library, not a honky-tonk."

"Who are we bothering?" Irene asked, happily transferring her frustration to the librarian. "There's no one around that can hear us but you."

The librarian bristled. "I can have you thrown out of here, you know…"

"We'll be quiet." Jonah held up a placating hand. "Really. We're sorry." He shot Irene a pointed look, silently imploring her to stop.

Irene glared at him but bit her tongue. The librarian cast them both an imperious glance and then stalked off.

"Whatever." Irene watched the librarian leave with narrowed eyes. Jonah tugged on her sleeve, refocusing her attention.

"Okay, fine, moving on," she said. She sat back in her chair. "So how about the spell thingy that lets you be dead? Where's that?"

Jonah wedged a finger into the pages and flipped about three quarters of the book open. "This whole back section is all spells, I think. I mean, that's what it looks like. That's where I found it."

Irene flipped through the pages, one at a time, studying each as she went. "Okay, this is totally creepy, by the way," she said. "I'm studying a book of 'magic spells.' Like magic is real or something." She slapped a page. "Okay, this says that this one is for warding off angels. Why would I want to ward off angels?"

Jonah shrugged. "You know, it doesn't make me omnipotent or anything."

His tone annoyed her and she gave him a flat look. "I think you mean omniscient, Mister Know-It-All. And watch your mouth."

Jonah emitted a squawk of outrage. Irene raised an eyebrow and he subsided into a simmering silence.

"Well?" she asked when he didn't say anything.

"Oh, am I allowed to speak now?"

"I never said you couldn't speak, Jonah. I said there was no reason for you to be a smart ass."

He looked like he was dying to make a sharp retort. She could tell they were both about to lose their temper. She took a deep breath, forcing herself to calm down. Honestly, she didn't even know what they were fighting about.

She flipped back to the page where it listed how long different cultures thought it took to arrive in the afterlife after dying. "You said it takes a week for dead people to show up in the land of the dead. When you first did the spell thingy to get into the afterlife…you thought you'd wake up a week later?"

Jonah ducked his head and traced a random pattern on the table with a fingernail. "Uh...no. I guess I didn't really think about it. I wasn't really sure what it would do."

"It could have taken a week, though?"

He shrugged. "I guess." He sounded annoyed.

"What would you have done then?"

"I don't know. I said I didn't think about it." He jerked away from the table as if stung.

"What about your mother? You keep saying how worried she'll be if you're late—"

"Leave my mother out of it."

"Didn't you even think? She would have been out of her mind with worry."

"You're a fine one to talk!" he cried. "You didn't even say goodbye to your mother." He glared at her for a second and then dropped his eyes.

She pulled back, stiff with anger. "That was a really shitty thing to say, and it's not true. You don't know me."

Jonah flushed and looked down. "I'm sorry...I...shouldn't have said that. You seem like you were a...nice...enough...lady. I know you're upset and wish this hadn't happened, but it did. So please stop taking it out on me."

Instantly, Irene was on her feet. She slammed her hands on the table and stood up, knocking her chair over. "Don't *ever* refer to me in the past tense again," she rasped, trembling with anger. "I'm still alive."

Instantly, the librarian appeared at her elbow. "Okay, that's it!"

Somewhere, in part of her mind, Irene realized that the nearby patrons—living patrons—had all gone silent when her chair had fallen over. She heard a nervous titter and then the normal sounds of low conversation and rustling paper returned.

"We're sorry!" Jonah cried. "It was an accident. We'll be quiet. Really. I promise."

The librarian turned an imperious eye on him. "Young man, I didn't get where I am today by listening to fudge and nonsense—"

That was the last straw. Irene had had enough—of everything. "Listen, you old bat, why don't you fuck off." The other woman gasped in outrage. Irene ignored her. "I'm having a really, really bad day, what with the being dead and all, and you're not doing anything to improve it. I don't know who elected you boss, but we're not going anywhere until we're good and ready, and I don't think there's anything you can do about it." Irene crossed her arms and defiantly glared at the other woman.

The librarian drew herself up with affronted dignity and turned on her heel without a word.

Jonah looked impressed. "Wow. You...that...you..."

"Exactly." Irene righted her chair and sat down. Two women at the next table stared at the chair for a moment and then hastily got up and left.

Irene pulled the book close again. "Okay. So, where were we?"

Jonah was looking at her as if he didn't know quite what to make of her.

"What?" she asked.

He shook his head. "You're very..." He seemed to be searching for a word. Then his eyes widened in alarm and he looked at his watch. "Holy crap! I've got to get home, it's almost dinner time." He stood up and began stuffing books into his bag.

Irene grabbed his shirtsleeve. "Hey, wait, you can't leave! We're not done yet."

"Don't worry. I'm going to keep helping you. I'll come back tomorrow."

"Yeah, but how will you find me again?"

He looked puzzled. "I'll just come to your house in the morning."

Irene shook her head. "I wasn't really planning on going home."

"Uh...then where are you going to sleep?"

"I don't know. I sort of figured I would have found where all the ghosts are already. I didn't realize this was going to turn into a...a...quest."

"Well look at this way—if you go home, you'll get a chance to pack and stuff." He frowned doubtfully at her. "You didn't bring anything, not even a toothbrush."

"Yeah, well the last time you said you'd be gone for just a day you disappeared for two days."

"I promise, I'll come right back in the morning."

"What's Plan B, if you don't?"

Jonah thumped his bag back down on the table and unzipped it. He reached in and pulled out the book. "Hang on...I think I saw something..." He flipped handfuls of pages, moving back toward the spell section of the book. "Here." He pushed the book across to her.

She frowned down at the page. "What am I looking at?"

"It's a spell. For locating things in the land of the dead."

"Whooo—eeeee." Irene twirled an index finger in the air. "I don't get it. How does this help?"

Jonah ducked his head, but his voice was steady as he said, "If I leave something of mine with you and then use this spell to locate it, then I might be able to find you wherever you are."

"If? That's a mighty big 'if'."

"So we try it out," Jonah said, impatience vibrating in every syllable. He climbed to his feet, muttering, "God, you're so impossible."

"Dead, not deaf."

"Well, honestly, you are. You sulk and you pout and you give up. You're such a...such a...such a girl! I don't have to help you, you know. I'm just doing it because I feel bad."

"You feel bad for me? That's a laugh," Irene snapped. "Speaking of childish, now who's two?"

"I'm not two, I'm fourteen!" Jonah shouted. "I'm allowed to act like a kid!" He thumped down on a chair and pulled off a shoe, followed by a sock. He jammed the shoe back on and then threw the sock at Irene. "Here, take my sock. It's stinky, just like you." Then, tucking the book under his arm, he stomped off, disappearing into the rows of bookcases.

"Hey! You can't throw dirty socks at me! Where are you going?" Irene twisted in her chair, trying to follow where Jonah had gone. "Get back here! I'm not done talking."

Jonah didn't respond. She flopped back in her chair, arms folded.

The seconds ticked by. She tapped a foot and frowned, but Jonah still didn't reappear. She scanned the room for any sign of him. He had left his backpack...so that meant he was coming back. Right?

She felt a niggle of worry jostle its way to the forefront and she stood up. Before she could take a step, the air in front of her shimmered. Then Jonah stood beside her. A self-satisfied smile spread across his face.

"What the hell...how did you do that?"

Jonah looked smug. "Just like I thought. The spell."

"I thought it let you find lost things, through...I don't know...that thing witches always do in the movies."

Jonah's brow furrowed with scorn. "Scrying? Hmph." He made a dismissive noise and then the self-satisfied smile replaced his frown. "It's better than that. It takes you right to the lost object."

"So as long as I keep your," drily she held up Jonah's sock, "stinky sock with me at all times, you can always find me?"

Jonah flopped down in a chair. "Appears so." Then he laughed at her holding his sock. "Alright, I'll find you something better. Like...here. Take my watch. Put it on so you don't lose it."

He unbuckled the watch and passed it over. On the loosest setting, it was still snug. "This has Mickey Mouse on it. Kids still like Mickey Mouse?"

Jonah shrugged. "I guess. It's old. I've had it since I was a kid."

Irene suppressed a smile at Jonah referring to himself as a kid in the past tense.

A stringent voice interrupted them. "Those two."

Their heads swiveled in unison and they spied the librarian, accompanied by a burly looking ghost man, bearing down on them with hostile intent.

Irene looked at Jonah. Jonah looked at her. "Time to go," Irene said. The librarian had a determined glint in her eye.

They grabbed their stuff and ran for the door, skirting the guard and the librarian, who was now shrieking at them in a rage. "And don't come back!"

"I'll be at your house at eight!" Jonah shouted. Then he shot her a cheeky grin and disappeared.

Irene skidded through the library's front door and then bounced down the steps, nearly tripping in her haste to keep up with her feet. She paused to get her breath. She checked behind her, but no one had followed her outside.

She couldn't believe Jonah had left her to the wolves like that. She shook her head, laughing despite herself at the look he had given her right before he disappeared.

She straightened up and looked around. The sun was sinking low, its orange rays glancing off the buildings in a dazzling light display. She suddenly felt restless again. The thought of going home to just sit on the couch seemed incredibly depressing.

She thought about going back inside to see if she could find Amy now that Jonah was gone. True, Amy did seem a little vapid but at least she'd be company. The militant librarian was probably on the prowl, though, looking for Irene to return. Irene wasn't keen to risk another run-in, so instead, she chose a direction at random and started walking. Maybe she could find some ghosts.

It was close to five. Office buildings were emptying, a steady stream of business-suit-clad workers flowing out of revolving doors, down the street, and into the subway station.

She passed a few ghosts sitting huddled on the sidewalk like panhandlers. Each was sunk deep into an overcoat or blanket, staring vacantly into the air. If it wasn't for the blue glow that marked them as dead, she wouldn't be able to distinguish them from the mounded lumps of the living homeless asleep on the street. She thought again of the pale young ghost woman in Salem, faded to nothing by decades of longing and despair. Irene shuddered and her quickened pace as she tried to shake the thought.

The temperature was dropping with the sun. The air felt cooler now, and Irene shivered.

She turned onto Newbury Street, crammed wall-to-wall with upscale shops and cafes. The street glowed from a mixture of streetlights and store windows. A nameless ache washed over her and grew stronger with each window she passed. Here were some clothing stores, filled with clothes she would never be able to buy. There, a salon advertising manicures that she could never have. She paused to watch the diners eating al fresco at Stephanie's—one of her favorite restaurants. She would never dine there again.

She halted in front of a shoe store, the kaleidoscope display of footware making her feel worse than anything else. She leaned her forehead against the glass, the ache now suffocating as it pressed down on her.

Irene thought again of the ghost girl she had seen in Salem, longing to enter that house. She understood exactly how the girl felt, yearning for something she knew was gone forever. Irene wanted to beat her fist against the window—to shout and scream and kick until she had pummeled her way through the invisible barrier that separated her from the living.

The glass felt cold. Irene lifted her head and to her surprise fog covered the glass, turning it a milky white beneath her. She stared blankly at the creeping haze as it spread across the glass, not understanding what she was seeing. A tightness crept into her chest making it hard to breathe.

Her hand flew to her chest as the tightness increased. What was happening? Was she having a heart attack?

The tightness turned to an ache and then a pain, as if an iron band clamped around her lungs, preventing them from expanding. She panted, her breath coming in short, sharp gasps as she tried, and failed, to draw in air.

The pain became a squeezing, crushing and wrenching, and she doubled over, wheezing with the need for air. Dimly she was aware that there were shadows, moving along the ground—smoke-like wisps, slinking and curling around her ankles. Liquid-nitrogen cold burned wherever the dark touched her, and she drunkenly she stumbled back. She turned, and behind her she saw...something big and black, a formless shadow gliding toward her, the wispy tendrils snaking from it like reaching, grasping arms.

She didn't know what it was and she didn't care. Malevolence rolled off it in thick, suffocating waves. What little air she could draw stuck in her throat; her heart swelled, threatening to burst with the need for oxygen. Somehow, she managed to straighten up, take a few tottering steps, and then *run*, run for all she was worth.

She ran without seeing, without hearing, without conscious thought. She brushed past the living, only vaguely aware that they were there. She followed where the street led — she rounded a corner, and then another one, and then another. She stumbled and fell to one knee, picked herself back up, and continued running.

The Prudential Center, all fifty-two stories of it, loomed before her. She threw herself against the door, tugging frantically, but a sharp jolt of static electricity made her jump back. She grabbed the door once more, and, again, she felt the sharp, searing pain numbing her hand and arm. She turned and ran, continuing down Boylston, brownstones flashing by in a blur.

A church bell tolled, and she knew she was near the Christian Science Center. Her legs burned where the smoke-like tendrils had touched her. Black dots danced before her eyes from lack of oxygen. She stumbled and threw a quick glance over her shoulder to see how close the thing was. She tripped then and dropped to one knee, panting, as she felt the burn of asphalt against her skin. She looked again, expecting the thing to be upon her, but there was only the clear night sky, the warmly glowing streetlights, the bustling street. It took a moment for her panicked brain to register that there was nothing there. She stared into the empty night, unable to believe her eyes. Nothing chased her. She was alone once more.

She was suspended, half in a sprinter's crouch, frozen with shock. Slowly, her brain began to work again. She realized she could breathe once more, the crushing weight gone from her chest, and she straightened up. The night seemed warmer, too, and she knew that the thing—whatever it had been—was gone for good. She remembered the sensation of suffocating, the feeling of despair that had washed over her, the bone-chilling cold, and she broke into a run again, heading for her car. Suddenly, she wanted nothing more than to be home, safe in her own bed.

Ten

Irene stood in the living room. It was nearly eight in the morning. Jonah would be here soon.

She had passed a restless night on the couch, afraid to go to bed. No matter how much she told herself to stop being a baby, she hadn't been able to go upstairs. Instead, she had stayed in the living room, edgily flipping through television channels.

She knew that when she and Jonah left to head back to the city it would most likely be for forever. She had no reason to stay now — the house no longer belonged to her. Madame Majicka had made that quite clear. At some point, her mother would come to pack up her stuff, the house would be sold, and then new people would move in. They would tear down her wallpaper, arrange the furniture in a ridiculous way, and replace her artwork with hideous, tasteless pieces. It was better to go before she had to see that.

The thought that her mother would come to clean the place out had prompted Irene to spend the morning picking up. Well, more accurately, removing evidence. She had removed the condoms and a couple of other embarrassing personal items from the bedroom, some revealing photos from her computer, and a large number of bottles from the recycling bin. She bagged everything up and snuck it into Jamaica's trash can.

Her eyes made one last, slow, sweeping trip around the living room, coming to rest on a collection of photos clustered on the sideboard. Her mother as a young woman—displayed more for aesthetic than sentimental reasons. Her and then-boyfriend—oh what was his name? Bill? Billy? Something like that—in Maui—displayed because she had looked really excellent in a bikini that day. The three musketeers—LaRayne, Alexia, and her—each hefting an Appletini. LaRayne on the left and her in the middle each draped an arm around the next girl. Alexia, on the far right, used her free hand to give the finger to the cameraman...or woman. Irene's brow furrowed. She couldn't actually remember who had taken the photo. Or when. Or, frankly, where.

Well, none of that was the point anyway. She studied the photo, noticing the fine details. The brilliant green of Alexia's contact-tinted eyes. LaRayne's heavy gold eye shadow. Irene's eyes paused on the gold chain around her own neck in the photo. A chunky series of interlinked rings, adorned by a dangling key-shaped charm. They used to joke about it—the key's meaning changing with mood and circumstance. It was the key to her heart. No, the key that locked or unlocked her inner bad girl. Even, on occasion, the key to the imaginary chastity belt they jokingly said was to blame for dry spells.

Where is that necklace?

She cast about in her mind, trying to remember when she had worn it last. She set the photo down and wandered upstairs.

A quick search through her jewelry box turned into a twenty-minute search. First, through coat pockets, and then the pockets of everything hanging in the closet. That, in turn, became a forty minute search of the clothes hamper, under the bed, and behind the dresser. Finally, she got down on her hands and knees and pulled all of the shoes out of the closet in order to check the floor more carefully. Inside the right half of a pair of fur-topped leather boots with three-inch heels she found the chain. She sat back on her heels, the necklace spread across the palm of her hand. She studied it for a moment. It hadn't cost a lot—in fact, it had been quite cheap—and now, along with all of her other stuff, it would pass to her mother — who would probably just throw it out.

Her hand curled protectively around the necklace, and she rose to her feet in one fluid determined motion. She looked around the bedroom, taking in the lamps on the matching nightstands, the comforter in a crumpled heap on the bed, the shoes scattered in front of the closet, the bra hanging from the dresser mirror. These things were important, damn it. They meant something. There were thoughts and feelings and memories attached to them. Now her mother would carelessly box them up and sell them at a yard sale or toss them in trash bags and leave them at the curb. Irene's hand tightened on the necklace.

As her eyes swept around the room one last time, she realized it was a disaster. It looked like burglars had hit the place. She sighed. Dead and still required to clean her room. Definitely not fair.

She was on her hands and knees putting shoes back into the closet when she heard a noise behind her. She turned her head and saw a pair of corduroy-clad legs. She gasped and spun around, throwing the shoe in her hand at the intruder.

"Ow!" Jonah rubbed his shoulder.

"Jonah? What the ffff…what are you doing here?"

"Jeez, take a pill," he said, giving her an indignant look.

"Did you use the spell?" she demanded. "Why didn't you just walk over and ring the bell?"

"I didn't want to waste time coming here if you'd already left."

"I said I'd meet you here, didn't I?"

"Yeah, well…" Jonah was surveying her bedroom with interest. He picked up a rhinestone stiletto and eyed it with a mixture of horror and fascination.

"Give me that." She swiped the shoe from him. "Look, I don't need you popping in when I'm in the bathroom or something, so how about we just agree that if I say I'm going to be somewhere at a certain time, I'll be there. Okay?"

Jonah nodded vaguely in agreement. He wandered over to the bed and sat on the edge, wiggling backward up onto it. "What happened in here? It's kind of…a mess."

"Why don't you wait downstairs?"

Jonah looked offended but didn't argue. He disappeared down the hall, and Irene sighed. She finished stuffing the shoes back into the closet and hurried after him.

He was in the living room, perched on the arm of a chair, slurping a soda. "Sure, Jonah, you can have a soda. Help yourself."

Jonah raised an eyebrow. "I can't even have a soda?"

"You could *ask* if you can have a soda," she said. "God, you just pop in like you own the place."

He eyed her, trying to gauge her mood. "You do know that, technically, you don't own it anymore either, right?"

She opened her mouth to argue and then closed it just as quickly. She might have just had this same conversation with herself, but somehow it stung when he said it.

"Yeah, I know. I'm dead," she said. "So all my stuff has passed to my next of kin." Then she added fiercely, "But until they come to get it, it's still mine!"

Jonah didn't seem to know what to say to this and apparently thought it best to change the subject. "I did some more research last night." He set the soda down and reached for the backpack sitting at his feet. He rummaged around inside and pulled out a wad of paper. The bag dropped down heavily, hitting the floor with a thud.

"What do you have in there, bricks?"

Jonah frowned but didn't answer. Instead, he smoothed the papers out on one knee.

Feeling that she'd been needlessly petulant, Irene settled herself on the couch, reclining against the cushions and spreading her arms out along the back to show her openness to hear whatever he had to say. She gestured with a hand for him to proceed. "Okay, whatcha got?"

"Okay, first...I didn't find anything more about guides to the afterlife — other than the Aztec thing I already told you about—except this one thing: Hindus and Zoroastrians put a light near the head of the deceased to guide them to the afterlife. Maybe that's what 'follow the light' means?"

Irene turned this over. "Okay...but a, I'm not sure how that would show me the way to the afterlife, and b, my body...oh." She stopped.

Jonah looked at her, puzzled. "What?"

"My body is still in the river, isn't it?"

He peered at her. "River?"

"I think...the car accident...I think I went off the road into the water where Route One-O-Seven crosses the river."

The curtain of blond hair swept over his face as he ducked his head, suddenly studying his papers intently. "I'm sorry," he said quietly.

Irene felt a prickling sensation behind her eyes and she blinked rapidly to push it away. She hated to think what a week in the water had done to her body. She hated to think of herself as despoiled, ruined beyond recognition.

Oh God, they'd show the body to her mother, force her to look at it to I.D. Irene.

Irene shuddered. There had to be a way to avoid that. She couldn't put her mother through that.

On the other hand, her mother needed closure. Irene couldn't just go missing. They needed to find her body—and soon. The longer they went without finding it, the worse it would be for everyone. "I should leave a note or something, telling people where to find my body."

Jonah's head came up and he frowned. "I don't think that's a good idea."

"Why on earth not?"

"I don't think you're supposed to interfere or change events around."

"Says who?" she asked, bewildered.

Jonah shrugged limply. "I don't know...the movies and stuff. You know, it's that thing about ending up as your own grandfather...which I've never really understood."

"Isn't that time travel?"

Jonah stared at her blankly for a moment, and then his face lit up. "Hey, you got one right!"

"Shut up!" She laughed. Grabbing a pillow off the couch, she threw it at him. He casually leaned out of the way and the pillow sailed past him.

"Okay, so here's the most important thing I found out," he said. "Ghosts or spirits or whatever it is we are right now are made out of energy, right?"

Irene looked down at herself, trying to switch gears and focus on what Jonah was saying. "Uh, I don't know. Is that what I am?"

Jonah gave her a look that said her interruptions were starting to wear thin. She held up her hands. "Okay, fine, but if I'm just a blob of energy, then how come I can't walk through walls and stuff?"

"Uh," Jonah said, thinking hard. "Well...some cultures think that when you die, your soul gets weighed on a scale, so I guess it would have to have mass and be solid. So I guess that's why...though the Egyptians thought it should weigh less than a feather so I guess it wouldn't have a lot of mass...but then again, they used the feather of the goddess Maat, which means it probably wasn't the same as a regular feather. I don't know if it was heavier or lighter than a real one...I mean, logically, you'd think it would be heavier...but since it was magical—"

"Jonah! Focus."

Jonah blinked. "Uh...sorry?"

Irene shook her head. "A feather..." she said in disgust. She sighed. None of this seemed to be getting her any closer to finding new ghost friends or the tunnel to the other side. She got up and started pacing, feeling edgy and restless. She went to the window, twitched back a curtain, and stared outside. When she turned around, Jonah was watching her carefully.

"My point," he said, a worried frown between his eyes, "was that there are people who believe the dead emit this sort of force field around them that distorts the light waves."

"What the hell are you talking about?"

Jonah huffed. "Your clothes and what you need to pack for the journey!"

"My clothes! What about them?"

"What Madame Majicka said about your clothes. About how she could see them."

"Of course she could see them."

Jonah sighed theatrically. "That's the point. They're not invisible—they belong to the land of the living, so shouldn't they look like they're floating through the air to people...alive people?"

Irene frowned down at herself. "Huh. She did say something like they showed or something..."

Jonah nodded. "Yes! Well your...your...ghost energy hides the clothes...well, anything you hold close to yourself. It distorts the light or something."

Irene surveyed herself again, trying to understand what Jonah was saying. "So...my clothes really are just floating through the air and mostly people can't see them...but sometimes they can?"

Jonah nodded. "Yeah. Apparently a lot of people think those are the shadows we see out of the corner of our eyes sometimes or the weird flashes of light you can't explain. Things like that. It's actually a ghost with something that belongs to the living."

"Okay...so this means what? I'm not going to walk around naked."

Jonah turned red. "Obviously, but I think it means you're only supposed to wear what you were buried in. That's why they bury stuff with the dead, and why ancient Egyptians buried their dead with *everything*—pets and servants and clothes and food. Even life-size replicas of boats and stuff. The Chinese emperors did it, too. Didn't you ever hear of the Terra Cotta Warriors? You can only take it with you if it crosses over with you."

"We just had this conversation...I haven't been buried yet," she said, a dangerous edge to her voice. "My body is at the bottom of a river...bloated...and rotting...and collecting barnacles..." She shuddered and pushed the image away.

Jonah made an impatient noise. "Okay, fine, not exactly buried, then. It's whatever you have with you when you wake up in the afterlife."

"You just changed what you said!" she cried, flinging up her hands in frustration. "You just said it's what crossed over with me…meaning what I woke up with, not what I was buried with. You're just making all this shit up! You don't actually know any more than I do."

"I am not!" Jonah cried. "I'm just repeating what the stories say about what happens in the land of the dead."

"Well, now technically the jury still seems to be out on whether this is the land of the dead or not. I thought this was the waiting room thingy and the point of the tunnel is to get me to the land of the dead so they can weigh my soul against a feather." Irene's voice dripped with icy sarcasm. Her eyes narrowed to dagger points. "So maybe, just maybe, Mister Know-It-All, it's not what I woke up here with. Maybe it's what I take with me when I go through the tunnel."

Jonah's eyes narrowed to match hers. "Madame Majicka said that which belongs to the living stays with the living and that which belongs to the dead —"

"I was there." Irene challenged Jonah with a hard glare, but he stood his ground. He crossed his arms over his chest and glared back.

"You know I'm right," he said.

They stood, locked in a silent battle of wills, for a long soundless moment. Irene gave in first. As much as she hated to admit it, Jonah was probably right. If the dead could just take whatever they wanted, then, logically, they would have helped themselves to enough stuff that people would have noticed.

She ground her teeth and practically snarled as she turned away from him. "Fine. Have it your own way."

She went over the list of what she'd had with her when she'd arrived home after waking up on the side of the road. She moved away and began picking up the strewn trail of items she had shed her first morning as a dead person. "Cell phone—fat lot of good that does." She moved out into the hall. "Purse...shoes..." Irene cataloged each item bitterly as she picked it up.

She tried to think what else she'd had with her when she'd woken up on the side of the road.

"You know," Jonah said from the living room, his voice raised slightly so it would carry to the hall, "it's really interesting the different stuff people think should be buried with the dead. Native Americans buried weapons. So did the Celts and the Romans."

"Slightly crumpled cocktail dress..." Irene called loudly from the hall as she headed up the stairs to her bedroom.

Jonah's voice floated up to her from downstairs. "The ancient Romans and Greeks buried money with their dead so they could pay the ferryman to get them across the river."

She grabbed the dress from the bedroom and then, from the bathroom, the jewelry she had been wearing along with the bobby pins from her hair. Her eyes swept over the bathroom one more time, looking for anything glowing blue.

"You know what's really weird?" she heard Jonah call up to her. "The Chinese believe that they can send stuff to the dead. They have this whole thing once a year called the Ghost Festival. They leave food out and burn money and little paper models of things like clothes and televisions and stuff for the dead. Cool, huh?"

She exited the bathroom and headed back downstairs.

"You know, it's like a kind of factoid Tourette's with you," she said as she re-entered the living room. She dumped everything on the couch. "That's it. That's all she wrote. All my after-worldly possessions. Oh look, no money, no weapons, no servants...not even a dead dog. I guess I'm kind of screwed, then."

Jonah moved to her side and surveyed the pile. He ran a hand over it, spreading the items out so he could see each one better. In addition to the items she had verbally cataloged, she had added her broken watch. Curious, he picked up the small purse and popped it open. Irene grabbed it from him.

"What do you think you're doing?"

"Jeez. Take a pill. I was just going to see what's in it."

"I don't think you need to see my tampons, thanks."

Red bloomed over his face and then quickly made way for a queasy green. "I can't believe you just said that," he said, mortified.

"Well, greedy goober, that's why we don't go through other people's things."

Jonah held up his hands and backed away. "Okay, okay."

She laughed at the look on his face. "For your information, it's just my driver's license, credit cards, lipstick, and perfume, but it could have been private — girly — stuff."

He glared at her, not enjoying the joke.

"Oh, and car keys," she said, suddenly remembering that she'd had them when she'd woken up dead. She spun around, her eyes scanning. "Car keys...car keys..." She left the room and returned a moment later, holding up a clump of keys. She shook them so that they jingled and then tossed them onto the pile. "My car too, I guess."

"What about the car?"

"What about 'what about the car?'"

Jonah rolled his eyes skyward in exasperation. "I mean, is there anything in it? Any other stuff that might be helpful?"

"Oh. Good thinking!"

She led the way to the driveway. Jonah went around to the passenger side and together they began combing through the car. Jonah was busy burrowing through the glove box when Irene, rummaging in the back seat, cried out, "Score!"

She wiggled backwards out of the car, pulling something from under the front seat. Jonah straightened up, looking expectantly across the roof. Irene held up a tall, thin bottle filled with an equally clear liquid. Jonah groaned. "Are you kidding?"

"Hey, listen, vodka makes life bearable."

"That's funny coming from someone who's *dead*."

"Yeah, well this is the only thing that's going to get me through the afterlife if it turns out there aren't any bars in the land of the dead."

Jonah groaned and shook his head again. Then he ducked back into the car to finish his inspection. It only took a few more minutes to complete the task of cleaning everything out of the car and lugging it back to the house.

"Okay, whatcha got?" Irene asked.

"Ketchup packets. Paper napkins. Pepper Spray. Two dollars and twenty-five cents in change. Four pens. Your turn."

Irene held the bottle up and teeter tottered it in the air. "Bottle of Grey Goose. Windshield scraper. One mitten. Two more pens. A pocket-sized book of Boston street maps. A thong. Power Bar wrappers."

Jonah started to reach for the thong. "Why do you have underwear in your—"

Irene slapped his hand away. "Why do you think?"

Jonah's expression changed to one of bewilderment.

Irene narrowed her eyes. "Don't you have a girlfriend or something?"

Jonah's face reddened, and then he ducked behind his hair and became very focused on the items Irene had added to the pile. Clearly changing the subject, he said, "Well, this is a little better, I guess."

"Ah, well, not so fast," Irene said smugly, allowing him to change the subject. "That was just the backseat. From the trunk we have: jumper cables, spare tire, tire iron, and jack— all of which I left in the car—a flashlight, a squishy beach bag slash basket thingy, suntan lotion, towel, and two-month old copies of Vogue and Cosmopolitan."

Irene's eyes swept the items again. As she looked at the pile, she let out a sigh that resembled the sound of a balloon deflating. "You can't be serious in thinking this is all I get to take to the afterlife. It's just junk. There's nothing of any use here. I've got no food, no clothes, no money. If you're right about the journey part, then I'm screwed."

Doubt shadowed Jonah's face. "Sorry," he said limply. "I think you're doing better than most people. These days, people mostly just get the clothes on their back and some jewelry or a personal memento. You've got a lot of stuff here, considering—at least you can eat the ketchup, and the pepper spray is a weapon."

She shot him an exasperated look. "I'm never going to eat plain ketchup." She looked around the room, seeing everything she would be leaving behind. "Well, I can see the argument for staying here then. Television. Food. Credit cards. Warm bed. A shower."

Jonah's look of disgust spoke volumes about his feelings on that idea. "Don't be lame. Even if you stay you can't keep any of it."

Irene sighed. "No, I suppose not. It's tempting to try, though." She reached out and pulled the crumpled dress and the shoes from the pile on the couch. "On that note, I think I'll get changed." She surveyed the thin slip of fabric in disgust. "Come on little dress. You and me are going to be spending some extended quality time together. God, if I'd known I'd be spending all of eternity in this dress, I would've worn the Cynthia Rowley. That, at least, has fabric that breathes."

Jonah took a step closer, squinting at the dress in her hand. "What were you doing...the night you died, I mean."

Irene shrugged. "Just hanging out with my girlfriends."

"Meaning?"

"Meaning," she said, a note of warning in her voice, "just getting a bite to eat, having a few drinks, dancing. You know, grown-up girl stuff."

A look that Irene couldn't interpret—Worry? Upset?—crossed Jonah's face. He looked like he wanted to say something, but he didn't speak.

Irene headed out of the room, saying over her shoulder, "I'll be right back."

A couple of minutes later, she reappeared. Jonah's eyes moved over her, from the thin criss-crossed double straps, across the deep red shimmer of rayon and lycra that set off her figure, down to the thigh-high hem that left most of her legs—and if she made the mistake of bending over, a whole lot more—exposed, to her feet, encased in the silver three-inch heels.

Jonah's eyes were as big as saucers, nearly bulging from his head. "That's what you're wearing to the afterlife?"

Irene eyed him with exasperation. "Hey, remember, this was your idea, not mine." Then she took in his fishbowl eyes and flushed face and smiled. She chucked his cheek as she walked past. "Maybe girls aren't so bad after all, huh?" she said. "Almost makes you want to spend more time with the living, eh?"

The shading on Jonah's face went from scarlet to maroon, and he stared furiously at the floor, as if trying to burn a hole through it. "Shut up," he muttered.

Irene laughed and then moved to the couch, grabbed the beach bag, and began stuffing items into it.

"Do you want my backpack?" he asked. "It would be easier to carry."

Irene gave him a pointed look. "It doesn't really go with the dress."

"So?"

"So I'd rather not look like a complete dork."

"Oh, but you don't mind looking like a…like a…" he burst out. The color had just started to fade from his face and now it leaped back. He ducked his head, letting the curtain of hair fall forward to hide his face.

Irene straightened up, hands on hips. "You better have been about to say 'a beautiful, sexy woman,'" she said sharply.

Jonah's head popped up and he looked alarmed at the introduction of the words "sexy" and "beautiful" into the conversation. A pained expression crossed his face as he realized he was in trouble. He couldn't call her beautiful and sexy, and he definitely couldn't say that she wasn't. She had trapped him very neatly between a rock and a hard place. Irene shot him a smug look. "Exactly," she said, hoping he'd learned to pick his words more carefully in future, and then turned back to the job of stuffing items into the beach bag.

He watched her hands moving back and forth, grabbing items from the pile and pushing them into the bag. "The Mickey Mouse watch doesn't really go either," he said, in a flat, dull, sulky tone.

"Oh, so what, now you're asking for your watch back?" She dropped the bag and spun around to look at him. He had a funny look on his face, as if he was caught between surprise and confusion. Irene replayed the words in her head and realized how they sounded. In fact, hadn't she said something similar to Dewie Chou in fourth grade when he'd broken up with her?

"No, you can keep it," he said, as if hurt she had offered to give it back.

"Just for the record, that doesn't mean we're going steady," she said drily.

He gave her the funny look again, eyebrows cocked — one higher than the other — eyes narrowed, and lips mashed together in a thin line.

"I don't know what that look means," she said, annoyed at how odd he was acting. Then, without waiting for an answer, she went back to filling the beach bag. When everything was in it, she picked the bag up by its straps and bounced it a couple of times, settling its contents.

She realized this was it. She was about to leave her home, possibly forever. Wanting a moment, and realizing she still needed to clean up a few things, she said, "I'll be right back."

She set the bag on the couch and left the room, heading for the kitchen. Jonah followed her, staying within arm's length of her, as if afraid to let her out of his sight.

Feeling smothered, she walked to the sink and turned on the water, letting it run until it was hot. Irene picked up a mug and began washing it, saying with impatience, "Unlike you, I can't disappear, so you don't have to follow me."

Jonah moved away, but only as far as the kitchen table where he pulled out a chair and sat down. In silence,

Irene washed the three mugs in the sink and put them in the dish rack to dry. She took one last look around the kitchen and then, turning out the light, she headed for the stairs. Jonah followed. She paused on the bottom step and spun around to face him. "For God's sake, wait down here. I'll just be a minute." Then she hurried up the stairs.

The key necklace was on her dresser. She found a plain envelope in the nightstand and stuck the necklace in it. She sealed the envelope, scrawled LaRayne's name on it, and stuck it back in the drawer. Anyone finding it would think she had set it aside to give to LaRayne and then forgotten it. She thought of Alexia and her mother, but she had no bequests to leave them. She frowned, thinking hard, but nothing came to mind. She snapped off the light and went back downstairs.

Back in the living room, she grabbed the beach bag and then, motioning for Jonah to precede her, headed for the hall. At the front door, she paused, giving one last look around. She felt a lead weight in the pit of her stomach as she took in all the memories, all of the mementos, all of the life she'd be leaving behind. Jonah saw the look on her face. "I'm sorry," he said in quiet sympathy, touching her arm.

"Fuck it," she said.

She stepped outside and pulled the door closed.

Eleven

Irene stowed the bag in the back seat. "So how long do we have till you have to go home?"

"I have to be home by dinner time. My mother expects me home after school, but I told her I might be late 'cause I had to work on a group project with some kids."

Irene chuckled. "Ah, yes, the classics. They never go out of style." They shared a conspiratorial smile over the roof of the car. Then they both opened their doors and climbed in. Irene started the car and they both buckled their seat belts.

"Okay, but so where are you really then?" she asked as she backed the car out of the driveway. "I assume you didn't go to school."

"In the attic."

Irene was silent for a moment as she navigated side streets and then choked with laughter. "The attic?" she echoed in disbelief.

"Shut up!"

The car slowed as it eased up alongside the curb. Irene put it into park and cut the engine. Jonah looked around in surprise. "Where are we?"

"We need to make a quick stop." She was out of the car and moving up the walkway before he had even unfastened his seatbelt.

He caught up to her and studied the house with a wary eye. "Who lives here?" He looked around at the neighboring houses and then his eyes lit up in recognition. "Hey, I know where we are...I met you over there for the first time..." He trailed off and then, a moment later, quietly added, "Your mom lives here."

Irene glanced at him. "How'd you know that?"

Jonah shrugged. "I just figured..."

"You pay attention too much," she muttered. She pushed open the door and stepped into the house. As Irene crossed the kitchen, she called out, "Mom?"

"She can't hear you."

"I know. I just don't want to startle her."

Irene didn't have to turn around to see the expression of mingled exasperation and disbelief on Jonah's face; she could just feel it. "You know what I mean," she said. "It's force of habit."

"Uh huh."

Irene passed through the doorway connecting the kitchen to the living room.

"Mom?"

However, the living room was empty. Irene paused and listened hard. "I think she's in the bathroom."

They stood there, awkwardly, waiting. Jonah began to hum the Jeopardy theme song. Irene shot him a warning look. Jonah then wandered over to an end table. He picked up the half-full glass of water sitting there and made it dance in the air. He accompanied the movements with spooky ghost-like noises. "Woooooohhhhhhhhoooooooouoo," he moaned.

"What are you doing?"

"Being a ghost."

"Well, stop it," she said. "What the hell is wrong with you? What if my mother walked in and saw you? You'd give her a heart attack!"

He grinned, completely unabashed. "Come on, it was funny, and you know it."

She shook her head, giving him an exaggerated frown to make it clear she did not think it was funny at all. He frowned back and set the glass down. He looked around the room in a bored, disinterested way. His eyes came to rest on the mantel, and he moved across the room, his attention drawn by the knick knacks and family photographs.

He snatched up a framed picture. "Hey, this is you!" Then he doubled over with laughter. "Look at your hair!"

Irene marched over and jerked the photo—her sixth grade school picture, taken only a week after an unfortunate incident in which she had tried to cut off all her hair after Tommy Barrett had called her rooster head—out of his hand. "That's quite enough out of you," she said, replacing the picture on the mantel.

Jonah straightened up but was still chuckling. He scanned the picture frames lined up in an overcrowded row. "Are these all you?"

Irene frowned at him. "So I had braces."

He started belly laughing again. "And pigtails. And freckles. And what's this one...what is that, chocolate ice cream on your face?"

"Shut up. Why don't you look at the ones at the other end, when I'm older. Look, here's one of me in my field hockey outfit from junior year."

Instead, he had stopped to stare at her high school graduation photo. He was frowning now, suddenly serious. His eyes slid sideways to her, then back to the photo. Then he turned away, stuffing his hands in his pockets, his shoulders hunched.

"What? What is that look for?"

He shrugged, scuffing a foot on the floor. "It's just...I forget sometimes...how old you are."

"Gee, thanks," she said. "I'm only thirty-six; I'm not that old."

He looked disconcerted. "I just meant I forget we're nowhere near the same age."

She wasn't really sure what he meant by that. She suspected there was a veiled insult in there somewhere, but before she could probe any further, her mother wandered in. Deborah Dunphy had a way of always appearing to be looking for something she had just set down—a sort of vague, distracted air, like she was trying to remember something hovering just on the edge of memory.

That passive, helpless, damsel-in-distress air drove Irene nuts. Irene felt her face contort of its own accord with the usual annoyance, and she tried to push the feeling away, tried to remind herself this was probably the last time she'd ever see her mother.

Deborah settled herself on the couch and seemed to be trying to decide on something. Irene crossed the room, tentatively settling herself beside her mother. Jonah moved closer, too, coming to stand on the other side of Deborah. Irene looked up at him. "What are you doing?"

"What?" he asked, irritated,

"Why don't you wait in the kitchen?"

"What for?"

"Because I want to talk to my mother *alone.*"

Outrage suffused Jonah's face, but he clamped his lips shut and stomped off to the kitchen without a word of argument.

Now that they were alone, Irene wasn't sure what to say. She had come because it felt like she should. She had seen the look on Jonah's face when she had told him she hadn't said goodbye to her mother. He had been shocked. He had thought her heartless, cold, unfeeling. Maybe she was; now that she was here, she couldn't think of a single thing to say. There wasn't anything unsaid between them. No secret confessions to make. No love that had been denied or unexpressed. They were two people with nothing in common who had done their best with each other. They had each held up their end of the mother-daughter bargain, discharging their respective responsibilities to the best of their abilities. There really wasn't much more to say.

Irene felt a nagging niggle of guilt again. Who was going to take care of her mother now that Irene was gone? She might feel relieved that she didn't have to do it anymore, and she might have told Mrs. Boine that she thought her mother should learn to take care of herself, but they had been thoughtless words, spoken in anger and frustration.

She knew her mother didn't have the ability to care for herself, and there wasn't anyone else to do it.

Her mother was as fragile, and just as substantial, as a wisp of smoke. She wandered through life the same way she wandered through her empty house. Irene could never be sure that her mother remembered to eat, let alone to call and have the oil tank refilled or to make out a check for the electric bill. Her mother might think Irene was "thoughtless" because Irene didn't enjoy listening to vapid, unfinished thoughts and trite, empty, half-remembered gossip about the neighbors; however, she always made sure her mother's needs were met. There was food in the fridge, the bills were paid, the lawn mowed, the driveway shoveled. Irene frowned and reached out to pat her mother's hand. Who would take care of those things now?

Her mother absently put one hand on top of Irene's, as if she had felt the gentle pressure.

"Mom?" Irene asked, leaning closer. "Can you hear me?"

Her mother appeared to be lost in thought, her gaze lax and far away. Irene put her other hand on top of her mother's, completing the four-layer hand-sandwich. Her thumb gently stroked the protruding veins of her mother's hand. Irene took a deep breath. "Mom, I'm leaving." She paused, trying to stop her voice from trembling. "I'm leaving, Mom. I have to. I'm...well, I'm dead." She gave a watery laugh. "Don't worry, though. Being dead is...well, really, it's kinda boring. It's just...ordinary.   I   mean,   it's interesting...mmmm...boring."   She   laughed   self-consciously. "Yeah, I guess I really do mean boring." She felt tears prickling her eyes. "Anyway, Mom. I just wanted you to know that I'm okay. There's nothing to be scared of, and I don't want you to worry." She studied her mother's profile, trying to detect any sign that her mother could hear her or even sense her presence, but there was none. Finally, biting her lip, she released her mother's hands and stood up. Her mother looked down at her own hands, tightly clasped together, one on top of the other, a confused frown on her face, and Irene knew that her mother had felt her. Her mother would dismiss it as a draft or imagination, but Irene knew that her mother had felt Irene's hand on her own, and that was enough. It had to be.

Irene turned, and without a look back, crossed into the kitchen. Jonah was peering into the fridge, the door held wide, and he jumped in surprise when he heard Irene approach. He turned around, a guilty look on his face. Irene made a noise of disapproval. Jonah shrugged defensively. "I was hungry."

"Come on."

"You're done?" he asked in surprise.

"Yeah." Irene hesitated in the act of pulling open the back door. "I could write her a note."

Jonah raised his eyebrows. "Saying what?"

"I don't know...telling her what happened and where my body is..."

Jonah shook his head back-and-forth in long sweeping motions that made the blond hair swing and swirl about his face. "No. Way."

"Why not?"

"She got a note about how you died...after you died?"

Irene thought about this, mentally weighing the pros and cons. "Well, she wouldn't be left wondering, you know, if there was something she could have done. They always tell you — when someone dies — that the person didn't suffer, but trust me, you always wonder."

Jonah shook his head again, this time with sharp, quick, side-to-side motions that made his whole body bobble. "So instead of wondering if you suffered, she'll wonder where the note came from, who left it, and if someone knows something about your death that they aren't saying — which would mean it wasn't an accident, or maybe it's a hoax and you faked your own death — "

"Yeah, okay, okay. I get it." Still, she hesitated in the doorway, refusing to leave. "I just..." She looked at him, torn and worried. "I'm not heartless you know."

Jonah looked surprised at this. "Yeah, I know."

"I do care if she gets upset or if she worries..."

Jonah's expression turned both earnest and bewildered, and he touched her shoulder lightly. "I know."

She started to speak, paused, took in a gulp of air, and then said, "It's just—"

Jonah cut her off. "I. Know." He took her arm and turned her toward the door.

She looked at him over her shoulder, a frown of regret and indecision etching deep lines around her mouth. Then she pursed her lips and said, "Okay."

Jonah stepped forward and nudged her gently. She let him propel her out the door. They exited the house and retraced their steps back to the car. Irene paused when they reached the sidewalk and glanced across the street. Mrs. Boine was holding court in her yard as usual. Irene waved.

Mrs. Boine fluttered a hand in the air. "Yoohooo, Irene."

"Come on," Irene said to Jonah. "Come meet my old babysitter."

Jonah's face twisted in a way that said he was doubtful this was going to be the treat Irene seemed to think it was. Irene laughed. "I just thought you might find it interesting to meet another dead person. That's why you're here, isn't it?"

They crossed the street, passed through the gate, and joined Mrs. Boine at the patio table.

"Oh Lord," she cried when she saw Jonah, "too young! Much, much too young, you poor thing!" She tried to fold Jonah into her ample bosom but he dodged away, moving to stand behind Irene.

"Don't mind him, Mrs. Boine. He may be young, but he lived a full and happy life." Irene managed to keep a straight face as she spoke. Jonah jabbed her in the back.

Mrs. Boine clucked sympathetically. "My, my, my. Well, I tell you, that's the right attitude, young man. Good for you."

Jonah leaned forward to hiss in Irene's ear, but she waved him away.

"We can't stay long, Mrs. Boine, we're on our way out. We're going to the city."

Mrs. Boine's eyes, suddenly shrewd, darted over Irene's face. "You're going to look for your angels and harps, aren't you?"

Irene nodded.

Mrs. Boine fanned the air with one hand. "You're young, Irene. You should go. Explore, travel, see new places. It'll do you good."

"You don't want to come with us?" Irene didn't really expect Mrs. Boine did, but felt politeness demanded that she make the offer.

Mrs. Boine settled herself more comfortably into the chair. "Oh, thank you, honey, but no. I ain't in any hurry. I got these grandkids that want watchin', and Heaven will still be there when I'm ready, I expect."

Irene hesitated, trying to find a way to tactfully frame her next question. "What about your husband? Don't you want to see him?"

Mrs. Boine fanned the air again. "Oh, I expect he'll keep as well."

Irene raised an eyebrow. "Don't you miss him?"

"Of course I miss him—and if he knows what's good for him, he's missin' me—but there ain't no hurry. That's the promise and the glory, Irene. We'll see each other again."

Irene was surprised. Mrs. Boine seemed rather blasé about the whole thing. Irene leaned forward to probe further, but Jonah laid a restraining hand on her shoulder. She turned to look to him, one eyebrow raised inquisitively. He gave an almost imperceptible shake of the head, and his eyes telegraphed a warning to drop the subject. Irene squinted a question at him, but his face remained impassive. With a frown, she turned back to Mrs. Boine. The whole exchange with Jonah had taken only an instant, and Mrs. Boine didn't seem to have noticed. She was offering Irene a chair and Irene sat. Then Irene asked the question she had wanted to ask from the start.

"Mrs. Boine, you haven't seen my father around, have you?"

Mrs. Boine's brow crinkled in thought. "Huh. Come to think of it, I haven't seen your father in…oh, I don't know…"

"Ten years?" supplied Irene helpfully.

"Oh my, yes, it must have been at least that long, now that I come to think of it."

"So he hasn't been hanging around here, then?"

"Oh my, no. Your father really wasn't one to loiter."

Irene tried to bite back her disappointment. No, her father wasn't the kind to just hang around, doing nothing. Still, the thought that he had abandoned his wife and daughter so easily hurt. Her disappointment must have shown because Mrs. Boine patted her knee in a motherly fashion. Then Mrs. Boine looked startled and peered more closely at Irene. "Good God, Irene, what do you have on?"

Irene jumped to her feet, annoyance sizzling through her—she was thirty-six year's old for God's sake. She didn't need a lecture on how to dress. "Well, we have to be going. I just wanted to say…good bye." Irene waved hastily and then made a beeline for the gate. Jonah scampered after her, trying to keep up.

"Wait, Irene!" Mrs. Boine called, waving after them.

Irene didn't pause as she hurried across the street. She unlocked the car and climbed inside without a backward glance. Jonah climbed in the passenger seat just as Irene started the engine. Without waiting for him to fasten his seatbelt, Irene threw the car into gear and stomped on the gas, sending the car shooting forward.

Jonah was thrown back against the seat. "Hey!"

"She always picked on how I dressed." The words crackled with anger. However, it wasn't really the catty comment on how she was dressed that was bugging her; it was the gnawing disappointment caused by the knowledge that her father had abandoned her. All that bullshit about the dead watching over us—ha! What a crock.

Jonah looked at Irene critically and said, "Well…"

"Don't start." She trod hard on the gas and the car accelerated.

"Okay, but could you slow down?" Jonah cried, clinging to the door.

Irene returned his deprecating look with one of her own. "We're already dead, Jonah."

"I'm not! I'm gonna be from heart failure in another minute, though!"

"Oh for pity's sake," she said, but the car slowed down.

There was a thick silence. Irene's anger slowly ebbed away, leaving in its place an urge to cry, though Irene wasn't sure why.

She looked at Jonah out of the corner of her eye, trying to think of something to say, something to talk about, something to break the silence.

"So," Irene said. "You're fourteen…so you must be in, what, eighth grade?"

His expression turned to one of scorn mingled with disappointment. His nose rose into the air a fraction of an inch. "I'm in tenth grade."

"Tenth grade?" she echoed. "How's that?"

"I skipped a grade."

"Uh, okay, chief, but that should only make you *one* year younger than everyone else, not two." She removed her eyes from the road long enough to give him a quizzical look.

He rewarded her with a thin smile. "My birthday is late."

Irene digested this with a frown. "Oh…so you mean you started school a year early?"

He shrugged. "I don't know, I guess. I just know that when I was in elementary school, I would just catch up to everyone else and then they would all turn a year older."

"Huh."

Jonah seemed to be mulling something over. Finally, he turned to her and said, "Can I ask you a question?"

"If you must."

"How did you die?"

"Car accident. You know that." Irene felt her face heat and she stared at the road ahead, not looking at him.

"I mean, like, how did it happen? Did someone hit you or did you swerve to avoid a cat or something? What?"

An unbidden image of wavering blue-green light danced before Irene's eyes. She shook her head, banishing the memory.

"I don't know. The last thing I remember was being out with my friends. Then I woke up on the side of the road."

She could see him out of the corner of her eye. He was watching her closely. A small pucker had formed between his eyebrows, and that look—Worry? Concern? Disappointment?—that she couldn't read was lurking in his eyes. He turned away, settling himself very gently against the seat.

"So...your sister. Tell me about her," she said, changing the subject.

He bounced up from the seat. "My sister? What do you want to know about her for?"

"Just making conversation. It's a thing people do."

"Oh." He was silent, thinking this over with great consideration. "Well, what about you? Why don't you tell me something about you?"

She noticed that, once again, Jonah seemed to be avoiding talking about himself. She looked at him assessingly, not really sure how to ask the obvious question. "Jonah, is there anything...going on—maybe at home...?"

"What do you mean?"

"Well, you seem really reluctant to talk about yourself. Whenever I ask anything, you get all weird and change the subject..."

Jonah gave her another scornful look. "I'm not being beaten or molested or anything like that if that's what you mean. Jeez! I just don't think you'd find my life very interesting, is all."

"Well, I asked, didn't I?"

"Yeah, and then you'll just make fun of me because I'm a nerd and I don't have a girlfriend."

She was so shocked by the accusation that she turned in her seat, staring at him with her mouth hanging open.

"Watch the road!" he cried, reaching out to grab the wheel.

She jerked her attention back to the road and straightened the car out, avoiding a near miss with a car passing in the other direction.

"That was a really unfair thing to say," she muttered.

Jonah had the grace to blush. "Sorry." He looked at his lap. "I didn't mean...it's just that we're really different."

"That's the point of getting to know other people, Jonah. To find out how you're the same."

He blinked at her, giving her that look of surprised admiration that both amused and annoyed her.

Irene slowed down to let two pedestrians cross the street. As the car started forward again, Jonah leaned back, relaxing against the seat, and said, "What do you want to know? My life is just ordinary." She thought she detected a trace of bitterness in this last part.

"I don't care. Tell me anything. All I know about you is that you're thirteen —"

"Fourteen."

"Fourteen, and like to read stories about death."

"You know where I live."

"And that you're a smart-alec ," she added. "Now spill. Tell me about your family...about your sister."

"What about my sister?"

"Well, for starters, is she a brainiac like you?"

"You know," he said, twisting in his seat so he could face her, "being smart isn't a bad thing."

"I know."

"Well you say it like it's an insult."

"Sorry." She shrugged. "I guess you just remind me of when I was in high school. Nobody wanted to be a nerd."

Jonah flopped back into his seat. "Tell me about it," he said, suddenly sounding furious. He kicked at the floor mat with a toe.

"The more things change..." she replied with a smile.

"So where did you fit in? In high school, I mean."

"Well, up until then, I sort of floated in between, getting okay grades, but not a nerd by any stretch of the imagination. Not popular, but not picked on. Mostly just invisible, I guess. Then during my freshman year I got my braces off and my boobs came in, and I became *really* popular."

Jonah snorted as if he had a very clear picture in his mind. "I bet you were like a cheerleader, too, weren't you? And prom queen and dated a guy on the football team…"

Irene glanced at him, wondering if they were still talking about her or someone he had a crush on. "No, I was never one of those girls. I played field hockey. You saw the picture."

"Field hockey?" He looked her up and down. "I can't really imagine you playing sports."

"Yeah, well, you have to do something to fit in and I'm not musical, I'm not artistic, I wasn't a nerd…but I am really tall." She shot him a smug, sly grin. "Besides, you get to hit people with a stick."

He stared at her in disbelief, trying to gauge if she was joking or not. Then he burst into gales of laughter when he realized she wasn't. She laughed, too.

"You're terrible," he said, but it was a compliment. He sounded impressed.

There was silence as Irene changed lanes. They were on the highway, heading toward the massive green steel bridge that spanned the Mystic River, and she was driving slower now, almost leisurely. However, Jonah still involuntarily clutched the door handle every time she changed lanes or sped up.

"So, what do you think is on the other side of the tunnel?" she asked.

"Well, I told you…there's probably going to be a hall of judgment kind of thing and then —"

"I meant the end result, what happens after the waiting room thingy and the judging and stuff. If everything we've been lead to believe is true like Madame Majicka said, then it's going to be either Heaven or Hell, right? There's only two choices. Since I haven't done anything really bad, like mortal sin bad, I'm expecting Heaven. What I meant was, what do you think Heaven is like?"

"Well..." Jonah had what Irene was coming to think of as his "professor" look—a thoughtful furrowing of the brow with his mouth quirking down that usually preceded a lengthy recitation of facts. "First of all, a lot of cultures think there's just one afterlife and everyone goes to the same place—no distinction between Heaven and Hell. Those that think that different people go different places usually offer three choices—Heaven, Hell, and an in-between place for people who aren't either really good or really bad."

"You mean like purgatory—or is it limbo? I can never keep those two straight."

"Purgatory. Yeah. The ancient Greeks called it Tartarus, the Zoroastrians call it Misvan Gatu—"

"Yeah, well I'm holding out for *Heaven*, thank you very much."

Jonah was silent.

"Thanks for the vote of confidence!" Irene cried.

"It's not that," he said quickly. "It's just...isn't Heaven supposed to be kind of boring?"

"It's Heaven. It's supposed to be, you know, *Heaven*."

"Yeah, but isn't it supposed to be all people sitting around on clouds, playing harps?"

"Yeah. So?"

They were sitting in traffic, backed up from the toll plaza in the middle of the bridge. As the car inched forward, Irene drummed impatiently on the steering wheel and craned to see what the holdup was.

"You'd like that?" Jonah said, drawing her attention back to the conversation. "Sitting on clouds and stuff?"

She glanced at him, but he was staring resolutely out the window. "Well, compared to the alternative of being roasted in a pit of fire, I guess it'll do."

There was a protracted pause. "I just don't think it sounds like you."

Irene shot him a dark look, which he also didn't see.

"Yeah, well, you don't know me very well, do you?"

They had reached the toll plaza and Irene rolled through it without stopping. Jonah shot her an incredulous look.

She returned his look with one of her own. "How was I supposed to pay?"

He frowned and looked away. There was another drawn out silence. Irene could hear the wheels turning in his head. Finally, he said, "The ancient Norse version of Heaven was called Asgard...that's where Valhalla is."

"That's the one where they sit around singing war songs and drinking grog all day?"

"Yeah...but I think its mead, not grog."

"Yeah, well, if it's alcohol, then I'm down with it."

Slowly they inched their way up the ramp connecting to the Central Artery — the elevated highway that ran through the center of the city. Even at mid-day, traffic backed up from the complicated merge that resulted from several major routes converging into one.

There was another lull in the conversation. Irene was starting to get the impression that Jonah was trying to make some point or arrive at some kind of conclusion. She maneuvered through the merge and then sped up as traffic thinned out and began flowing again. From there it only took a few minutes to reach their exit.

"Muslims think there are forty virgins waiting for them."

"Yeah, I'm hoping that's not it," she said. That sounded more like Hell to her.

"Yeah. What's so great about virgins, anyway?"

Irene laughed. When she realized that Jonah wasn't joining in, she risked taking her eyes off the road. He was staring at his lap, the fingers of one hand tracing abstract designs on the palm of the other. She realized he was serious and was waiting for an answer. She choked, mid-laugh.

"Oh," she said, trying to think fast. "Uh...well, I guess they beat big, fat, singing women."

Jonah looked at her as if she'd lost her mind. "What?"

"You know — the ones on horses that swoop out of the sky. With the helmets with the horns and the long braids."

"Oh, you mean Valkyries!" He gave her an exasperated look. "Yeah, I guess..."

"We're here!" Irene said brightly, relief flooding through her. There was no way she was going to answer a teenage boy's questions about sex.

She put the car into park and cut the engine.

Twelve

"Okay, so what's the plan?" she asked.

"We should go back to the library. We didn't get a chance to try and translate the book."

"I think we're banned from the library."

"Okay, then, if we're looking for a tunnel, shouldn't we check out actual tunnels?"

"What, you mean like the Sumner or Callahan?" she asked, referring to the traffic tunnels that ran under Boston Harbor, connecting the suburbs to the north with Boston.

"Yeah, and the bridges, too, just to be sure."

Irene made a face. Despite all the evidence to the contrary, she was still holding out hope that she could move to the city and life would continue much as it had before, just populated with dead, rather than living, people.

She made a face. "I told you before, I want to know what's on the other side before I go anywhere. So I'd rather keep looking for other dead people."

"We tried that yesterday, remember? How about we try one of my ideas now?"

"Oh, all right." She hated to agree, but for some reason she hated the accusation that she was being bossy and selfish even more. Since they couldn't walk through the tunnels, she restarted the car and eased back into traffic.

First, they tried the Central Artery tunnel, descending into the fluorescent cavern that burrowed under the streets of Boston. Then they tried the tunnel that connected the airport and East Boston. They drove through without seeing anything of interest there either.

"Well, how can we find it if you're whipping by at eighty?" Jonah cried.

"I'm only doing fifty, and there's no place to park and no place to walk."

Arriving in East Boston, Irene looped around and took the Sumner Tunnel, the narrow, dingy, fluorescent-lit, mile-long cavern that carried inbound traffic under the harbor and back into the city. There was also nothing remarkable there. She refused to make another loop through East Boston in order to check out the Sumner's sister, the Callahan, which carried outbound traffic.

"Well, maybe these tunnels are too new," Jonah said. "There's always the subway tunnels — they're really old."

"I'm not wandering around in subway tunnels," she said emphatically, ending the discussion. Then she remembered that the subway's blue line went under Boston Harbor and as a compromise, suggested they ride the train through the tunnel and back.

As they drove through the city, returning to the North End to park, she said, "So what do you want to do for a living? Other than mortician I don't see all this death research leading to any kind of career field."

Jonah shrugged and scuffed the floor mat with his foot. "I don't know. Something in an office, I guess."

"Well, that narrows it down." She looked at him from the corner of her eye.

He shrugged again, looking glum. Irene tried to think back to what she had wanted to be at his age. Nothing came to mind. She felt a twinge of sympathy and tried to offer up some ideas.

"You could be one of those guys who goes and digs up ancient ruins, like an archeologist or whatever. You know, digging up old burial sites and whatnot."

He didn't seem happy with this suggestion. "Everything good's already been discovered." He gave the carpet a vicious kick.

"That's not true," she said. "You've already discovered something really amazing, something no one else knows about, with the book and your visits to the afterlife and all, and that was just an accident. Imagine what you could do if you were actually trying."

He flushed and shot her a grateful look.

She wasn't used to giving advice—certainly, not any that people actually listened to—and she felt a small rush of pleasure at the thought that she might have actually helped him.

She parked and they walked the few blocks to the Government Center T station. As they passed an upscale coffee house, Irene sighed. "I really miss coffee." Her eyes lingered longingly on the coffee-sipping patrons visible through the window.

At the subway station, they descended down into the steamy, fluorescent-light-filled cavern below and then down again to the Blue Line platform. The smell of oil and hot metal filled the air, intermingled with the odors of roasting cashews and urine. Luckily, a train arrived as they reached the last step so they didn't have to linger there.

They rode the subway three stops without talking—the racket of the train making it impossible to hold a conversation—exited the train at Maverick station, crossed over to the inbound platform, and rode the three stops back into the city. They found nothing of interest.

They spent the rest of the day exploring by foot as many tunnels as they could think of—the underground passages at Northeastern University, the tunnel connecting Park Street station and Downtown Crossing station, and the glass enclosed walkway along the Charles River T stop.

"Technically, I think this is a bridge," Irene said. This led to Jonah insisting they check out bridges next. So they wandered over the foot bridge in the Common, the bridge at Boston University, and the pedestrian walkway over Storrow Drive.

In all of this, they still only managed to glimpse a handful of ghosts. Jonah urged her to approach each one they saw, but she felt weird about it. What was she supposed to do, sidle up to them and whisper, "Psst, hey Mack. Where can I find the tunnel to the afterlife?" like some kind of drug deal?

"I don't understand. Where is everyone?" she asked finally. Why had she been left behind?

Jonah gave her a worried look. "I don't think people are meant to stay here."

Before she could stop it, the lurking concern that had been nagging her for some time burst free. "What if it's because they all died, for real? What if there is nothing else? What if it is like the headless chicken scenario and I'm just waiting for my brain to catch up to the fact that I'm dead, and then I'll just...stop or disappear or something?"

He looked at her for a moment. Then he slipped a hand into hers and gave it a reassuring squeeze. Surprised, she looked at their joined hands. Oddly comforted by the gesture, she felt the fear subside, and she smiled gratefully.

He squeezed her hand again and then released it. "For what it's worth, I don't think this is the end," he said. "There's too many stories about what comes after. I just think everyone moved on."

"Then why doesn't anyone come back?"

"Maybe they can't. Maybe the people who believe in reincarnation have it right and everyone did come back, just as someone else. Or," he added, "maybe what comes after this is so great, no one wants to come back. Either way, I don't think you should worry."

"Oh, Jonah," she said, sagging with relief. "You know...mostly you're annoying, but sometimes you're all right."

He grinned.

Irene, feeling more confident about the future than she had in days, had a sudden inspiration. "Okay, you know what? Let's go back to the library and see if we can find that girl...what was her name? Amy? Yeah, Amy. Remember?

She said something about knowing a bunch of other dead people."

"I thought you were afraid to go back?"

"That was then. Amy is the one solid lead that we've found, so I'm willing to risk another run in with Attila the Hun."

Jonah's grin instantly disappeared, replaced by a small pucker across his forehead, but he didn't say a word.

They were in luck: halfway back to the library, as they were cutting through the Common, they ran into Amy.

"I was just looking for you!" Irene exclaimed.

"Hello," Amy replied. "It's nice to see you again." She looked distracted and didn't seem to want to stop and chat.

Irene frowned, suddenly feeling awkward. "Um, you had mentioned that you knew of some places that were good to hang out, meet people…"

"Oh sure, that's easy. Try Flanagan's on Charlestown Street. You can't miss it." Then, clearly eager to be off, Amy excused herself and hurried away.

"Charlestown Street?" Irene muttered. "I've never heard of Charlestown Street…" She reached into her bag and pulled out the street map. Together, she and Jonah combed through every square inch of it, but couldn't find the street listed anywhere.

"Maybe she meant Charles Street?" Jonah pointed to the map.

Irene shrugged. It was as good an idea as any, though she didn't hold out a lot of hope. They had been there earlier, checking out the Charles Street subway stop and hadn't seen anything unusual or ghostly in the area.

She folded up the map and they set off. Unfortunately, Charles Street was fairly long, bordered on one end by the city's largest hospital and on the other by Chinatown. They walked the entire thing but found nothing.

The sun had sunk low in the sky and the streetlights were coming on. Jonah looked at his watch. "It's getting late," he said, reluctantly. "I really have to go."

"Really?" she asked with a sinking feeling. It occurred to Irene that she still had no place to stay. She'd left her house that morning with the intention of never returning, and, in fact, the thought of going back seemed incredibly depressing. She'd said her goodbyes, and already it was starting to seem like something remote and unconnected to her, something from a dream. She didn't really want to go and sit there, bored and alone, surrounded by mementos of everything she'd lost, everything she would never have again. She had fully expected to just be able to show up in the city and find a new apartment and new friends, and she hadn't really made a "Plan B" in case that didn't happen.

Jonah looked oddly pleased that she wanted him to stay. "I'll be back tomorrow," he reassured her. He looked at her more closely. "You gonna be okay?"

"Of course," she lied. "Why wouldn't I be?"

When he continued to stand there, she said, "I thought you were going."

"I'll walk you back to your car," he said, and she was both touched and amused by his gallantry.

Jonah seemed to think she was still worried that there was no actual afterlife; as they walked, he related stories of living people who had supposedly gone into the afterlife, usually to bring back a loved one. Irene half listened, lost in her own thoughts. When they reached the car, Jonah said, "Okay, I've got to go. I'll meet you at your house at eight again, okay?"

"Uh, plan on meeting me here," she said quickly, not really wanting to explain why she didn't want to go home. "I'll probably get an early start." The last thing she wanted was Jonah—who was so organized that he probably even ironed his underwear—to know how impetuous she had been in leaving the house. She wasn't in the mood for snarky comments on her lack of preparation and forethought. He would also probably tell her to just go home. He wouldn't really understand why she didn't want to, and she wasn't prepared to explain.

Jonah frowned but nodded, and then he disappeared.

Irene climbed in the car and sat there, trying to decide what to do. The sun was nearly down—the horizon was silver, the stars already visible overhead. She started to turn the key, steeling herself for the drive home, when she glanced at the gas gauge. How was she going to fill the gas tank in the afterlife? Did they make ghost gas for ghost cars?

She put her forehead down on the steering wheel, as a wave of despair and frustration washed over her.

Put on your big girl pants! she told herself fiercely. She'd never cried or felt self-pity when she was alive, and she wasn't about to start now. She sat up, shoving the feelings aside. *So you're homeless and there are big scary monsters out there. So what?*

Somehow, the pep talk wasn't helping.

She turned the key just enough to power the radio. She turned it on and was surprised to find that it worked. She scrolled through the channels until she found one that she liked. She rummaged in the beach bag and pulled out the towel. Draping it over her like a blanket, she reclined the seat and tried to sleep.

Thirteen

When Jonah showed up the next morning, he handed her a cup of coffee — glowing blue.

"I didn't know how you like it," he said, tumbling creamers and sugar packets into her hands.

She almost threw her arms around him. "Oh my God, Jonah, I love you forever!" She took the lid off the Styrofoam cup and took a gulp, straight, with no cream or sugar. It was still piping hot and it burned as it went down her throat. "Oh God," she said with a sigh, eyes closed, "this is really good!"

Jonah shook his head, smiling in amusement. "Glad you like it."

While Irene added cream and sugar, Jonah reached into his backpack and pulled out a piece of paper. "I have something else. I found this list…"

Irene glanced over and saw the words "Most Haunted Places in Massachusetts" splashed across the top of the page.

"…so I figured there are supposed to be ghosts here — "

"Huh," she said, scanning the list over his shoulder. "Wait, Danvers State Hospital? We're not doing that one."

"Why not?" he asked. "We have a car."

"It's not that. Danvers State was a mental hospital. Don't you watch horror movies? Nothing good ever happens to people who visit old mental hospitals, trust me."

He looked at her suspiciously, as if he thought she might be joking but wasn't quite sure. "Well, there's plenty of places to start here in the city," he said. "The Majestic Theater, the Everett Theater, Berklee College of Music, BU..."

"Those are all over the place," Irene said doubtfully. She reached into her bag and fished out the map. After a short argument about how to attack the long list of sites, they plotted each one on the map. Fort Warren, the supposedly most haunted place, was too hard to get to, being located in the harbor and reachable only by ferry, so they ruled that one out. There were four sites — the two theaters plus the two sites related to Emerson College — that were all clustered together in the theater district, which was just a short walk away, so they decided to start there. As they set off, Jonah said, "I have to leave early today. I have a biology test this afternoon."

A wave of surprise washed over Irene, followed quickly by embarrassment. She had forgotten that Jonah was still alive and, technically, supposed to be in school. She felt a momentary twinge of guilt and wondered if maybe she should send him home.

"You okay?" Jonah asked.

On the other hand, he seemed to be keeping up with his schoolwork just fine, so these absences must not be that big of a deal. And it wasn't like she was his mother — it wasn't her job to tell him what to do.

"Uh, yeah," she said. "Come on, let's go."

It was another nice day. The intermittent clouds kept the sun from beating down on them, and they enjoyed the walk down Tremont Street. They detoured into the Common to look for the two ghost women who were supposed to haunt the park. They found no sign of them. Then they continued south. When they reached the theater district, the two theaters were closed, the doors locked tight.

"Duh," Irene said. "I didn't think. It's eleven o'clock in the morning. Of course they're not open."

Next, they decided to head over to the two music schools. They retraced their steps back to Boylston and hopped on the subway. They took the green line back to

Park Street station, where they switched to the red line for one stop and then switched to the orange line.

"I am not going to miss this," Irene said as they stood on the platform waiting for a train. The lonely strains of a saxophone trembled in the air from a nearby street musician, his music case lying open hopefully in front of him. "Switching trains three times just to get around the corner — ugh."

Jonah was peering down the tracks. "You know," he said, "these *are* tunnels, and there's a white light down there…"

Irene gave him a dry look. "That's an oncoming train."

The rush of the train, followed by the squeal of brakes as it pulled into the station cut off whatever he might have said in retort.

They found nothing unusual at either school — or, at least, more unusual than is generally found on a college campus full of musicians — though Jonah did seem fascinated by everything he saw. Irene led him around, describing college life — meal plans, dorms, lecture halls, electives. Jonah seemed a little young for fake I.D.s, fraternities and sororities, and the side effects of binge drinking, so she left those facets out.

Hours later, Irene leaned against a wrought iron fence, tired and dejected. "Well, this is a little more needle-in-a-haystack than I expected." They had roamed all over both campuses, finding nothing but college students. Irene thought again of the millions and millions of dead that should be here and, again, felt a momentary rising panic. *Where was everybody?* Why had she been left behind?

Jonah checked his watch. "I've got to go," he said reluctantly.

She waved him off, despite a twinge of panic at being left alone. "Yeah, okay."

"See you tomorrow." The words hung in the air as he disappeared from view.

Irene frowned, not sure what to do next. There was still the Boston University campus to check out, though she didn't hold out a lot of hope that she'd find anything there. Her feet hurt and she was hot and tired. She dug in her bag, looking for the map. Her hand landed on the bottle of vodka and she pulled it out. She contemplated it for a moment, then unscrewed the top and took a drink. Suddenly, she wanted a nap. She hadn't slept well—not that she'd expected to be comfortable in the car. She decided to go back to the car for a quick rest and then to head back to the theaters.

She was too tired to walk all the way back. To avoid the hassle of switching trains three times, she walked two blocks over to Huntington Avenue so she could catch a green line train directly back to Government Center.

She strolled down the street, enjoying the sunshine and light breeze. The sensation that someone was following her crept over her so stealthily that she wasn't aware of it until she felt the cold, burning as it wrapped around her ankle. She didn't have to look to know what it was: the nameless, formless terror from the other night.

Terror swept over her and she bolted.

She dodged down streets, zig-zagging her way toward the car, heart pounding in terror. The shadow stayed with her, following every bend, every twist she put in her path.

She could tell when the creature got closer—the air burned with cold as she sucked it in, trying to fill her lungs. Twice she stumbled, her ankles twisting beneath the force of running in four-inch heels. The second time, a tendril caught hold of her, wrapping around her thigh. It was as if someone had jabbed a red-hot poker through her leg, and she screamed with the searing pain of it. Her leg buckled and she stumbled. She managed to stay on her feet, and she forced a burst of speed out of her rubbery legs.

Her head was swimming, black spots twinkling before her eyes, and her lungs were on the verge of exploding. Any second now she was going to pass out.

She wasn't going to make it to the car. In fact, she wasn't going to make it at all. She was spent.

She was running along a street of close-packed storefronts She veered to the right, grabbed the nearest door handled, and tugged. It opened and, without thinking, she tumbled in, falling to the floor. The door closed behind her.

She lay there, panting, as she tried to catch her breath. Her heart hammered in her chest and she thought it might explode.

The thing slammed into the door and the glass rattled. Irene heard a nervous chuckle and looked up.

She had stumbled into a barber shop. The barber was frozen mid-snip, his attention arrested by the banging of his front door. Two other customers, waiting their turn in the chair, were also gaping at the door, which continued to rattle and shake as the shadow threw itself against it.

"Guess the wind's picked up," the barber said. His customers chuckled and they all went about their business as if nothing was happening.

It can't get in, Irene thought wildly. She didn't understand why but she wasn't about to question it.

She took long, deep breaths, willing herself to calm down, to think, to be rational. The door continued to rattle with the thing's efforts to enter the shop.

Little by little, the black terror faded as her breathing slowed. Her heart, however, still thumped like machine gun fire with panic. What if that thing found a way to get into the shop?

She stood up slowly as pain rippled through her. She had wrenched her left ankle and her thigh still burned. She lifted the hem of her dress and saw a thin, angry red line encircling her thigh, almost as if someone had garroted her leg with a wire. She dropped her dress hastily. She felt branded, as if somehow tainted by the welt.

The shadow creature emitted no noise, but Irene could tell it was in a rage. It continued to rattle the door for several terrifying minutes. Then, all of a sudden, the noise stopped. Irene listened hard, waiting for the assault to resume, but the silence stretched on. She didn't dare hope it was gone; she was afraid it had simply gone around the corner to wait for her. She limped over to one of the chairs and sat down.

Two hours later, when the barber started locking up, she still wasn't keen to leave, but she clearly had no choice unless she wanted to spend the night here. She slipped out while the barber was washing up in the back. The sun was down and the streetlights cast a jaundiced glow on the sidewalk. There was the chill of autumn in the air, but nothing more. The thing was gone. Slowly and painfully, she made her way back to the car, tears silently tracking down her cheeks as she went.

Fourteen

Irene was up early the next day, after having spent another restless night in the car. Fortunately, though the burn on her thigh still hurt, her ankle was better and she was able to pretend everything was fine when Jonah arrived.

The scene from last night kept replaying itself in her mind. She couldn't understand why the shadow hadn't been able to get through the door, or, more importantly, why she had. She remembered the first attack—she had tried to get into the Prudential Center and hadn't been able to.

"Do you mind if we check something out?" she asked.

Jonah shrugged his agreement. She thought for a second and then struck out for the nearest collection of office buildings and stores. At the first store they came to, she stopped to try the door. She jerked her hand back quickly, shaking it vigorously, as she felt a jolt of electricity. "Ow!"

Jonah blinked in surprise. "You okay?"

Irene frowned. "Yeah, but I have a question for you. How come sometimes I get a shock when I try to open a door?"

Jonah shook his head "I don't think it's anything special, just a little static electricity." He grabbed the door handle but pulled back his hand with a yelp. "Ow!"

Irene gave him a smug look. "Just a little static electricity," she said. "You know, this happened to me before...I don't think the dead are allowed into places like this."

Jonah looked at her and then at the door and then back again. "What? Into department stores?"

"Any stores. Mrs. Boine said the living have ways of keeping us out and making life hard for us."

"We went into the library."

"Yeah, that's what I don't get. We can get in to some places but not others."

Jonah's face squinched with deep thought. "Well, I guess...would you want ghosts coming into your store? They're invisible, they can make stuff float through the air, and they have no money. They'd just scare your customers and rob you blind."

The sound of muttering drew Irene's attention. She looked around, finally settling on two men — clearly homeless, if judged by their tattered and scruffy appearance — sitting on the sidewalk nearby.

"Pooka?" the first man was saying. Despite the warm sun overhead, he was bundled in a canvas trench coat that had perhaps once been a tan or camel colored. He had the ghost glow.

"Nawwww," the second, who, Irene realized, was not blue, answered. He took a deep, phlegmy breath through his nose and then hawked a wad of spit onto the ground. "Boggie, mebbe."

"But 'e's dead?" the dead one asked.

"Near dead, mebbe."

They were staring at Jonah with puzzled frowns. Jonah bumped her, trying to surreptitiously push her aside. "Excuse me, do you know why we can't get into the store?"

Irene nudged him. "Don't encourage them," she hissed.

"Ooooo, 'e talks to us," the dead one said. He nudged his friend. "Pluck up, Robert."

A woman walking by tossed a coin into the battered hat lying upturned on the ground in front of the two men and tugged her young child closer as she hurried past. Irene felt a flush of embarrassment and rooted through her bag for spare change, feeling shown up by the woman. "Uh...here," she said, tossing a couple of quarters into the hat. Then she grabbed Jonah's arm and tried to pull him away. "Let's go," she said in a low voice.

The non-dead man fished out the coins Irene had tossed into his hat and went rigid with anger. "Do I look dead, you God-damned fool?" he bellowed indignantly, holding the glowing coins in the palm of his hand. Several people walking by skittered off the sidewalk, putting distance between themselves and the enraged beggar. The dead man climbed to his feet, holding out a hand.

"Give here..." he said.

"I'm sorry, I don't have any more money," Irene said, backing away and pulling Jonah with her.

"No, wait," Jonah said, trying to pull out of her grip.

"Now, Jonah!" Irene pulled hard on his arm. "Move it!" She started down the street, towing Jonah behind her.

"Those guys might be able to help us." He tried to yank his arm from her grasp.

"I don't need any help from a couple of homeless lunatics, thanks."

"God, you're such a pain sometimes." He wrenched free of her vice-like grip and ground to a halt in the middle of the sidewalk. "Could you stop being so rude and angry for two seconds and just listen?"

Irene whirled around, furious at his tone. "Excuse me? Please don't talk to me like that. Try to remember that I'm an adult and you're a—"

Jonah's face twisted into an enraged scowl, purple-red splotches of anger blooming like fireworks across his face. "I'm not a kid! Will you stop treating me like one? *You* asked for *my* help, remember?"

"Yeah, well, I've changed my mind if you're going to be a jerk about it. Anyway, if I remember correctly, you were thrilled to have an excuse to get out of school, so it's not like I twisted your arm."

"I came because you begged me to!" he shouted. "*Oh Jonah, I need your help!*" he mimicked in a nasty falsetto.

Irene's jaw clenched with anger. "You are such a little shit sometimes, you know that?"

Jonah looked ready to explode. Then, with an obvious effort, he took a deep breath and said very calmly, "Look, we're wandering around, lost, no plan, no idea where we're going, and you won't even talk to the people who might be able to help us find the tunnel—"

"I'm not looking for the tunnel!" Irene cried. "I'm looking for dead people!"

"Those guys were dead!"

"Cool dead people that I can hang out with. That girl, Amy, was the only person I've found like that so far, and *you're* the one that didn't want me to talk to her."

Jonah looked flabbergasted. "I thought you wanted to go through the tunnel?"

"No, I don't want to go through the fucking tunnel!" she shouted. "You're the one who keeps going on about it."

"Well, then what do you want?"

"*I* want to be alive again. That's what I want. I want my life back. But apparently that's not going to happen." Irene angrily brushed at her cheek, swiping away the tears that had embarrassingly spilled over.

Now Jonah looked alarmed, the anger ebbing from his face. "Are you going to cry?"

"Yes, God damn it! Yes, I'm going to cry!" she shouted. "Do you know why?" Her voice rose with each syllable. "Because it's a normal, human reaction to a fucked up situation!"

Jonah backed away, his hands raised as if to ward off an attack. Irene's shoulders slumped as tears tracked down her cheeks. She hated this. She hated all of it. The wandering around. The not knowing why she was stuck here. The not knowing where she was supposed to go or what she was supposed to do. Most of all, the fear that the shadow creatures were lurking around every corner. She'd had a life once, a great life. Now it was all shot to hell.

"Do you want...should I...give you a hug?" Jonah asked tentatively.

"No, I don't want a fucking hug," she raged at him, sending him scuttling backwards another few steps. She snatched the bag from her shoulder and threw it against the nearest wall. "I want you to go over there," she flung out an arm, pointing to a distant corner of the street, "and leave me alone, and just wait...wait until I'm done."

Jonah took another couple of steps backwards, but kept a wary, watchful eye on her, as she turned away, scrubbing at her eyes with her hands.

She looked at the beach bag, which had thumped against the brick and then slid jaggedly down the rough surface to settle on the ground in a lumpy puddle. Her arms dropped in weary frustration as she realized what she had done. "Oh shit. I hope the vodka didn't break." She hesitated, as if afraid to look, and then moved to the bag, squatting beside it to rifle through the contents. She pulled out the bottle and, still squatting, held it up to the light for inspection. Then in one quick movement, she lowered it, twisted off the top, and took a long drink.

"I think I liked it better when you were crying," Jonah said drily, sidling closer but staying out of arm's reach.

Irene lowered the bottle, resting it on one bent knee. "I don't know why crying bothers you so much." She twisted the top back on the bottle, stowed it in the bag, and slinging the bag over her shoulder, stood up.

"My sister cries. All the time."

Irene could imagine. His sister had looked, from the pictures, like the type to use tears as a weapon to get what she wanted. Irene felt another prickle of tears at the thought that Jonah saw her the same way—a manipulative prima donna who kicked and cried when she didn't get her own way. She straightened up, blinking back the sudden surge of new tears caused by the bitter thought that she used to hang out with people who actually liked her. The feeling of being all alone returned. She whirled around and stalked off, leaving Jonah by himself, as she tried to get hold of herself, tried to figure a way out of this mess.

"Hey!" Jonah said, catching up to her. He grabbed her arm but she kept walking, trying to shrug him off as she went. He kept a tight grip on her and tugged her arm again, gentler this time, but insistent. She stopped with a sigh and looked at him, feeling brittle and bleak.

"Irene..." His voice was choked with worry and she was surprised to see deep and genuine concern on his face. "Come on," he said gently. "Look, there's some benches over there. Why don't we take a break? Just for a minute? Come on. Sit down."

She deflated as her anger fled, and she placidly followed as he led her to a seat. He crouched in front of her and leaned forward, peering into her face, his eyes big with worry. "Look, I'll do whatever you want, okay? Just tell me what you want to do. Do you want to go home? Do you want to keep looking? What?"

Irene shook her head. "I don't know. I don't know if I want to go through the tunnel or not. I keep hoping there's a third option, you know?"

He stood up and moved to the bench, sitting down beside her. He shrugged out of his backpack and swung it around to his lap. "Okay. So let's have some lunch and strategize a bit, okay? We still haven't exhausted all the possibilities. There are still places on the 'Most Haunted' list, all the places on the Freedom Trail, which are really old and likely to have ghosts, there's the cemeteries..." He trailed off as he rummaged in the bag, nearly disappearing inside it. He emerged holding a sandwich, wrapped in plastic, which he passed to her.

She looked at the sandwich as if it was a foreign object. She sniffed it gingerly — tuna fish — and then looked at Jonah. "You brought sandwiches to the afterlife?"

"How else are we supposed to get food?"

She had to bite back a laugh. He was so ridiculously rational, so absurdly practical. She felt a sudden rush of affection for him, despite herself; it was simply impossible to stay mad at him. "You know, technically, I guess I don't need to eat anymore."

He shrugged. "Yeah, but I thought you might like to, anyway."

She looked at him, at a loss for words. "You really are incredibly sweet, Jonah." She had almost said a 'sweet kid' but managed to catch herself at the last second.

His ears turned pink and she thought he looked pleased in the instant before he ducked behind his hair. He'd found a second sandwich, which he now unwrapped and bit into.

She followed suit. She chewed in silence for a moment, her brow furrowed. "This sandwich tastes weird."

"What do you mean?" he asked, tearing off another bite.

Irene chewed thoughtfully, savoring the taste. "Well...it tastes like a sandwich. I mean, I can actually taste the tuna and the bread..."

Jonah's face clearly said that he thought she had lost her mind.

"I just realized that nothing has really had any taste since I woke up here—or, at least, it has all tasted off—but these sandwiches actually taste...real. So did the coffee you brought me."

Jonah chewed thoughtfully for a minute. "Everything else you've been consuming has been from the land of the living, right?"

Irene nodded.

"I think maybe it's because when a person dies just their essence crosses over. I mean, you don't actually have a body now, right? So it's like you need the essence of food rather than actual food. These sandwiches came through with me so I guess they're ghost sandwiches now. The actual sandwiches are with my body."

Irene looked glum. "So I'm a ghost woman, eating a ghost sandwich...and look, now I'll feed this ghost cat."

There was a small black and white cat sitting on its haunches, watching Irene intently with intensely green eyes. Irene broke off a bit of sandwich and tossed it to the cat. The cat stared at Irene for another moment and then bent its head and sniffed gingerly at the bit of sandwich. It pulled back with disgust and lifted an indignant gaze back up to the humans.

"I don't think that cat is dead. It's not blue," Jonah said through a mouthful of sandwich. He was thoughtful for a minute. "We've got a cat. She's always staring at things that aren't there." He chewed. "I guess there is something there after all."

Irene watched the cat absently, not really paying it any mind. It seemed to resolve itself to the fact that no better food was forthcoming. With a look of deep discontent, it leaned down, took the bit of sandwich into its mouth, and proceeded to chew it with delicate distaste.

"If the cat isn't dead then how come it's eating an invisible sandwich?" Irene asked.

"The Egyptians thought cats were the guardians of the afterlife," Jonah said, apropos of nothing.

Irene shook her head. Jonah seemed distracted suddenly, and she suspected she wasn't going to get anything coherent out of him until he finished thinking out whatever thoughts were churning in that brain of his.

She watched the cat, which appeared to be watching her. No, not watching so much as...assessing. In fact, it seemed to be judging her. She shifted her weight and looked around for something to throw at it, to scare it off.

When she turned back, the cat was gone.

"Did you see that?" she asked. Jonah's brow knit with confusion. "Oh forget it," she huffed in exasperation.

He shrugged and turned back to his sandwich, taking a big bite and chewing intently. He seemed to be eating it in a circle, attacking all of the crust edges first, before tackling the middle. Irene shook her head and looked away to hide a smile.

She sat back against the bench and looked out over the street. Why were there so many people out? Didn't they have to work? She realized that all this daytime activity was almost like another world, squashed side-by-side with her own—or, at least, the one she had just vacated. While other people were at their jobs, there was a whole other species of human that was out jogging, walking the dog, sunbathing, or reading a book. She tried to imagine what they did when the "regular" people appeared. When the office buildings emptied at five o'clock, where did the "recreationists" go? Did they trundle off to jobs, disappear underground, or blend into the crowd of regular people? She had a sudden uncomfortable feeling there were a lot of things about the world—existing just under the surface—that she had never noticed.

She turned to Jonah. "Madame Majicka said that all the legends about death and burial and whatnot are true."

Jonah nodded slowly, still intent on his sandwich. "Yeah."

"Okay, but, so far, none of them have been true. I don't know a single story where the afterlife is just the regular world and you just go on living your life, forever."

"Well, actually, the ancient Sumerians believed the afterlife was just like real life, only kinda gray and washed out. The Hebrews had Sheol, which was a similar kind of idea."

"So this is it? The Sumerians had it right? Life just goes on and I need to get a job and keep paying the bills and all that?"

Jonah bit into his sandwich and took his time chewing it. The rustling of the world in motion swirled around them—birds chittering, leaves whispering, and traffic humming and swishing. Irene realized there were three worlds layered together here—the "regular" nine-to-five world, the world inhabited by the "other" people who thronged the streets while others were at work, and then the world of the dead who drifted through both worlds, unseen.

Jonah swallowed. "I think, well…maybe death and life aren't connected."

"What do you mean?"

"Maybe the stories are wrong. Maybe living isn't the point of death and maybe death isn't the end of living. Maybe they're just different."

A faint echo of Amy's voice tickled her memory—*Just because you're dead doesn't mean your life is over.*

"Maybe it's like…moving to another country," Jonah continued. "Like France."

Another faint echo, this one from Madame Majicka's self-help book, danced across her memory — *It's not about a right and a wrong way. It's about choices.*

"If you move to France, things are…different, right? They talk a different language and eat funny foods. So like…it's the same, but it's different. You know? Like…a new era kind of thing."

"So I have a choice? I can move to…'France'…or I can stay here?" she said.

"Yeah, exactly."

"I don't know about that, but it's as good a theory as any, I guess." She wadded up the plastic wrap from her sandwich and tossed it on the ground.

Jonah frowned.

"What?" she said. "It's the invisible essence of litter, not actual litter."

Jonah continued to eye her until, with a groan of exasperation, she picked the plastic wrap up and stuffed it in her bag. "Fine. Happy?"

"Effervescent," he said around the last mouthful of his sandwich. "So now what?"

Irene shrugged. "I don't know. I feel like…like I'm floundering a bit here."

"Well, we could start by going back and talking to those guys."

"What guys? You mean the winos?"

Jonah sighed heavily.

"I mean the probably-very-sweet homeless men?" she amended.

Jonah cocked an eyebrow, challenging her to reject his idea. Irene took a deep breath and hauled herself to her feet. "What do I have to lose?" she asked, spreading her hands to indicate that Jonah should lead the way.

They went back to the store, but the sidewalk was now empty. They walked up and down the street as they checked the alleys and cross streets surrounding the store but there was no sign of the men.

Irene and Jonah walked in silence for a few minutes, returning by unspoken, mutual agreement to the exploration of the city. At the next intersection, Irene saw two dead priests, in full, formal dress, ringing hand bells. "The church is always open, sister," they said to her as she passed.

Really? she thought. *Even now they're still trying to recruit? It's a little late, isn't it?*

The light changed and she and Jonah crossed the street, entering Back Bay, a residential area populated with iconic Boston brownstones. The streets were neat and clean here and fall pots and window boxes of mums and brightly colored leaves lined steps and wrought iron railings.

"So," she said to Jonah, wanting a distraction, "tell me some of these afterlife stories. The ones that are supposed to be true."

"Well, you know all the common ones, right? Like Charon, the ferry man who takes you across the river, and Cerebus, the three-headed dog that guards the entrance to Hades."

"Yeah, sure, of course. The 'common ones'." She made air quotes. "Or, conversely, Saint Peter and the Archangel Gabriel and the pearly gates and all that."

"Yeah," Jonah said, a little hesitantly.

Irene laughed. "I guess your family isn't too big on church, huh?"

Jonah shrugged. "My grandparents are Presbyterians...Unitarians...Episcopalians, something like that."

"Yeah, well, you might want to add something to your research about current views on the afterlife. I think all your stuff is a little out of date."

Jonah frowned, looking hurt and a little puzzled. They walked on, the silence stretching out. Amidst the numerous lithe, Lycra-clad joggers, a middle-aged man was walking a pocketbook-sized dog on a pink leash. Irene watched as the man leaned against a wrought iron fence, his stomach straining the yellow fabric of his polo shirt as the dog did its business.

"There's the Rainbow Bridge," she added, prodding Jonah to continue the conversation. The man walked off, leaving the droppings behind.

"Huh?" Jonah said.

"Rainbows are supposed to be the bridge to Heaven."

"Who says that?" he asked with a trace of bewildered suspicion, as if he thought she was pulling his leg.

Irene shrugged. "I don't know. We had a dog when I was a kid and it died, and everyone kept talking about the Rainbow Bridge, the Rainbow Bridge, the Rainbow Bridge. That's where animals meet us in the afterlife. Supposedly. I just know it was all kind of sappy and didn't make me feel any better." She remembered thinking that her dog, Pebbles, was going to have to wait an awfully long time to see her again. That didn't seem very fair to Pebbles. Plus, how could she ever get another dog, knowing Pebbles was sitting in Heaven, waiting endlessly for her? *Poor Pebbles.* Doggie Heaven had sounded an awful lot like the pound.

"Which reminds me, where do you think all the dead animals are? Shouldn't this place be crawling with them? I mean, I don't think animals have the ability to conceptualize either a tunnel or an afterlife, let alone the idea of 'moving on,' so one would suppose they'd all be stuck here, wouldn't they?"

Jonah looked around in surprise, as if he hadn't really considered it before. "Huh. I guess that's true. So where *do* they go?" He frowned in concentration, and Irene could imagine him mentally flipping through every piece of afterlife knowledge he possessed. She suppressed another smile.

"Huh. I don't know." His frown deepened for a moment. Then he shrugged. "You know, there are a lot of bridge metaphors in afterlife mythology. A lot of Native American tribes think the Milky Way is a bridge to the afterlife. The Zoroastrians thought you had to cross a bridge the width of a hair to get there."

Irene lifted a foot, displaying her stiletto heel. "That would be difficult in these shoes."

Jonah laughed. The subway tracks ran above ground here and a green line train rumbled by, momentarily interrupting their conversation.

When the train was gone, Jonah said, "The Norse had a bridge, too, and if someone tried to cross it before their time, the guardian shook it so they'd fall off." He paused and then added after a moment's thought, "I think it must have been a rope bridge."

Now it was Irene's turn to laugh. "You're so weird." She realized it was her turn to add something, so she thought for a moment and then said, "Well, there's supposed to be lakes of fire. In Hell, at least. I remember reading *The Inferno* in college, and I definitely remember the lakes of fire."

"Oh God, there's everything! There's burning lakes, razor sharp mountains, deserts, rivers, icy sharp winds, forests…everything!"

Irene picked up her foot again, once more indicating her shoes were inappropriate for a journey that contained such things.

Jonah chuckled. "Well, the Sumerians think you have to be naked to get to the land of the dead, so I guess that would solve your problem."

"They're the ones who think the land of the dead is the same as the land of the living, just grayer?" she asked, hitting the button for the walk signal as they waited at a corner.

"Yeah. There's this famous poem about it that describes the land of the dead as 'the house where one goes in and never comes out again, the road that, if one takes it, one never comes back.' Isn't that creepy?"

Irene smiled at the little-boy side that was peeping out. "And you're just dying to see this in person, huh?"

Jonah went on, with obvious relish, clearly enjoying the gruesome description. "It also says it's the place where the inhabitants live on dust and their food is mud."

"Great," Irene said, her voice heavy with sarcasm. "Can't wait to go." The conversation was light-hearted and playful, but, subtly and faintly, a glimmer of worry was starting to worm its way into Irene's mind.

Then Jonah giggled. "They said you get ferried across a river to the palace of the king of the underworld, and then you have to take off all your clothes in order to enter the palace." Jonah giggled again. "Isn't that weird?"

Irene smiled but she shook her head.

"There's even a myth about this goddess who tried to take over the underworld. She had to leave behind a piece of clothing or jewelry at different places during her journey. I think it's funny to imagine her leaving clothes strewn all over the underworld and wandering about naked."

Irene gave him a dry look. "Well it's good to see you're a normal boy in some regards." When he shot her a questioning look, she laughed. "Aren't there any stories about good things in the afterlife? Like living on clouds and playing the harp all day, that sort of thing?" She jabbed the button for the walk signal again.

"Well, most Native Americans think that everyone who has died before you, like your family and friends and stuff, meet you in the afterlife. I've always liked that idea. Like you die and then there's a big party and everyone you've ever known comes."

Irene smiled wistfully. "Okay, that would be cool." Her heart jumped at the thought of seeing her grandmother.

"I think my most favorite of all is the ancient Romans, though," Jonah continued. The light finally changed and they crossed the street, turned left, and continued on.

"Uh, where are we going?" Jonah asked, looking around as if noticing the scenery for the first time.

Irene looked surprised. "Uh…I don't know. I thought you were leading the way."

Jonah shook his head. "I was following you."

"Well, I was following you," she countered.

They both laughed.

"Okay, fine, let's go this way." She pointed, indicating a cross street that would take them back the way they had come. They were both silence as they navigated a series of cross walks.

"So, you were saying something about the Romans," Irene said once they were safely across the street.

"What? Oh, yeah, the Romans. They thought the afterlife was the real life and the land of the living was a prison where we all have to spend some time."

Irene could see their point. She liked living, wanted to be alive again, in fact, but a lot of life did seem like prison — family responsibilities, work, bills. Death, at least, was a release from all that. Only, as she was discovering, the part that was left didn't really seem very interesting without all that other stuff.

"They thought the body was just an outward representation or projection of the spirit or soul, and that we can control what it looks like, based on what we think we look like and how we feel and whatever. They thought we were a race of immortal beings, like gods, that share a universal consciousness. Like, we all share one mind and can hear each other's thoughts and stuff. They thought that we all knew this, too, deep down inside, and that we can feel the universal consciousness while we're in the land of the living. You know, like, if we all just kind of stop and listen, we can sense how we're all connected and how there's more than what we can see all around us."

Irene's pace slowed. "Wow. That's really beautiful. I like that."

Jonah nodded. "Isn't it?" He said in a low voice, as if to himself, "We're all gods."

"It'd be nice if it's true, huh?"

Jonah shrugged. "I guess it is."

Irene hit his arm playfully. "So, in the afterlife, we're all going to be naked gods eating mud on a boat?"

Jonah laughed.

"So does this mean other things are supposed to be true, too, like elves and fairies and whatnot?"

Jonah frowned. "Maybe. No. I don't know. Those don't really have to do with the afterlife, do they? I think they're just stories — like mythology and stuff. Like, I don't think Medusa is real."

"Oh, elves are just made up but a three-headed dog is real?"

Jonah shrugged in bewilderment, as if to say he didn't know one way or the other.

"Okay, well then obviously angels are a given," Irene said. "But what about...imps and demons? Those are supposed to live in Hell, which is part of the land of the dead. I mean, if you've got a three-headed dog, then you have to give me demons." She'd been joking but it struck her that maybe it wasn't a joke. There was something out there, something dark and malevolent, and it had attacked her.

She shivered. "I think demons are real." The words spilled out of her before she could stop them. She hadn't meant to tell him—she didn't want to scare him—but suddenly she couldn't stop herself. "There's something out there. Something chased me last night, after you left, and the day we went to the library. I was walking back to the car and there was...something. Something scary. I don't know what it was."

"What do mean?" he asked.

"I don't know," she repeated, feeling helpless and stupid. "It was a monster. An honest-to-God monster. It was big and black, and it didn't look like anything I've ever seen before." She remembered the pain and the cold and she shuddered. Jonah slipped a hand into hers and gave it a reassuring squeeze. She smiled gratefully. He smiled back. He held on to her hand for a minute longer before giving it another squeeze and then letting it go.

"It'll be okay," he said. "I won't let anything eat you."

"Gee, thanks."

Fifteen

They spent the next couple of days continuing their explorations of the city, trying every place they could think of to look for either a tunnel or other dead people, even going so far as to participate in a "ghost tour" of the city. They had giggled their way through the entire thing. At night, when Jonah went home, Irene slept uneasily in her car. She was careful to always be out walking around by the time Jonah showed up each morning so he wouldn't know.

"So how long are you here for today?" Irene asked.

"All weekend." Jonah looked smug. "I told my parents I was sleeping over at a friend's house this weekend so I don't have to be home until Sunday night."

"Your parents really have no clue that anything is going on?"

"I told you—I'm an honor student. Why would they think I was anywhere but where I'm supposed to be? As long as I get good grades, they don't much care what I do."

She wasn't really surprised—she had gotten away with a lot worse in her time. Jonah was right: parents could be so clueless about their kids.

They decided to visit the State House. Jonah had never been inside and wanted to see it. Frankly, they didn't have anything better to do, so Irene agreed.

They slipped inside and skirted the metal detectors.

"Huh," Irene said, looking around.

"What?"

"I just realized we can go anywhere. Like...I can literally go anywhere in this building — all the behind-the-scenes places you're not allowed when you're alive: private meetings, people's secret files..."

Jonah smiled. "See? Being dead isn't all bad." He grabbed her hand and pulled her toward the wide, marble stairs that swept up to the second floor. "Come on! Let's see if we can go all the way up to the dome."

Just then two living men in business suits — very likely legislators — came down the stairs, talking earnestly together. Two dead men dressed in outfits that Irene had only ever seen in paintings — satin knee breeches, matching white stockings, and long coats — trailed them. In fact, if she wasn't mistaken, they looked an awful lot like the people featured in the paintings that hung on the walls around them.

The two dead men were arguing.

"My dear Sir, you know as well as I that to raise taxes during this current economic climate would be disastrous!" the heavyset one said.

"What would you have the man do? Shall the state declare bankruptcy?" The thinner one leaned forward and said in the ear of the living man he trailed, "Stick to your guns, my boy! Don't let them roll you up."

The two legislators clearly had no idea that two of their forebears were dogging them. They walked on, deep in uninterrupted conversation. As the quartet passed by, Irene heard the heavyset one say, "Nothing will be gained by shouting at each other in this ill-mannered way. Come, let us discuss this in a civilized manner over a pint."

The thin one clapped his companion on the shoulder. "I beg your pardon, my dear Sir. You are, as always, the wiser man."

The two broke away from the men they were following and headed for the door. Irene turned to Jonah. "Come on, let's follow them," she hissed.

"What? Why?"

"Because it sounds like they're going to a bar or something. It's very likely the place that girl Amy was talking about."

Jonah looked longingly up the stairs. "Yeah, but —"

"Come on." Irene didn't wait for an answer. She turned and followed the men out the door.

Jonah trailed after her, clearly disgruntled at having to give up the tour of the State House.

"Oh, cheer up," Irene said, piqued by his sulking. "We can see the State House any time."

Ten minutes later, on a dingy side street, they found themselves in front of an old, low, ramshackle wooden building that looked like a leftover from the set of a western. A faint blue aura surrounded the place, and Irene's heart sped up. The strains of some kind of folksy Irish ballad wafted through the air.

"This must be it," she said. She grinned slyly. "It gives new meaning to the term 'dead drunk.'"

Jonah frowned up at the wooden sign hanging above the door, where the word "Flanagan's" was written in peeling blue letters. "That's not funny."

"Actually, it kinda was. Lighten up." She pulled open the door and the music grew louder, now accompanied by the burble of many voices talking all at once.

Jonah hung back, looking reluctant. "I don't know about this…"

"Look, it's blue," Irene said, wanting to be inside already. "There are dead people in here and I need a drink. So come on."

Jonah shifted his weight from one foot to another. A crinkle appeared between his eyebrows. "Maybe you shouldn't drink so much," he said, looking at the ground.

Irene froze and then backed out of the door, turning to face him on the sidewalk. "What is that supposed to mean?" she asked coldly.

"Nothing. Just…you drink a lot."

"Jesus Christ! First of all, you aren't the boss of me. Second of all, I'm an adult — I can do what I want. Third of all…piss off and mind your own business."

Irene pulled open the door again and put a foot over the threshold.

"Irene..." Jonah said, clearly miserable.

She spun around. "You know what? You're right, this is a bar. It's no place for a *child*. So why don't you go home."

Jonah blanched, as if she had slapped him. He looked at her, his eyes wide with hurt, and Irene regretted the words but was now too angry to admit it. She pursed her lips and marched inside, leaving him standing outside on the sidewalk.

The smell hit her as soon as she was through the door. It was a familiar cocktail of cigarette smoke, stale perfume, and booze—the tangible atmosphere that pervaded every bar of a certain class. The kind of place where working stiffs from the middle shelf of life—accountants, secretaries, aerobics instructors, teachers, software programmers, store clerks, and the like—went to get comfortably sloshed and pick up members of the opposite sex.

What had seemed like a burble of noise while standing on the street outside turned into a sledgehammer of solid sound. Voices talking and laughing, plates and cutlery banging and rattling, music thrumming, and inexplicably, what seemed to be a sort of nineteen sixties beat poet—black turtleneck, beret, sunglasses, and all—on a stool in the corner, adding broken threads of sound to the mix.

As Irene's gaze swept across the landscape, taking in details, she realized the place was more than a meat market. In fact, it seemed to be every kind of bar there ever was rolled into one. Memorabilia plastered the walls so thickly it was impossible to distinguish the underlying wall material. License plates, postcards, farm implements, autographed posters, old records—the eye got lost trying to identify discreet objects. They were crammed and layered until they made a kind of textured, three-dimensional wallpaper. The ceiling was made of exposed wood beams giving the place the feel of an old barn, and the scattered light fixtures glowed with a dull, yellow light, evoking an old Irish pub. An oak counter ran along one wall—polished smooth by time and use. Stools topped with black vinyl and deep wood-framed chairs with padded black leather—the type of reading chair you might find in an old-fashioned library or office—added to the old tavern feel of the place. The cheap, square, plastic kitchenette dining tables topped in orange or white Formica around which the chairs were arranged, however, did not.

Even the patrons seemed snatched from a dozen different locales. The beat poet in the corner. A boisterous group of Lager-drinking rowdies singing Danny Boy, drunkenly and off-key. An earnest looking group of men with graying beards and patches on the elbows of their tweed sports coats engaged in a lively debate that seemed to require a lot of table pounding. The maudlin drunks, scattered about by themselves, slumped head in hands over their drinks. The college frat boys who were egging each other on with shouts of "Chug! Chug! Chug!" as a member downed shots. Irene shook her head in disgust. They must be freshmen—who shouts 'chug" while drinking shots?

The only consistent element in the entire place was the faint, pearly glow that surrounded every person and object, suffusing the air with a rippling sheen, like oil on water. Irene realized that everything in here was dead. This was a completely ghost establishment.

Once inside, she was immediately accosted by a middle-aged man with a shock of dirty blond, corkscrew hair and an old-fashioned handlebar mustache who said to her, "Why aren't ghosts good at telling lies?"

"Excuse me?" Irene replied. She turned to look at Jonah for clarification, but he wasn't there. He must have taken her advice and gone home. She felt a momentary twinge then dismissed it.

"Why aren't ghosts good at telling lies," the man repeated.

Irene was bewildered. "I have no idea."

"Because you can see right through them!" The man chortled so hard his mustache swayed.

"Uh..." Irene wasn't sure what to say to this so she sidled away. The man happily pounced on someone else, and she heard him say, "What did the bartender say when the ghost ordered a brandy?"

She looked around again. This time, in addition to the different social groups, she noticed other differences. Hairstyles. Facial hair. Clothing. She felt her breath catch in her throat. There must be four hundred years of history crammed into this one room.

She continued to make her way through the crowd to the bar. As she went to scoot between two occupied tables, she realized too late there wasn't enough room. Wedged between two chairs, she leaned down to apologize when she stopped short as she recognized the face that had turned to look at her. "Amy!" she exclaimed.

Amy, who was part of a small group at one of the Formica tables, looked up. "Hello...you!" she exclaimed, as if seeing Irene was the highlight of her day. "Everyone, this is..."

"Irene," Irene supplied. "Irene Dunphy." She waved at them.

The small group consisted of a limp young man with wavy, slicked-back, brown hair and dark, intense eyes, who was lying across the table, one temple resting in the palm of a hand, his other hand dangling a lit cigarette; a twenty-something girl with severe, blue eyes and a soft, pretty mouth who was dressed as a ballerina—complete with pink leotard and matching tutu; and a plain but solidly built woman Irene instantly nicknamed "Poopie Patty" due to the sour expression she wore combined with her close resemblance to Peppermint Patty from the Charlie Brown comic strip.

Inexplicably, from somewhere in the back of the bar came the muted sound of a group of people shouting, "Hooray!" Irene started to look around for the source of the noise but was distracted from her search by Amy inviting her to sit down.

Gratefully, Irene sank into the proffered chair. "Is this the place you were talking about?" she asked. When Amy nodded, Irene said, "You said it was on Charlestown Street."

"Patty" laughed. "Amy gets confused sometimes. She forgets they renamed the street in nineteen-oh-eight."

Someone passing by put a shot glass in front of Irene. "Er, thanks," she said to the air, turning to look at her unknown benefactor, but whoever it was had disappeared into the crowd. From somewhere in the near distance came the muted roar of people once more shouting, "Hooray!" Irene hoisted her glass in silent solidarity with the cheerers and swallowed her drink in one gulp. Then she frowned — the shot glass was full of beer. Who put beer in a shot glass?

Amy leaned toward her. "Did you ever find what you were looking for at the library?"

"No." Irene made an exaggerated moue of displeasure. "The Nazi guarding the place chased me out before I could find what I wanted."

The limp-looking young man sitting to Amy's right chuckled. Amy shushed him with a wave of her hand and made a sympathetic clucking noise.

"You can't mind Doris. She's just angry about being dead. Sometimes she takes it out on other people."

"Who isn't angry about being dead?" the limp young man echoed, taking a drag on his cigarette.

"Okay, fine. Angry dead people," Irene said. "Not unreasonable; but why is she guarding the library, of all places? And for what, against who?"

"People get attached to things," Amy said with a shrug.

"Meaning...?"

One of the tweed-coated "professor types" set several more shots down on their table and walked away.

"Meaning she liked her job so much she kept showing up even after she died." Amy shrugged again and took a sip from one of the shots.

Before Irene could challenge the notion that anyone would continue working at a job they didn't get paid for — and that shots should be sipped — Jonah was at her elbow, causing her to nearly swallow her tongue in surprise.

"Jonah? I thought I told you to go home?"

He shot her a look that said "as if." Then he looked around the table, taking in her companions. His eyes lingered on the ballerina.

The ballerina noticed his stare. "Car accident," she said abruptly, her eyes daring him to comment.

"Hey! Me, too!" Irene said. She grabbed a drink and hoisted it in salute to the ballerina. She paused just as the glass touched her lips. "Ah...why the outfit?"

"It was a very *bad* car accident."

"Ah." Irene tried, unsuccessfully, to reconcile these two pieces of information.

"Are you ready yet?" Jonah asked impatiently, cutting into the conversation.

"No, I am not ready yet! I *just* sat down. If you don't want to hang around, then why don't you go home for a few hours, okay?"

The mulish look returned, making his face sharp and ugly. Irene raised a hand and pointed toward the door. "*Don't* even start."

His eyes flashed with anger but he didn't say a word. Instead, he spun around and marched away, disappearing into the crowd.

"You might want to slow down a bit," drawled the limp young man, taking a drag on his cigarette. He had a lazy way of speaking, as if forming words was almost more effort than it was worth.

Amy shushed him with a wave of her hand. "Oh, leave her alone, Ernest."

The handle-bar-mustache jokester stopped on his way past their table and leaned over the ballerina's shoulder. "Hey! Hey guys, what kind of mistakes do ghosts makes, eh?"

Ernest rolled his eyes. Everyone else looked annoyed.

"Boo-boos. Huh? Huh?" He laughed and slapped the back of the ballerina's chair so hard she was jolted almost out of her seat. "Good one, huh? How about this one? What kind of street does a ghost live on, eh? Huh?"

"Maurice, take a hike..." Ernest said, blowing a ring of smoke toward the ceiling.

"A dead end!" Maurice chortled, ignoring Ernest. "Get it? A *dead* end." He laughed again and then, waving cheerily, he moved away, heading for the next table.

"That guy is such an ass," muttered Ernest. He pulled a new cigarette from his coat pocket and lit it off the end of the first.

"Well, at least he doesn't mind being dead," Irene replied.

Amy shook her head. "I don't know how he keeps coming up with new ones. I've never heard him repeat a joke."

From somewhere in the bar there rose another chorused shout of *"Hooray!"*

Irene set her glass back down on the table and her brow crinkled. "What I don't get is that, for this place to exist, it would have had to cross over with someone, right? So someone would have to have been dead here...for a while."

"Poopie Pattie" shrugged. "People die. No one finds them for weeks. It happens."

While it might be true, the rather cold-hearted way of stating it so baldly surprised Irene. "I'm sorry, I didn't get your name?" she asked.

"Nellie."

"I'm Itza," the ballerina chimed in.

"It wasn't that uncommon during my time to wake a person for a week to make sure they were really dead," Amy said.

"This place has been here...well, forever, I guess, to judge by the décor," Ernest added. "It has all the hallmarks of an institution—the floors are sticky, the drinks are weak, and the help is surly. Welcome to the club!" He hoisted his glass and polished off the remains of his drink.

From somewhere amongst the background noise another chorus of "hoorays" rose above the general hubbub.

"What are people shouting about?" Irene asked, craning her neck to find the source of the noise. The others shrugged and didn't seem in the least interested or concerned.

Someone dropped off another round of drinks — all in shot glasses. This time it was shots of whisky. Irene blanched in disgust. "I don't suppose there's any chance of getting an Appletini?"

Ernest nearly spit out his drink. "Listen, princess, beggars can't be choosers. They serve whatever's available. Drink up or pass it over."

Irene laughed. She couldn't help it. "I feel like I'm at the mad tea party."

Amy gave her a blank look.

Irene stared back. "You know. Alice in Wonderland?"

"Oh," Amy said blankly.

"For Christ's sake, you work at a library!"

Amy shook her head. "Oh no. I *live* at the library."

"You what? I'm sorry. Maybe I'm slow, but what do you mean you *live* at the library?"

"What?" Amy asked defensively. "Look, I tried living in a regular place but it didn't work out. My roommate was all like, 'Waahh, who keeps turning on the lights? Waahh, someone keeps moving my stuff around. Waahh, I hear strange noises.' I only borrowed her jacket for one day, and I was going to replace the milk. It was such a headache."

Irene digested this for a moment. Then she leaned forward, resting an elbow on the table. "Let me guess...she was still alive, and you...weren't."

Amy threw up her hands. "Yes, but I never complained about the things that happened when *I* was alive. Lights and noises at the boarding house or where my stockings kept getting to. It turns out there were *two* people bunking with me the whole time, and they never once helped with the rent, plus one of them was a man, the masher!"

Irene groaned and shook her head. "Okay, but...how did you end up at the library?"

A chorused *"Hooray!"* rose up above the background noise for a moment.

Amy shrugged. "Oh, I don't even remember. It was ages ago. Someone probably told me about it. You bunk where you can."

"Exactly how long have you been dead?" Irene asked.

Amy made a non-committal gesture, as if the question was irrelevant. "Oh, who knows? It's been forever."

Irene looked at Ernest.

"Uh..." Ernest seemed to be doing a calculation in his head, then he hoisted his glass. "This year marks my ninety-fourth"

"About eight-five for me," Nellie said.

"Eighty-five!" Irene exclaimed.

"I've only been dead fifteen years," said the ballerina with a haughty sniff.

Irene took a swig of her drink to wash away the surprise. She wasn't sure why she was surprised when she knew there were people from the entire span of American history in this very room; but this small group had seemed so...normal.

Ernest touched her hand. "Hey, princess, just a word of advice, a sip is as good as a gulp to the dead. You're better off making it last."

Irene frowned. She wasn't sure what he meant, but his unsolicited advice annoyed her. She met his eyes and deliberately polished off the drink. His mouth quirked in a sardonic smile and he leaned back in his seat. He lifted his cigarette in ironic salute as if to say, "touché."

She turned away and looked at her other companions. "Is there anyone famous here?"

The others shrugged. "Define famous," Itza said.

"You know...like George Washington...or Ernest Hemingway or...Clark Gable."

The small group gave another collective shrug.

Their apathy bewildered her. "How can you not know?" Irene looked at Ernest again. "I mean, in a hundred years you must have bumped into someone famous, right?"

Ernest blew a cloud of smoke across the table. "Listen, sweetheart, I come for the booze and the laughs. Who wants to hear some dead bore droning on and on about what a big man he was when he was alive?"

Another round of drinks appeared and Ernest snagged one, lining it up next to the one he was still working on.

Irene looked around the table at the others. They all shook their heads, indicating Ernest was right — going on about your life was a huge faux pas.

"What's done is done," Nellie said taking a sip of her drink.

"Nellie was famous, you know. She was a Ziegfeld girl," Amy chimed in. "You don't see her going on about it, do you?"

"What's a Ziegfeld girl?" Irene asked.

Ernest laughed. "See?"

"A show girl," Itza said. "Around the turn of the century."

"Hey, I'm not that old," Nellie retorted. "I was on in twenty-eight!"

Irene tried to reconcile Nellie's plain face and stocky physique with the little she knew about showgirls. However, Jonah's reappearance prevented her from probing any further.

This time she sensed his presence before she actually saw him. One minute she knew the space to her right was empty and the next she knew there was someone in it. She also knew without looking that it was Jonah.

"Ready?" he said.

"No," she replied, refusing to look at him.

Out of the corner of her eye, she could see him looking at the collection of empty glasses in front of her.

"How many drinks have you had?" he asked.

She bristled in irritation. "Are you kidding me?"

He folded his arms over his chest. "I think you should stop now."

"I'm not drunk!"

Jonah flashed her a dark look. "That's why you should stop *now*."

She glared at him and then purposefully took a swig from the nearest glass, her eyes never leaving his. He set his jaw, turned, and stalked off, disappearing into the crowd.

A *"hooray"* chorus sounded in the background.

"Who keeps shouting?" she asked, exasperated. The random and intermittent cheering was beginning to feel like Chinese Water Torture.

Her companions shrugged — it seemed to be their favorite gesture. Irene couldn't tell if it was because they didn't know or didn't care. Amy was gazing around the room, as if looking for something. "I think it's our turn to buy a round," she said. "Ante up."

Itza shrugged. "What do you want from me, the shirt off my back? It's not like this thing has pockets."

"Oh come on, Itza, you never have anything," Nellie complained. "What about those earrings you're wearing?"

Itza put a hand to one of the diamond studs. "I'm saving these!"

"Oh don't mind her," Amy said to Itza while pulling two cigarettes out of her purse and handing them to Ernest. "Here."

"Where *do* you get these?" He kissed the cigarettes and then secreted them in a jacket pocket.

"That's my little secret," Amy replied. "Now put in for me."

Ernest rummaged in his pockets and then threw two quarters and a pair of socks — all glowing blue — on the table.

Nellie threw a nickel onto the pile. Ernest and Amy looked impressed and each made a low noise of admiration.

"Uh…I don't really have any money on me," Irene said. "I've got a little change, but…" she shrugged apologetically.

"That's okay, they take trade here," Itza replied.

Irene's brow furrowed. "What do you mean, trade?"

"You know, stuff. Cigarettes are big. Candy. Soap. Anything really. Just as long as it's dead."

"Uh…okay." Irene dug through the beach bag, ignoring the fact that ghost currency seemed to bear a frighteningly close resemblance to prison currency.

"Come on, guys," Amy said. "This isn't enough to get us the good stuff. We need some more. Doesn't anyone have anything else to add?"

"Get ready to lose the earrings, glamour puss," Ernest said to Itza.

Itza put a protective hand to her ear again, covering an earring with a finger and thumb. "I'd rather eat live meat."

"Hang on." Irene started pulling things out of the bag. "I've got some old magazines..." — which was met with frowns of disapproval — "a few pens..." — met with ambivalent shrugs that indicated these were not a first choice but might have some value — "...um...a bottle of perfume..." She held it up, expecting jeers. Instead, someone behind her snatched the bottle from her hand. She turned in her seat and saw a stringy man — lean and knobby like gristle — trying to hang onto the bottle.

"Here! Here!" he cried as several other men attempted to wrestle it from him. Pandemonium broke out. People were coming from all directions now, pig piling onto the knot of fighters, each grabbing for the bottle. Irene half jumped, half fell out of her chair in an effort to move out of the way.

"Give it here! I want it," one shouted.

"No, me!" cried another.

The bottle disappeared into a morass of flying elbows and fists. Irene looked at her tablemates in bewilderment, too flabbergasted for words. Amy, Itza, and Nellie had all clustered around the far side of the table, putting it between them and the fighters.

"Ooh, God," moaned someone from deep inside the throng. "Laura!"

The crowd broke apart as the bottle's current possessor rose up like mist, the slim vial clutched in his hands. He had the top off and he was holding it under his nose, inhaling deeply, his eyes closed. The others fell back, watching him with silent, greedy longing.

"Oh, God," he moaned again. He shuddered and then after a moment of stillness, he passed the bottle to his left, his eyes still shut. The man there took it, holding it gingerly in his beefy hands and took a cautious sniff. His face went slack and dreamy, as if he was lost in a blissful trance. In a fog, he passed the bottle on. "Sarah…" he mumbled absently.

Irene looked at her tablemates again. "What's going on?" she hissed in a whisper, afraid to interrupt the strange ritual.

Ernest looked grim. He stepped forward and snatched the vial out of a surprised hand. He held it out to Irene, his hand trembling as if holding the bottle was a great strain.

"Maybe you ought to keep it," she said, afraid to take it back. She looked at Amy for guidance.

With an impatient hiss, Ernest thrust the bottle into her hand. "Don't be so quick to part with your stuff."

She blinked in surprise at the rebuke and stood there, gape-mouthed. Ernest turned back to the knot of men, who stared at Irene, as if waiting for something. "Get!" he shouted. "Go on. Show's over."

Reluctantly, the men drifted away. Ernest righted an overturned chair and sat down. The others followed suit.

He picked something up off the floor and swore, throwing it back down with disgust. Irene saw it was a cigarette, only partially burned down, but hopelessly trampled. He pulled out a fresh cigarette and a half-empty pack of matches, lit the cigarette, and took a deep, calming drag. "So," he said to Irene, exhaling slowly, "what else you got to offer, princess?"

"I don't understand," she said, looking around the table. "What did I do?"

Amy clasped her hands together, and Irene saw that they were shaking. "It's nothing. It wasn't you."

Irene looked at Itza and Nellie, hoping they would shed some light on the matter. Itza avoided eye contact.

Nellie alone seemed unaffected by the incident. She shrugged. "Memories. You never know what will trigger one."

Irene's brow furrowed as she turned this over. She still didn't really understand, but Ernest was prodding her again, so she let it go.

"Come on, ante up." He nudged her with his elbow. "I'm thirsty."

She glanced at the collection of full glasses in front of him. "What are you doing, stockpiling it?"

He gave her a lazy, half grin. "If you pace it just right, you never have to stop drinking."

She hesitated, half amused, half bewildered, unsure if he was joking or not. Then she reached for her bag again, pushing the perfume to the bottom of it. "Uh...well, I've got some ketchup packets..."

"Boy!" Ernest cried. He gestured with his hands, indicating she should produce them. Irene raised an eyebrow but complied. "There's like six of 'em here!" he exclaimed. "Glamour puss, keep the earrings. This round's on her."

"Really? Ketchup?" Irene shook her head. She tumbled the ketchup packets onto the pile at the center of the table. Jonah had been right; the ketchup packets did have value. He'd never let her live this down. Then she remembered his disapproving frown, and she angrily pushed him out of her mind.

"Whoa, Whoa," cried Ernest. "Take it easy, princess." He handed back several of the packets. "No need to spend it all at once."

Irene looked at the packets in her hand, shook her head again, and then tossed them back into the beach bag. Meanwhile, Ernest had passed back everyone else's contributions to the kitty. Then he grabbed one of Amy's hands and slapped the two remaining ketchup packets into it. Amy dutifully got up and trundled off to the bar.

"Hooray!" slipped into a dip in the background burble of noise.

An awkward silence fell over the group as they sat waiting for Amy's return.

"How did you die?" Irene asked Nellie, trying to fill in the lull with small talk.

A chill seemed to descend over the group.

"It's not really polite to ask that," Ernest said as he lit a new cigarette from the butt of the current one and then tossed the stub.

"Speaking of slowing down," she replied, giving him an incredulous look. "What's with the chain smoking?" He grinned ruefully. "Can't let 'em burn out. I'm almost out of matches."

Amy returned and set five shot glasses on the table. Ernest snatched one up crying, "Whoa, this is the real stuff!"

"Yeah," Amy said. "Greig nearly fell over with surprise when I slapped that ketchup down on the counter."

Everyone hoisted their glasses to Irene, who was bewildered but went with it.

As soon as the liquid touched her lips, Irene understood what Ernest had meant. This drink tasted...like she remembered. It tasted potent and rich. It tasted real. Everything else she had drunk so far had tasted like an imitation or a memory rather than the actual thing. She realized it must be like the tuna fish sandwiches or the coffee—this liquor must have crossed over with a dead person. Everything else must have been "alive," belonging to the living. Suddenly she understood about the perfume. It had been "real" to the men. It was dead, having crossed over with her, and they had been able to use it to evoke the memory of perfumes they had smelled in life—and, most likely, the women who had worn them. Irene shuddered with revulsion as she realized the men had been reliving intimate moments from their lives—a kind of olfactory pornography. "Eww!"

She took another swallow to wash the bad taste out of her mouth. Unexpectedly, the memory of the dark shadows that had chased her rose to her mind. She set her drink down.

"Hey, can I ask you guys something? Have you ever seen this like...I don't know...big, scary shadow-like thing lurking about?"

Amy nodded. "Mmm, the Uglies. Stay away from them."

"Mmm," the others chorused.

Hooray sounded in the background.

"Knock it off!" Irene cried to the room in general. Nobody paid any attention. She turned back to the table. "Okay, but what are they?"

"You ever hear the saying 'handsome is as handsome does'?" Ernest asked.

Irene nodded.

Ernest shrugged as if to say 'there you go' and took a deep drag on his cigarette.

Irene noticed everyone seemed to be casting glances at Nellie. Irene looked from Nellie to the others. The discrepancy between Nellie's profession and appearance once again stood out to Irene, but she couldn't for the life of her figure out what it all meant.

Irene's thoughts seemed to be heavy and slow…there was something hovering on the edge of her brain, but she couldn't quite grab it. She realized the drinks must finally be catching up with her. She shook her head, trying to clear it.

"Wait, are you saying…what was it he said?" She tried to recall Jonah's words. "The…Chinese…or Hindus…something about…we project what we look like…yeah, that was it!" She snapped her fingers. "We project what we think we look like." She looked around the table. They were all looking at her as if she had lost her mind.

"You okay, sweetheart?" Ernest asked.

Irene smacked the table with her hand. "Yes, I'm fine. I just realized it's another true story. That's why you all look so young even though you're really old now. Right?"

Amy looked offended. "I'm not old!"

"How old were you when you died?"

"Twenty-three," Amy replied.

"Yeah, and you've been dead…what? A long time, right? Yet you look like you're not a day over twenty…maybe twenty-five."

"Well, you don't age after you die," Nellie said as if this was the most ridiculous thing she'd ever heard. Everyone else laughed. Irene flushed.

190

"Okay, fine, but still, you don't look twenty-three," she said to Amy.

Amy smiled, grabbed one of the drinks that a passerby had left, and saluted Irene with it. "Thanks!"

Irene laughed, grabbed a drink, and downed it in a quick rush. Then she grimaced with disgust. "Ugh. This must be live stuff."

Ernest chuckled. "The new kid is learning."

Irene rummaged in her bag and pulled out several more ketchup packets. She pushed them toward Amy. "Here, go get us something worth drinking, will you?"

Amy shrugged and then complacently took the ketchup and went off to fetch them all another round.

"That's not going to endear you to Greig," Ernest said.

"What, he doesn't like to make..." She started to say "money" but quickly changed it to "ketchup."

"No, it's just that the good stuff doesn't come along all that often. He likes to make it last."

"Is that why everything is served in thimbles?" she asked.

He smiled. "It only takes a drop to make you remember."

Before she could reply, Itza stood up. "I'm calling it a night, guys."

They all waved to her and Irene watched the pink tutu disappear into the crowd. She wondered what time it was. It must be getting late.

As if on cue, Jonah appeared beside her. "Are you ready yet?" he asked, his arms folded across his chest.

"I totally bought a round of drinks with ketchup packets!" She snorted with laughter.

"You might have needed those," Jonah cried.

"Yeah, I did," she agreed. "To buy drinks."

"I meant for food."

"No matter how hungry I get, Jonah, I'm not going to eat ketchup straight from the packet." She slapped at his arm. "Hey. Hey. What do you have in your backpack? Got anything I can use as trade?"

He jerked away from her. "No."

"I think you should totally go home and get me some stuff."

"What, so you can buy drinks with it? No way!"

She frowned at him. "Don't be an ass."

He shook his head, his lips pursed in anger. "It's getting late."

"Then go home and go to bed."

"What about you?"

"What about me?"

"What are you going to do, sleep here?" he asked.

"I don't see how it's any of your business where I sleep."

Jonah's mouth fell open—Irene wasn't sure if it was due to outrage or surprise—and he turned eyes smoldering with speculation and anger on Ernest.

"As if!" she said. "Not that it's any of your business. Now buzz off."

"Gee, thanks," Ernest said, clearly not bothered in the least by Irene's dismissal.

"No offense," she replied.

"None taken."

"You can totally stay with me tonight," Amy interjected, appearing with their drinks. "Tomorrow I can show you around if you want. Come on, it'll be fun!"

"See? I'm sleeping over at Amy's," Irene said in a perky falsetto. She grabbed a drink and drained it in one long swallow. She set the empty glass down on the table with a deliberate thump. "Now hit the bricks."

Jonah shot another suspicious look at Ernest. "Fine," he said, his voice flat. Then he was gone.

"I must be very drunk," Amy said sitting down, "because that boy totally just vanished."

"Is that your brother?" Ernest asked as he pushed a drink across the table to Nellie.

Irene shook her head. "No."

Amy grabbed Irene's wrist, turning it so she could look at the watch. "Oh my God, is that the time? We have to go."

"What? Why?"

"Doris gets us all up at six."

"What? Why? We're dead. Why do we have to get up at any particular time?"

"She doesn't want us hanging around in the basement when the staff arrive. She says it gives them the heebie-jeebies."

"But we're dead," Irene argued. "They can't see us...can they?"

"No, but you know how the living are. Wah, wah, wah— 'it's creepy down there.' Wah wah wah—'there are odd noises.' Wah wah wah."

Irene rolled her eyes. "Christ! Being dead just keeps getting better and better. I can't even rest in peace." However, Amy continued to prod her, so she reluctantly rose to her feet. "Night, all."

Ernest made a vague gesture goodbye with his cigarette hand. "Princess, it was a pleasure."

"Oh, we'll be back again tomorrow," Amy said, looking at Irene for confirmation. Irene nodded.

Ernest smiled. It was the first time all night Irene had seen him do so. "Au revoir, then," he said, giving Irene a small, enigmatic smile.

It was dark outside and the streets were empty. The ghost-light from the bar spilled over to the sidewalk, the street, and the nearby buildings, casting an eerie glow on the surrounding area.

"What do living people see when they look at the bar?" Irene asked.

Amy shrugged. "I don't know. Never thought about it. I don't suppose they see anything, just an empty lot."

Irene laughed. God, she'd forgotten how good it felt to turn off her brain for a while, to relax and just have fun and go with the flow. No worrying, no questioning, no figuring things out. Compared to Jonah's relentless spewing of facts and incessant badgering to investigate every damn thing, Amy was a breath of fresh air.

Irene laughed again.

"What's so funny?"

Irene slipped her arm through Amy's. "Nothing."

The walk back to the library was uneventful. Amy didn't say much and Irene, who was feeling thick-headed and fuzzy, was glad of it.

Amy led Irene around to the side of the library and there Irene was surprised to see a door, surrounded by a faint blue glow.

"What's that?" she asked. Amy looked at her. "I mean," Irene amended, "I know it's a door, but...but...what's it doing there?"

Amy pulled the door open and gestured for Irene to pass through. "Oh I don't know. You find them around sometimes on old buildings. Leftover from renovations or fires and whatnot."

Still, Irene hesitated. "It's not locked?"

Amy shrugged. "What would be the point?"

Irene supposed she understood what Amy meant. If the dead wanted to get into a place who was to stop them. They could pick locks, smash windows, and break down doors without anyone seeing them. Besides, what would the dead—well anyone, really?—want to break into a library for, other than for a place to sleep? Might as well leave a way for them to get in as not—hence the unlocked ghost door.

"Have you found a lot of stuff like this?" Irene asked, as Amy led her down a short flight of stairs. "You know, secret doors and invisible bars and things like that? Stuff that's just for us...for the dead."

"Some...not a ton, but there's some."

Dim overhead emergency lights offered a sparse and watery light that only allowed Irene to see a few feet in front of her. She stuck close to Amy, afraid that the dark would swallow Amy up if she allowed her to get too far ahead.

Amy seemed to be leading her through a labyrinthine path of discarded furniture, filing cabinets, and haphazardly stacked boxes. Irene realized they were in the library's basement. Occasionally they passed hidey-hole sized spaces that had been dug out of the debris, populated by sitting or lying figures—all glowing blue, some rolled in blankets, most without.

Amy led her farther into the maze, finally stopping at one of the hollowed out "rooms." Amy exchanged a few words with someone inside, passed over what looked like a couple of cigarettes, and received a bundle in return. Then they continued on their way through the maze.

"Did you just buy those blankets with cigarettes?" Irene asked.

Amy laughed. "Not even. We're just renting these."

Irene followed as Amy ducked into an empty space in the maze. Irene guessed this was where they were bunking down for the night.

Amy had gotten a sleeping bag and a blanket, the choice of which she offered to Irene. Irene hesitated and then took the blanket.

"Where do you get all the cigarettes?" she asked.

"I'll show you tomorrow." There was a mischievous note in Amy's voice. "You have to promise not to tell anyone, though."

"Cross my heart," Irene said.

Amy spread the sleeping bag on the floor and then climbed in. Irene followed suit, trying to make an impromptu sleeping bag out of the blanket. It was too small, however, so she spread it on the floor, laid down on top of it, and flipped a corner over her feet and legs.

It struck Irene that she had no pajamas. She felt a flutter of alarm in the pit of her stomach as she realized she would be sleeping in the same dress for the rest of her...eternity. She hadn't showered, washed her hair, or brushed her teeth in days. She hadn't felt a need, really, but still, it seemed wrong not to do those things.

She thought of the few possessions she did have and recalled the bottle of vodka in her bag. She thought about pulling it out and offering some to Amy, but then realized that slim amount of vodka also had to last all of eternity. Better to save it.

She pulled the bag closer, resting her head on it like a pillow. The darkness seemed solid and close, pressing in on her. The thick, oppressive silence seemed to have weight, and it bore down, crushing her. She rolled onto her side and brought her knees to her chest.

"Do you miss it?" she asked. "Having stuff, I mean. A place to live, your own blankets, that sort of thing."

"Oh no," Amy replied. "I prefer this. It's footloose and fancy free, you know. I'm not tied down like I was in life."

Irene thought of her house, her shoes, the key necklace, and all the other stuff that had seemed so important. She felt a pang. It still seemed important. Maybe in a hundred years it wouldn't, but right now, she missed it.

She tried to remind herself that the tradeoff for losing her stuff was the freedom to do what she liked. "What do you do all day?" she asked.

There was a rustle beside her as Amy shifted in the sleeping bag. "Oh, there's always stuff to do, you know."

When Amy didn't elaborate, Irene said, "Like…?"

"I'll show you tomorrow."

Irene heard a sound, possibly a faint, high-pitched squeak, and tensed. "Are there rats here?" she asked. "If there are rats, I'm going home!"

"Don't be silly."

Could live rats bite dead people, Irene wondered? *Were there dead rats?* She reached down and tugged the blanket more firmly over her feet, tucking the loose end under her legs. She lay still for a moment, and the silence started to intrude again.

"Can I ask…is this what you expected?" she said. "I mean, life after death…you know, didn't you expect…more?"

"I guess I never thought about it."

Irene grunted. "Me either." Her thoughts swirled in a dizzying eddy, muddled and fuzzy. She turned on her side and closed her eyes to quiet her brain. Even with her eyes closed, the dark pressed in on her, heavy and thick. She curled into a ball and prayed for sleep.

Sixteen

As promised, Doris came marching through at six a.m., banging a plastic bucket like a drum.

Irene groaned and tried to roll herself up in the blanket. Amy, chipper as always, sprang up from the sleeping bag — Irene had the impression she hadn't been asleep — and urged Irene to her feet. "I don't suppose there's a shower...a toothbrush...anything?"

Amy simply laughed.

You're dead, Irene reminded herself. *You don't need to brush your teeth. You don't have any teeth to brush.*

Around them came the rustling of dozens of dead collecting their things and setting off for the day.

"Do you like living here?" Irene asked. "It seems kind of..." she hesitated, searching for as inoffensive a word as possible, "shabby."

Amy didn't seem offended. "It's not so bad. I only come here when I want a break or to get in out of the weather or, like last night, after I've drunk the real stuff. After a while you'll find you don't really need to sleep at all."

Amy stopped to hand the blanket and sleeping bag back to their owner, and then she led the way through the labyrinth, up a set of stairs, and out to the street where they blinked in the early morning light, bright compared to the dimness of the library's basement.

"So what do you want to do today?" Amy asked.

"I don't know," Irene said, suddenly excited. "What is there to do? I want to do whatever it is you usually do. I want to see the sights and meet people and just get out and have some fun!"

Amy stared into space, her brow furrowed, as if she was thinking hard. "I know, I'll take you to the museum. That's my favorite thing to do. I can show you some of the sights on the way."

They turned right and headed down Copley Street.

"Now that place has an interesting story." Amy pointed to a ghostly building, long and squat. Two stories high, it was rough-hewn, raw, and unfinished looking. A rustic farmer's porch ran the length of the building and disappeared around the far side.

"It was a boarding house—oh, I don't know, ages ago—and the couple who ran it poisoned one of the boarders and then hid his body under the floor."

"Interesting is one word for it. Is it still a boarding house?"

"They serve meals—just live stuff, nothing dead, so it's not really worth it."

They weren't that far from where Irene had first encountered the shadow monster—the Ugly. "Not to switch the subject, but the Uglies, what are they exactly? Where do they come from?"

"Bad people," Amy said, leading her left onto another street.

"Yeah, but..." Irene insisted, still not understanding.

Amy stopped short and spun around. "Some people are just bad. They know they're bad and they hate themselves."

She turned abruptly and continued on.

We project what we think we look like.

Irene's mind rebelled at the sudden understanding— the idea that, not only were people's appearances not fixed, but also that their self-perception could be so distorted they become monsters—actual, real-life monsters. Her stomach knotted in fear. She grabbed Amy's arm. "Can they hurt us?" she asked.

"We're already dead, aren't we?"

"Is that a no?" Irene persisted, remembering the bone chilling cold and the terror of her encounters with the creatures. Her hand instinctively went to the scar on her thigh.

Amy shrugged. "Honestly, I don't know, but everyone's afraid of them. Just stay away from them."

Irene was frustrated by Amy's lack of both information and helpful advice, but it was clear Amy had nothing else to say on the matter.

The art museum came into view, the long, classically Greek-looking building of white marble stately and dignified. Irene and Amy had no problem slipping in through the front door. Sound bounced around the vaulted ceiling and wide, airy space of the lobby, amplifying the burble of conversation and footsteps of the museum's visitors into a hubbub of noise.

Irene looked around, trying to orient herself — she couldn't remember the last time she'd been here — but Amy didn't give any of the exhibits a second glance as she led the way past the two wings flanking the entrance hall. She appeared to be looking for something in particular.

"Watch out for Herman," Amy whispered as they passed through the rotunda and then to the left. "*Don't* touch his statue!" Out loud she said, "Hello Herman," addressing a ghostly middle-aged man with flyaway hair. He was propped up by an umbrella, leaning on the handle while the tip rested on the floor, while worshipfully gazing at a full-sized marble statue of a half-naked woman, her gleaming white Grecian robe forever caught in the act of slipping from her shoulders and falling to the floor.

"Amy!" he said warmly, turning ever so briefly from the statue and then, quick as lightning, pouncing on two living women who had drawn closer. "Git! Git!" he cried, poking at them with his umbrella. Unable to see or hear him or feel the blows from his umbrella, they examined the statue at their leisure. All the while he was berating and castigating them in an attempt to drive them away. Finally, the women moved on.

"Keep clear!" Herman cried, jumping toward anyone in the sparse crowd who came within a foot of the statue. Those passing by flowed around him without noticing.

Irene slowed down, unable to tear her eyes away, amused by Herman's antics.

"Get off you filthy little bugger!" he cried, whacking a little boy—who had stopped to trace the line of the marble robes with an inquisitive finger—over the head.

"Jimmy!" called his parents and the boy started, looked around wildly, and ran to catch up, oblivious to Herman's ministrations.

Herman wiped his forehead, as if sweating heavily, and leaned on his umbrella for a moment. Irene looked at Amy, trying her best not to laugh. Amy wore the same expression, and the two women moved hurriedly off to convulse in giggles out of earshot of Herman.

"What's his deal?" Irene asked.

Amy lifted one shoulder in a bewildered shrug. "People get attached to things."

Irene's eyes goggled. "Yeah, but it's not even his. It's a museum piece."

This time Amy shrugged with both shoulders. "What can I say? Some people are just strange. There's a woman who comes every day and sits and stares at one of the paintings upstairs."

Irene shook her head. "I really can't imagine spending eternity that way."

"Oh, she's not dead." They had arrived in the Art of the Americas wing and Amy slowed down to scan the crowd as they strolled through the galleries.

"I thought we were going to look at the pictures," Irene said when Amy passed through yet another gallery without looking at a single piece of art.

Amy shook her head. "Oh no, I've seen them. It's the people that we're here for." She seemed to be following someone and she darted ahead, slipping into the next gallery. Irene couldn't remember the last time she had been to an art museum so she took her time, slowing down to check out the paintings. She realized she now had all the time in the world. She could take up a new hobby if she wanted. Become an expert in any topic. She idly tried to think of something she was interested in. Annoyed, she realized she couldn't think of a single thing she'd want to study.

She looked around for Amy and found her two galleries ahead, hovering near a family of four who were studying a painting of women with parasols parading in a park. Irene hurried over.

"That's so interesting..." Amy was saying. She turned to Irene. "Todd was just explaining how they made paint in olden days by grinding up sticks of clay and mixing them with oil and water."

Confused, Irene looked at the family again and confirmed that they were, in fact, alive. The family moved away from the painting, and Amy went with them. Irene followed.

"There's something weird about the perspective in this one," the living woman in the group said.

"Mmm," Amy said. "You're right. Something seems a little off."

"It's the hands. That's one of the characteristics of the American Folk Art style—the hands are always out of proportion to the body," Todd said.

Amy laughed, a tinkling, fake giggle that grated on Irene's nerves. "Wow, Todd, you really know a lot about art."

The little boy, perhaps seven years old, pointed. "What's that sign say, Daddy?"

"It's the name of the painting and the date it was painted," Todd replied.

Amy leaned down to the boy's level. "It says Samuel Dap, seventeen eighty-three."

Irene watched as Amy followed the family to the next painting, worry lines crinkling her forehead. Amy's behavior was bizarre. The family obviously couldn't see or hear her, but Amy was acting like they could, like she was part of their group, part of their conversation.

Irene followed the quintet for a few more minutes before she realized what was going on.

You never know what will trigger a memory, Nellie had said.

Like the perfume for the men in the bar, Amy was trying to evoke memories of life, trying to recreate feelings and thoughts by pretending to be part of this family's outing.

Irene was torn between pity and disgust. While Amy's actions were understandable, there was something sick about them—something parasitic and grotesque—and Irene suddenly felt uneasy. Was this what her life was going to come to if she stayed here? If, instead of going through the tunnel, she chose to linger in the land of the living, would all her thoughts and feelings and memories fade away until she had to try and steal them—vampire like—from the living?

Irene shifted uncomfortably suddenly wanting to be somewhere—anywhere—else. "Look, art's not really my thing…"

Amy looked surprised. "Oh, well, okay. We can go if you want. There should be a good crowd at the bar by now."

This sounded a lot safer to Irene. With a sense of relief, she followed Amy out of the museum and down the street.

"Did you have a family?" Irene asked, assuming Amy had picked this family because they reminded her of her own.

"No," Amy said. "I never married. I was an old-maid." The smile faded from her face and she looked grim. "I was a teacher. I went to work. I went home to a rooming house. Life was pretty drab." There was bitterness in her voice now. "It was different back then. It was impossible for a woman like me to find a husband. You weren't allowed gentleman callers at the boarding house, except Sunday afternoons. No visitors of any kind after seven p.m. any day of the week. They barred the door on you if you weren't in by eight. Life for a single woman back then was...' Amy's mouth twisted with resentment. 'It was unseemly to go out alone to the theater or dinner. Not that I made enough money to do those things, anyway."

Irene didn't know what to say to this. Amy seemed to realize her bitterness was making Irene uncomfortable, because the frown smoothed away and she smiled. "Now I do it all. I do everything I didn't do when I was alive. I go to the museums. I sightsee. I travel." She giggled. "I play cards for money, I drink, I meet men."

It was strange to hear Amy describe the life Irene had lived as ideal. Amy didn't talk of big, life-defining moments like a dream trip to Venice or running a marathon or jumping out of an airplane. Her dreams were of the little things that had served as the filler of Irene's life, the things Irene had done to fritter away time while she was waiting for life to start.

Amy held out her pleated, pale blue skirt. "You modern girls are so lucky. You don't know what hell is until you've worn a corset, trust me. I got this outfit off a girl who liked my dress and wanted to trade." Amy motioned with her hands, indicating the tight-waisted, puffy shouldered style of the turn of the century. "My hair was a little harder," she said indicating her short curls. "Though I've found that if you can just imagine things a certain way hard enough, then you can make it so."

Irene didn't know what to think. For a while now, she'd begun to worry that maybe there had been more to life, that maybe she'd missed out. And now, here was Amy, saying nope, that had been pretty much it, that Irene had had the best one could hope for. That this, in fact, was as good as it got.

Irene swallowed hard, suddenly feeling queasy. She quickened her pace, wanting to be at the bar. She needed a drink. A big one.

Seventeen

The next few days passed in much the same way. Each morning, Amy led her to the science museum, the aquarium, the natural history museum at Harvard, the zoo — pretty much anywhere Amy could follow living people around and pretend to be with them — and then to the bar in the afternoon when Irene restless and bored. The bar held a rotating cast of characters — usually some combination of Itza, Nellie, and Ernest, with additional faces that were becoming familiar: Maurice, the jokester; Herman, the obsessed art lover; Shanquil, a very angry, young woman caught in gang crossfire who spent her days poltergeisting those responsible for her death; and countless others who all seemed to be clinging to something just out of reach.

Jonah popped in occasionally, usually when she was in the bar, his visits growing farther and farther apart as he grew angrier and angrier at her for spending so much time there. The angrier and more disapproving he grew, the more Irene dug in and refused to leave.

On the fifth day, when Amy proposed taking her to the arboretum, Irene said, "Please, I love hanging out with you, really, but no more museums. There's got to be something else we can do."

Amy looked a little crestfallen, but after thinking hard for a few minutes, she said, "Well, I can show you where I get the cigarettes. That might be interesting." Irene got the feeling Amy was running out of things to show her.

Amy led her across town and then down a dizzying series of narrow alleyways, into a part of the city she had never been in before. The triple-deckers were old and dilapidated, hardly even upright. Rugs and laundry were slung over deck railings and sloppy, overflowing trashcans gave off an odor so foul it clogged Irene's throat and made her gag.

The few people around were all Asian, and Irene assumed they had crossed into Chinatown at some point.

"Where the hell are we going?" she asked, trying to find a dry path through the rutted and uneven cobblestones that paved the way. *I really hope that's water*, she thought.

Amy pointed. The alley ended in a sort of courtyard, formed on two sides by buildings that ended in a brick wall, ancient and crumbling.

They came to a stop in front of the roughly textured bricks, whose original terracotta color had long since been darkened by age and dirt to the color of dried blood. There were niches in the wall—some carved by human hands, some made by the brick crumbling away—and Amy hunted amongst these little crevices, looking high and low. Irene saw a living woman a few feet away, facing the wall, muttering to herself. Her head was bowed, her hands tightly pressed together in front of her.

As Irene watched with puzzled curiosity, the woman reached up to one of the niches and then turned and left, shuffling, shoulders bowed, down a dark, narrow cross-alley. Shadows swallowed her up and she disappeared from sight. Irene moved closer and saw that the woman had left, in one of the hollows, a piece of paper, crisply folded into the shape of a tiny crane. Irene fished it out and studied it. A bit of writing caught her eye and she smoothed the smoothed the paper open. She stared uncomprehendingly at the Asian characters handwritten on a page splashed with tiny wet spots.

She turned to Amy, who was still hunting along the wall. "What is this?" she asked.

Amy hardly glanced at the paper. "Probably a letter."

Irene's brow creased. "I don't get it. What's it for?"

"Ah!" Amy reached into a nook and pulled out a glowing pack of cigarettes. She brandished the pack triumphantly for Irene to see.

"I don't get it," Irene repeated.

Amy took the letter from Irene's hands, folded it into a square, and returned it to the niche. "People leave stuff here for the dead. Letters. Gifts." She brandished the cigarettes. "These show up every month like clockwork."

Irene looked from Amy to the wall and back. "Those cigarettes are dead...how...?"

Amy shrugged. "I don't know, it just does. You find these sorts of places around—shrines to the dead. They're like little post offices—people leave stuff and then—poof!—it gets sent over to us."

"Yeah, but—"

Amy made an impatient gesture. "I don't know. It just happens. Gravestone in a cemetery, wooden cross on the side of the road, or a pile of rocks in the back yard. If it's a shrine or memorial to someone dead, then it works."

"Okay, but why would someone send cigarettes to the dead?" Irene asked, still confused.

"Oh, people send all kinds of stuff. They send whatever reminds them of their loved one. If Grandpa was a big smoker he gets cigarettes. If Dad loved baseball he gets a season ticket."

Irene thought of the beer can she had seen on the grave in Salem, seemingly so long ago. She had thought it was litter, but now she wondered if it had been left on purpose. Then she thought of the pebbles lined up on the graves—there must be some very pissed off dead people out there wondering why their relatives sent them nothing but rocks.

"Well, okay," Irene shifted her weight from one foot to the other, "but isn't that stealing? Those cigarettes are meant for someone."

"Finders keepers," Amy said without hesitation. Apparently, like thieves, there was no honor among the dead.

A loud blast of horns and drums drew their attention, followed by the sharp crackle of firecrackers. "What's going on over there?" Amy asked, turning to look down the cross alley that led to the next street. She started cautiously toward the alley, motioned for Irene to follow, and then surged forward without waiting.

They emerged into a thick crowd of people watching a Chinese-dragon parade down the street.

"Oh my God, it's Ghost Festival!" Amy grabbed Irene's hand and began pulling her through the crowd.

"Ghost Festival?" Irene asked. Something dinged in her memory. Jonah had said something about a ghost festival. She racked her brain, trying to remember what he had said. Something about...the living sending stuff to the dead...

"Yeah, all these foreigners have one, you know. They're really superstitious, but I'm not complaining. It's like Christmas." She tugged sharply on Irene's hand. "Come on!"

She dragged Irene down a side street, away from the crowd. Irene noticed things laid out on the sidewalk. She slowed down, trying to get a closer look, and realized it was mats covered with dishes of..."Hey, that's food!" she cried.

"Yeah," Amy said, still tugging her down the street, "but it's all nasty Oriental food. God, what is it with these people? Doesn't anyone have anything good? I'd kill for a pork chop or even a Skybar."

Irene pulled her hand free. "Okay, slow down for a second and please explain to the new girl what exactly is happening here."

Someone knocked against Irene and a man—glowing blue—dropped to all fours in front of the closest mat of food. "I haven't eaten anything in months," he moaned and began shoveling food into his mouth with both hands. Repulsed, Irene took a step back.

She tried to remember the last time she had thought about food—it seemed so long ago that she had stood in front of Stephanie's thinking that she hadn't eaten in days. It seemed a lifetime ago. She still wasn't hungry, but the sight—and tantalizing smell—of the ghost food stirred the memory of hunger and her "stomach" growled.

You don't have a stomach, she reminded herself.

"Come on," Amy said, "before all the good stuff is gone!" She bee-lined down the street and disappeared around a corner, leaving Irene behind. Irene slowed down, trying to get a good look at the items laid out on the sidewalk. On closer inspection it turned out that it wasn't just food laid out for the dead. There were small items such as soap, candy, jewelry, flowers, and money. There were also elaborate paper models of larger items: sailboats, cars, even animals. Irene stooped and picked up a paper horse—delicate and precise. It was beautiful, obviously folded with care. She reached down and scooped up several more paper items, turning them over in her palm to study them—paper money, some sort of building that was either a pagoda or a house, and a motley collection of animals, mostly birds.

She meandered down the narrow street, the air cooler here from the tightly packed buildings, stopping to explore the contents of each display with fascination. She found a cigarette lighter at one—just a cheap, convenience store item—but it was glowing blue so she slipped it into her bag to give to Ernest next time she saw him.

Food seemed to be the most popular item left for the dead. She passed many empty plates and quite a few dead, greedily eating. The paper animals seemed to be the least popular, judging by the number that she found left behind. She picked up a few more, holding them in her palm like pebbles.

She heard Amy shout her name. She absent-mindedly dropped the paper items into her bag and ran to catch up. She found Amy around the corner, happily munching what turned out to be a hamburger from a local fast food chain.

"God, this is good," Amy said.

"Really? Someone left a bag of fast food for the dead?"

Amy held out the remainder of the burger, offering it to Irene. Irene shook her head. "You are so lucky," Amy said, polishing it off. She burrowed into the bag and pulled out some fries. "We didn't have anything like this during my time."

"It seems like a rather smart-assed move to me—leaving fast food." Irene couldn't believe it was a serious offering to the dead, on par with the meticulously folded paper animals.

Amy wrinkled her nose. "I'll take a hamburger over a paper cow any day!"

Irene raised an eyebrow.

"Think about it," Amy added. "If you thought the dead were hanging around, pining away for the things they enjoyed when they were alive, which would you send them...a..."—she snatched up one of the paper animals—"...pig? Or a television? Stewed cabbage or a hamburger?" She dropped the tiny animal to the ground and took Irene's arm. "Let's see if we can find some dessert. I adore dessert."

They wandered down the narrow street, checking both sides and the alleys leading off of it. At one point, Amy cried out in elation at finding a pack of playing cards and then promptly had to fight off another young, dead woman who tried to wrestle them away from her. There were a lot of wind chimes, which Irene and Amy had a good laugh over, wondering what possible use those could be to the dead, and a lot of paper money that Amy impatiently told Irene wasn't of any use when she saw her picking it up. "Coins are the only money that matters," she said.

"Why?"

Amy shrugged. "Just are."

There were other dead people with the same idea. Their numbers seemed to ebb and flow—Irene and Amy would be alone on a street and then there would be a flood of dead, jostling and jockeying to get close enough to pick through the offerings. Sometimes they would turn the corner onto a crowded street, which would be deserted a moment later. Irene began to notice a sort of uniformity to the dead—most had bland good looks with no distinguishing features. Very few were overweight. Very few were too tall or too short. Very few men were bald, very few women were flat-chested. Irene wondered if this was another manifestation of projected self-image—the same effect that created the Uglies. After all, if she actually had to sit down and draw her own face from memory, what would she come up with? Would it be deadly accurate—blemishes and all—an idealized version, or just a vague resemblance? After all, how much time did she actually spend looking at herself in the mirror? Her mother's face, heck even Jonah's face, was probably more recognizable to her than her own.

There were very few living people out and about, and Irene thought this was odd—the library had been busy enough, for a Saturday, and the streets between there and here had been, not crowded, but busy. Here, however, the streets seemed deserted, and Irene began to wonder if perhaps the living were purposely avoiding the area. For some reason it reminded her of Halloween—it was a silly ritual, an excuse to dress up and have fun, but, when you got right down to it, the whole point was the fiery pumpkins left burning outside to scare off ghouls. After trick or treating ended at eight o'clock or so, people generally stayed inside with their doors locked and their lights off. Was this just another example of the living subconsciously knowing the dead were about but trying to ignore the fact?

Amy and Irene collected quite a few candles. Irene remembered the flashlight in her bag and kept an eye out for batteries but didn't find any. Amy sighed the next time they found a candle. "How do people think we're going to use the candles and cigarettes—they never send any matches!"

Irene had second thoughts about giving Ernest the lighter she had found until they found another one, overlooked under an empty plate by those who had gone down the street before them.

They zigzagged through the streets, turning off onto smaller streets and alleys as much as possible in the hopes of finding less traveled areas. Amy pointed out items of interest on the houses, especially talismans against the dead, as they passed. Bundles of sage, iron nails over doors, and, in one case, a line of sand spread across a porch.

Irene was confused. "Why sand?" she asked.

Amy laughed. "Why anything that people believe? In my day, we thought spitting dried beans at a ghost would drive them off. Why beans? Why do you have to spit them? Now that I think about it, I realize it was idiotic. As a child, however, I always carried a handful of beans in my pinafore pocket, just in case." She pointed to a red mark, painted above a door. "That, however, does work. We can't go in there."

They seemed to have reached the edge of Chinatown. They circled back, returning by way of a street they had already examined. Instead of sticking to the sidewalk, Amy went up and down the front stairs of each building, stopping to peer in the lower windows.

"What, exactly, are we looking for?" Irene asked, following her up onto a rickety porch and watching as Amy craned on tiptoe to see through the dirt-encrusted window.

"Here!" Amy tried the front door. It was unlocked. They slipped into the house.

"This is breaking and entering," Irene hissed in a low voice.

"Not today it isn't. We're invited."

In the front room was a large table covered with a red tablecloth and an array of food. Plates and silverware lay in formal place settings. At the place of honor sat a steaming bowl of something that emitted a foul odor. Irene pinched her nose. "Ugh, what is that smell?"

Amy laughed. "Fermented cabbage. It's a traditional offering."

"Screw that! Who would want it?" Irene cried.

Amy laughed again. She reached out and snagged a handful of roll-like objects from a tray. She handed one to Irene. "Red bean paste buns. I love these things!"

Amy looked for a pocket to put the buns in then looked at Irene and motioned for her to open her bag. Amy then upended the plate into it, which, by now, was bulging dangerously with their combined treasures. They heard voices from the next room and Amy motioned to Irene that they should leave.

"Why did we have to leave?" Irene asked once they were outside. "They can't hear us...can they?" She felt a surge hope at the thought that the Ghost Festival might signal a special day when the living could see and hear the dead.

Amy shook her head. "No, but there's no point in antagonizing people. The living only send us stuff as long as they don't believe we exist."

"Don't you mean as long as they *do*?"

Amy gave one of her characteristic shrugs. "Isn't that the point of superstition — something you believe because it *might* be true, not because it's actually true?"

Irene was impressed. "Wow, that's deep."

Amy laughed. "I *was* a teacher."

They continued up the street, gazing in windows. Finally, Amy looked up at the sky. "It's getting late."

Irene was surprised to see that the sun was almost gone, the sky darkening to pre-dusk. For the first time since she'd died, the day had flown by.

"Do you mind if we skip the bar tonight?" Amy asked. "I don't want to lug all this stuff around. Tomorrow we'll go to the market to trade it all in. Okay?"

The thought that she might be able to get rid of some of this stuff was a welcome one; Irene was getting sick of lugging her stuff around all the time. Jonah had thought she was lucky because she had so much stuff, but now she wasn't so sure.

Speaking of Jonah — she hadn't seen him in two days. Her heart sank. He was probably gone for good now.

Which is fine, she thought fiercely. She didn't need him. She'd done what she set out to do: she'd made new friends and started a life, as a ghost, for herself here in Boston.

Somehow, none of it felt as exciting as she'd hoped. It still felt like something was missing.

Eighteen

"You have to get here pretty early to find anything of use," Amy said as they wandered up and down the rows of ghostly vendors lined up outside the gates of a neatly manicured cemetery.

Doris had walked through pounding her bucket drum at six a.m. as usual. They had collected their stuff, and then Amy had led her two blocks to the subway station. They went three stops and then exited to the street, where they waited for the bus. The bus was a little trickier to manage than the subway, as the drivers didn't stop unless someone—someone living that is—was getting on or off. Five buses had gone by before someone living had shown up to wait at their stop. Then it appeared that no buses were coming ever again. Time had ticked by as Irene tried valiantly—but unsuccessfully—to find a topic of conversation on which Amy had more than two or three words to say.

When Irene had finally expressed impatience at waiting any longer, Amy had said, "Oh don't worry. There's no hurry."

She realized Amy was right. There was no need to hurry—ever again. There was no job to get up for, no appointments to go to, no aggravating responsibilities like filing taxes, getting her car inspected, or driving her mother to the eye doctor. There was no need to invent dead uncles or alien abductions in order to bug out of work after a night of over-indulgence. No need, in fact, to ever again break up a party because she had to get up early the next day. She could stay out as late as she wanted, drink as much as she wanted, lie in bed for as long as she wanted — for the rest of...forever.

Well, that's what I wanted, right? Irene thought.

Somehow that thought didn't give her the same sense of euphoria as it had when standing on her front step a lifetime ago thinking the same thought. Worrying that she was becoming one of those people who are never satisfied, she pushed the unsettled feeling away.

The bus arrived and Irene's attention became focused on the careful negotiation of getting onto the bus undetected. They had to follow closely enough on the heels of a living person to ensure they were on the bus before the doors closed but not so close that they caused a scene by bumping into them.

The slow, jolting ride had seemed to last forever. No one had gotten on or off at the stop they wanted, so they'd had to ride three stops farther, resulting in a long walk to their final destination — a neat, moderately-sized cemetery.

"My feet are killing me," Irene said. She tried to remind her feet that, technically, they couldn't hurt any longer, but they didn't believe her. She kicked off her shoes. The grass was soft and cool underfoot and she let out a sigh of relief.

Arrayed around the fence, just outside the cemetery, was a motley array of people — both dead and alive — selling goods out of shopping carts or laid out on the grass. Apparently, this served as the formal market system for the dead.

They wandered up and down the row of vendors. Amy traded most everything she had picked up for cigarettes and coins, keeping a few candles and the deck of playing cards. Irene, still not entirely sure what had value in the afterlife, chose to keep everything. Every time she went to trade an item, Jonah's disapproving face appeared before her, preventing her from getting rid of anything.

Once they finished transacting business with the vendors they proceeded into the cemetery. Amy led her up and down the orderly rows of headstones, and Irene disinterestedly followed along, her shoes dangling by their straps from loose fingers. In addition to the living people who were there—visiting graves and trimming the grass—Irene could see quite a few dead people scattered about. They all seemed to be doing the same as Amy—hunting for something.

Irene shifted her shoes to the other hand. "What, exactly, is it that we're looking for?"

"Nothing in particular, just anything that might have been dropped. The place already looks pretty well picked over, though."

"What do you mean 'dropped'?" Irene asked.

"You know, people—when they wake up—often leave stuff behind, due to the shock and all."

Irene turned this over. She supposed if she had woken up in a cemetery, instead of by the river, she might have freaked out a little more than she had.

"The best are the streakers."

"What, streakers as in...streakers? Like...naked people?"

Amy nodded. "Yeah, they leave everything behind. They just kind of freak out at being dead. They're total kooks."

"No way!"

Amy nodded earnestly. "Uh huh. Really! I saw one once."

"What happened?"

Amy shrugged. "He started screaming, then he ripped off all his clothes and ran off, still screaming." She grew thoughtful. "I got a good haul that day."

Irene saw neat rows of flat stones on some of the headstones, same as she had in Salem. She knew that she and Jonah had discussed this ritual, but his answer had been unsatisfactory. She pointed to the rocks. "I've always wondered why people do that."

Amy shrugged. "It's better when they leave coins."

Irene felt an odd sense of unease at the implication that the dead removed items from other dead peoples' graves. It seemed rather like grave robbing.

They traveled down a long row to the far side of the cemetery. Irene stopped dead at the sight before her—a pile of glowing blue coffins, heaped haphazardly before a small cluster of ghosts working industriously to take them apart. Irene blinked.

"What the...?"

"Oh that," Amy said dismissively. "Coffin reclamation."

"Coffin what?"

"What did you think happens to all the coffins? They come, too, you know; but who's going to keep theirs? I mean, honestly, what would you do with it?"

"Okay, fine, but what do *they* do with it?" Irene asked, pointing to the men, women, and even a few children, who were busy tearing the coffins apart. She could see several people working to tear the linings out, carefully setting the fabric aside in neat stacks. Others were pulling off the metal pieces—decorations and handles—and tossing them into piles. Another crew seemed to be dismantling the box—taking off the lid and breaking down the sides.

Amy smiled in amusement. "You do know that there's a whole underground conduit of goods from one place to the next, right? Where do you think Greig gets all the live stuff he sells us?"

Irene frowned as she puzzled over this for a minute. "Yeah, but—"

Amy shrugged. "I don't know. I never asked."

Irene wanted to probe further the idea that people were trading goods back and forth across the invisible divide that separated the living from the dead, but a sudden flash of green light on the far side of the cemetery drew her attention. It was so brief Irene wasn't sure she had seen it. "What was that?"

"New arrival," Amy said dismissively.

"You   mean...that's   what   happens   when someone...crosses over?"

Amy nodded, looking bored. "Well, I've got everything I wanted." She gave Irene an inquiring look. Irene nodded, feeling disappointed that Amy wasn't more interested in the newly crossed over person, but then Irene realized there wouldn't be much to see — just another ghost, standing next to a coffin. She supposed it wasn't all that exciting, after all. *Sorry, dude,* she thought. *You'll just have to figure it out by yourself like the rest of us.*

Amy turned and headed back through the rows of gravestones. Irene followed, limping slightly and wishing for the hundredth time that she had worn her gladiator sandals the night she died, instead of the stilettos.

Nineteen

Ernest, Nellie, and Itza were waiting for them at the usual table when they arrived. The bar was crowded as usual, with all the regulars: the beat poet, the frat boys, the college professors.

"Princess!" Ernest raised his glass when he saw them. "What luck, you're just in time to buy a round."

Irene gave a mock grimace and fished some change out of her bag.

Everyone booed. "We want the good stuff," Ernest complained.

"Patience, my friend, patience. The night is young, and I need an aperitif to get me started."

Itza took the coins and dutifully went to get drinks. Ernest, looking at Irene, pulled out the empty chair beside him and patted it. She smiled warmly at him and sat down, kicking off her shoes under the table.

"God, it feels good to sit," she said. "I can't believe I have to spend the rest of my life in these shoes!"

"So get some new ones," Nellie said, not unsympathetically.

Ernest leaned closer to Irene. "I rather like your shoes," he said. "And all the rest."

Up close, she could see that his eyes, which she had thought were black, were actually a dark blue.

"We were just at the market," Amy said. "No shoes."

Itza returned with their drinks. "What are we talking about?"

"Irene wants some new shoes," Nellie said.

Itza took a seat. "Mmm, shoes are hard to come by." Itza and Nellie screwed up their faces in contemplation.

"Scalper might..." Itza said finally.

Amy frowned and shrugged half-heartedly. "Maybe," she said without much enthusiasm.

Irene looked from one to the other. "Scalper?"

"What's wrong with Scalper?" Nellie asked.

"He's a bit dodgy, is all," Amy replied.

Ernest laughed. "Beggars can't be choosers."

Itza chimed in with, "He's alright."

"He's a *character*," Amy countered, as if this was the ultimate condemnation. "And he's expensive."

She pulled out the deck of cards and held them up. There was a ripple of approbation from their companions.

"Who's Scalper?" Irene repeated.

"If the market is a strip mall, then Scalper is Rodeo Drive," Itza said. "He has unusual and hard-to-get items."

"Yeah, but most of it is of no use on this side," Amy protested. Then she added, "What are we playing?"

Everyone spoke at once.

"Poker," Irene said automatically.

"Bridge," Itza suggested.

"If anyone had shoes, it would be him," Ernest added, still on the first conversation.

"Pinochle," Nellie said.

"Well, unless I can buy shoes with ketchup, I assume that at some point I'm going to need some actual money," Irene said to Ernest.

Hooray! people shouted in the background.

Amy began to deal the cards. "I vote for whist."

Ernest let out a long stream of smoke. "Everyone takes trade. You'll be fine."

Amy dealt a card to Ernest. He tossed it back. "I'll play whist when hell freezes over, kitten."

Amy turned to Irene.

"I'm out," she said. "I don't know how to play whist."

The others offered to teach her, but she waved them off. "I'll just watch."

She observed the game play for a bit, sipping absently at her drink. She wasn't sure if the women were actually playing — and if so, for the fun of it or just to kill time — or trying to invoke memories of enjoyable times they'd had when they were alive. The play was slow, with lots of contemplative pauses, dreamy, faraway looks, and little talking. Irene had the uncomfortable feeling that there was some deeper meaning to the game that she just wasn't seeing.

After a while, she turned to look at Ernest, who had fallen silent. He was studying her intently, his blue eyes studying every inch of her face. He noticed her looking at him and smiled thinly. He took a deep drag on his cigarette and then sat back, careful to blow the smoke away from her.

"So what's your story?" she asked, deciding to break the taboo against talking about their previous lives.

A slow, self-deprecating grin slid across his face. "It's a sad one, I'm afraid. Born to a life of wealth and privilege. Then, at the tender age of nineteen, called up for the war and blown all to hell."

At first she thought he meant World War Two, but then remembered he said he had been dead more than ninety years. She did the math in her head and realized he must have died during the first world war.

She smiled, making a joke to take the edge off his words. "That *is* a tragedy. I was just about to ask you if you wanted to get out of here and go do something, but if you're only nineteen, you're too young for me, and if you're over a hundred, you're way too old."

He raised his drink to her in toast. "Then here's to the agelessness of death."

Her smile widened as she raised her own glass to his and they both took a drink.

Someone set another round on the table. Itza sighed and reached for a glass. "I never thought I'd hear myself say this, but I miss Coca-Cola."

Nellie heaved a heartfelt sigh of her own. "I miss chewing gum."

"Chewing gum!" Amy cried, setting down her cards and digging through Irene's bag.

This reminded Irene of the lighter she had picked up for Ernest. She waited for Amy to finish, then pawed through the bag, and pulled the lighter out.

Amy handed the gum to Nellie. Nellie looked surprised and touched at the same time. "For me? A whole pack?" she said.

Amy picked up her cards again, nodding. "Yeah, I came across it the other day and I owed you."

Ernest gave her a suspicious look. "I wish I knew where you find this stuff."

Irene interrupted this exchange by handing him the lighter. "Merry Christmas," she said.

Ernest was taken aback. "Princess, I'm touched. I only wish I could return the favor." He flicked the lighter and grinned with delight when the flame appeared. He lit a new cigarette and stubbed out the old one. Amy laughed.

Meanwhile, the game continued. Itza laid down a card. Nellie frowned and stared at her own hand with deep contemplation. Then she threw down what appeared to be the winning card. The other two women groaned and tossed their cards onto the table. Itza scooped up the deck amidst an animated rehashing of the hand and began to shuffle.

Irene felt Ernest's eyes on her again and turned her head. He was studying her, and he suddenly leaned forward, coming in close, and said, in an undertone. "How about it, princess? You and me...?" he nodded toward the door. She met his inquiring gaze with a searching one of her own. His eyes crinkled with amusement, as if he felt a little self-conscious, and then he reached out and, ever so gently, tucked an errant strand of hair behind her ear, his fingers whisper-soft against her cheek.

Indistinctly, in the background, she heard Amy and Itza haggling over some point of the game. Then it seemed that the volume of the background noise rose for a moment and, just as suddenly, went dead silent. She pulled away from

Ernest and looked around. Itza, Nellie, and Amy seemed to be staring at something on the floor behind them. Irene craned her neck and saw a shattered tableau of spreading liquid and glittering fragments of glass. Someone had dropped their drink.

"What happened?" she asked Amy, but Amy didn't answer.

The moment passed and people went back to whatever it was they were doing. The burble of background conversation returned.

Irene turned back to find Ernest slouched against his seat, his direct gaze fixed and unwavering. She felt the blood rush to her face, hot and uncomfortable. Guys usually stared at her breasts or legs; she wasn't used to one staring at her face as if he was trying to memorize it.

He gave her another lopsided, slightly self-deprecating grin, as if realizing he had embarrassed her. Then, as quick as it had come, the smile left his face, replaced with a fierce scowl. His eyes narrowed and slid away to something over her shoulder. Irene started to turn to see what was going on behind her, and Jonah's face came into focus, leaning over her shoulder, wedged between her and Ernest.

"What are you doing here?" she asked, her heart sinking. Having him find her in the bar—as if she had never left—was the last thing she wanted.

Jonah didn't answer. Instead, he said to Ernest, eyeballing him with belligerence and suspicion, "You still here?"

"Jonah!" she barked, mortified, half turning in her chair and nearly knocking heads with him.

Jonah straightened up, casting her a disgusted look. Irene turned back to Ernest. "Ignore him, he was raised by wolves."

Ernest laughed, but it sounded rather brittle. "I thought he wasn't your brother?" There was a question in his eyes, and she couldn't be sure, but it seemed like there was more space between them than there had been a minute ago, as if he had moved his chair away. She heard Jonah make a noise that sounded like a cross between someone clearing their throat and throwing up.

Irene felt her hackles rise. She flashed Ernest a smile, put a hand on his, and gave it a reassuring squeeze. "No, like I said, just a stray I picked up."

There was the distinct sound of something fragile being broken from somewhere behind her. Irene braced against the sound, her shoulders hunching up around her ears. "Tragic really," she said to Ernest through gritted teeth, a warning in her voice. "He died so young." She narrowed her eyes and, barely turning her head, hissed at Jonah, "Go away, I'm busy!"

Jonah snorted. "Yeah, I can see."

"You're behaving like a child."

Jonah stalked off, melding into the shifting crowd. Irene tried to ignore the sounds of dissatisfied foot stomping and items rattling that circled around behind her, instead fixing her attention back on Ernest. People around them seemed to be staring, and Irene felt the prickly hot rash of humiliation warring with the molten heat of outrage from head to foot.

"So...you were just suggesting somewhere...*less pesky*." These last words erupted in response to Jonah throwing himself into the empty chair beside her. Amy seemed to have left. Irene glanced around the table and saw that Itza and Nellie had left as well. Very likely, she thought, in response to Jonah's tantrum.

Irene forced a smile to her face and said to Ernest, "Does your place have a proper bed? I'm sick of sleeping on the floor."

Jonah hissed and then coughed in a way that sounded suspiciously like gagging. He began shuffling the empty glasses on the table, clinking them together nosily.

Ernest seemed distracted, looking from Jonah to Irene. "Uh...huh? Oh, yeah. I live at the hotel."

"Hotel?" Irene exclaimed. "Perfect!"

Her chair shook from a well-placed kick by Jonah. He leaned toward her, spluttering in outrage. "You're not gonna...with him?"

"Jonah!" she snapped, clutching the edge of the table so hard she thought it might snap in two. "Go. Away. I mean it!" Her voice was deadly, warning of impending violence if he didn't listen.

Jonah looked at Ernest. "What do you want, anyway?" he demanded. "Can't you see she's busy? She can't talk right now." His fists balled up and he leaned across the table, crackling with aggression. Irene was struck by the crazy notion that bantam weight Jonah was about to launch himself at Ernest who, while no heavy weight himself, was a full grown man, and she put a restraining hand on Jonah's arm, the anger replaced by a sudden, rising alarm.

Ernest gave Jonah a level look. "I would think that it's obvious what I want, mate."

Jonah tensed like an over-wound spring under her hand, and she tightened her grip while shaking her head at Ernest. "He really is only fourteen," she warned.

Ernest, whose posture matched Jonah's aggressive stance, slowly relaxed, easing back into his seat, though he still looked grim. "Then he needs to settle down, doesn't he? 'Cause he sure seems to think he owns you."

Irene's voice turned dangerous. "No one — *owns* — me."

Ernest grunted. "Then why don't I go get another round of drinks while you two sort this?"

Irene nodded, pushing Jonah back into his seat. His eyes, flashing with anger, followed Ernest across the bar until Ernest disappeared into the crowd.

As soon as Ernest was out of earshot, Irene exploded. "What the hell is wrong with you? Have you lost your mind? If you hadn't noticed, I don't need your help at the moment."

"He's a creep," Jonah said nonchalantly, reclining in his seat as if nothing had happened. "I don't like him."

She stared at him, blinking in disbelief. Finally she said, "He isn't for *you*."

Jonah scowled, his expression turning truculent, and he sprang up, trembling with fury. "*I*. Don't. Like. Him," he repeated.

Irene threw up her hands. "Are you off your meds or something?" She spluttered for a moment, too angry to be coherent. "Ernest is right. You're too young and I'm too old for you to be acting like this. You don't own me, Jonah. I'm a grown woman and I can do what I want with whomever I want. If you think throwing a colossal tantrum is going to get me to leave, then you're nuts."

Jonah crossed his arms over his chest. "So you're really going to stay then, and not go through the tunnel?"

"What does that have to do with the price of tomatoes?"

His face went from white to red in an instant and he uncrossed his arms explosively. "So that's it, then?" He was rigid, his movements stiff and jerky. "You're going to...with that guy? You don't even know him!"

She was taken aback, the hot lava of anger and embarrassment turning instantly to ice. She stared at him, breathing hard, as if he had slapped her. "I haven't made up my mind what I'm going to do," she said, the chill in her voice warning him that he was on dangerous ground.

"If you stay here, then I'm leaving, and I'm not coming back," he warned.

She was shaking now, her arm twitching with the urge to slap him, and she dug her nails into her palm to stop herself. "Fine. Why don't you take your watch then?" She started to unbuckle it.

"Keep it," he snarled, two white spots of rage on his checks. "It hasn't worked since I gave it to you, anyway." He clenched his jaw, took a breath so hard his nostrils flared, and then was gone.

"Fuck!" She grabbed a glass and smashed it on the table, enjoying the satisfying jangle of breaking glass. She was suddenly ashamed, but for what, she wasn't sure. What right did Jonah have to tell her what to do? How much to drink? Who she could sleep with? He wasn't her brother, he wasn't her father, and he sure as hell wasn't her boyfriend —

and if he thought her having sex with Ernest had anything to do with him, he was dead wrong, that was for sure.

"Okay, time to go," Ernest said, appearing beside her. He put a hand under her arm and urged her up. "Greig takes exception to people smashing up the place — do you know how hard it is to replace glasses?" Ernest guided her through the crowd and out the door. Once outside, the cool air hit her face, soothing against her flushed cheeks.

"For his own good, I hope that kid doesn't show his face in here again," Ernest said grimly, giving her an inquiring look.

Hauntingly, the look in Jonah's eyes when he'd asked if she was going to stay burned in her mind's eye. "He won't," she mumbled, anger and frustration creating a bitter sludge in her stomach. Then she remembered the look on Jonah's face when he delivered his ultimatum and the defiance bubbled up within her again. Who was he to tell her what to do? She didn't owe him anything.

She looked at Ernest, a determined glint in her eyes. "How far is it to the hotel?"

Twenty

The hotel turned out to be a quick walk from the bar — only two blocks — and Ernest seemed to sense that she was in no mood to talk. She was still seething with anger and barely noticed anything around them as they passed. It wasn't until they got into the elevator at the hotel that she finally took note of her surroundings. When Ernest hit the button for their floor, she was so surprised that all thoughts of the fight with Jonah were washed away.

"Thirteen?" she cried. "I thought buildings didn't have a thirteenth floor?"

However, there, out of place at the very top of the numbered list, was a button, sparkling faintly with ghost aura, clearly labeled "13."

He looked amused. "If the building has more than twelve floors, princess, it has a thirteenth floor."

"Yeah, I know *that*, but they always leave it off, don't they?"

He gave her a lopsided grin. "Obviously not."

She huffed in exasperation. "Well, obviously I see that *now*."

He laughed. "Haven't you heard the old superstitions about tithing to the spirits — farmers leaving a portion of their crops in the field, that sort of thing?"

"Uh, I'm a city girl. Not so much with the farmers and crops." She thought for a moment. "Though, I guess I remember some fairy tales from when I was a kid — about

Brownies and how you had to leave them a bowl of cream at night or they'd get mad and wreck your house." She said this with a tinge of embarrassment. She had gone through a phase, when she was four or five, where she left bowls of milk around the house in the hopes of luring a Brownie out into the open. All she had done was make the dog sick.

"Yeah, well, same sort of thing with buildings. To keep ghosts from wreaking havoc in the place, most hotels set aside an entire floor for the dead."

They stepped off the elevator and he led her down the hall. The furnishings, glowing faintly, were impeccable — done in rich shades of gold and antique olive green. Dabs of pink wove through the green of the carpet and the heavy gold satin curtains framing floor to ceiling windows pooled on the floor. The crystal and brass of the chandeliers, the side tables, and even the flower vases glowed warmly in the soft light. The overall feel was of antique opulence, tasteful and understated.

Halfway down the hall, a ghost woman, in a flowing white dress that might be a bridal gown, was wailing at the top of her lungs and wringing her hands. A hotel employee — alive and looking harassed — was trying to reason with her. "Madam, please! I'm sure we can find a way to..."

Ernest's lips twitched as he pulled a key out of his pocket. "Matilda's at it again, I see. She has a fit at least once a week, just out of spite." They stopped at the last room and Ernest turned the key in the lock.

They stepped across the threshold, and he shut the door behind them. Inside, the room was as richly furnished as the hall, but in an old-fashioned, faded sort of way. A soft, yellow light emanated from the antique gas lamps on the walls.

"Drink?" he asked, heading for a decanter on the desk.

"No, thanks. I'd better not. I already had quite a few tonight. Anymore, and I won't be upright for this."

He looked at her oddly, and she realized what she had said. "No pun intended," she added. He laughed and then she did, too.

He came closer, standing almost nose-to-nose with her. "It's not really a problem, princess," he said, his voice soft and close. "We didn't have any of the real stuff tonight. You welched and didn't buy us a round."

He studied her face for a moment and then, almost brusquely, tucked a wisp of hair behind her ear. The flash of humor was gone and the blistering intensity was back—he was staring at her with the same searing, searching look he'd given her in the bar. She was gratified to feel the familiar flutter of desire, deep and low. She focused on it, using it to block out everything else—the worry, the fear, the guilt, the bad feelings from the fight with Jonah.

She saw his eyes glint—a nanosecond flash in the dusky light—and then he was kissing her, hungry and fierce. Whatever fears she'd had about being able to have sex vanished—he was solid beneath her searching hands.

They tumbled onto the bed, clothes flying, and she was just as impatient as he, clawing at his jacket, his shirt, his pants.

There was a tussle for supremacy, her trying—impatiently—to straddle him, him trying to flip her onto her back. He won. Then his mouth was on her, moving across her skin, and she lay there, looking at the ceiling as he drifted lower. The sensations were there—flickers of pleasure, coiling tension, aching need—but distant and pale, as if it was all happening to someone else. She squeezed her eyes closed, trying to blot out everything else, trying to feel the here and now, trying to make it real. Anything to distract her, to drive away these feelings. Anything to forget Jonah's face, his accusations and disappointment.

It didn't work. The harder she tried to focus on the feelings, the weaker they got.

"Stop. *Stop!*" She pushed against the smooth, solid wall of Ernest's chest. He rolled off of her and she sat up.

"What? Is something wrong?" he asked.

She swung her legs over the edge of the bed, feeling sick to her stomach and angry with herself. "I'm sorry," she said, leaning over to snag her panties off the floor. "It's just not working."

He grabbed her arm. "Wait a minute…"

She went rigid and gave him a freezing stare. "Take your hand off of me."

He let go as if he'd been scalded, holding up his hands in surrender. "Okay, okay, take it easy, princess!"

She bounced up and pulled her panties over her hips. "Look, it's not me, it's you…I had a great time…yada, yada, yada."

His mouth quirked in a wry grin and he settled back against the pillows, adjusting the sheet around his hips. "Don't you have that backwards?"

"Whatever." She stood up and slipped her dress over her head.

"Did I do — or not do — something…?"

"No, it's not that. It's just…it feels…weird." Like everything else, it was only a memory of a feeling, hazy and blurred. She wanted to kick herself. She had no body. Of course she couldn't have sex. She could only remember — and her memories wasn't that great.

Ernest's smile was both wry and bitter. He pulled a cigarette from the pack on the nightstand, lit it using the lighter she had given him, and then took a long drag. "Is this your first time?" he asked.

"Of course it's not my —" she said dismissively, hunting for her shoes.

He held up a defensive hand. "I meant, since you died."

She straightened up, her shoes clutched to her chest. "What difference does that make?"

"It's just…you get used to it after a while. The food tastes funny, the booze doesn't make you drunk, the sex feels…weird." He stumbled over her chosen word. "The cigarettes," he gestured with a hand, "have no flavor. It's all just part of the package, I guess."

They thought the afterlife was the same as this life, just pale and washed out. The people are gray. They eat dust and their food is mud.

Jonah's words washed over her and she felt a surge of panic, stronger now than ever before. She jammed her bag onto her shoulder and headed for the door.

Ernest, watching her carefully, wore an expression of resigned disappointment. "It's not the end of the world," he said. She hesitated, hand on the doorknob. He added, "You know, I rather like you." His voice was full of uncertain longing, as if he was hoping against hope that she'd stay. He flashed her a sweet, lopsided smile. "You're not the usual."

She shook her head, flustered and irritated. "I'm not looking for love, just a lay." She threw open the door and walked out.

She kicked herself all the way back to the library. How had she managed to screw things up so badly?

She hesitated in front of the entrance, not really wanting to face Amy. It had been a rotten day all around, and she didn't really want to explain what had happened — or didn't happen — with Jonah or Ernest. Then she thought of the Uglies and knew that she didn't want to stay outside, either.

She opened the door, but instead of heading to the basement, she continued to the main floor of the library. It was dark and she fished out the flashlight. She shone the beam around, the book-lined walls looking alien and strange in the dark. She trundled over to the bank of computers and fired one up.

She stared at the blinking cursor, hesitating to put form to her fears, as if typing the words would somehow make them real.

Isn't that what superstition is...

She took a deep, heartening breath and typed, her fingers flying over the keys: *dying in the afterlife*. It was almost a relief to write them, to let the fear out.

She hit enter.

To her surprise, dozens of entries appeared. She scribbled call numbers on a scrap of paper so thoughtfully provided for that purpose by the library staff and then went hunting.

It took a little bit of trial and error to find the right section, but eventually she ended up with a small stack of books, which she spread on a table. She skimmed the first book, intermittent words and phrases sticking out:

…Egyptians believed that you could die in the afterlife and that this death would be permanent…believed that if something happened to their mummified bodies or to their name, they would cease to exist…destruction of Hatshepsut's images, name, and temple by Tuthmose III were an attempt to deny her immortality by destroying her Ka in the afterlife…

That answered that question. She slammed the book shut. The dead could die, and die for real. Oblivion — that was what awaited anyone the Uglies got hold of.

Well, that was certainly a vote for moving on.

Moving on. She groaned. She still had no idea where the tunnel was. She went back to the computer and started a new search. This one was a little harder. "White light death" and "tunnel to the afterlife" both just turned up dozens of references to near-death experiences. "Lighting the way for the dead" didn't turn up anything.

Through a convoluted series of inter-related searches, she finally found something relevant in an article about the Chinese Ghost Festival:

"…fourteen days later, lanterns are lit — often this includes floating candles placed on rivers — to guide the dead back home…"

Jonah had said something about a culture that placed candles next to the corpse — at the head — to guide them to the afterlife. She thought back, trying to pick out that one fact from the morass of information he had dumped on her over their several days together. She wished now that she had paid more attention when he had been rambling on about all the different death rituals.

She typed "lanterns of the dead" into the search box and got back some interesting reading on stone towers in France used to hold lanterns that marked the position of cemeteries. She wasn't sure how this helped, but it seemed to be one more indication that people thought the dead needed to see some sort of light to find their way to the next life.

She thumped the book in frustration. None of it made any sense. She slumped, head in hand, and gazed into space, lost in thought. How was a lit candle supposed to guide her to the afterlife?

Maybe they lined a path?

No, it sounded like a single candle was enough.

Okay, well, how did the living know where the land of the dead was, anyway?

They must know...they were the ones putting out the candles and lanterns.

Cherchez la lumiere. Follow the light.

No...not follow — it came to her in a flash, dredged from the depths of her memory — to look for. "Cherchez" meant "look for."

Look for the light.

Where?

What light?

She was staring absently into space, eyes unfocused, her mind wandering. The light from the flashlight was in her field of vision, off to one side. As she gazed at nothing, the steady beam of light seemed to waver, flickering and dancing before her eyes, and then suddenly brightened, filling her entire field of vision, blotting out everything else. Psychedelic spots of color danced in front of her eyes and then seemed to melt and run in golden rivulets that swirled and churned and joined together to form a river of molten light. She felt a jerk, as if someone had grabbed the front of her dress and yanked her forward, and then she was falling...

She resisted, digging in, pulling back. She blinked and jolted upright, startled. She shook her head, blinking rapidly, and her vision cleared. She looked around. She was still in the library, still at the table, the flashlight there, untouched, books spread out before her.

She shook herself mentally. She must have fallen asleep. That was all. Nothing had happened.

Yet...there had been something...familiar...in the vortex of light. Something half-remembered or half-forgotten, she wasn't sure which. She absently surveyed the table and her belongings spread out there and realized she hadn't been staring into *space*. She'd been staring into the soft glow of the flashlight. Into its beam of *light*.

"No, it couldn't be..." she said out loud.

She grabbed the flashlight and pulled it closer. Holding it to her chest, the light pointing to the ceiling, she looked straight down, into the beam. The light was searingly bright. Her eyes watered and spots danced before them. She squinted and moved her head, trying to find a comfortable position. She relaxed her eyes, trying to hold the light in her field of vision while looking past it, as one did during an eye exam.

The light flared and turned golden, twirling into an eddying pool so thick it looked like molasses. It was beautiful, warm and welcoming. She wanted nothing more than to join it, to embrace it, to slip into it and become part of it. She stopped holding back and let herself go. Once more, she felt herself falling forward, falling into the light.

Suddenly, she couldn't breathe. It was as if an elephant sat on her chest, crushing her. She flailed, trying to surface, and she couldn't move, her limbs weightless and weak. She felt, rather than saw, the light, now green-blue, fading away around her, fading to black. All around her was a rushing, roaring, bellowing sound, as of a hurricane. Her heart pounded against her ribs, as if hammering to be heard, hammering to escape.

She drew back, wrenching herself away from the inextricable pull of the tunnel to the other side, forcing herself to look away.

She blinked and the library reformed around her once more. Her heart was still pounding, her breath coming in short, sharp bursts. She put a hand protectively to her chest, over her heart, and felt her eyes prickle with tears.

You don't have a heart, she told herself fiercely. *You're dead.*

Yet, she had felt the moment in the vortex when her heart had stopped. Her heart. *Hers.* It was a violation, a personal affront, deeply offensive and uncontrollably terrifying. The panic didn't subside, and it was several minutes before she could take deep, even breaths again. She stared at the flashlight as if it was a deadly snake.

So, that's what they meant.

Follow the light.

The tunnel had been there all the time. Like Dorothy, she'd had the power to leave all along. Now she was free to leave whenever she wanted.

If she wanted.

She picked up the flashlight and hit herself in the head with it, castigating herself for an idiot.

All the stories are true. The stories are also very literal.

She repeated this like a mantra several times, hoping that this time it sunk in.

Irene wasn't sure what to do next. She could leave, if she wanted. She just wasn't sure she did. She wasn't sure what she had just experienced, but it hadn't been pleasant. She felt deceived, lied to, and tricked. A comforting promise had lured her forward and then it had been pulled away, replaced with cold, harsh punishment.

There was something on the other side, of that she was now sure. She had felt it. She didn't know what it was, and she didn't know if it was any better than what was here, any safer than the Uglies.

She felt a sudden stab of longing. She wished Jonah was here — she could use his advice. She winced as she remembered how deliberately cruel she had been about going into the bar and then sleeping with Ernest just to spite him. Jonah had just been trying to protect her — perhaps overzealously and with a possessive jealousy that was alarming and more than a little uncomfortable, but protective nonetheless.

She grimaced ruefully. The only person she needed protecting from was herself. She should have handled them better. She'd been unkind, and now she wished she could apologize.

"If wishes were horses..." she muttered, furiously stuffing items into her bag. There was no point crying over spilled milk, as her grandmother used to say. Jonah had left, and she didn't doubt him at his word—he was gone for good. She could track him down and apologize, but she wasn't sure what good that would do. He hated her now—as she deserved.

You're a big girl, she castigated herself. *You can do this by yourself.*

Of course she could. It was just that she preferred to do it with him, rather than without. She sighed and headed for the basement to look for Amy.

Twenty-One

Doris marched through at six a.m., but Irene was already awake. She hadn't been able to sleep, her mind churning with everything that had happened and everything she had learned. However, she still wasn't any closer to a decision on whether to go through the tunnel.

"Still want to go see Scalper?" Amy asked.

Irene nodded, instantly diverted. "Oh, we have to go — I'm dying of curiosity!"

This time they struck out in a westerly direction from the library, walking the six blocks to where Scalper was tucked into a dead-end alley.

The trader's appearance was a rag-tag assortment of styles, epochs, and what appeared to be found objects. He sported buccaneer knee boots — worn to a dusty gray — baggy trousers, and a green, plastic rain cape — the five-dollar kind sold at zoo and amusement park gift shops. Brooches, paperclips, nails, buttons, and various other small objects covered every square inch of his clothes so that the underlying fabric was barely visible. Everything glowed with the familiar blue sheen of the dead.

"'Allo gorgeous, what can I do for you, then?" he greeted them, giving Amy an air kiss on each cheek.

"I'll leave you to it," Amy said with a roll of her eyes. Then she moved off to look at Scalper's wares, set up on an impromptu table made from a plank laid across two trashcans.

Irene noticed the trace of a Cockney accent. "British?" she asked, wondering if he'd come to America before or after he'd died.

"Well today's Tuesday, ain't it, love?"

Irene's forehead puckered in confusion. She opened her mouth to ask the obvious question and then shut it again with a shake of her head. What was the point? The dead never seemed to give a straight answer to anything.

He was looking at her, sizing her up. Eyes so dark they were almost black lingered as he looked her up and down. "Can I just say, love, that you are *working* that dress."

She smiled despite herself.

"It's a shame, really. I don't have anything your size to trade, or I just might take it off you," he said, a teasing glint in his eyes.

"I'm sure we could work something out," she said.

"Tempting, very tempting." He slapped his hands together and then rubbed them against each other, as if relishing the thought. "I only deal in hard goods though, love."

Irene's eyes twinkled. "Funny. So do I," she said, matching his tone of sly innuendo. She was unable to help herself. He was too ridiculous and his playful mood was infectious.

He laughed appreciatively and waggled a finger at her. "Naughty, naughty minx. Now what can I do for you?"

"I'm looking for a new pair of shoes."

"Well, but them's you got on is lovely!"

"Yeah, well, I need some walking shoes." *Or*, she thought, *quite possibly hiking boots if Jonah's mountains and such are real.*

"Ah," he said with regret. "Unfortunately, love, we don't have any in stock just at the moment. If you care to come back another day…"

Irene's lips twisted in a rueful grimace. "My friend…" — she looked around for Amy and saw her looking over the items for sale—"said that you buy things...dead things..."

"You're wanting cash?"

Irene nodded.

"Well then," he said, bowing her toward the refrigerator-sized cardboard box behind him with a flourish. "Step into my office."

"Your office is a cardboard box."

"Yes," he agreed, as if this was the most natural thing in the world.

"Okay, just so long as we're all clear," she said.

She felt ridiculous standing there, her head and shoulders hunched so she'd fit in the box, but Scalper seemed to think this was normal.

"So," he asked rubbing his hands together in what appeared to be anticipation. "What you got?"

Irene rummaged in her bag and began pulling out items, naming each one as she did so. "Magazines." Scalper shook his head in distaste. "Pens?"

"Oooh..." He plucked the two pens she offered out of her hands. "What else?"

"Um...ketchup..." She dangled a packet from one hand, the top edge pinched between her thumb and forefinger. Scalper suddenly went very still, like a wolfhound catching its quarry's scent.

"How much you want for that?" he asked, his voice quivering with suppressed excitement.

Irene glanced at the ketchup and then back at Scalper. "What is it with ketchup?"

Scalper licked his lower lip and then pinched it between his teeth. Reluctantly, as if afraid of revealing too much, he said, "Well, it's the real thing ain't it?"

"Okay, I get that not too many people get buried with food, but please don't tell me you just eat it plain?"

"Well, no, love, but somethin' like that takes the edge off the live stuff, don't it?"

She contemplated the ketchup packet for a minute. *Gives a whole new spin to seasoning*, she thought.

"Okay, maybe I'll keep the ketchup." She moved to put it back in the bag.

"Now, now, don't be hasty," said Scalper quickly. "I'm willing to offer you coins, if you insist, but take a good look around. I'm willing to bet you see something you'd like in exchange."

She glanced over the items laid out on the improvised table. A green, heart-shaped stone, winking and twinkling with a strange light, caught her eye. It hung on a cheap leather cord and made her think of carnivals and fairs.

Scalper saw her looking at it. "Good choice! It brings out the color of your eyes."

"My eyes are brown."

"Exactly!"

Irene was barely able to suppress an eye roll. "Okay, fine, I'll take the necklace for the ketchup." God knew she didn't need it—she could see Jonah's disapproving look—but for some reason it drew her attention.

He waved his hands in consternation. "I can't do it, love. That's a special item, that is. Coins only for that one. It's worth a lot, but I'll make you a special deal."

"Coins?" she asked, incredulous. "How many coins?" *How much spare change did he think she had?*

"*Small* coins," he amended. "Pennies or dimes."

"Are you nuts?" She frowned and looked at the necklace again, ready to dismiss it, but there was something about the way it glinted. Reluctantly, she dug down to the bottom of the bag. "Listen…I've got…one…three…four…six…six dimes." She held them out for him to inspect. "That's it."

"And a packet of ketchup," he added.

"And a packet of ketchup," she amended, adding one to the dimes in her hand.

"Done!" He snatched the items out of her hand. He ran over to the table to get the necklace and Irene thought that she had never actually seen anyone gambol until now. He came back, holding out the necklace.

Irene shook her head, feeling she had missed something, and took it from him. "Uh, thanks," she said. She tied the cord around her neck. The pendant felt warm where it nestled against the bare skin above her breasts.

He seemed to be holding his breath as he watched her tie the necklace on. When she was finished and had lowered her hands, he let out his breath and his face suffused with approval. "Lovely. Just lovely."

"I know it's in bad taste, but can I ask, what did you do when you were alive?"

He smiled cheekily. "Oh, same thing I do now, mostly. Bought things. Sold things. Found things." He winked. "Lost things."

Irene surveyed the improvised shop. Amy was talking to another shopper. She seemed to be haggling, or possibly debating, over an item with the other woman. Irene turned back to Scalper.

"You know the tunnel...to the afterlife?"

He nodded. "Yeah."

"You don't happen to have anything that describes what's in the tunnel or what's on the other side, do you?"

He shook his head. "'Fraid not, love."

"Do you know what's on the other side?"

He shook his head again. "'Fraid not."

"Well, can I ask, why haven't you moved on? Aren't you in the least bit curious to see what's on the other side?"

Scalper drew himself up, looking offended. "I haven't moved on *yet*, love. The optimal word being yet. Doesn't mean I won't ever. I just got some things here I want to do first."

Irene's look turned first suspicious and then disbelieving. She pointedly ran an eye over the makeshift table, as if to say, "*This* is what you're putting off the afterlife for?"

"Listen, love," he said, indignantly, "I ain't never seen Hawaii, Pair-ee, the Great Wall, or the Cubs win a World Series. Before I move on, I'm going to sit on a tropical beach with a fruity drink—one with an umbrella in it—and watch the sun set over the ocean. I'm going to take one of those boat rides on a canal in Venice—the ones where the little

Eye-talian fellas push you 'round with poles. I'm going to swim the English Channel. I'm going to go hang gliding and bungee jumping and deep sea diving. I'm gonna do it all. No regrets. No stone unturned. That's me."

"Okay, point taken."

Scalper grabbed the front of his rain poncho and tugged on it sharply, as if to straighten it. "I should think so."

At that moment, Amy came up and slipped her arm through Irene's. "Are you ready yet? Let's get out of here." She tugged Irene away.

"I'll be seein' you, love," called Scalper, and somehow the words seemed sinister, more of a threat than a promise.

"So did you get what you wanted?" Amy asked.

Irene shook her head. "Somehow, instead of getting cash, I ended up spending cash. Now that I think of it, he stole two pens, too. I'm not really sure how he did it. It's definitely a talent."

Amy gave her a rueful look. "Yeah, that's why I try to avoid Scalper. So what did you get?"

Irene lifted the necklace for Amy's inspection.

"That's pretty."

"Yeah," Irene said, fingering it. "It only cost me six dimes."

"Six dimes?" Amy cried in dismay. "That's outrageous!"

"It's only sixty cents," Irene replied, thinking Amy had misunderstood.

"It's six *dimes*," Amy corrected. "That's extortion."

"Gee," Irene said drily, "and that isn't even counting the packet of ketchup."

Twenty-Two

Maurice met them at the door. "Who does a ghost invite to his party?"

"Hey, Maurice," Irene said, not pausing as she headed for their regular table.

Maurice followed. "Give up?" he asked. "Anyone he can dig up. Get it? Anyone he can dig up!"

As they made their way through the crowd, Maurice fell away, heading off to pounce on someone else.

Irene wasn't keen on seeing Ernest again, but she needn't have worried. Only Itza and Herman were at the table. Almost as soon as they sat down, Itza said, "It's our turn to buy." As usual, Itza had nothing to contribute to the kitty. Irene threw in three of her pens and two candles she had picked up at the Ghost Festival. Herman took their "money" and went to get the drinks.

Amy and Itza didn't seem inclined to talk, so when the drinks came Irene focused on her glass, letting her thoughts wander. Her mind kept replaying the conversation with Scalper: *I haven't gone yet* — yet *being the optimal word.*

For some reason, his words made her sad. She wondered when he would reach the point where he was ready to go. She thought of Amy, enthralled with the ever-changing world of the living. How could you ever leave if you kept waiting to see what happened next? Or kept thinking there was just one more thing you wanted to do? Didn't there have to come a point when, if you were truly going to move on, you just had to "cut bait" and do it? Just had to say, "Screw it, this is good enough," and then just go?

Herman left, apparently finding them all dull company. Irene frowned at her companions. "Can I ask you something? Have you ever thought about, you know, leaving?"

Amy looked blank. "Leaving?"

"You know, moving on." She set her drink down. "I mean, I get why you stay—so you can do all the things you didn't get a chance to do when you were alive—but does there ever come a point when you're done? Where it's enough and you're ready to move on?"

Amy started to shrug and Irene got angry. "No, don't shrug; answer the question. Do you ever imagine a day when you would leave?"

Amy stared at her coldly and then said, rather frostily, "I don't know. I expect I'll leave some day."

Irene looked at Itza. "What about you? Why have you stayed behind?"

There was a blank silence. Finally, Itza shrugged. "I haven't decided *not* to go."

Irene puzzled over this for a minute—at first she didn't understand what Itza meant. Then it came to her. Itza hadn't made a conscious choice to stay behind. She meant to go...tomorrow. After one last hoorah, one last chance to enjoy all that life had to offer. The same as Scalper. The same as Amy. Very likely the same as the hundreds of others who had ended up here in the bar, here at last call. Tomorrow had turned into the next day and then the day after that and then the day after that and years had passed. Just like Irene.

It's about choices.

Madame Majicka had known. The words were right there in that book she had tried to give Irene. Irene groaned.

We make our own afterlife, she realized. *We make our own hell.*

She repeated her mantra—the stories are all true. *Heaven. Hell. Limbo.* They all existed. Only the stories were all wrong. There was no omnipotent judge, meting out reward and punishment. No tests. No criteria. No good deeds or mortal sins toted up. No set of scales to balance. Instead, each person served as their own judge and jury. Each person chose his own reward or punishment. If you thought you deserved a reward, you got one. If you thought you should be punished, well, you got that, too. If you just didn't know what you deserved, then the universe waited, ever so patiently, for you make up your mind—even if it took an eternity.

Irene's head began to swim and she suddenly felt sick to her stomach. She pushed back her chair, the sound of the legs scraping the floor harsh and shrill.

"*Hooray!*"

She rose unsteadily to her feet, gripping the edge of the table for support. "I have to go," she said, forcing the words through her constricting windpipe.

"Hey, where are you going?" Amy asked.

Irene just shook her head, grabbed her bag, turned, and fled, pushing blindly through the crowd. She didn't pause when she reached the door, just pushed through it and tumbled out onto the sidewalk, the sunlight too bright after the dimness of the bar.

The door closed behind her, cutting off the faint sound of cheering that followed her out onto the street. She blinked rapidly, trying to adjust to the sparkling daylight. Her stomach clenched and she doubled over, prepared to vomit. She wretched, but nothing came up.

Stop it! she told herself savagely. *You can't throw up—you don't have a stomach. You're dead. You have no body—no mouth, no throat, no stomach muscles, nothing. So stop it!*

She felt her body relax, little by little, as she laid out the bare truth to herself.

You're dead. You can't actually feel *anything. Not anymore. Not ever again.*

For once, her body believed her. The world stop spinning and she straightened up, cautiously opening her eyes. She looked around, the bile in her throat fading away. She took a deep breath.

Now what?

She felt an ache, deep and low. She wished Jonah was here.

Well he's not here and you have no to blame for that but yourself, she told herself fiercely. *So put on your big girl pants.*

She knew what she had to do; she'd just been procrastinating this whole time. Time to stop stalling. She needed to find out what was on the other side, she needed to know what she needed to have when she crossed over, and, then by God, she needed to go through that tunnel.

She set her jaw and with a determined glint in her eye, she turned left and started walking.

A half hour later, she started to severely regret her decision to strike out on her own. The sky opened up, like someone had turned on a fire hose. Fat, driving sheets of rain spilled from the sky, sending pedestrians fleeing for cover.

Irene dodged backward into a recessed doorway, flattening herself against the wall in an attempt to keep dry. She began to shiver and goose pimples broke out across her arms and chest.

"You're not cold," she told herself, but the trick didn't work this time. Her brain could not ignore the evidence of her eyes — she was cold and she was wet.

She hunched up, curling hedgehog-like into a ball and found that this put the top of her head outside the overhang's protection. She straightened up, pushing back into the recess, but grew cold again in an instant. She bounced back and forth between the two positions several times. "For God's sake!" She wrapped her arms around herself. *What I wouldn't give for a towel.*

A towel!

She reached for the beach bag, lying forgotten at her feet. She pulled out the towel, shook it, and then draped it — blanket-like — across her chest and arms. Then she slid down to the ground with as much grace as her dress allowed, trying several different ways of arranging her legs in an attempt to protect her modesty before giving up and just pulling her knees up to her chest.

Irene's teeth chattered. She burrowed farther under the towel, which was quickly becoming sodden, pulling her knees tighter against her chest. As her eyes adjusted to the gloom she began to pick out human-sized mounds scattered along the opposite sidewalk—in doorways, in alleys, and one brave living soul across a subway grate right out in the open getting drenched. The living and the dead were both present, mingled indifferently together.

Jesus. Death—the great equalizer. I'm a freakin' MBA for Christ's sake and now look at me!

She sighed and laid her forehead on her knees.

Vaguely she became aware of a repetitive sound—a low, deep booming. It took a moment for her to realize it was the sonorous peal of a church bell. She raised her head, listening hard. *Yes, most definitely a church bell.* The sound made her feel hollow and sad. She felt something on her cheek. She put up her hand and found that her face was wet. She wasn't sure if it was rain or tears. She laid her head back down and waited for the rain to stop.

Sometime later, she came to with a start.

She had been sleeping.

It was night now. She squinted, trying to bring the world into focus through her sleep-blurred eyes. There were shadows moving out in the rain, which was lighter now, but still coming down in a steady stream. She squinted harder and the images resolved themselves into people, moving together in a pack or maybe a processional. The droning buzz that she heard hovering just above the sound of the rain became words, and she realized that it was chanting. The people walking in the rain, surrounded by the now familiar blue-glow of the dead, were chanting.

"Pax tecum. Pax tecum. Pax et bonum."

The scene was surreal. It seemed like a dream and she pinched herself, to be sure that she was awake. A small band of what were clearly priests, despite the assorted styles of clothing they wore, were moving together in a small, slow parade. She recognized the black robes and white collar of a

Catholic priest, but the others were a mystery: white frilled robes, somber dark suits, plain white or black robes covered in surplices of various colors, and even a robe of what appeared to be burlap tied shut with a rope. The headgear and facial hair were just as varied. When she noticed a set of mutton chop sideburns on a man wearing an Abraham Lincoln-like hat and another wearing a hairstyle—bald in the middle surrounded by a wreath of hair—that she had only ever seen on depictions of Friar Tuck, she knew she was seeing a collection of people that spanned hundreds of years.

The procession was led by a nun and what Irene—a non-practicing Protestant—assumed to be an altar boy, both shaking hand bells. Every person's silhouette shimmered with the pearlescent glow that marked the dead. Something seemed to be running before them down the street—a large, black, shapeless mass dodged sideways and disappeared between two buildings. Irene felt a jolt. The Uglies—and they were afraid of the priests!

"Sanctity for the dead. Peace for the dead," the procession chanted, drawing closer.

Individual members of the group would break off to head down side streets or into buildings. When one headed in her direction, their purpose became clear: they were rounding up the dead.

Irene struggled to her feet, tangled in the sodden towel. She poised for flight, ready to run, if necessary. The man approaching her was dressed in a simple black dress shirt—no white collar—and plain black slacks. He moved through the rain as if he didn't notice it, despite a complete lack of protection—no raincoat, no umbrella, no galoshes. He was older; in fact, one of the oldest dead people she had yet seen. He looked to be in his sixties and his tall, thin frame was emaciated by age. His thin, white hair was cropped short. He gave her a warm, comforting smile. "The church is always open to you," he said, passing within a few feet of where she stood, frozen with surprise and fear. Then he continued down the street and the rain swallowed him and all the rest up.

She sank to the ground, still not sure she wasn't dreaming, and wrapped her arms around herself to try and stop the shivering. The night was still again except for the rhythmic patter of the rain. She laid her head back down, her thoughts tumbling over in confusion, and for some reason, she felt even sadder than before.

This time, when she awoke, the rain had stopped. The sky glowed silver in the lightening dark. It was the pre-dawn. The sun would be up soon. She rose shakily to her feet, feeling stiff and cold. The sodden towel dropped to the ground and she left it. She straightened her wet dress as best she could, the slippery fabric now clinging like Saran Wrap, and stepped out of the alcove. She looked around, trying to orient herself. Where was she? More importantly, which way was the car?

She hesitated and then turned left. In two blocks, she crossed into a nicer area of town — the financial district, judging by the wide, well-kept sidewalks and the tall, modern skyscrapers rising like redwoods above her.

An alley branched off to her right. Irene heard a rustling sound at her feet and looked down in time to see a rat, surrounded by a blue glow, scurry out of the alley and run past her. She felt a jolt of amusement as she thought to tell Jonah she had seen a ghost animal, and then her heart plummeted when she remembered that she wasn't likely to have the opportunity.

She looked into the alley as she passed. It was longer than she expected, running about fifty feet back. It was dead-ended by a wall of bricks — the backside of an abutting building. A feeble campfire burned low, and something turned on a makeshift spit over it. Irene paused, blinking in surprise. A figure crouched beside the fire, facing in her direction. Man or woman, the person wore a dark trench coat and a baseball cap pulled low, obscuring their face so that she could not tell if it was a man or a woman. At that moment, the person looked up and then slowly rose to his or her feet, unfolding skyward. The motion seemed to go on for a long time and when it was finished the figure towered over Irene so that she had to crane her neck to look him in the face—she figured anyone that tall had to be a man. The baseball cap obscured his eyes, but Irene had the distinct impression that he was looking directly at her, despite the fact that he was not blue. She noticed, too, that the trench coat fit oddly—it appeared to be at least one size too big, loose, and ill-fitting across the shoulders and waist, but pulling tightly across the chest.

"Hello?" she said, taking a tentative step forward.

There was no response.

"Can you see me?"

"I see you." The voice was low and deep, like the lingering resonance of a vibrating bass note. The words came out long and slow, as if it took a great effort to form them.

Irene took another hesitant step forward. "How? You're not dead."

"I see you," the man repeated. Something flashed white in his face and Irene thought he must have smiled. She wasn't sure why but she suspected she should be glad she couldn't see it clearly. Irene's gaze darted around the alley as she tried to assess the situation. Her eyes came to rest on the spit and she realized with mounting horror that a skewered rat was cooking over the fire.

She shuffled in place, her feet unable to decide if they wanted to move forward or back. "Uh…my name is Irene."

The man stiffened, as if suddenly on alert. "You give me your name?"

Irene felt a flutter of panic. She had a sudden sense of overwhelming danger, as if she had made a terrible mistake.

He seemed to understand her sudden fear because she saw a flash of teeth again. "Your name—it is of no use to *me*."

Irene bristled, angered by the feeling he was purposely trying to intimidate her. "Oh yeah? Well, then, why don't you give me *your* name?"

Another smile. "It would be of no use to *you*."

"Okay, you know what…" Irene took a step back, "sorry to have bothered you." She backed away, keeping him in sight, as she headed for the street.

"Samyel," he said, with reluctance, his teeth flashing.

She paused. "Samuel?" she repeated.

Another flash of teeth, this time accompanied by what sounded like a rustling noise. "Close enough." Somehow, she knew that he was laughing at her.

There was a faint glimmer when he moved that she couldn't quite place—it wasn't the pearlescent blue glow of the dead. The glow seemed to be more of a brittle, silver shimmer, like shards of a mirror reflecting a bright light. She couldn't decide if he was dead or alive.

She realized he was looking her up and down, and while she couldn't be sure, she thought his eyes lingered on her hips, her stomach, her breasts. She took a step backwards.

"Don't get any ideas," she warned, too late.

He took two long strides toward her, emanating menace, and she panicked. She turned and fled, blind terror consuming her. There was a long, low, deep noise behind her, and somewhere deep in the recesses of her brain she recognized it as a snarl. She pounded down the alley and out into the street. She ran blindly, stumbling in her heels, her only thought to put as much distance between her and the savage, unnatural thing behind her.

She risked a glance backward. Then she slammed into something solid. She recoiled from the impact, falling backwards onto her behind, feeling—rather than hearing—someone say, "oomph" as she did so. She looked up and saw Jonah. He was shaking a foot and glaring at her in exasperation.

"Ouch," he said matter-of-factly, looking down at her. Then he held out a hand to help her up.

She stared at him in stupefaction, not understanding how he could be there. He shook his hand at her, encouraging her to take it.

She remembered Samyel, and she looked behind her. The street was empty. She turned back to Jonah, staring at him uncomprehendingly. Then she started, coming to, and grabbed his outstretched hand. "Oh Jonah!" she cried climbing to her feet and throwing her arms around him, unrestrained relief washing over her.

Jonah stood there rigidly as she hugged him. "Er, get off?" he said, but it sounded more like habit than annoyance. "Look, are you going to do this every time you haven't seen me for a few days?"

Irene laughed shakily and let go. She looked at him, but he looked down, suddenly shy. He took a step back and held out one clenched hand. Hanging from it was an olive-green man's suit coat. He looked up and met her eyes. "I brought you a jacket," he said.

Irene hesitated for a second, instinctively defensive. The small gesture seemed like censure, but his face was a careful blank as he watched her closely, silently waiting for her to take the jacket. The anger faded. Not censure — a peace offering. She took the jacket, hesitated, and then shrugged into it. It was big enough to nearly wrap around her a second time. She tucked the edges under her arms and clamped her arms to her sides to hold the coat in place. She felt oddly comforted and protected by the coat, as if he'd just given her a Kevlar vest.

"Thanks," she said, somewhat grudgingly. "How did you find me?"

He grabbed her wrist and held up the wristwatch. Just as quickly, he dropped her arm again.

"Oh." She looked at Jonah for a minute, feeling like she should say something more.

Jonah's face suddenly sharpened and he took a step toward her, tensing. "What's wrong?" he asked.

Irene realized that she was shaking. She remembered Samyel and quickly glanced over her shoulder again. The street was still empty, with no sign of him. "Uh…nothing. Just a creepy guy. We should go."

Jonah craned his neck, trying to see behind her.

"Not creepy like homeless wino kinda creepy," she said, grabbing his arm and trying to turn him around. "I think he was a serial killer."

Jonah scoffed. "I don't think there's any such thing."

"Of course there are serial killers." She tried unsuccessfully to push him forward down the street.

"Of people who are already dead?"

"I mean it, Jonah, the guy was seriously creepy, and I think he was dangerous. He was roasting a rat on a spit!"

Jonah didn't seem to be taking her concerns very seriously, and in fact, this new piece of information seemed to intrigue rather than frighten him. He stepped around Irene, heading for the alley she had just left.

"If you get murdered, I'm not going to save you," she warned, trailing behind him.

Jonah turned his head and shot her the cheeky grin that so often both exasperated and amused her. "Come on," he said. "It's empty. There's no one here."

It was true. Samyel had disappeared.

Jonah was looking around the alley with bright eyes, taking in the fire, the scattered crates, and the roasting rat. She hesitated, not sure what to say to him.

"Jonah," she said at last, "I think maybe you and I—"

"Come on," he said gently, taking her by the hand and leading her, like a child, closer to Samyel's fire. That was it. No apology, no explanation needed. She felt her heart pinch, and she suddenly wanted to cry, though she couldn't say why. She made a great show of fanning her skirt before the fire in order to dry it.

Jonah was watching her and seemed to know what she was thinking. He cracked a thin smile and said, "You know, this doesn't mean we're going steady."

She tried not to smile but couldn't help herself. "Don't be such a smart ass."

A self-satisfied grin spread slowly across his face, from ear to ear. He crouched down near the fire and picked up the spit, holding it out to her. "Toasted rat?" he asked.

"Uh, a world of no, thanks."

He shrugged and surveyed the rat critically with one eye. Then with another, deeper, shrug—as if to say, "Oh well,"— he pulled off a piece of meat near the thigh and popped it in his mouth.

"You did *not* just do that!" Irene cried, pulling away in disgust.

Jonah chewed thoughtfully for a minute, letting his mouth fully experience the flavor. He swallowed. "Tastes like—"

"DON'T say it," she said with a warning look.

He grinned. "No, it really does."

She shook her head. He coughed slightly, as if something was stuck in his throat, and he swallowed again, laughing. "Actually, not really. I'm also not entirely sure this is done." He cast the skewered rat aside.

Irene laughed. "That will teach you."

Jonah wiped his hands on his pants and looked around the alley. "What are you doing here, anyway?"

"Being lost, mostly."

Jonah raised an eyebrow and straightened up. Irene sighed in resignation. "I tried to take your advice. I was trying to do research."

The other eyebrow went up.

"Then it started to pour and I ended up sleeping in a doorway. Now I'm cold and wet, and then there was this creepy guy in the alley…"

Jonah stared at her in amused disbelief. She bristled with irritation. "You know, I survived perfectly well for thirty-six years without you."

"I don't see how," he replied.

"Hey, listen, no one asked you to—"

"So I should just go home, then?"

Irene bit back what she was about to say and uneasily shifted her weight from foot to foot. "No," she conceded with bad grace. "You should stay here and help the senile, incompetent, old woman."

Jonah gave her a smug smile. "Don't be so hard on yourself. You're not senile. Yet."

"Just incompetent and old?"

He laughed and dodged away, as if afraid she was going to swat him. "Why…why you…you…" she stammered, laughing.

The fire was between them now and he gave her an arch look across the flames. "I hope you are about to say handsome genius."

She sputtered for a moment, taken aback by the way he had so neatly turned her own words on her. Then she laughed. She couldn't help it.

"You're getting awfully cocky," she grumbled.

"Yup." He grinned as he dropped into a cross-legged sitting position on the ground.

"It's not really an attractive quality."

His eyes crinkled with laughter. She looked for a place to sit and decided on an upended milk crate. She smoothed the hem of the coat over her knees.

"Just so you know," she said, "I'm not a complete idiot. I did manage to find out some stuff while you were gone."

"Really?" he said, as if he found this hard to believe.

"Yes, really!" She bristled, ready to launch into a tirade about all she had accomplished while he was gone, but he headed her off by laughing. "I was just joking."

She shifted on the milk crate, trying to find a balance between comfort and modesty. "You know, I can't always tell when you're joking."

He looked up, meeting her eyes. For a moment, his expression was as frank and unwavering as Ernest's. "Ditto," he said.

They stared at each other for a long moment.

Irene looked away first. She swallowed hard and looked into the fire, wrestling with herself, and then said, "I found the tunnel."

His eyes widened and he sat up straighter. "What? How? Where…?"

She let out a half-laugh, brittle and dry. "When they say the stories are all true, they really mean it. In the most literal sense. It's just like I said in the park, the tunnel is everywhere. Literally, anywhere you look. Just follow the light. Any light." She pointed at a nearby street light. "Like that. Just stare at it for a minute."

He stared at the light and then looked at her. "What? What am I supposed to see?"

"You have to stare at it until your eyes go out of focus. You know…like one of those 3-D magic eye things."

He tried again and then shook his head. "I'm not seeing anything." Frustration sounded in his voice.

"Well, you're not doing it right."

"Me? Why is it my fault? You're not explaining it right!"

"There's nothing to explain. Just stare at the light until you go all cross-eyed."

He tried again and then shook his head, indicating it still wasn't working.

"Okay, well try another light…" She pointed at the fire. "Try that."

He stared hard, not blinking.

"Anything?" she asked after a minute.

He shook his head, still not breaking eye contact with the flames. She looked into the fire herself, letting her gaze go lax. The flames swirled and ran together and she felt them pulling her forward, into the golden vortex, just as before. She blinked and pulled back.

"It's there," she said. "I can see it."

He looked at her, his face a mask of confusion. "Maybe it doesn't work on me."

"Why wouldn't it work on you?"

"Maybe…maybe because I'm not really dead?" There was something in his voice—fear maybe—that raised goose bumps on her arms. She stared at him, a sinking feeling in the pit of her stomach.

"Jonah…" She couldn't breathe. She saw his shoulders jerk, like a spasm, and knew he understood as well as she did what this meant. He shook his head, as if he refused to believe it.

"You can't go with me," she whispered. She began to shiver, despite the heat of the fire, and tears prickled in her eyes. She looked away, trying to hide her disappointment. "I should have known…it makes sense. You said it yourself. People go and they don't come back. It's a one-way trip. If you went…"

He jerked to his feet. Worry bleached his face. "You don't have to go!" he cried. "I thought you were going to stay?" She heard tears in his voice. "You could stay," he repeated in a hoarse whisper. "Other people do. I'll visit you and we can do stuff..."

She shook her head, not looking at him. "I can't stay, Jonah. You know it as well as I do. I have to go."

"I don't get it. Why did you change your mind? You were so dead set on staying. What happened?" Now he sounded angry. "Is it that guy?"

Everything she'd been holding back—all the fears she had refused to voice, all the bewilderment and confusion she had refused to acknowledge, all the frustration she had refused to give in to—suddenly burst forth. "Because this place sucks! People work...for no money. Because there isn't any money. Because there's nothing to buy. There's nothing to eat, nothing to drink, nothing to do. We just trade the same junk back and forth. I traded ketchup packets for booze, and I already had booze! I traded *ketchup*, for something I already *had*. Dimes are suddenly the most valuable form of currency. It doesn't matter anyway because even if we could buy stuff, we have no place to put it. We're all homeless. Everyone sleeps at the library or on the street!"

The anger burned out as quickly as it had flared. She deflated and tears trembled in its place. "It's like...this place is all used up. Just like you said—it's all washed out, faded and gray. There's nothing new here for the dead. Whatever you died with—not just stuff, but thoughts, experiences, emotions—that's it. That's what you're stuck with. It's not real life anymore, Jonah.' Her voice cracked. "It's a memory—a memory of life. And I can't stand it."

His eyes were dull under his deeply furrowed brow, but he nodded.

"So, are...are you going to go now?" he asked, struggling to hide the quiver in his voice.

"No, not yet. There are a few things I need to do first." She stood up and smoothed out her dress, now dry from the fire, trying to exude a nonchalance she didn't feel. "Like get my car." She looked around the alley. "I don't suppose you know where it is…in relation to here, that is?"

He gave her an inscrutable look. "Where's the map?"

"Map?"

"Map," he repeated.

"Oh shit, the map!" She dragged the beach bag closer and rifled through it. "I completely forgot." She found the street map near the bottom of the bag and pulled it out. She spread it wide on her lap and then looked around the alley. "Of course, a map only works if you know where you are."

Jonah shook his head. "Wait here," he said.

"I really am a smart, capable woman," she called after him.

She heard a scoffing laugh. He went to the end of the alley, looked in both directions, and then returned, dropping back into a sitting position beside her. He snagged the map from her and, pulling it into his lap, bent his head to study it. After a minute of close study, he folded the map, handed it to her, and rose to his feet.

"Come on."

They were only two blocks from the car.

She cried out in surprise when the car came into view. He looked like he was going to say something smart-ass, and she cut him off, saying, "Smart. Capable. Woman."

He raised his eyebrows but didn't say anything.

As they drew closer to the car, she said, "Look, it's almost morning, so there's no point in going all the way home just to turn around and come back again, but I'm really tired. I'd like to rest a bit before we do anything else." She stowed the bag in the back, climbed in, and then settled back in her seat.

"So you just want to sit here?" he asked, incredulous.

She reclined her seat and turned on her side, facing away from him, so tired she could hardly keep her eyes open. "It's been a long couple of days, Jonah. While you've been sleeping in a comfortable bed, I've been sleeping on a basement floor and in doorways out in the rain."

"It hasn't been a picnic for me either," he said quietly.

She turned quickly, looking at him over her shoulder. His eyes were dark and unreadable. He looked like he wanted to say something. She turned away and pulled the coat tighter around herself, tucking it under her chin.

"What have you been doing since…since I saw you last?" she asked.

She heard him shift in his seat, and she thought he probably shrugged. "Going to school. Stuff."

She lay there, waiting for him to say more, but he didn't. The silence stretched out and the darkness began to feel thick and oppressive.

"I thought you had left for good," she said softly.

She knew he was still there. She could feel it, could feel him staring at her, his eyes burning into her back.

She hunched down into the coat farther until it nearly covered her ears. "Why did you come back?"

He didn't answer right away. She could hear him turning over answers in his brain. Finally, he said, "I just wanted to be sure that you were okay. I wasn't planning on staying."

She watched the threads of dawn snaking around the edges of the buildings. He seemed to be waiting for her to speak. She wasn't sure what he wanted or expected her to say.

She heard him shift in the seat and knew he had turned his back on her. The air vibrated with…hurt? Embarrassment? Frustration? She knew that, once again, he was disappointed in her.

"Jonah—" she said, her voice heavy.

"I'm going to go home." His voice was low and muffled. "Just for a minute. I have to make my mom think I went to school. I'll come right back."

She could tell the minute he disappeared. The car felt empty without him and a sick ache gripped her stomach. She shivered and burrowed deeper into the coat, clenching her eyes against the bitter burning tears that assailed them.

Twenty-Three

She came full awake with a jolt. Jonah sat in the passenger seat, watching her.

"Do you know that you snore?" he asked.

She frowned at him, disoriented and cobweb-brained. "Who are you and why are you bothering me at this ungodly hour?" She rubbed the sleep from her eyes.

"It's nine-thirty," he replied.

She craned to see all around her head in the rearview mirror. "Is my hair sticking up?"

He surveyed her critically. "No."

"I want food." She self-consciously patted her hair anyway and then opened the car door.

He tumbled out the other side. "I brought some more sandwiches."

"*Real* food."

"Real live or real dead?" he asked.

"Real *breakfast*."

She smoothed her clothes, patted her hair one final time, and then said, "Come on," motioning him to follow her. They headed down the street. Jonah was in a buoyant mood, and his head was continuously in motion as he twisted and craned to gawp at the buildings, the sidewalks, the window displays, and even the light posts. Irene strode along, glancing at him from time to time out of the corner of her eye. She had trouble not laughing. She wasn't sure why he found everything so interesting, but he seemed to be in an exuberant mood, delighted with everything he saw.

After a while, she found his mood catching. She began to study the landscape, too, and they began trading trivia and arcane facts, pointing out odd-looking people, and sharing snatches of personal trivia. His favorite sandwich was peanut butter and banana. Her favorite candy was black licorice. His dream place to visit was the moon. Hers was Paris.

"Yeah, Paris would be cool," he said. "There's miles and miles of catacombs under the city where all the dead people are buried."

"How do you manage to make everything about the afterlife?" she cried, torn between amusement and exasperation.

He shot her a cheeky grin. "It's a gift."

It took a little hunting and a few wrong turns, but she managed to lead him to the dead boarding house.

The inside was as roughhewn as the outside. The floors were plain boards and the trestle tables and benches were unfinished.

They sat down on opposite sides of the table—the rough wood of the bench scratching the bare skin on the back of Irene's legs and thighs. A surly ghost-woman with frizzy hair hustled over and sloshed glasses of not-dead water down onto the table. Then she glared at them, hands on hips.

"Do you have a menu?" Irene asked.

The woman glared harder. "You'll eat what we have."

"O-kay...then, uh, what's the question?"

The waitress thrust her hand under Irene's nose. "This ain't a charity! Money then food."

This led to a prolonged negotiation that started with a request for more cash than Irene had, which Irene countered with offers of some cash plus gum, cigarettes, or candles, and ended with Irene paying for breakfast with her earrings. Though her face still looked stiff and unfriendly, the waitress seemed satisfied as she pinned the earrings to her own ears and there was a swing to her hips as she sashayed off to get their food.

Jonah was playing with his silverware, arranging and rearranging it until the three pieces were perfectly parallel.

Irene filled him in on her adventures—the market, Herman, the Ghost Festival, and what she had learned— the Uglies, how perception changed the way you looked, and how the living could send stuff to the dead. He hung on every word, his eyes growing bigger and bigger until they threatened to swallow up his face.

It hadn't felt that way at the time, but seeing it all through Jonah's eyes, she could see how it was all kind of...cool. A whole secret world, layered right below the real one, visible only to those with the eyes to see it. Irene looked around at the rough and shabby restaurant and for the first time appreciated how special it was. It shouldn't exist. It was crazy that it did. Yet, here it was. Here she was.

"So, I've been thinking..." she said, as the waitress returned to drop a metal pie plate of sausage, scrambled eggs, and something runny—possibly Hollandaise sauce—in front of each of them. The waitress then stomped off without a word. As Amy had said, the food was from the land of the living, so Irene dug through the beach bag and pulled out the last two ketchup packets. She handed one to Jonah. He raised an eyebrow.

"It'll make the food taste better," she said, spreading the contents of hers across her plate.

Jonah watched her take a bite and then seemed convinced it was okay. He tore open a corner of his ketchup packet and formed a little lake of it on his plate. He speared a sausage with his knife, dipped a minute bit of the end into the ketchup, and nibbled the end. He made an appreciative face, as if surprised that it tasted good, and then proceeded to stuff the rest of the sausage into his mouth.

"So, I've been thinking," she repeated, picking up what she had been about to say before. "The next couple of days, before I go, you and me, the adventure of a lifetime, just like you wanted, right? We'll go check out everything ghost related—I'll show you the market...whatever you want. What do you think?"

His mouth was hanging open, a sausage suspended halfway to it. "Really?" he said.

"Really." She looked down at her plate. "You didn't have to help me but you did. You skipped school, you lied to your parents. I do recognize that's a big deal. So we'll just kick back, relax, have fun for a couple of days. Deal?"

Now he was looking at her suspiciously. "Who are you and what have you done with the real Irene?"

"God, I hope that's not what you really think of me." She was only half joking.

"No," he said, his ears turning pink as he ducked his head and became intent on shoveling food into his mouth. "You're okay."

"Gee, thanks," she said dryly. "That's almost the Good Housekeeping Seal of Approval."

He looked at her blankly.

She laughed. "Come on, finish your breakfast, Gulliver. Adventure's waiting."

Twenty-Four

Jonah was in raptures over the market. He ran around like an overexcited puppy, gawking at everything in sight, trailing exclamations like a kite tail—"Wow!" "Look at this!" "Holy cow!"

Irene let him go. It was funny to see him so feverish. She wondered if he had much opportunity to cut loose in real life. He was pretty tight-lipped about his life on "the other side," but she thought she had a pretty clear picture. He was tall for a fourteen year old and short for a tenth grader. Two years younger than his classmates, he had to compete for friends, social status, and dates with boys who had jobs, cars, and facial hair. He was smart, conscientious, courteous, sweet, and considerate—in other words, a social pariah in the cut-throat world of high school popularity. Plus, given how easily he kept up with his schoolwork despite missing so many days, school obviously posed no challenge. No wonder he spent all his time doing whatever he could to avoid school.

She'd seen the pictures of his stolid parents and his vain, self-centered sister. She couldn't imagine that a dreamy, imaginative boy who believed in magic and who looked for the best in everyone fit in well there, either. Sure, they didn't beat him or anything. They just wouldn't have the interest in or time for anything he was interested in. She perfectly understood how frustrating and lonely that was.

Jonah materialized at her elbow and grabbed her hand. "Come on, come see!" he cried, tugging on her arm. She let him pull her over to one of the vendors, who was selling an array of ghostly swords.

"Isn't this cool?" Jonah asked, picking up one of the swords. "They're from all different time periods, all left behind by dead people. I think this is Roman! It's hundreds of years old. I think you should get it."

Irene choked in surprise. "I'd look cute with a sword."

He frowned down at it. "It's not very long, and it's pretty light. It'd be okay for a girl."

"I was thinking more that it doesn't go with my outfit."

When he looked furious, she laughed. "Joking!" she said hastily. "I was joking. Besides, what do you think I need a sword for?"

He gave her a sidelong glance. "Just in case."

The Uglies flashed through her mind. She remembered them fleeing before the procession of priests. Somewhere in the recesses of her brain she made the connection. She whacked Jonah in the chest with the back of her hand.

"Wind chimes!"

"Wind chimes?" he said, starting so badly he nearly skewered her with the sword.

"They're bells."

"Uh, you've gone kind of incoherent."

"The Uglies can't stand the sound of bells! They stopped chasing me when the church bell began ringing, and the priests I saw were ringing bells. That's what the wind chimes are for."

"Yeah, I guess," he said. "Bells are supposed to ward off evil spirits. That's one of the reasons that churches have bells." He looked at her in amazement, clearly impressed. "Wow."

"Yeah, yeah," she said. "Don't get mushy on me. Look and see if anybody's selling some bells or wind chimes."

They combed through the vendors, finally finding one who was selling a variety of improvised bells—a tambourine, a big, black wrought-iron triangle like the type used to call farmhands to dinner, a set of sleigh bells, a tiny hand bell formed of delicate china, and a dainty set of metal chimes shaped like a pan-flute. Jonah advocated for the wrought iron triangle, arguing that it was the loudest, but Irene picked the metal chimes, on the basis they would be the easiest to carry. The negotiations over price took a while because Jonah wouldn't let her trade the pepper spray, which the vendor was perfectly willing to take as payment.

Irene argued that the pepper spray was useless since there was no way it could work on beings that, technically speaking, had no eyes or nose.

"It's not actual pepper spray," he reminded her. "It's the essence of pepper spray, and you need a weapon."

"Yeah, but still, if someone has never been sprayed with pepper spray before then they're not going to feel it. They need to be able to remember what it feels like…"

"Then fine, trade it for a sword."

"You and that sword! The best offense is a good defense. I'm better off getting the wind chimes."

In the end, she had to trade the two chocolate bars she had picked up during the Ghost Festival, which she had really wanted to hang onto.

"After vodka, chocolate is the thing that makes life bearable," she moaned to Jonah as she tucked the wind chime into her bag. "I hope these stupid things are worth it."

They continued shopping. Jonah generously traded a sweatshirt he had in his backpack for a blanket, which he then handed to her. "Just in case," he said, not looking at her. His ears were pink again. She hid a smile as she tucked the blanket into her bag. She knew he'd think she was being condescending if she said that someday girls would find his gallantry irresistible, so instead, she pretended to look at a jar of marbles.

She continued shopping, looking for flashlight batteries — without success — while Jonah wandered off to watch the coffin reclamation work. He came back, his face shining with excitement, and he related every minute detail of what he'd seen.

"Did you know they send the stuff on to the afterlife? They were pretty tight lipped about how they do it, but apparently there are whole cities of the dead on the other side, and they use the wood and stuff to build things!"

"Cities, huh? Well, that's good to know." Maybe things on the other side wouldn't be so bad, after all.

She was picking through a collection of items in a shopping cart manned by a non-dead man—clearly homeless—who watched her with eagle eyes. The man had long, dirty fingernails, and he sucked on one, cleaning it cat-like, as he waited for her to finish.

Jonah noticed what she was doing and stopped mid-sentence. "What are you going through that for? Remember, you can only take dead stuff with you."

"You know, I am smarter than I look." She shot him a dry look. "I know I can only take dead stuff through the tunnel. Since I'm going to be here for a while longer, I thought there might be something useful. However, I was wrong." She turned away from the cart. "You see everything you wanted to see?"

Jonah nodded. "Yeah...but are you sure you don't want to get that sword? I really think—"

"No," she said firmly, steering him toward the exit.

She led him next toward Chinatown, wanting to show him the "post office" wall where the living could send things to the dead and all of the different charms—the lines of sand, the bundles of dried sage, clusters of nails, and the painted symbols—used to keep ghosts out. She knew he'd love all that stuff. In fact, he'd probably get so excited, he'd have a heart attack.

They crossed the street, dodging around pedestrians and cars. Irene knew they were near Chinatown now, running parallel to it, and she hunted for a cross street that would take her directly into the neighborhood.

They rounded the corner and Irene halted, feeling like someone had thrown ice water over her. His back was to her, but there was no mistaking him—the trench coat, the baseball cap, the sheer improbable height of him. It was the man from the alley.

Samyel turned at that moment, almost as if he knew she was there.

She stepped back, crushing Jonah's foot, and then whirled around, knocking into him. "What the—" exclaimed Jonah.

"Run," she hissed. "It's him!"

Irene was pushing Jonah—trying to turn him around, trying to get him to run—but suddenly Samyel was there, in front of them. With preternatural speed he had overtaken them and was now blocking their path. In the daylight, she could see that he wore dark glasses and had jet-black hair hanging in a sheet almost to his waist.

"Irene." Samyel said her name, and she went cold at the sound of his voice slithering over the syllables. His lips drew back and Irene's mouth went dry with fear. She had the insane idea that he was trying to smile, but it was all wrong. His teeth, small and sharp, were bared, as if in a snarl and his lips were locked in a grotesque rictus, a parody of a smile. "I was mistaken," he said in his strange, rasping voice. "Your name is of use to me."

Jonah, turned, thrusting Irene behind him. "Get away from her!" he cried. He snatched the wind chime out of her bag and shook it threateningly at Samyel.

"Jonah," Irene hissed, pulling him backwards, away from Samyel, "I don't think that works on him. He's not dead!"

There was a snarl and Samyel raised a hand, striking out at Jonah. Irene reacted instinctively. She shoved Jonah out of the way, shouting his password as she did so, "Supercalifragilistic…"

Jonah disappeared.

Samyel advanced on Irene and she backed away. Her back hit a wall and her heart sank. There was nowhere to run, no way to escape. Samyel came closer, raising a hand, fingers curled into claws. Irene, blinded by panic, did the only thing she could think of—she lashed out with a well-placed stiletto to the groin. To her surprise, she connected. Samyel faltered and put a hand to the spot as if he had felt something — though apparently not the searing, gut-curling pain she had hoped for.

There was a dry, grating sound, like dead leaves rubbing together. Irene realized it was the sound of Samyel laughing — at her.

"Pain," he said, when he finally stopped laughing, as if identifying an interesting scientific specimen.

It dawned on her that she should have run when she had the chance. He had her cornered. Frantically, she scrabbled backwards, her back against the wall. *"For God's sake, you're a ghost!"* she berated herself. *"He can't hurt you."* She didn't believe that, though. After all, she had hurt him — however minutely.

Samyel had stopped advancing after she kicked him. Now he seemed to be studying her. Then, to her surprise, he said, "I have passed through the underworld door. Nothing grows and nothing dies. All that was and would be, is."

She blinked, stupefied, not sure what he meant. It almost sounds like a password or a message of some sort.

Then Jonah was there, charging forward, head down, arms wind-milling. She grabbed him by the shirt collar and yanked him back. "Wait...stop!"

"What are you doing?" he cried, frantic, grabbing her roughly by the shoulders as if trying to both hug and shake her at the same time. "Get out of here...Go...Run!"

For a moment, there was a tangle of limbs as he grabbed her and she grabbed him, each to push the other out of harm's way. She won, managing to get him — straining to break free — half beside, half behind her. She spoke to Samyel as she held Jonah at bay with an arm thrown across his chest.

"What do you want?"

Samyel stretched out a hand toward her, seeming to reach for her neck. She grabbed the collar of her coat, pulling it closed about her throat, and said with daggers in her voice, "So help me God, if you try anything, I'll jimmy kick you into another time zone."

Samyel froze for an instant and then, with infinite care, he reached out with a single finger and tapped Irene's coat, directly over the place where the stone pendant that she had gotten from Scalper rested. "Utukku," he said.

Beside her, Jonah, who was quivering with adrenaline, jerked forward as if to attack Samyel. Irene pushed her arm against Jonah's chest to restrain him. She looked at him, to see if he'd understood what Samyel had said, but he didn't see her. He was glaring at Samyel through slitted eyes.

Samyel seemed to be waiting for an answer. He tapped the necklace again. "I seek passage."

"Passage? What do you mean, passage?"

"I wish to travel…when you return."

She felt Jonah stiffen the same moment she did and knew he had calmed down enough to hear and understand what Samyel was saying. She released him and stepped away, straightening her dress and pulling the coat tight around her with chilly dignity. "Are you crazy? You just attacked us!"

"I?" he said, and he sounded genuinely surprised.

Irene opened her mouth to argue and then stopped as the scene replayed in her head. She realized that she had been more frightened of Samyel's appearance than any of his actions. There was something…unnatural…about him, strange and aberrant, as if he just shouldn't be. She had instinctively reacted with revulsion and fear, before he had even done anything. In hindsight, his actions hadn't been particularly alarming—he'd taken a swipe at Jonah, that was true, but only after Jonah shook the wind chime in his face—and he had stopped advancing after her one feeble kick.

"Take you *where*?" she asked suspiciously, folding her arms across her chest. Jonah made a choked sound of protest.

"Come." Samyel gestured, indicating that they should follow him. "We must go."

"Go? Go where?"

"Away. Inside. Or they will see."

"Who will see what?"

The dark glasses revealed nothing as he stood impassively for a moment. "Everyone."

Samyel *was* attracting a lot of attention. The crowd moving around them was giving him a wide berth, and he was the focus of a lot of strange looks, which just confirmed that he wasn't dead—people could see him. Irene knew that it looked like a seven-foot tall man in a trench coat and dark glasses was talking to himself in the middle of the sidewalk. It wouldn't be long before the cops came to investigate.

Irene gestured for Samyel to lead the way. "Fine. Let's go."

Irene heard another choke of protest and glanced at Jonah. There was a silent exchange of mouthed words, pantomimed gestures, and angry, exaggerated looks.

"Don't be crazy," Jonah hissed. "You can't go with him!"

"You're the one that always wants to stop and talk to every weirdo we meet," she countered. "And what do you mean 'you'? We're both going."

"Uh uh," Jonah said. "This is your idea. If you get murdered, I'm not saving you."

With an exasperated look, she motioned for Jonah to follow and set out after Samyel, who was nearly out of sight. Jonah reluctantly followed. Irene gave him a wry look as they trailed, side by side, a few feet behind Samyel. "You know, at some point, we're going to have to talk about your propensity for picking fights with people bigger than yourself."

"What's propensity?"

"A really bad habit that you should stop."

Jonah's expression turned unreadable for a long moment, as if he was debating with himself, and then he looked away, stuffing his hands in his pockets and bowing his head to stare at the sidewalk as they went.

"I've changed the password, by the way, so you can't do that again," he said darkly.

She grabbed his arm, pulling him to a halt. "Jonah, listen to me. It's not that I don't appreciate you trying to protect me. I do. Even when it's annoying and misplaced, like with Ernest. You're the bravest, sweetest guy I've ever met, but I'm dead. You're not. I'm already probably going to Hell for dragging you along on this adventure. Don't add being the cause of your death to my list of crimes, okay?"

The tips of his ears had turned pink and his head was down, shoulders hunched. Then, to her surprise, he suddenly looked at her, his eyes inquiring as he searched her face. She didn't know what he was looking for, but he was gazing at her so earnestly that she blushed.

Before she could say anything further, Samyel called to them. He had halted a few feet ahead of them, in front of a squalid, boarded-up building. He held aside the board covering a first floor window, indicating they should enter. Reluctantly, knowing that her conversation with Jonah wasn't finished, Irene went to see what Samyel was pointing at.

She peered into the gloomy interior. There was a rustling noise—as of skittering rodents—and she drew back. "You're kidding, right? There's no way I'm going in there."

Samyel stood impassively, silently waiting for her to enter. She looked at Jonah but he wasn't any help—he just shrugged as if to say it was entirely up to her. She sighed, thought to herself, *this is such a bad idea*, and then climbed through the doorway into the darkness beyond.

She groped in her bag and managed to find the flashlight. She clicked it on and shone the light around. As expected, it was a dingy rat's nest of filthy, torn furniture, discarded appliances, old blankets, and garbage. She didn't look too closely, suspecting that she should be glad she couldn't see the fine details. There was a smell in the air—mold and decay along with something sharper, more foul—and she hoped it was just the smell of unwashed bodies or rotting trash, rather than something dead.

She could also see people and realized with a jolt that it was a squatter's camp—for both the living and the dead. She shuddered, feeling both pity and revulsion. It reminded her that while she wanted to give Jonah a few days of enjoyment, she couldn't let him lull her into staying too long. She didn't want to end up like these people — worn away to nothing and living off scraps.

Jonah came up beside her, followed by Samyel who, still wearing the dark glasses, moved unerringly through the dark as if he didn't need the light.

"Alright, talk," Irene said. "What do you want?"

Samyel tilted his head, as if confused by the question. "Passage."

She frowned. There could only be one place that he'd want her to take him, but the request didn't make any sense. "Let me see if I understand this. You are alive and I am dead. You want to get to the afterlife, and you want me to take you with me — through the tunnel — when I go. Does that about sum it up?"

Samyel nodded. "Yes."

"Uh huh." Irene waited for him to say more, but he didn't. In fact, he seemed to be waiting for her to speak, for her to give him an answer. "Okay, let's start at the beginning. Why do you want to cross over to the other side if you're not dead?"

He stared at her, his face an unreadable mask behind the sunglasses. "My business."

"Okay, yeah, but if you go through the tunnel with me, won't you...die?"

He gave her the imperturbable, blank-faced look again, this time cocking his head a minute amount, as if the question puzzled him. Irene had to concede that the question might not actually make any sense — what, after all, did it mean to be dead? It was supposed to mean the cessation of life. However, despite supposedly dying, here she was, still...alive. She realized with an inward groan of frustration how woefully inadequate the English language was to describe her current situation.

"I mean, if you want to get to the land of the dead so badly, can't you just kill yourself? What do you need me for?"

He let out one of his low, rasping chuckles but didn't answer the question.

"Uh huh. Okay, well try this on for size—how exactly am I supposed to bring you along? I'm not entirely sure you'll fit in my bag."

She heard Jonah hiss and knew he was worried she was going to aggravate Samyel. However, Samyel didn't seem bothered by her sarcasm.

"You will open the tunnel. I will be able to cross."

"So we just hold hands and jump in together?"

Samyel remained impassive. Irene took that as a yes.

"I will pay," he rasped in his slow, strange voice, as if sensing that he hadn't convinced her. "With a…favor. To owe."

"Yo, man, shut up!" someone called from the dark. "People are trying to sleep."

Irene looked Samyel up and down. "You would owe me a favor?" she asked incredulously. "Okay, well, first of all, I'm not sure what kind of favor you could do for me, and certainly not before we left—"

"Not here," he corrected, his voice echoing faintly in the empty space. "There."

Irene blinked in surprise. "In the land of the dead, you mean?"

"Yes. I…will come if you call me." This he said with great reluctance, as if he was hesitant to promise such a thing. "I will…assist you."

What was it Madame Majicka had said—*you need a guide. Just spread a little goodwill around and one will generally show up.*

Apparently, here was hers. So all she had to do was this one teensy tiny favor of very possibly making the very big mistake of letting him into the land of the dead. There was probably a very good reason why he couldn't get there on his own.

On the other hand, it wasn't going to cost her anything to take him with her and she might even benefit from it. The danger of possibly dying in the process was his problem, not hers. So why not take him?

"Okay, fine…" There was another hiss from Jonah. She reached out with her elbow but he was out of reach.

"Not yet. I need more…time," Samyel said.

"How much time?" she asked suspiciously.

"A day. A month. Hard to know until I have finished."

"A month?" she cried. "Well, fuck that. I'm leaving in a few days. You're either ready when I am or you get left behind. I'm not hanging around here for a month to satisfy you, that's for sure." Then she stopped to reconsider. "Well, actually, maybe I can work with that…" She began to think out loud. "I want to get that book from Madame Majicka, and I want to go through your book again"—this was directed to Jonah—"to see if there's any 'know before you go' tidbits…"

Jonah had drawn closer to her and now he tugged on her arm. "Irene…"

"…and I still want to show you some stuff,"—also to Jonah—"like the dead post office…"

Jonah tugged harder. "I can't stay here for a month," he said quietly.

It took a moment for the words to sink in. Then she started with alarm and grabbed him by the shoulders so forcefully she was very nearly shaking him. "Well you can't leave me alone with *him!*"

Samyel's lips pulled back in a ghoulish smile, revealing his sharp, shark-like teeth. "I don't bite," he said, chomping his teeth together in a grotesque display that reminded Irene of a chattering wind-up toy.

Irene looked at Jonah again, shaking her head forcefully back and forth. "No. Way."

His expression was obscured by the dark, but in the pale light of the flashlight she could see worry etched in sharp relief on his face. "I know!" he hissed in an undertone. "I don't think you should be alone with him, either. I think we should leave."

She cast a furtive glance at Samyel over her shoulder. He saw her fearful look and he smiled his horrid smile again.

"Jonah, I think we need him…well, I mean, *I* need him. I think he's the guide that Madame Majicka talked about.

Plus, it will be good to have a friend on the other side..."
She shifted uncomfortably. "I...I still don't know what's
on the other side, and I'm not sure I'm going to be able
to...to really do it, unless—"

"I don't think he qualifies as a friend."

"Jonah," she pleaded. "Please...I really do need you
this time—"

"What do you want me to do?" he cried. "You know I
can't!"

Irene had a sudden inspiration. "Look, you'll just have
to lie."

"To who?" he asked, bewildered.

"To your mother. Tell her...tell her you're going on a
school field trip."

He looked at her as if she had lost her mind. "Are you
crazy? She'd know if I was going on a field trip...there's a
permission slip...and...and...they have to pay..."

"Okay..." Irene said, thinking fast. "So make up a
permission slip. You kids these days and your
computers," she added satirically, "the things you can
do."

"Why is she just getting this to sign a day before I
leave?" Jonah asked in a flat, irritated tone that indicated
his resistance to the idea was weakening.

"Because," Irene continued smoothly, "you are a
scatter brain who put it in your backpack and then forgot
about it."

"Of course."

"The letter will say that parents just have to provide
spending money because..."—she thought for a moment
and then continued, her voice rising in triumphant self-
satisfaction—"because the students did fundraising to
pay for the trip."

"Uh huh."

"And...ah...that's it. Easy."

Jonah cocked his head and glared at her through his
eyelashes. "Uh huh. Easy."

"Look, I used to do this kind of stuff all the time," she
said. "Trust me."

"What about my body? What am I supposed to do with that for a month?"

"Go to my house. There's a key under my neighbor's door mat."

The whispery, rustling-paper laugh sounded. "We are agreed," Samyel said as if the conversation was finished.

"A month is too long," Irene replied. A month was long enough to settle into a routine, to start enjoying herself, to change her mind. Then a month would turn into two, and then six, and then a year and entropy would trap her here like Amy and all the rest. She didn't want that. No matter what horrors awaited her on the other side it had to be better than a creeping, lingering irrelevance. "I'll give you two weeks."

"More time."

"Fine, three weeks. Final offer."

When he didn't say anything, Irene assumed that he agreed to her terms. She turned back to Jonah, who was shaking his head. "What about school? They're going to call my parents to find out where I am."

"So forge them a note, too."

"Saying what?"

"Use your imagination," she said, turning him in an about-face. She moved her hands to the small of his back and propelled him forward with a small push. He turned to look at her with a mixture of irritation and worry.

"Look, I'll go to a hotel and get a room—because I'm certainly not staying here. It will be safe there, lots of dead people around. I'll be fine until you get back."

Jonah opened his mouth to protest but Irene cut him off. "Hurry," she mouthed with a meaningful look. He sighed, shrugged in resignation, and then, shaking his head, vanished.

Twenty-Five

As they moved through the revolving door, the lush interior of the hotel lobby came into view. A middle-aged man — dead — dressed in an understated but handsome black suit with an eye-catching red and gray tie got into the revolving door as they got out. Irene looked around. She hadn't really paid attention before when she had crossed this lobby with Ernest. She had been too angry, too determined, to pay attention to anything other than getting to his room.

The lobby had an old-fashioned, baroque opulence. Crystal chandeliers dangled from a gilt ceiling. The floor was white marble.

Irene took it all in, trying to figure out how ghosts went about renting a room. She saw that there were a couple of ghosts standing in the queue that snaked its way through a red-velvet rope line in front of the registration desk. Annoyed at having to wait — being dead really didn't seem to come with *any* perks — she reluctantly joined the line. Samyel, busily surveying the ornate ceiling of the lobby, followed more slowly, coming up behind her a few moments later. He didn't try to make conversation. They both just stared straight ahead.

The line inched forward in starts and stops. After a while, Irene noticed that the woman standing in line behind her was standing quite a ways back. Irene looked at Samyel with a critical eye. "Look, you're scaring people. Why don't you go over there" —she pointed to a couch—"and wait. I'll take care of this."

Ten minutes later, Irene reached the front of the line. A young man and a young woman, both alive and with the fresh-scrubbed look of prep school students, were huddled around one computer terminal, working in tandem to check people in. Another, slightly older man—also alive—with spiky blond hair and a round, acerbic face was typing furiously on another terminal a short distance away. As Irene reached the front of the line, the blond man looked up from his typing and beckoned her forward with a nod. His name tag identified him as "Chet."

Irene did the clichéd head turn in either direction to see who he was looking at. The woman behind her leaned forward, directing an inquiring look at him. "Are you open?"

"I'm sorry, ma'am, I'm not," he replied. "But you are next in line." Then he looked at Irene again, giving her a meaningful stare. Irene pointed to herself and he nodded sharply.

Irene stepped up to the counter. "Uh, how much for a room?"

He gave her an odd look. "How long will you be staying with us?"

"Uh, I don't really know…"

Chet typed furiously on his console. Irene was amused. She finally understood what the people typing away on computer terminals behind the counter at airports and hotels—and not assisting any customers when the line was a mile long—were doing. They *were* helping customers—dead, unseen customers.

Chet laid a key card on the counter. "Thirteen-twelve is all set," he said.

"Oh, uh…I'm sorry, I need two rooms…"

Chet gave her a look that seemed to convey a feeling of apology without actually being apologetic. "I'm sorry, but space is limited. We ask parties to share a room."

"Well…okay, but my…'friend,'" she pointed to Samyel, "is alive so I think he needs a regular…"

"Can he see you?" Chet asked, a note of superciliousness creeping into his voice.

"Well, yes, but…"

"Then he can see your room."

Irene took a deep breath to control her rising frustration. "Okay, fine, but don't you want my name or anything…?"

Chet lifted his eyes from the computer terminal in front of him just long enough to flick them to the key still sitting on the counter. "We just ask you to be considerate of our other guests," he said and then went back to typing. That seemed to be it. She was clearly dismissed.

Irene shrugged in resignation, took the key, and went to collect Samyel.

Samyel seemed faintly alarmed by the elevator. He hesitated before stepping in, looking the interior over as if he expected a man-eating tiger to jump out at him. "It is very…confined," he said, stepping gingerly into the gilded box.

They navigated the thin crowd of the dead, wandering or lounging in the hall aimlessly and reached their room, mid-way down the corridor. Irene couldn't help shooting a glance down the hall, seeking Ernest's door with a pang, as she unlocked their room. Inside, she was immensely relieved to see two double beds as well as a small couch since she'd forgotten to ask for separate beds.

She tossed her bag on one of the beds and then rounded on Samyel. "So…are you going to tell me what your deal is? You're not living, you're not dead…for God's sake take off the glasses, at least. We're indoors."

Samyel didn't pay her any attention; he was too busy studying the room. He slowly circled the perimeter, touching everything tentatively, as if checking to see if it was real. Irene sighed and turned away, finding his actions both annoying and unsettling.

Out of curiosity, Irene went to the nightstand and opened the drawer. Sure enough, there was a Bible there, glowing blue. She pulled it out, exasperated, and flipped it open.

"Book of the dead," Samyel said, dismissively, turning to look at what she was doing.

Irene, thinking he wanted to see it, closed it and handed it to him.

There was an irritated hiss. "I do not read the tongues of men," he said haughtily, as if offended.

She blinked in surprise. Not sure which part of that sentence to attack first, she settled for what seemed the most obvious: "So I take it English isn't your first language?"

He laughed then, a long, hard, full-bodied chortle that went on for a long time. She tossed the Bible back into the drawer and slammed the drawer shut. "What's so funny?" she demanded when he didn't seem inclined to stop.

With difficulty, he got control of himself. "My English must be *very* good. You speak with no mouth. You hear with no ears."

Her brain sputtered to a halt. "What? What do you mean?" But she wasn't stupid. She understood him well enough. She was dead. Technically, she no longer had a mouth—or vocal cords or ears—so how was she talking to him? Telepathy? Electromagnetic waves? Shared hallucination? There wasn't an option that wasn't terrifying and problematic.

"You know what?" she said, pointing. "That's your side of the room. Why don't you go there and stay the hell away from me."

With a low, sandpapery laugh, he complied. Irene rubbed her hands up and down her arms. She was suddenly cold, and she knew it had nothing to do with the temperature. She pulled the jacket tight around her and sat down on the couch to wait for Jonah.

Twenty-Six

At some point she had gone to bed. When she awoke, Jonah was propped up on the couch studying the big, black book.

Three weeks to kill. Three weeks until she left behind the land of the living forever.

She sat up and threw back the covers. "When'd you get back?"

"A while ago."

"And? Any problems?"

He was engrossed in the book and gave a kind of shake of the head that included his shoulders — a vague, indistinct wobbling motion that she took to mean no. "I have to check in by phone once a day."

She looked at the other bed and saw that it was neat and empty.

"He's gone," Jonah said without looking up.

"Gone? Gone where?" She swung her legs over the edge of the bed.

Jonah shrugged. "He was gone when I got here."

"Is he coming back?"

Jonah raised his head, his expression exasperated. "I. Don't. Know. He. Was. Gone. Before —"

"Okay, okay. I get it." She stumbled out of bed, yawning. "So I'm just supposed to sit around waiting for him to come back?"

Jonah gave her another look.

Hastily, she added, "That was a rhetorical question. I just meant that if we decide to go out, he'll have to wait for us to get back to let him into the room since there's only one key." She had gone to sleep still wearing the suit coat over her dress, wrapped securely in its olive-green folds. Now she shrugged out of the jacket, carefully draping it over a chair back. When she turned around, Jonah was watching her closely. He ducked his head, turning his attention back to the book. She crossed the room and sat down on the couch beside his legs, nudging his feet out of the way with her hip.

"What do you want to do today? I promised you adventures."

He sat up, swung his feet to the floor, and shifted closer, moving the book so it spread across both their laps. "I think we should go through the book and make a list of everything we know about the afterlife."

She grimaced. "That's your idea of adventure, huh?"

He made an impatient sound. "We can go out later, if you want. I just want..." He looked at her and then quickly looked away again, but not before she'd seen the worry in his eyes.

She put her hand on his and gave it a quick squeeze of gratitude, feeling very protective of him suddenly. "Yeah, okay. You're right. I need to be prepared."

He relaxed, looking relieved.

She pulled a pen out of the beach bag and then, realizing she didn't have any paper, pulled out one of the magazines and found a page with a lot of white space. Pen poised above the paper, she said, "Okay, so what do you want on this list?"

"I think we should try to make a map of the afterlife. We should find out everything we can about what the place looks like."

"What do you mean?"

"Well, like...here..." —he flipped pages—"it says how many levels there are to the afterlife."

"Well, yeah, but you said it could also be just the hall of judgment and then straight to Heaven, without anything in between."

"It's probably both. Madame Majicka said all the stories are true."

"Well, how could it be both? That makes no sense."

Jonah sighed impatiently. "Look, I have an idea about that, okay, so can you just—"

She held up her hands in surrender. "Okay. Fine. I won't give you a hard time. You're in charge. I'll just do what you say."

"Finally!" he said, pushing the book toward her again.

In retaliation for the wise crack, she playfully hit him in the arm with the magazine. He laughed.

They worked for the next hour, slowly flipping through the book without talking. Occasionally, one of them would say something like:

"Is that an *f* or a *t*?"

"It's a *k*."

"Didn't I see something about a bridge a few pages back? Do you remember what page that was?"

When they were done, Jonah closed the book with a thump while Irene sat back and stretched like a cat. Then she took up the list they had made.

"Okay, so we've got…a hall of judgment. A river crossed by boat. A river…" She squinted at her handwriting, "of fire crossed by a bridge. Wait…really? I think there's some logistical problems with that—"

"Just keep reading."

"Uh…a bridge made of stars. City slash village of the dead. Forest. Mountains. Desert…Oh come on!"

"Keep reading."

"Oh for God's sake…uh, a castle slash banquet hall…Okay, how is this helping me exactly?"

"Look, I think I can make a map. This is all the stuff the book seems to indicate is real. So if we look at the stories where these things appear, we'll be able to figure out which order they come in and where they are in relation to each other."

She eyed him for a moment, admiration warring with concern over just where this idea had come from. "You've given this a lot of thought, haven't you?"

He looked uncomfortable for a moment. Something about his face, his discomfort, the sudden furtive air about him worried her and made her heart thump with uncertainty.

"Jonah, promise me you're not thinking of doing something stupid."

He sprang to his feet, pacing away from her impatiently. "I'm doing this for your benefit, not mine," he said hotly.

"Yeah, okay, I know." She felt guilty for her suspicions but still wasn't able to shake them. "I just —"

"Look, why don't we go out and do something now," he said, grabbing his backpack. "We can finish this later."

She hesitated, not sure what she could say or do to either reassure herself Jonah was fine or dissuade Jonah from whatever course of action he was considering if he wasn't.

"So, do you?" Jonah asked.

"What?"

"Do you want to go out?" He pursed his lips. "You're just standing there, staring into space."

She decided to drop the subject, as reluctant to pursue it as he was. She just had to trust that Jonah, who was in many ways more of an adult than she was, knew what he was doing.

She grabbed the jacket, shrugged it on, and then picked up the beach bag. "How about we go back to Madame Majicka's?"

Relief flooded Jonah's face. "Yeah, I wouldn't mind going back there."

They left the room, and he shot her a quizzical look as they stepped into the elevator. "Why do you want to go? You hated her."

"Yeah, but it turns out that book she showed me wasn't as batty as I thought it was."

The sun was out and the streets crowded with fall tourists. People with guidebooks and cameras strolled by or stood clustered on the sidewalk, while people with briefcases or overloaded shopping bags pushed past.

When they arrived at the magic shop, they found it closed. Irene wiped at one of the dirty windows with the hem of the suit jacket.

"Do you see anything that says when she's open?" she asked.

Jonah was peering, hands cupped around his eyes, through the window. He shook his head.

Irene stood back for a moment and then banged on the door. Jonah snorted, but wore a reluctant smile of admiration as he said, "You really don't take no for an answer, do you?"

She raised an eyebrow. "What would be the point of that?"

She rapped a few more times. No one answered. Well...that was disappointing. She thought for a moment, wondering what else they could do with what remained of the afternoon.

"While we're in the area, let's go back to Chinatown," she said, thinking of the aborted attempt to show Jonah all the anti-ghost charms she had discovered.

Jonah agreed and they retraced their steps back to the main street and then followed this for several blocks as Irene described the different ways the living tried to ward off the dead. As she had expected, Jonah was fascinated by both the "post office" wall and the different charms the living used to protect their homes.

Once they reached Chinatown, they took their time exploring. Each time she stopped to point something out to Jonah, he would pull out the book and start flipping furiously through pages, apparently looking for any additional insights the book might provide on a particular charm's effectiveness.

"Are you worried I'm going to come back and haunt you?" she asked him drily the fourth time he did this.

He made a non-committal noise and kept reading.

The afternoon flew by. Soon the sun was sinking low in the sky so they began heading back. Office buildings emptied out and the streets became more crowded.

They passed two dead women waiting at a bus stop, and Irene smiled when she overhead one say to the other, "I wish they'd buried me in something like that!"

They cut through the Public Garden, stopping to watch the swans lazily gliding over the water. "So, what do you think of Samyel?" she asked.

"I don't like him," Jonah said promptly.

She bit back a smile. "Care to be more specific?"

Jonah gave her a sidelong glance. "I think we should follow him. See what he's up to."

"Yeah, okay, Sherlock."

"I'm serious!" he insisted, turning pink.

"Yeah, well, I'd rather get my tongue pierced," she said. "I have no interest in what he's doing."

Jonah suddenly seemed furious. "I don't understand how you're not interested in stuff."

"I'm not interested in weirdos who might possibly be psychopaths. There's a difference. The less I know the better off I probably am."

They navigated around a group tour taking photographs in front of the "Make Way for Ducklings" statues.

"You know," Jonah said, "there are supposedly lots of otherworldly things in the afterlife."

Irene wasn't sure where this strain of conversation had come from, but was relieved to have avoided another fight.

"Yeah, I remember," she said. "Like the exhibitionist goddess who leaves her clothes all over the place, the three-headed dog, the goddess with the feathers who weighs your heart on a scale…"

Jonah looked impressed. "You have a good memory," he said.

Irene chuckled. "That's the first time a guy has ever complimented me on my memory."

Jonah's ears turned slightly pink but he didn't look away; instead, he just gave her a mock glare of exasperation. "Well, anyway, there's lots of otherworldly things in the land of the living, too—spirits, ghosts, death portents, and even demons. Like there's lots of cultures that think women who die while giving birth come back as bad spirits that try to lure people to their deaths. The Chinese and Japanese believe in all kinds of other bad spirits, too—people who commit suicide, girls who die before they get married. The Navajo believe in the Chindi, which is the spirit of a dead person that can make living people get sick and die."

"Well, they're not far off," she replied. "There are the Uglies—people who come back as...well, I guess you can call them monsters or bad spirits."

Jonah, clearly having warmed to his subject, was talking fast now, his words coming in a rush. "And that's just things that started out as people. There are other things, too, like in Ireland they believe in Banshees and the Welsh have a pack of dogs that hunt in the underworld called the Cŵn Annwn."

"Yeah, okay, this is all fascinating but I thought we were talking about Samyel?"

Jonah gave her another slow peeping glance. He stuffed his hands into his pockets and studied the sidewalk as they walked.

"Oh. You think he's one of these other things?" she said.

"Maybe." He kicked a non-existent pebble. Irene waited for him to work up to whatever it was he so obviously wanted to say. "I really think you should have something to protect yourself."

"You and that sword! The best offense is a good defense," she said primly, pulling the wind chime out of her bag and shaking it, causing it to tinkle melodiously.

"Yeah, well, bells don't work on Samyel."

She laughed. "I'm still not getting a sword."

Jonah cracked a smile, but he still looked worried.

When they returned to the hotel, Samyel was standing in the lobby, waiting for the elevator.

"Where have you been all day?" she asked. Samyel stared at her impassively from behind the ever-present sunglasses.

She rolled her eyes. "Whatever. I'm probably better off not knowing. Did you manage to do whatever it is you need to do?"

"No."

Before she could retort, a familiar drawl interrupted them. "Princess."

All three of them turned. Ernest was there, cigarette in hand, blowing a stream of smoke, his expression even more laconic than usual. She couldn't tell if he was pleased or annoyed to see her. His eyes were as dark as ever, smoldering as they caught and held hers. Suddenly she couldn't remember why she had walked out on him. Something telegraphed between them and her stomach fluttered.

His eyes left hers to sweep over her companions.

"Junior," he said, nodding to Jonah, who wore a deep scowl.

Jonah's hands clenched in response.

"I see you've picked up a spare," Ernest added, eyeing Samyel. Samyel's only response was to curl his lip in disdain.

The elevator slid open behind them. Jonah grabbed her arm and pushed her into it. Ernest's face was unreadable as the doors closed, blocking him from view. As soon as the doors opened on thirteen, Jonah said, almost angrily, "I have to check in with my mom" and disappeared before Irene could say anything.

"I suppose you have an opinion?" she said to Samyel as she unlocked their room.

Wisely, Samyel said nothing.

Twenty-Seven

Once again, Samyel was gone when she woke up. Jonah was sitting cross-legged on the floor studying the book.

"Don't you sleep?" she asked him.

He shrugged, lost in deep concentration.

"I'm going to take a shower," she said, tossing back the covers and trying to untangle the coat, which had twisted up with the sheets during the night.

"There's no towels," he said without looking up.

"What?"

He lifted his head just long enough to flash her a quick grin. "Ghosts don't need to shower."

"Well, Irene Dunphy does," she said. "Can you go back to my house and get me one?"

He rolled his eyes but shut the book and disappeared. He returned in a few minutes and handed her the towel.

When she came out of the bathroom a little while later, toweling her hair dry, Jonah was standing over Samyel's bed, sprinkling something onto it.

"What are you doing?" she asked with a mixture of curiosity and exasperation.

Jonah looked guilty, as if she'd caught him doing something wrong. Irene came closer and took the small bottle from his hand. "Sage?" she said. "Did you get this from my kitchen?"

He looked even guiltier.

"Are you seasoning him so we can eat him later?" she asked drily, handing him back the bottle.

Jonah turned pink and ducked his head. "Sage is supposed to protect against evil spirits," he muttered.

Irene frowned. "I think it's supposed to be hung outside the door, not sprinkled in the bed."

Jonah stuffed the bottle into his backpack without another word. Irene didn't want to hurt his feelings any more than she already had, so she changed the subject. "So, today...how about we go and look at some bridges? I know you had suggested that a while back."

He flashed her a look of surprise. "What's the point? You already found the tunnel."

"Yeah, I know," she said, pulling on her shoes. "I was just thinking about your map idea and how all the stories are true, but in really literal and weird ways. I don't know...it's hard to explain, but it seems like bridges and tunnels are special for some reason. They're mentioned so often in the stories, so I thought we should check it out, just to be thorough."

Jonah looked both astonished and impressed. She straightened up with a sigh. "Okay, stop giving me that look. I got my MBA from Bentley you know. I'm not a total idiot."

His ears pinked again and he ducked his head. She laughed. "Come on."

As they drove over the massive cable-stayed Zakim Bridge, Jonah pointed out that, like their expedition to check out tunnels, they couldn't see much if everything went by in a flash.

"There's no place to stop," she said. "We'll get run over."

"I don't think we..." Jonah stopped and then appeared to change his mind. "Actually, I have no idea if we can get run over or not."

Irene was so surprised to hear him admit he didn't know something she almost drove off the road as she stared at him in shock. "Are you feeling all right?"

"Watch the road!" he yelled, grabbing the door handle.

Irene laughed. "Settle down. We're fine." She laughed again as Jonah shot her a sour look. "Look, this bridge seems too new to have any mystical properties so let's move on."

Jonah wasn't entirely convinced by this logic but agreed to try the Tobin, a fifty-year-old green, steel monstrosity that stretched north from Boston to the working class city of Chelsea.

They drove over the outbound lower deck without seeing anything unusual. Irene got off once they reached the other side and turned around. They drove back into Boston over the upper deck; they didn't see anything unusual there either. Jonah wanted her to stop the car so they could get out and inspect the bridge more closely. As there was no place to stop on the upper deck, she had to loop all the way around again. They went back into Boston, circled around, went back up over the Zakim, and then back across the lower deck of the Tobin toward Chelsea. Halfway across the bridge there was a small pull out for construction vehicles and Irene pulled into it. They got out of the car and instantly Irene felt buffeted by the wind, much stronger here than it had been in the city. The bridge bounced and swayed gently beneath her feet.

"What's wrong?" Jonah asked, looking at her face.

"I don't like heights much," she said, knowing that she was turning a delicate shade of green that matched the nearby girders.

Jonah seemed surprised by this. "You're scared of both rats and heights?" He said this as if he found it hard to believe that Irene was afraid of two such pedestrian things. She was quick to correct him.

"I'm not scared of rats. I just don't like them."

She tried to walk a few steps, but the rocking and swaying of the bridge was like being on a boat, and she wobbled drunkenly.

Jonah's expression became a cross between disbelief and concern. "Maybe you better wait in the car."

That actually sounded like a great idea to her. She got back in and watched anxiously as he strolled the length of the bridge, peering over the railing into the water, gazing up at the underside of the upper deck, and studying the sturdy, steel supports. Then he strolled back past the car and kept going in the other direction.

There was no place to safely walk—not even a breakdown lane—and the cars passed frighteningly close to him. As he became a speck in the distance and then disappeared from view, her heart climbed into her throat. This was such a bad idea. In fact, probably the worst idea she'd ever had.

Time slowed, ticking by second by second. Jonah didn't reappear. Where was he? Had something happened to him? Had he been struck, fallen, or, God forbid, jumped? She thought of his evasiveness when she'd asked about how much thought he'd put into mapping out the afterlife.

Her heart thudded within her chest. She had the car door open and was halfway out of the vehicle when he reappeared, a black dot growing larger as he strolled leisurely toward her, hands in pockets.

He looked at her as he approached, appearing perfectly at ease, as if he had just returned from a walk on the beach. "What?"

She couldn't speak. She just stared at him, her eyes wide as relief washed over her, and then, without a word, got back into the car, where she sat, taking deep, calming breaths. He went around and climbed in the passenger seat.

"Did you find anything?" she asked and was surprised to find that her voice didn't shake.

"No," he said, giving her another curious look. "I think it's like before...I think this bridge is too new. We need to find something older."

She took one last deep breath, restarted the car, and pulled into traffic, continuing northbound.

"How about a break?" she asked as they crossed into Chelsea. Her hands, clutching the wheel in a death grip, were still shaking. "I was just thinking about the beach the other day. Revere Beach is only like twenty minutes away—why don't we stop? Do you mind?"

The surprised expression was back and he looked at her closely. "No, that sounds cool."

There were plenty of places to park—after all, it was a weekday in late September. People were at work, the kids were back at school. She felt a pang as, once again, she was reminded that life had gone on without her. Days were passing, seasons turning, and she hardly noticed it at all.

They took off their shoes and strolled barefoot on the beach, picking up seashells and trying to skip rocks across the water. Neither of them knew the secret of this particular skill, so they ended up doubling over with laughter each time one of them tried and, invariably, the rock hit the water with a plunk and then sank beneath the waves. Finally, out of breath, and nearly sick from laughter, they gave up.

To Irene's astonishment, they found a dead ice cream stand—the cart, vendor, and wares all glowing blue. In exchange for a bit of the perfume—hardly more than a thimbleful—she procured two sugar cones—one with black raspberry for her and one with cookies and cream for him—and they walked the beach, licking the cones in blissful silence. One advantage of dead ice cream, it turned out, was that it didn't melt in the sun, and they were free to eat it as slowly as they liked.

They stopped to watch a surfer bobbing gently in the waves, waiting for a worthy swell. "You know, I notice there's nothing about an ocean in any of the stories," Irene said absently, watching the breakers rock the surfer as he sat astride his board. "Why do you think that is?"

"The Etruscans thought the afterlife was under the ocean and that you had to ride a seahorse to get there."

"Who the hell were the Etruscans?"

Jonah shrugged and took a bite of his ice cream. Irene shivered. "Ugh, how can you stand to bite it? Doesn't that make your teeth hurt?"

He laughed. "Of course not. Technically, I don't have any teeth right now. Try it."

She gave him a doubtful look, but took a tentative bite anyway. She shrugged. "Well, okay, but I still like licking it better."

There was a lull in the conversation as they both focused on their ice cream and the waves. Jonah's eyes slid sideways to her. "Are you really going to take Samyel with you?"

She looked at him in surprise. "Yeah, of course I am. I said I would, didn't I?"

Jonah looked away, suddenly intent on watching the surfer struggle to his feet as a wave approached.

"Do I seem like the kind of person who doesn't keep her word?" she asked, hurt. "What have I ever done to make you think that?

"No, it's not that," he said quickly, looking at her, an unreadable expression in his eyes. "It's just...well...if you can take Samyel, then you can take me, right? We're both alive..."

She shook her head, suddenly scared. "Jonah, no!"

"Why?" he asked, dropping his eyes.

"What if you get stuck there, and can't get back? Or what if crossing over makes you die for real?"

"Yeah, but Samyel —"

"Jonah, I don't care what happens to Samyel. I do care what happens to you. As much as I wish you were going with me, I'm not willing to risk your life."

He looked at her again and now there was something shimmering in his eyes that she couldn't name — something sweet and gentle and hopeful. She flushed with embarrassment and looked away.

"I don't think —" he said.

"Jonah, *please*. Don't ask me again. I'm not going to take you, no matter what."

She braced for a tantrum, but he seemed to accept her answer, as if it wasn't wholly unexpected.

"We should go," she said.

They made their way slowly back along the beach, munching down the last of their cones. When they reached the car, he paused, hand on the passenger door. "Today was a good day," he said. It came out like a statement, but there was a question in his eyes as he looked at her over the roof of the car.

"Yes," she agreed with a smile. "Today was perfect."

My one perfect day on earth.

His eyes lit up for a moment as if he was pleased. Then, out of nowhere, a black cloud descended over his face and he scowled, as if suddenly angry. "I have to call my mom," he said abruptly. "I'll see you back at the hotel." He vanished, leaving her bewildered as to what she could have possibly done now to aggravate him.

"Teenagers," she muttered, climbing into the car.

Twenty-Eight

Irene's time on earth continued to tick down.

Over the next couple of days they continued with "adventure" excursions, Samyel disappearing each morning before Irene got up and returning to the hotel late each night. When Irene had asked him what it was he spent all day doing, he replied, "I go to see with my eyes. I go to hear with my ears," which had put an end to the conversation.

Madame Majicka's stubbornly remained closed, to Irene's annoyance.

"How does this woman stay in business?" she asked in exasperation after one visit, to which Jonah just shrugged.

Meanwhile, Jonah continued his "bad spirit repellent" experiments. Samyel hadn't seemed to notice the sage flakes in his bed. Nor did he take any notice of a crucifix hung on the door, garlic left under his pillow, or a handprint stamped on the door frame in red paint. This last attempt drew an irate visit from the hotel manager, though, who threatened to throw them out if they did any more of that sort of thing.

This morning, Jonah had booby trapped the room by sprinkling sand—apparently scavenged from their beach excursion—across the doorway. Now he was gone to check in with his mom while Irene finished getting ready.

"Irene!"

She was in the bathroom when Jonah bellowed her name. She yanked open the door. "What? What's wrong?"

"Big trouble!" He looked more agitated than she had ever seen him. His eyes were wild and his face white. "Someone came to your house and found my body!"

"What?"

He nodded. "Yeah, they called the police who called my parents. It's a disaster!"

She sank down onto the bed. "Holy shit!" She put a hand to her head, her thoughts a jumbled mess. "Well...what's happening? Where are you now?"

"In the hospital! As soon as I opened my eyes everyone started asking me questions and my mom was crying and then my dad was shouting at the policeman. I freaked out and came back here. What are we going to do?"

"Wait, no, this is perfect!" she cried, bouncing up, elated. "You can tell them where my body is."

"Are you nuts? They were asking me what I was doing at your house, how do I know you, did I know what had happened to you, that kind of stuff. They think that either you did something to me or that I did something to you!"

"Wait...what?" She felt the color drain from her face. "Are you saying that your parents—*and my mother*—think that either I'm some kind of child molester or that you're some kind of deranged lunatic?"

"Dis-As-Ter," he said, dropping weakly down onto the bed.

She sank down beside him and put her head into her hands again. "Holy fuck. Well this is just great. Here I was, worried that people were going to forget about me. Fat chance now. I'm going to go down in the history books right next to Lizzie Borden and Jeffrey Dahmer."

Jonah started to laugh. She lifted her head and looked at him. "It's not funny!"

"It kinda is," he said, wiping tears from his eyes.

"I'm having a hard time seeing the humor." Her first instinct had been for her own reputation, for what people would think of her, but now she realized the problem was a lot bigger than that. "You're in a lot of trouble," she said ruefully. "It's all my fault. I'm really sorry. I didn't think. I shouldn't have made you come with me. This was stupid."

He flashed her a grin. "It's okay. Honestly. Don't worry, I'll figure something out. Besides, I'm going to be a lot more popular at school now. I'm all over the news."

"Well, that's one way to look at it." She laughed, despite herself. Then she quickly grew somber again. "I really should make you go home, now, before this gets any worse."

He scoffed. "How are you going to make me go home? Besides, sending me home *would* make it worse. They can't do anything to me while I'm here."

"That's avoidance...and trust me, it doesn't solve anything."

Jonah wasn't listening. He pulled some paper out of his backpack and kneeled down at the coffee table. "Where's that list we made a few days ago?"

Irene pulled the magazine out of the beach bag and handed it to him. She watched him for a moment, her stomach churning with guilt. "I really think we need to figure out a plan to keep you out of jail."

He didn't answer. He just bent over the paper and began sketching.

"You know, it's really annoying when you ignore me," she said in a sing-song voice.

He looked up and grinned. "Come help with the map." He held a pencil out to her.

She took it, looking doubtful. "You want me to spend the afternoon coloring?"

He grinned again and then bent his head back down to his work. After a minute, she kneeled down beside him. "Okay, fine, what am I drawing?"

"The river Lethe is supposed to be to the east somewhere."

"Uh, can you be more specific?"

He shrugged. "Just put it wherever you think it goes. Just...make sure it's east."

A couple of hours later they were surprised when Samyel walked in. It was still early afternoon.

Irene didn't bother to lift her head from the mountains she was penciling in as she asked, "What are you doing back?"

Samyel didn't answer.

"Always good to talk to you." She set her pencil down and stretched. Suddenly, she felt restless and oppressed, as if Samyel's presence had sucked all the oxygen from the room. He reminded her that the clock was ticking on her time left on earth. She'd managed to successfully distract herself from all the worries, all the concerns— What waited on the other side? Was Samyel a demon? Was she going to Hell?—over the last few days, but the doubts sprang free now, crushing her beneath their weight.

She felt a sudden need to get out, to get away, to escape. "Let's take a break," she said to Jonah. "Let's try Madame Majicka's again."

"Uh…okay," he agreed reluctantly, setting his own pencil down.

Unexpectedly, Samyel said, "I will go with you."

Irene froze, hand on her bag, both surprised and aghast at the idea. "That's really not necessary," she said, hoping she sounded considerate, rather than horrified.

Samyel's lips pulled back and he chattered his teeth together in one of his horrible smiles. "It would be my pleasure."

There didn't seem to be any way to tactfully dissuade him, so without another word, they headed out. It was overcast and cool outside, but not unpleasant. The blustery, hat-snatching wind of late fall hadn't arrived yet and the clouds seemed to have kept most of the tourists—fearful of a downpour—inside. Even though it was early afternoon, the sidewalks were deserted, and even the traffic was unusually light.

Not unexpectedly, Madame Majicka's shop was closed. Jonah, seeming to sense an impending temper tantrum, put a hand on Irene's arm and said, rather quickly, "Why don't we walk around for a while and come back later?"

They ended up wandering through the Common. Samyel slowed as they passed a stone statue of a serene and beautiful angel, holding a bowl of water above the words "Cast thy bread on the waters for thou shalt find it after many days."

Samyel halted. He seemed to be studying the figure, turning his head this way and that, as if trying to get a good look at it. Irene couldn't read his mood behind the sunglasses — she couldn't tell if he was merely curious or incredulous.

Finally he said, "This is an angel?"

Irene nodded. "Yup. More or less. Sometimes they have halos."

"This is how you see them?" There was a teasing hint of something dark and dangerous in his voice, and she had the impression he was laughing — but she wasn't sure if it was at her or the statue.

"Uh, yeah, I guess. If one believes in them, that is."

"*You* believe in such things?"

"Cloud-sitting, feather-winged, harp-playing things? No. I don't."

There was a low, raspy whisper of laughter. "Very wise."

Irene felt a prickle of unease. Samyel was hinting at something, something she was sure had to do with the afterlife and what waited for her beyond the tunnel.

"What's on the other side of the tunnel?" she asked.

He stared at her blank-faced, and for the millionth time, she had the urge to snatch the sunglasses from his face and grind them underfoot.

"You have to give me something or I'm going to leave your ass here."

He shifted his weight, and she had the sense that her threat had actually made him worried. He didn't say anything though, and she thought he wasn't going to answer. Then, with what appeared to be great reluctance, he said, "Home."

Home? Her heart leapt. She had been right; he did know what lay through the tunnel!

"So what's it like on the other side, then? Is it like this?"

He was silent again and she had the impression he was searching through a catalog of possible responses for an answer. "I do not know."

"Of course you know. If you've been there before then you have to!"

"You and I are going to different places."

That stopped her. How was he supposed to be her guide if they weren't going to the same place? More importantly, how was she supposed to take him to some place she wasn't going?

A sudden surging realization pushed these thoughts aside. If he was a demon, as Jonah suspected, then home for him would be whatever Hell-like place existed. If, as he said, they were going to different places, then that meant she wouldn't be going to Hell — she'd be going somewhere else. It might not be Heaven, but it wasn't Hell.

Her stomach lurched buoyantly and she suddenly wanted to cry in relief. A thousand thoughts and questions tumbled through her mind, all competing to be heard. Before she could latch on to any single one, though, Jonah called to her, interrupting the conversation. He had kept walking — unaware that she and Samyel had stopped. He had finally realized they were lagging behind and was calling to them. Irene hurried to catch up.

"Okay?" Jonah said, shooting her a quizzical look.

Irene grinned. "Effervescent."

Twenty-Nine

The next day, Jonah suggested they check out some of the old cemeteries in the city. "I'd love to meet a pilgrim or a founding father," he said, eyes shining.

Sixteen days left.

Despite Irene's revelation of the previous day, she didn't really want to double cross Samyel—after all, she didn't really want to get on the bad side of a demon—so she decided to honor their bargain and wait out the full three weeks.

Irene smiled in amusement at Jonah's desire to meet a pilgrim. "Yeah, I guess that might be cool." She didn't point out that anyone still hanging around on this side would probably, and more easily, be found at the bar. She knew how that conversation would go.

They headed out to the Old Burying Ground, one of the oldest cemeteries in the city. After an hour walking around the small, black headstones—most worn almost smooth—hoping for some sign of the dead, Jonah realized the plan was flawed. "No one's been buried here for a long time. Everyone will have woken up and moved on ages ago." He leaned dejectedly against a tomb and kicked at the ground. Irene wished she could give him this. She could imagine the rapt look on his face as she introduced him to Alexander Graham Bell or Thomas Jefferson.

The bells of the church across the street began to peal, marking the hour. Sudden memories of the tunnel—the golden light, the suffocating weight, the crushing pain—surfaced, shattering Irene's buoyant mood. She'd been procrastinating finding out anything further about the afterlife because she'd been afraid of the answer. However, now that she knew she wasn't going to whatever demon-infested place Samyel was going, she felt brave enough to finally find out—and who better to ask than a priest?

Irene straightened up and nodded at the church. "Hang on a sec. I want to run in here."

Jonah eyed the building with alarm. "Are you going to pray?"

"No, smart ass, I'm not going to pray!"

He followed her as she crossed the street and climbed the granite steps.

"The doors are locked," Jonah pointed out when Irene pulled on them.

"Thank you, Mister Obvious."

He frowned. "I see sarcastic Irene has returned."

She gave him a quelling look and led him down the stairs and around the building. As she had thought, there was a ghost door there. Jonah looked impressed when she pulled it open, and they walked inside.

The interior was cool and dim, the walls dappled with shifting flashes of color filtered through the stained glass windows. They headed down the nave, past the endless rows of gleaming wooden pews—Jonah craning his head to study the vaulted ceiling overhead—to the chancel, where they found a ghost priest polishing the altar.

He looked up as they approached, a welcoming smile on his face. Irene recognized him as the priest she had seen in the rain—older, perhaps in his sixties, with close-cropped white hair, wearing a simple black dress shirt and pants.

He came forward, holding out a hand. "Howdy! I'm the Reverend Jim."

He shook hands with both of them as they introduced themselves and then he offered them a seat in the front pew. They all sat down, with Irene in the middle.

"So, death or dogma?" the Reverend asked, a hint of a southern drawl coloring his words.

Irene blinked in surprise. "Come again?"

The priest chuckled. "Most everyone who comes here is looking for answers regarding either death in general or Heaven and Hell in particular. Which are you?"

Irene hesitated. Now that she was actually faced with a priest, she didn't know what to say. She had a momentary flare of panic—perhaps it hadn't been such a good idea to come here. She had never been religious. God had always just been a faint concept, lurking in the background, like oxygen or gravity—presumed to exist but never actually consciously thought about. She stiffened with defensiveness at the thought that she might be required to pass some sort of dogmatic test before the priest would help her.

Reverend Jim smiled reassuringly. "Why don't I get us some coffee while you think on it?"

Coffee! *God, how she missed coffee.* "Is it dead?" she asked.

He said in a gentle but firm voice, as if correcting a small child, "Yes, it's spirit coffee." He left to fetch it.

"Spirit coffee?" she mouthed to Jonah, but he didn't seem amused. He was banging the front of the pew with his heels as though bored. There was a worried pucker across his face.

Irene poked his leg. "Quit that."

His drumming dwindled to a stop. "What is it, exactly, that we're doing here, again?"

"Just chill, okay? This will only take a minute."

Jonah huffed and stood up. He started to walk away, then stopped and, half-turning back to her, his voice dangerous, said, "Do *not* go back to treating me like a little kid."

Before she could respond, the priest returned with a tray holding three cups of coffee. He set it down on the pew between them. "So, what can I do for you?"

"Well, I'm just wondering about...about the other side?"

The Reverend took a sip of coffee and gave her an amused, but kind, look. "You know, my vocation doesn't give me any special insights into what the next world looks like. You know the old sayin' about doctorin' being about comforting the dying? Well, preacherin's about comforting the living. It's about helping people get through this life as best they can. If people live right in this life, then the next one takes care of itself." Her disappointment must have shown because he added, "Personally, I believe in Heaven. Perhaps not the literal description, but Heaven nonetheless."

"I notice that you didn't mention God in any of that."

"Would you find it comforting if I did?"

She blinked at him, a dozen tart responses flitting through her mind. She finally settled for, "What kind of priest are you, exactly?"

"I'm not — a priest, that is. I'm a preacher."

"What's the difference?"

"Well, when you get right down to it, not much. We're all in the God business, but if you want to be precise, I'm a Baptist, not a Catholic."

Irene ran an eye over the church's interior. "Uh, isn't this a Catholic church?"

Reverend Jim shrugged. "Beggars can't be choosers. When you've been carrying the load for a couple hundred years and someone offers to take it up, you gonna argue with him about the shape of his hat?" He smiled and slurped his coffee. "There's a rabbi manning the Episcopal Church two streets north and a Hindu at the Unitarian Church. It's all one and the same when you get right down to essentials."

"Yeah, but —"

He nudged the neglected cup of coffee in front of her. "You're not drinking your coffee."

Reluctantly, she picked it up and took a sip. Jonah had wandered back up the aisle, hands stuffed in his pockets, and now he drifted closer.

Seeing Irene's continued confusion, the minister leaned toward her. "Sister," he said, "at this stage of the game, people ain't comin' to church for a sermon, ain't comin' to hear the finer points of religious doctrine. They either believe or they don't. They want answers, maybe some comfort, maybe a kick in the pants. So a rabbi's as good as a priest, a shaman, or a traveling preacher."

"Well okay, but why are you sticking around here if you believe in Heaven? You're not in any kind of hurry to cross over? To find out what happens next?"

"Being a priest isn't a job you put down at the end of the day. It's a calling, a lifetime commitment."

"Yeah, well, you're dead, so—"

"An eternal commitment, then," he corrected. "The point is, we each got our own reason for choosing to turn around and linger here."

Jonah inched closer, coming to stand beside them.

"What do you mean 'turn around'?"

"Well, you know, most people just pass straight on through to the next life, but some of us, we see death and turn back."

"I don't understand what you mean," she said, setting the coffee down. She saw, out of the corner of her eye, that Jonah was listening intently. "I was alive, and then the next thing I knew, I was dead. I don't remember there being anything in between."

The preacher, his forearms resting on his legs, clasped his hands together and leaned forward. "Let me ask you a question. How did you die?"

An expanse of blue-green light intercut with swirls of white foam flashed through her mind's eye. Irene tensed. "I'm told that it's bad manners to ask that," she said, trying to make light of the question.

The preacher's gaze was frank and unwavering. "It is only if you're embarrassed by the answer."

She straightened, anger turning her spine to steel. "I'm not embarrassed!" she said hotly. "It was a car accident. It could have happened to anyone."

Jonah put a hand on her shoulder. She looked up into his worried face. "What?" She looked back at the priest. "What?"

"What kind of car accident?" Reverend Jim asked.

"Just...an accident. What does it matter? Dead is dead. There was no tunnel. No light. No skeleton with a scythe asking for my hall pass. Nothing."

"Did you cause it? The accident, I mean."

"No!" She started to look at Jonah, to repeat the denial, but then checked herself. "I mean...I might have fallen asleep at the wheel, but I only hurt myself, so what does it matter? I didn't kill anyone."

Jonah's fingers tightened on her shoulder — she couldn't tell if he was trying to give her a comforting squeeze or restrain her. She saw the priest exchange a glance with Jonah over her head. Jonah said her name — a soft, tentative whisper — but she refused to look at him. Anger — and something else she didn't want to name — bubbled up to wash hotly over her. She jumped to her feet. "Fuck you! You don't know me! You don't know anything about me!"

"You're going to have to face it sooner or later, whatever it is, if you really want to get to the other side," the preacher said placidly. "You'll have to go through death. There's no hiding and no going around."

"Irene..." Jonah's voice was pleading. He reached for her again but she stepped back, stumbling over the pew. "You know what? Fuck both of you!"

With that, she turned and fled, the echoes of her pounding footsteps tap-dancing across the vaulted ceiling.

Half a block away, she got hold of herself. Panting, she slumped against a building as a hot wave of anger and shame washed over her. She struck out, beating impotent fists against the wall, ashamed of herself. She let out a scornful laugh. When had she become such a watering pot, bursting into tears over the least little thing, letting people goad her into feeling angry or ashamed? What had Mrs. Boine called her — a trooper, for not crying at her father's funeral. Alexia had called her unflappable one night, when a yuppie stockbroker had gotten handsy — refusing to take no for an answer — and Irene had simply dumped her frozen Mojito on his crotch and gone on talking as if nothing had happened. When Aaron cheated, had she cried? No. Not one single tear. When Hal, whom she had gone so far as to move in with, had left, calling her an ice princess and slamming the door behind him, had she blubbered? No, not even then.

So why was she crying now? Hadn't she made up her mind to go, to face the lakes of fire and icy winds and razor sharp mountains? Why the sudden attack of nerves?

The priest's words echoed in her mind. *You're going to have to face it sooner or later.*

Blue-green light danced across her mind's eye and then Alexia and LaRayne's laughing faces as they leaned on the cab. *Want to ride with us?*

If only Alexia or LaRayne could see her now, weeping against the side of a building, out in the open where anyone could see, how they would laugh.

That thought was enough to stop the tears cold.

Irene took a watery breath and wiped her checks with the heel of her hand.

Deep down, she knew why she was crying — she knew what waited for her through the tunnel. She recalled the crushing weight and the searing pain she had felt when she discovered the tunnel — it was the same feeling as when the Uglies attacked her. It was death. It was the bald, ugly reality of dying. It was the moment when you stopped pretending you were still alive, that nothing had happened, that nothing had changed. It was the truth, plain and simple. All of it. The whole enchilada. The moment when all illusions would be stripped away.

She was going to have to relive her death, plain and simple. She was also going to have to relive her life and face some ugly facts about it — facts that had been nagging at her since she'd died but that she'd been ruthlessly avoiding.

Her death had hurt — that she knew — and she had been terrified and alone. That was all she could remember — all she wanted to remember. There was more, though, and none of it good. She didn't know if she was strong enough to face it.

Jonah came into view, dropping from a run into a casual saunter. He didn't look at her as he approached, but, instead, rolled to a stop and slouched up against the wall beside her to stare at the sidewalk in front of him. After a moment he said, "So...that went well."

It worked—she laughed. "Shut up!"

He grinned and risked a peek at her.

"I'm sorry," she said. "Really. I didn't mean what I said."

He brushed it off with a shrug. "So, who do you want to go yell at next?"

She shook her head, a snort of laughter escaping. She wasn't really in the mood to do anything else, so they headed back to the hotel.

Samyel was in the room. He must have gotten the manager to let him in.

"How was your day?" she asked, tossing her beach bag onto the bed and then sitting down beside it.

Samyel's face was as impassive as ever.

She kicked off her shoes and leaned back so she could wiggle her toes appreciatively. "Whatever. It's not like I care. I was just making conversation. The clock is ticking."

Jonah, who had seated himself cross-legged on the floor to rifle through his backpack, looked up when she said this.

"Don't look at me like that," she snapped, suddenly feeling constrained and irritated.

Jonah frowned and looked down at his lap. He reached for his backpack again, pulled out the book, and bent his head over it, becoming engrossed. Meanwhile, Samyel had curled up on his bed and appeared to be asleep.

Irene felt a little frayed, as if she wanted to laugh and cry at the same time. She looked around the room, taking in the scene. When she had imagined her life, was this how she thought it would end—trapped in a hotel with a fourteen-year-old boy with a death fetish and a demon from the afterlife?

Maybe that was the problem. She hadn't pictured her life—it had just sort of happened on its own. She had never had a burning ambition—ballerina, fairy princess, and racecar driver had all been extremely short-lived fads, and after age six, she couldn't remember a single thing she had wanted to do with her life.

Her eyes fell on her bag. The bottle of vodka was peeking out the top.

Irene couldn't stop Reverend Jim's words from running through her head: *You're going to have to face it sometime.*

Unbidden, an image of her heart being weighed on a scale came to mind.

She reached past the bottle, her hand hesitating only slightly over it, and pulled out a magazine, spreading it open on her lap in hopes of finding a distraction. She turned the pages absently, not really seeing them, as unwelcome thoughts continued to intrude.

Maybe Hal had been right—maybe she was cold. She couldn't think of a single thing she had been passionate about, a single cause she supported, a single person she had loved fiercely, a single moment so beautiful it had etched itself on her heart. When she reached the afterlife, what would her judges make of that? What would her grandmother and father?

She didn't even realize her eyes had strayed to her bag—to the bottle of vodka—again until she felt herself instinctively reaching for it and then she was holding it to her lips in an attempt to wash the thoughts away. When she lowered the bottle, Jonah was staring at her. Angrily she capped the bottle and stuffed it back into her bag. She jumped to her feet.

"I'm going out."

Jonah jerked as if he had been stung. "Out? Out where?"

Her eyebrows arched up in annoyance. "Just out." She angrily buckled on her shoes, not looking at him.

"Do you want to play a game or something? Cards, maybe?" Worry lines marred his forehead.

She hesitated, wanting to say one thing, meaning to say another. "Jonah," she finally said impatiently, "I don't need you to amuse me every second of the day. I'm a grown woman. I'm perfectly capable of entertaining myself."

He started to protest, but she brushed past him, the door closing behind her with a snap. She took the stairs two at a time and pushed her way out onto the street. Once outside, she felt better, less suffocated. She took a deep breath of the cool evening air, feeling the crisp touch of fall in it. The few stars visible above the city lights were cold and bright, and the moon, big and full, was low in the sky.

Unbidden, images flicked across her mind's eye, like flashcards—demons and goddesses, a heart on a scale, a pointing finger of condemnation, a lake of fire. She stood there, grasping the railing, looking at the sky, feeling nauseous.

"Princess," said a quiet voice behind her.

She turned around. For once, he wasn't smoking. He was simply standing there, looking at her with those dark, intense eyes, his hands stuffed in his pockets, looking almost shy and uncertain.

She didn't know what to say. "Hello" seemed too little and anything else seemed too much. She looked up at the stars again.

"Jonah says that there were people who believed that our time on earth was a prison, and that death releases us, but I'm starting to wonder...maybe it's the other way around."

He didn't say anything. She felt him move closer, standing so they were almost, but not quite, touching. She knew he was studying her. She could feel his eyes boring into her.

"How can you stand to stay here?" she asked wildly, turning to him. "Don't you want to do something— anything—just to escape?"

"Yes," he said, the word full of meaning. He reached out and touched her cheek, tenderly, with a single finger, and gave her a wistful smile. Then his look turned searching as he studied her face. Her breath caught in her throat. He leaned in, hesitating just a second, his lips a hair's-breadth from hers, and then he kissed her, his lips tender and soft. She let him, her eyes drifting closed, for just a moment. Then she gently pulled away.

"We tried that already," she said with a quiet smile, but her heart was pounding.

"I can do better." His mouth hovered just a heartbeat from hers.

Her lips twitched, on the verge of a smile. Then her gaze drifted down to his mouth and she felt a rush of desire. She looked up and she knew her eyes were saying, "Yes." He leaned in and she shivered in anticipation, expecting his lips on hers. Instead, he planted a gentle kiss on her forehead and then, taking her by the hand, led her back into the hotel.

Thirty

She closed the door as noiselessly as she could so as to not wake Samyel and Jonah, cringing at how loud the latch sounded. Then she turned around and saw that she need not have bothered — Jonah wasn't asleep. He was sitting on the couch, paging through the book. He didn't look at her. She froze, trying to assess his mood.

"I thought you'd be asleep," she said cautiously.

He grunted.

She relaxed. It didn't look like he wanted to fight. She set the bag on the floor and took off her shoes.

"I think we should go to the library," Jonah said abruptly, still flipping through the book and not looking at her.

"What, now?"

"Why not?"

"It's like three a.m.!"

He locked eyes with her for a fraction of a second, and there was something — anger? accusation? — in them. "You said we can get in any time." His voice was stiff. He went back to flipping pages.

"Yeah, I've already seen the library. Spent all the time there I care to." She really didn't relish the thought of seeing Doris, the dead librarian, again, or, for that matter, Amy. She had just sort of left Amy hanging, running off without a word after several days of being bosom buddies, and she didn't really want to explain why.

She flopped on the bed. Ernest *had* been better this time—he had been tender and sweet, and very thorough. The sensations had been real enough, in their way, to blot out everything else for a time, but it had still only been a faint echo of the real thing. She left feeling both the pleasurable lethargy of satiation and a heavy, frazzled melancholy—as if she was on the verge of breaking into a million little pieces. What she really wanted was to curl up, hedgehog-like, in the sheltering olive-green coat and sleep for a thousand years. She rolled onto her side and closed her eyes, trying to blot out everything around her.

"It will just be for a few hours," Jonah persisted. "Then we can go do something fun. Together."

She didn't move. "Define fun when one is dead. There's not a whole lot of options."

Jonah's voice grew terse. "You're doing that thing again that I hate."

"Argh!" she cried in frustration, bolting upright. "Fine! Let's go. God, you nag like an old woman. Anyone with any consideration would see that I'm trying to sleep."

"It's not *my* fault you're tired," he retorted.

She stared at him, trying to judge exactly what he meant by that. He was looking at her oddly, almost as if he hoped he had made her mad. A triumphant gleam flashed in his eye, just for an instant. Then he turned away to stuff the book in his backpack. "Besides, you're dead. You don't need to sleep anymore."

They didn't speak as they exited the room and made their way across the lobby. Once outside, however, she led him across Tremont, heading west.

Nervously, Jonah said, "I thought we were going to the library."

"I have a better idea."

He seemed to realize she was in a dangerous mood, because he didn't say anything else. A few minutes later they stood in front of the magic shop, which, unsurprisingly, was closed.

A ghost woman, dressed in fluttering rags, sat on the ground in front of the shop. "Penny for my bread, dear boy?" she croaked to Jonah in a cracked, high-pitched wheedle.

Irene was about to say something curt to the woman, but a meaningful look from Jonah made her bite back her words. She pursed her lips and then, nodding at the shop, said to the woman, "Do you know when this place is open?"

The beggar looked behind her as if astonished to find a building there. "What, this?" she squeaked in surprise. "Fits and starts, I suppose."

"Gee, thanks," Irene said. She surveyed the shop again and came to a decision. She began digging through her bag, hunting for the tire iron. She encountered a stray coin and she fished it out, absently tossing it to the woman. "Here."

She started to return to the search through her bag but stopped, frozen by surprise at the beggar's response to the coin.

The woman cackled with greedy relish, brought the coin to her lips, and kissed it. She jumped to her feet, a flurry of dust exploding upward from her lap.

"So long, suckers!" she cried, holding the coin aloft in one triumphant fist. She looked up, squinting at a nearby streetlight, seemed to concentrate for a moment, and winked out of sight.

"What was that about?" Jonah asked.

Irene was less impressed. She went back to digging through her bag. "Who knows, Alice? This place is a nut house."

"You know, it seems like coins are really valuable. Maybe you should stop giving them away."

"Too late," she said absently, pulling the tire iron out of her bag. "That was my last one."

She used the tire iron to beckon to Jonah that he should follow her as she led the way down the side of the shop and around the corner to the back. The alley that ran alongside the building opened up into a small pocket of asphalt rimmed with a tall wooden fence, which provided total privacy for the collection of odds and ends that littered the space. An old oil drum, cardboard boxes, and a mattress, all in various stages of decay, cluttered the space.

"What are we doing?" Jonah asked nervously, looking over his shoulder.

"Using the self-service check-out." She pointed. The back of the building contained only two features—a sturdy metal door and above that, a transom window, open about an inch.

Jonah looked doubtful. "The door's locked."

"The window, stupid."

Four-alarm panic spread across his face. "You can't be serious! You can't break in here, that's illegal!"

"Have you seen any undead cops? Who's to stop us?"

He shook his head. "You can't even fit through there."

"Yes we can."

"How are you even going to get up there?"

"I'm noticing a lot of 'you' being used suddenly."

"This is your idea, not mine." He put up his hands and backed away. "I'm not doing this."

"What are you scared of? Do you think she's going to turn us into frogs or something?"

"That's witches," he said, still shaking his head in refusal.

She made a cradle with her hands and held it out for his inspection. "Look, I'll boost you up."

"No. Way," he said.

"Oh, for God's sake!" she huffed, thrusting the beach bag at him. She marched over to the oil drum, and, by grabbing the rim with both hands and heaving, managed to rock it up on edge. She paused to give Jonah a smug smile and then, through a combination of rocking and shoving, managed to walk the barrel into position under the window. She stood back to admire her work.

"I need a boost up."

He stared at her, wide-eyed, as if he couldn't believe his eyes, and shook his head.

"Oh for God's sake," she said. She looked around, trying to find something to use as a step stool. Finally, she grabbed the edge of the barrel and started to hoist herself, like a gymnast mounting a balance beam, up on to it. Then she dropped back to the ground. "Turn around."

"What? Why?" Jonah asked, clutching the beach bag to his chest like a shield.

"Because this isn't going to be very ladylike and I don't want you looking at…" She made a vague motion with her hand and he got the picture. He turned crimson and whirled around with a cry of horror — "Aaackkkk!"

She hoisted herself up. She was able to get one leg up onto the drum by pulling her dress up around her waist. Then, with a bit of tricky balancing, she managed to both get fully on the barrel and stand up. She pulled her dress down and brushed her hair out of her face.

"Okay, you can turn around," she said, eyeing the window. "Where's the crow bar?"

"What, this?" he asked picking the tire iron up off the ground. "It's a tire iron." He handed it up to her anyway.

She inserted it against the open edge of the window and pushed, trying to force the window open wider. "Crow bar," she grunted through gritted teeth.

The window slid out half an inch with an ear-splitting screech. Jonah hunched his shoulders against the noise. "Jesus!"

Irene laughed. "What's the matter…afraid I'll wake the dead?" She looked at him. "Get it? I made a funny. You can laugh if you like."

"Did you?" he said absently, gazing around the narrow alley as if he expected to be arrested at any moment.

Irene sighed. "I don't know how someone so young got to be such a stick in the mud." Then she attacked the window again, redoubling her efforts. With a drawn-out, shuddering groan, the window slid open another half an inch.

Irene was panting, and she rested for a minute.

"Uh, Irene…"

She ignored him and applied pressure to the crow bar again, but the window refused to move. She pushed harder, putting all her strength into it.

"Irene..." Jonah said again, a note of urgency in his voice.

"This is stuck," she said. "Why don't you come up here and help—there's enough room—"

"Irene!" Now he sounded quite frantic.

"What?" she snapped irritably, looking down at him.

The back door stood open and Madame Majicka—clad in an immaculate charcoal gray pantsuit—looked up at her. Irene froze. The two women stared at each other for a moment.

Madame Majicka spoke first. "I suppose you want some tea."

"I don't suppose there's any way to convince you that I don't," Irene countered, but she was talking to herself. Madame Majicka had disappeared back inside.

With only a touch of awkwardness, Irene managed to get down off the oil drum. She snatched the bag from Jonah. "Some look-out you are!" she said. They followed Madame Majicka back inside.

"So, how can I help you?" asked Madame Majicka, setting the tea tray down on the same table as before.

Reluctantly, Irene sat down on one of the stools, dropping her bag down beside her. Jonah, upon entering the store, had made a beeline for the merchandise displays and now seemed engrossed in perusing the wares. Irene noticed things she hadn't seen the first time she had been here: jars of preserved flowers—gently glowing blue—and vials labeled things like "fresh linen," "the beach," and "Christmas."

Madame Majicka handed over a cup of tea. Irene hadn't noticed when she was here before, but the cup Madame Majicka handed to her was glowing blue, while the one she used for herself was not. Irene was impressed despite herself. Madame Majicka, for whatever reason, appeared to be the real deal—a living, breathing psychic who lived in both the land of the living and the land of the dead.

Irene settled onto the stool and took a sip of tea. To her surprise, it was actually quite good—for tea.

"When I was here before, you showed me a book...about the afterlife."

"Oh, yes?" Madame Majicka asked. "Be careful of that, dear," she called to Jonah. "It sings."

Irene turned but Jonah had already put down whatever he'd had and was now looking at a rack of books. Irene turned back to Madame Majicka. "Uh, yeah…about the book…"

Madame Majicka rose, went to the counter, and pulled out the guidebook. She set it in front of Irene. "This one, dear?"

"Yes, that's the one. I was wondering if it's for sale?"

"Oh my dear girl, but it's a gift! I want you to have it."

Irene's eyebrows arched upward in surprise. "Really?"

"Of course!" Something over Irene's shoulder drew the psychic's attention. "If that's Richard, be a dear and tell him I'll get back to him later."

Irene turned and this time Jonah was hastily replacing a white cloth over something that looked suspiciously like a crystal ball. Irene turned back around again.

She picked up the book and thumbed through it — *look on the bright side, make the best of things*. A wave of guilt for taking her anxiety out on Jonah washed over her. She should apologize after they had left the shop.

She closed the book with a snap and slipped it into her bag. "Well, thanks. I really appreciate it." She stood up. "Well, I'm afraid we have to go now. Jonah?"

Jonah came over, carrying a book. "How much is this?" he asked.

"That one?" Madame Majicka asked. "That one costs something dear but not precious."

"Is that the same as between a hair and a whisker?" Irene asked.

Jonah gave her an exasperated look. Irene shrugged. "It's something my grandmother used to say."

Jonah shook his head, as if the sayings of grandparents were unfathomable nonsense, and then looked at Madame Majicka. He seemed to be thinking. His face crinkled with uncertainty and he studied the book, appearing to debate with himself whether or not it was worth the price. Then he shrugged off his backpack, set it on the ground, and rummaged inside. "Let's see…"

The whole exchange mystified Irene, but Jonah and Madame Majicka seemed to understand each other.

"What are you looking for?" she asked.

Jonah's head was nearly inside the backpack, muffling his voice. "Something with sentimental value but not worth a lot."

"Oh." Irene turned this over for a minute. "Well, how about your watch?" She started to unbuckle it.

Jonah jumped up and put a hand over hers, stopping her. "No!" His vehemence took Irene by surprise. He hastily crouched back down, as if embarrassed. Then he stood up again, something in his hand. "Here." He thrust the item at Madame Majicka. It was a wadded up T-shirt.

"It's got my favorite cartoon character on it," he said, carefully avoiding looking at Irene. "Well, it was. I'm too old for cartoons now."

Madame Majicka smiled. "Done!"

Jonah stuffed the book into his bag but not before Irene saw the title: *Communicating Beyond the Void*. Her throat was suddenly dry and she felt the prickle of tears. She wanted to both hug and shake Jonah. She hastily turned away and swiped each eye with a finger before Jonah saw and became exasperated with her. She understood now why he didn't like tears: he hated the powerless feeling of seeing someone in pain and not being able to help.

"Okay?" Jonah said.

She pretended she had been looking at a nearby display, which just happened to be the one of giant, dried insects. She shuddered and stepped back.

"Yeah, just dandy. Ready?"

Madame Majicka ushered them to the door. Irene was halfway through when she stopped and turned, asking, "Is it going to hurt?" She bit her tongue, wishing she could take back the words as soon as she'd spoken them but there was nothing she could do — they were already out there. She reluctantly finished the question. "When I go through the tunnel, I mean. Will it hurt?"

"My dear, how could it hurt?" Madame Majicka asked. "You're already dead. Any pain you feel now is all in your head." Then she shut the door.

Irene was halfway down the street before she realized that Madame Majicka hadn't really answered the question at all. Irene did still feel pain.

Maybe that had been Madame Majicka's point.

Thirty-One

Ten days to go.

The good news was that Jonah seemed to have gotten over her interlude with Ernest. However, the bad news was that he seemed to be keeping a close eye on her, refusing to let her out of his sight and insisting they go to the library every day to work on translating the book.

She tried to be a good sport, put aside her anxiety, and throw herself into the work as a way of apologizing for her behavior, but Jonah's constant monitoring — and the implied censure and disapproval that went with it — chafed, and she wasn't sure how much longer she could tolerate it. At least they had avoided running afoul of Doris — who nevertheless kept a close eye on them, continuously hovering within earshot — and had only seen Amy once, at a distance. Amy had waved but hadn't seemed inclined to stop and talk.

After three days, however, Irene had begged for a moratorium. "I can't do it, Jonah," she said. "I can't spend another day cooped up in that library. Go if you want, but count me out."

Irene sighed and let the curtain fall as she turned away from the window. Jonah, having reluctantly agreed to a day off from the library, was gone at the moment, checking on his body and seeing if there was any developments in her missing-person case. Alone in the empty room, terrifying flash card images of the afterlife — Sisyphus endlessly rolling a stone up the mountain, Damocles under the pendulum sword, Satan immersed to the waist in a lake of fire — played over and over in her head.

She had a sudden urge to throw a chair through the glass. To smash the lamps and the mirror and anything else that would break. To crush, tear, and destroy until everything was in ashes around her. She gritted her teeth, looking wildly around the room for a distraction. She spied the book from Madame Majicka's shop on the bed, amidst the up-ended clutter she had been trying to organize. She crossed the room and sat down on the bed, drawing the book into her lap.

Words and phrases popped out at her. *Life goes on.*

She thought again of the inadequacy of the English language to describe her situation. Maybe they should call it a post-corporeal existence, rather than death. She thought of Jonah's analogy that dying was like moving to France. *This was my life when I lived in America. This was my life when I lived in France. This was my life when I had a body. This was my life when I didn't.*

She felt a shiver of unease. What, exactly, was the point of life without a body? Maybe, if death had been more like the movies — if she could walk through walls, possess people's bodies, control them through subliminal messages whispered in their ears while they slept, or any of the other cool superpowers Hollywood ghosts seemed to possess — then she could see why the universe introduced this new stage of existence. Without that, though, she didn't see why people had to lose their bodies if being dead didn't change anything else.

A: The good news is, you can only die once.

Well, the book was wrong about that. You could die for real in the afterlife. The Uglies were just one of what she had no doubt would turn out to be an endless array of ways for a person's spirit to be permanently obliterated.

She felt a sense of both grim satisfaction and mounting panic at the realization that the book didn't know everything. She hated its smug, smart-ass tone, but at the same time, it was the only solid information she had so far about what to expect on the other side.

Q: Is this Hell?

She noticed that, once again, her source material was mum on whether or not there was a God, a supreme judge of right and wrong.

She felt the unease again, stronger now, like a boulder on her chest. She spied the bottle of vodka on the bed and grabbed it. She unscrewed the top and swallowed a mouthful. She breathed out, slow and steady, as the vodka burned away the invisible hands wringing the air from her lungs like water from a sponge.

If all the stories were true, then surely Hell—and eternal torment and damnation—must be true, too. The flashcard images resurfaced.

She flung the book away from her, as if it had turned poisonous and deadly. Her heart thudded in her chest. The urge to scream, to yell, to beat her fists against the walls returned, stronger than before, and she clenched her jaw with teeth-aching severity to stop herself. She raised the bottle again, and her hand shook as she held it to her lips. She drank longer this time, wanting to feel the vodka burn its way through her chest. At least it was something—something real and solid to hang onto.

She felt sick now, her stomach churning with nerves and vodka. Blind, boiling rage swept over her. She was sick of waiting. Sick of inaction. Something, *anything*, needed to happen. She took another swig from the bottle, gulping greedily at the burning pain of it.

Jonah chose that moment to reappear.

He turned a furious shade of red. "I've only been gone a few minutes!"

"Give me a break." She capped the bottle and stuffed it in the bag, her face heating. "It's not like I drink all the time, Jonah. I haven't had a drink in days."

"You were drinking just the other day!"

"Oh my God, call AA—I had about three shots worth of vodka four days ago! Jesus Christ, you're such a Puritan."

He turned his back on her and stalked to the other end of the small room. His foot hit the front of the couch and she wasn't sure, but she thought he had kicked it.

"Why don't we go out and do something?" His voice was stifled, his back to her.

"What do you suggest?" she asked irritably. "I think we've seen everything there is to see."

"I wish you'd stop staying stuff like that," he said, suddenly miserable. "Don't you realize how amazing all of this is? None of this stuff should exist—this hotel room, the diner, the bar...it really is like magic. I just wish you would realize—"

"Jonah, don't try to make me someone I'm not," she said, turning away from him. "Stop trying to control me and change me."

He was quiet for a minute. "We could...look for another market...around other cemeteries, maybe." He turned around. "We could—"

"Oh, the market is useless!" she snapped. "Everyone keeps anything of any importance for themselves. I'm not going to find anything I need."

"I still think you should get a sword—"

"For the last time," she shouted, "I'm not getting a sword!"

Jonah seemed to withdraw, as if trying to make himself as small and unobtrusive as possible. "Are you going to be in a bad mood all day?" he asked quietly.

"Yes," she said emphatically.

She jerked to her feet, marched across the room, and opened the door with such force it banged into the wall.

"Where are you going?" he asked.

"Out."

"Out?"

"Yes. Just out. Once again, I'm a grown woman, Jonah. I'm allowed to go out, whenever I want."

"Aren't you going to take your bag?" he asked.

"Oh, I'm so sick of carrying that thing!" She slammed the door behind her.

Once in the hall she tried to breathe, but her breath seemed stuck in her chest. The wailing woman in white was there, doing her thing, the flustered hotel manager pleading with her to be reasonable. Irene felt a sense of grim satisfaction at the scene. She completely understood the woman's point: she, too, just wanted to screech at the top of her lungs.

Irene turned and stalked down the hall to the last door. She banged on it, waited two seconds, and then banged again. The door opened. Ernest, looking completely unsurprised, leaned against the doorframe and swung the door wide so she could enter.

She stalked in. "Do you have something to drink?"

His mouth twisted into a sardonic smile. He silently crossed the room to the decanter and poured them each a drink. She tossed hers back and felt it wash away the anger, leaving only a scum of bitter determination in its wake. She looked at him expectantly, her eyes hard.

"Do you want to talk first," he asked lazily, "or should we just get right to it?"

Her eyes narrowed. He laughed and came close, sliding a hand into her hair to cup the side of her face.

"You know, I'd like you just as much if you were just a little bit nice to me," he said as his lips closed on hers.

As before, the sensations were stronger than the time before. She wasn't sure if it really was getting better or if she was just forgetting what this had actually felt like—the intensity, the heat, the realness—when she was alive.

After, they lay in bed. He was rubbing her head and she was letting him because she was too listless to get up and leave. She dreaded going back and facing Jonah. He was going to hate her before long. Which might not be so bad; right now it was like pulling a Band-Aid off a little at a time. She wished they could just get it over with, just get to the disappointment and resentment and the part where he, like everyone else, got fed up and left. Besides, maybe then he'd stop visiting the afterlife.

She heard the slow rush of breath as Ernest blew out a cloud of smoke. "Are you at least going to say goodbye this time?" he said.

"Don't get attached; I'm leaving. Going through the tunnel. Soon." In less than ten days, to be exact. Less than ten days and she would be leaving everything behind — for good.

She turned her head, craning her neck so she could look at him. "You could come with me."

He was studying her, looking for something in her face. "You could stay."

"No, I couldn't." Icy fingers of dread gripped her insides at the thought. No matter what waited for her on the other side, it had to be better than this endless nothing.

He shifted slightly. As if reading her mind, he said, "What's going to make the other side any better than this one?"

"Well, for starters, you could come with me."

"You could stay," he repeated, and she heard him grinding out his cigarette. "This isn't so bad."

Her expression turned questioning and she sat up so she could look at him more fully. Deep lines of sorrow etched his face and suddenly he looked older, worn and tired. "Is there a problem?" she asked.

He was quiet for a moment, his dark eyes probing hers. When he finally spoke, his voice was heavy with regret. "The thing is...things were hard. After the war. I got injured. Pretty bad. And...I just couldn't..." His voice shook. "So one day, I took my service revolver and blew my brains out. So...you see...no matter how bad this is, whatever's waiting for me is worse."

Her heart sank.

Suicide.

A crime considered so heinous, so against the laws of nature, that most cultures believed it to be punishable by eternal torment. She didn't know if the Catholic Church had relaxed its prohibition on suicide victims being buried on consecrated ground, but she did know they still preached that suicides went to Hell. She remembered Jonah mentioning in one of his endless litanies that several Asian cultures believed that suicide victims came back to torture the living. All in all, suicide victims had every reason to fear the afterlife. How terrible must one's life be to still, knowing all the horrors that awaited you, choose death?

A dull ache throbbed deep inside her. "God, I'm so sorry…" A lump formed in her throat and she tried to swallow it.

"Don't fret, princess." The laconic drawl was back. He gave her a half-smile.

She didn't know what else to say, so she kissed him, pulling him to her and offering him the comfort of her body

Thirty-Two

Irene listened to the sound of Samyel moving around, followed as usual by the door opening and then closing with a snap.

Mercifully, Jonah had been out when she returned this time. She had crept into bed and spent a few restless hours falling in and out of sleep.

She sighed and sat up, awake now.

Jonah was sitting on the couch, flipping through the book. She hadn't heard him return.

"Really, do you sleep?" she asked, running her hands through her hair. "What is it with you and that book? You have your nose stuck in it every second of the day." She threw back the covers and climbed out of bed, suddenly feeling angry and out of sorts.

Jonah closed the book and sat up carefully, giving her his full attention. "I'm looking for something you can use to protect yourself against Samyel. Plus, he said something to you, a word, and I'm trying to find it."

"Oh, please," she huffed, guilt for giving him crap about reading the book when he was doing it for her making her even angrier. She flung herself back down into a sitting position on the edge of the bed. "Obviously he's not going to kill me before we go through the tunnel, and if he's planning on killing me on the other side it's not like there's anything you can do about it."

Jonah was watching her closely, his eyes assessing. She waited, but when he didn't say anything, she scowled and burst out with, "Look, it's gonna be whatever it's gonna be whether or not I'm prepared. Everyone else just goes through the tunnel without all this ridiculous build-up."

He got up and crossed the room to where she sat. He looked down at her for a minute and then, gingerly, sat down beside her. "What's up?" he asked.

"What do you mean?"

"I know you try to pick a fight when you're worried about something."

She stared at him for a moment, not sure what to say to that. Then she snorted. "You really think you've got my number, don't you?"

He flashed the cocky grin that so often preceded something purposely provoking. "Honestly, you're not that complicated."

"Why you...you little..."

"Handsome genius," he interjected, still grinning.

She punched his arm, but she laughed, too.

He grew serious again. "So...what's wrong?"

She shook her head and looked away, suddenly embarrassed. "Why don't you go home, Jonah? Huh? I think it's time."

He shook his head and smiled. "Seriously, I'm not going to fight with you today."

"I'm serious. You should go home."

"I want to stay."

"Jonah, you've already missed so much school and everything...it's been weeks."

"I'm in a coma. It's a perfectly acceptable reason for missing school."

"Jonah," she said, exasperated, "I'm not good at this, okay? The waiting around...dealing with uncertainty...things are just going to get worse. *I'm* gonna get worse. You should go. Before..." She meant to say, "before you hate me" but she couldn't bring herself to say the words, afraid he'd say that he already did.

"Look, I'm gonna stay—until the end, okay?" He looked at her and there was that nameless something— gentle yet insistent—in his eyes.

She sighed and looked away.

"So, are you going to tell me what the problem is?"

She smiled despite herself. "You're like a dog with a bone sometimes, you know that?" She looked at him again. He smiled but kept his eyes on her, silently demanding an answer. She sighed again. "You know, you keep asking all kinds of questions about Samyel but you've never asked anything about me. Not that I care, but it's just that…well, it's as if I'm not even a person to you—just someone to kill time with. You've obviously got your own set of assumptions and ideas—none of them flattering, apparently—but you've never bothered to ask."

Jonah's gaze was gentle and steady. "I never asked because I didn't think you'd want to talk about your life. You're so mad about being dead."

She looked away. After a minute, she said, "Not that you asked, but I was the Manager of E-Commerce Strategy for the biggest department store chain in the Northeast."

He didn't say anything. She looked back and he was watching her carefully. She sighed. "You're right. I was mad, but not anymore. Everything seems really long ago." She smiled weakly.

When he still didn't say anything, she smiled for real and said, "No, really. You're right, I'm a brat sometimes, but I can see how…" She searched for the right word. "It's like there's a reason for everything, like all that lame stuff they say about us just not knowing what it is, is true. I'm excited…" She hesitated. "Well, maybe not excited exactly, but you know what I mean—to get to the next life and find out what everything was all about, to get some answers, to experience some magic and mystery— like a three-headed dog."

It was sort of true and it sounded better than that she was growing eager to put this life and all its mistakes behind her. The longer she contemplated the past, the less she liked what she saw. Plus, staying here meant stasis. Moving on was the only way she was going to have a future.

He was quiet for a minute, tugging a loose thread on the comforter, and she was afraid she'd made him uncomfortable, but then he said, "So, what is an e-commerce manager anyway?"

She laughed, relief flooding through her. "It means I figured out how to sell shit to people over the Internet."

One side of his mouth quirked up in a half-smile and he looked at her from the corner of his eye. She laughed again. "Well, when I put it that way, it does sound like a waste of time. It didn't seem like it at the time, though."

After that it was easy to talk about her life—she told him about how, when she had gotten her job, she had celebrated with a weekend in the Florida Keys with LaRayne and Alexia. She told him about her childhood dog, Pebbles. About snorkeling in Hawaii. About bumping, quite literally, into the governor in the doorway of the Union Oyster House restaurant. About the guilty pleasure of honey roasted cashews from a cart at the State Street T Station. "I don't know why, but they always remind me of fall."

"How come you never got married?" he asked.

This made her squirm a little. "Just never met the right guy." She shrugged in what she hoped was a casual manner.

"Did you have a...a boyfriend...when you died?" He glanced at her out of the corner of his eye as if he thought maybe this was too personal.

She gave him a dour look. "No."

He didn't seem to be getting the hint to change the subject. "Do you think people can fall in love after they die?"

She had no doubt he was thinking of Ernest, so she changed the subject by recounting the one time she had tried skiing—and the broken arm that had resulted.

"Do you have any regrets?" he asked.

She was both impressed and disconcerted by the point-blank brutality of the question. She was also surprised to find that the question didn't upset her. She was able to answer it with perfect equanimity. "I hope they find my body before I leave."

"Do you know where you'll be buried…when they find your body, I mean?"

She shook her head. "I have no idea." She suddenly realized all the details her mother would have to take care of—Irene's funeral, her burial, cleaning out and selling her house. She didn't know how her mother would handle it all, and she felt a great, hot wave of guilt roll over her. "God, I hope she doesn't cremate me!" Irene wondered what would happen to her—her spirit, that is—if her body was destroyed.

"Don't worry—they had urn reclamation at the market, too. Burning is a way of sending stuff to the dead—the essence still arrives in the afterlife intact. Like, for instance, during the Chinese Ghost Festival they burn the little paper models of animals and money and stuff in order to send it to the dead. Also, the Vikings used to set their dead adrift in burning boats to send them to Asgard—"

"Yeah, well, I'm still not big on cremation. Whatever she does, I hope it's not maudlin. God, I hate that!"

Jonah nodded. "I had to go to my grandfather's funeral. I didn't like it. It was creepy."

Irene tried to imagine what she wanted for a funeral. "I don't want it to be sappy, but on the other hand, I don't want people acting as if it doesn't matter—like a jazz funeral kind of thing. Those just seem wrong. Maybe a nice gospel choir or something like that. And I want a teary eulogy from all my old boyfriends, saying how I was the best thing that ever happened to them."

Jonah laughed himself silly at that.

"Oh yeah, Mister Smarty Pants," she said, poking him in the arm. "What's your funeral going to be like?"

"I want to be buried at sea," he said promptly.

"What?"

"Or I want a casket shaped like a rocket, and I want them to send me into space."

Irene started to laugh and then realized this actually was a good plan—clean, neat, and effective. It was strong and memorable without being sappy. "Wow, you're good."

He grinned.

They spent the rest of the day making up more and more elaborate funerals for themselves, Jonah peppering the conversation with information on burial rites from a dozen different cultures.

When Samyel returned that evening, she asked as usual, "When are you going to be ready to go?"

"Soon," he said.

"Is that one day? Three? A month? I'm getting sick of waiting."

He had no answer for her.

Aggravated, she hissed to Jonah, "Okay, fine, you win. Tomorrow, let's follow him."

When the door clicked closed the following morning, they both sprang up—she from the bed and he from the couch. Wanting to travel light and quick, they left their bags in the room.

Samyel bypassed the elevator and headed for the stairs. The stairs were noisy and they were sure he could hear their footsteps. They hung back, trying to use distance to muffle the sound.

However, Samyel didn't pause on the way to the ground floor. He crossed the lobby, pushed into the revolving door, and spilled out onto the street.

They followed him around Copley Square—where he seemed to be going in circles—then past the Prudential Center, down Huntington, and past the Christian Science Center fountain. Then they followed him as he circled back toward downtown, zigzagging through the back streets of the Fenway.

"I think he's sightseeing," Irene said irritably after two hours of this.

"No," Jonah said after a thoughtful pause. "I think he's looking for something."

For a while, Samyel seemed to be on to something because there was a long, straight beeline for the North End, where they, once again, spent a couple of hours zigzagging up and down cramped and crowded side streets filled with the smells of Italian pastries and pizza.

"Is it my imagination or does he keep sniffing the air, like a dog?" Irene asked as they peered around a corner, watching Samyel waiting at an intersection.

"Not your imagination."

Irene leaned against the building, enjoying the feel of the cool stone against the bare skin of her back and shoulders — she'd forgotten the jacket in their haste to leave the room. The days were definitely getting cooler. There was more than a hint of fall in the air now. However, if she stood in the sun and closed her eyes, she could trick herself into thinking it was still summer.

She shivered as the cold seeped into her, feeling like ice. She pulled away from the building and rubbed her arms. The feeling persisted. She turned to see if Jonah felt cold too, and saw a smoke-like tendril creeping along the ground toward them.

She grabbed Jonah's arm and pulled him toward her, away from the shadow. "Jonah…" she said, panic in her voice. He looked at her and then turned to see what she was staring at.

"We have to go," she said urgently, tugging him with her as she scuttled backwards. "It's them. It's the Uglies."

The air was already thin. She couldn't breathe, couldn't think. Panic washed over her. She turned to run and suddenly there was a wall of shadow, thick and dark, looming before her. She screamed and the air froze inside her lungs. The creature rose up, towering over her, blotting out the sun, the buildings, the world. Everything became a terror-induced blur.

She felt Jonah tug her backwards. She stumbled once, twice, then got her legs under her, turned, and ran. The tendril of smoke that had approached from behind was attached to another, different Ugly, advancing like a fast-moving wave of fog rolling off the ocean, blocking the way. She turned her head wildly, searching for a way to escape.

She spied an alley, opposite them, and she pulled Jonah after her as she dove toward it.

It was a dead end.

She hit the chain-link fence stretched across the far end, blocking the way forward, at a run, rebounding slightly and grabbing onto it as if she could pull it down with her hands. Pain knifed through her from the lack of oxygen and the burning cold as the Uglies filled the alley's opening, cutting off the only escape.

Irene clung to the fence as she doubled over, gasping for air like a beached fish. The world bobbed before her eyes and black spots blotted out everything. Beside her, Jonah clutched his chest with both hands, his breathing sounding like a file on metal.

"Wind...chi..." he rasped.

She managed to squeeze out a single word in response: "Ho...tel."

The shadows advanced down the alley, the swirling tendrils flowing along the sides of the buildings. Jonah slapped at her, pointing back down the alley, but there was no room to maneuver past the Uglies.

Irene's vision dimmed and she was on the verge of passing out, the world fading from view as her knees went weak. With the last of her strength, her lungs bursting with need, the entirety of her consciousness focused solely on the searing, white-hot agony consuming her, she grabbed the fence and tried to climb. She only managed one step before the darkness overcame her. She felt the Uglies' burning-cold fingers curl around her ankle and then she was falling...falling...falling endlessly.

Somewhere, far away, she heard a church bell ring.

Thirty-Three

She and Jonah lay on the ground, gasping, panting, and shivering, unable to move, unable to breathe, entombed in a soul-chilling cold so thick it felt like they were wrapped in layers of solid ice as the Uglies retreated, driven away by the church bell.

Eventually, Irene and Jonah managed to drag themselves, by aid of the fence, to their feet. Barely conscious, they slowly and painfully made their way back to the hotel where they each rolled themselves in a comforter and lay trembling with a chill that wouldn't subside. Despair washed over Irene, and she sobbed noiselessly for hours, racked with pain and terror, until she was empty, wrung dry like a dishrag.

Silence descended. Worried about Jonah, she crawled out from under the blanket to check on him. He was sitting on the couch, immersed in the book. When she got up, he looked at her, his face so pale it was almost translucent, and Irene felt sick to her stomach for the danger she had put him in.

"I want you to go home. Now," she said.

His voice was surprisingly strong and steady after the ordeal they had just been through. "No. Absolutely not."

"Jonah—"

"You can't make me," he replied, crossing his arms over his chest. He wasn't even arguing. He was matter of fact.

Her first instinct was to argue, to demand, but reluctantly she had to admit, he was right—she couldn't make him. Her shoulders slumped in defeat and she turned away.

Things were quiet for the next couple of days. They decided to stay inside, where it was safe. Jonah used the time to try a variety of charms against Samyel: holy water sprinkled on the bed—he had apparently nicked it from the church when she was talking to Reverend Jim—salt spread across the threshold, and a horseshoe nailed to the door—procured from God only knew where—all with no effect.

To Irene's frustration, there was no change in status in the land of the living. Jonah's body was still in the hospital, surrounded by a team of baffled medical practitioners and investigators. With nine days to go, Irene's body still hadn't been found.

"What are you going to tell them?" she insisted for the hundredth time, pacing around the room, while he dug like a burrowing raccoon through his backpack.

"Oh, I'll make up something," he said airily, and when she protested, he added, "I'll tell them I was breaking in to steal stuff to support my drug habit."

"Jonah!"

"Oh, alright," he said, flapping a hand like he was shooing a pesky fly. "I'll tell them…I'll tell them I saw some kids picking on your neighbor's dog. I knocked on her door and no one answered, so I went next door to tell you. Your front door was open, I went in, no one was there, and next thing I knew, I was in the hospital. They'll think I had a seizure or something."

"That will never hold water," she said scornfully. "What about the note you forged to the school and your parents about the field trip?"

He shrugged. "I'll get in trouble for lying and for skipping school—probably be grounded for the rest of my life—but…whatever." He went back to digging through his backpack.

She couldn't argue with the logic—especially since she didn't have any better ideas—but she felt a twinge of unease at his use of her favorite word.

She turned the conversation over in her mind again. While the solution to Jonah's problem wasn't great, at least it was a solution. However, no one had found her body yet and she couldn't think of any way to help that process along without creating more problems than she'd solve.

She stalked to the window and pulled back the curtain. She hadn't lied when she told Jonah that it no longer hurt to think about everything she had lost — her job, her home, her friends, the sensual joys of living — sex, drinking, food, the feel of sand through bare toes, a warm cup of coffee in cold hands, the smell of roasting cashews mixed with the hot, burning metal and oil smell of the subway. Whether or not her body was ever found would not change the fact that these things were gone.

What she hated was the thought of her mother *wondering* for the rest of her life, hated the thought of the open-ended rawness of it. When she had left her home for the last time, she had regretted that she had no gift, no final message, to leave her mother, but she had been wrong: her body was the gift — her body and the closure that would come with it.

"I really hate to go before they find my body," she said.

Jonah raised his head from the backpack. "You know, we could ask…" he hesitated, as if he thought she wasn't going to like what he was about to suggest. "…Madame Majicka to help — she's alive, you know. She can call the police, leave an anonymous tip."

Irene dropped the curtain and spun around as wild, blazing hope surged through her. She stared at him, too overcome to speak.

Jonah didn't seem to know how to interpret her silence. His forehead crinkled with concern.

She gave him a reassuring look while choking back a laugh. "You really are brilliant, Jonah. It's a great idea."

He seemed relieved and embarrassed at the same time. He stood up, apparently giving up on whatever he'd been looking for in the bag. "Okay. I'll go right now if you want." He looked around the room. "Where is the wind chime?"

"No, absolutely not," she said. "It's too dangerous. I'll go."

He shook his head. "I'll be okay. I'll take the bells and I'll use the locator spell to teleport there and back. If I get into trouble, I can always return to my body."

She blinked at him. "You can do that...teleport there, I mean?"

He carelessly tossed his head. "Oh sure."

He made it all seem so easy and her so useless, so disposable. She crossed her arms, covering her mouth with a hand as resentment and shame wrestled inside her. Finally, she said, "I'm the adult. I'm supposed to protect you." Which just made her feel worse. Of the two of them, Jonah was clearly the more capable.

He gave her a gentle but unrelenting smile. "Just don't do anything crazy while I'm gone, okay?"

"Jonah..." she protested, but he reached for her bag and snatched up the wind chime. He stood for a moment, as if he wanted to say something, then he flashed her another reassuring smile and was gone.

It was only after he disappeared that she realized the likelihood of his finding the shop open was extremely low. However, to her surprise, when he came back twenty minutes later he reported that, against all odds, Madame Majicka had been in and had agreed quite readily to help. The timing was perfect — given the news stories and accompanying requests for people with information to come forward that had been generated by the discovery of Jonah's body at Irene's house, an anonymous tip that a woman in a silver BMW had been seen driving erratically on the Lynn Marsh Road late one night several weeks ago wouldn't seem suspicious or out of place.

For the first time since she'd died, Irene found herself looking forward to tomorrow, rather than dreading it. The next couple of days passed in relative quiet. With only seven days until she left remaining, Jonah seemed determined to cram as much afterlife knowledge into her head as he could in between frequent trips to his body to check on the progress of the search for Irene's remains.

"You know, one thing that's always bothered me," she said, when he mentioned again the idea that all of your family and friends waited to assist you in the afterlife, "is what happens to people whose spouse dies and then they remarry. Like my Uncle Robert—he's going to have two wives when he gets to the afterlife. How does that work?"

Jonah didn't have an answer for that. They took turns inventing different scenarios as to how this might play out.

"Well, maybe the first wife found someone else in the afterlife and got remarried, too," Jonah said.

"Or maybe she's waiting with one of those Welsh demon dogs on a leash to rip him apart for cheating on her," she countered.

In between these conversations Jonah distracted and amused Irene by tormenting Samyel, when Samyel was in, with questions about the afterlife or, when Samyel was out, continuing with his subtle demon and ghost repellant experiments—both of which Samyel ignored.

"He's got that impassive Terminator vibe going on," Irene whispered to Jonah. "Maybe he's a robot."

It took two days for the police to find and pull Irene's car from the river. Three days after, Irene and Jonah were in her car, heading to Salem for her funeral. Samyel had volunteered to come as well, and Irene had promptly quashed that idea, instructing him instead to get a move on, the clock was ticking.

There were two days remaining.

Clouds hung heavy and low in the sky. Occasionally a single ray of sunlight would appear, haloing whatever it fell on. A raw breeze threw clusters of fallen leaves into their path and it brought with it the smell of the ocean, heavy with the tang of seaweed. It was, she thought, a proper day for a funeral.

She studied the scenery as the car crept down familiar streets. It was clichéd, but it really did seem like a lifetime ago that she had last been here. Everything looked strange and different. Now, in a way she couldn't before, she could see everything around her as a series of components from different eras and ideas, layered on top of each other. She could see the jigsaw nature of the housing, the roads, the stores—sea captain homes built in the seventeen hundreds stood next to brick condominiums built last year; a Wiccan shop abutted a surplus army and navy store; schmaltzy tourist attractions stood next to sites of important historical events.

She had always thought the world around her was a single, cohesive background to everyday living, tightly woven and knit in a dense and impenetrable fabric, a kind of irrelevant wallpaper to the more important things in life. Now she wondered if perhaps all the background stuff was actually the most important part. A person had only to find a single, distinct thread to pull and the entire thing broke apart into a million fascinating and wondrous pieces to be admired, studied, collected, understood, or questioned. It wasn't good and it wasn't bad—it was, as Jonah often said, just interesting.

She remembered a long-ago family vacation where her father had insisted on taking her on a tour of a rope factory. She had been immeasurably bored, impatient to get to the beach, having just gotten her first bikini. To her knowledge, her father hadn't had any particular interest in rope, so she couldn't understand his fascination with learning how it was made. Now she did. She even understood that Jonah's obsession with afterlife myths, Mister MacKenzie's fixation on his lawn, and ex-boyfriend Theo's pre-occupation with basketball brackets were not weird or annoying—something to be mocked. Instead, they were beautiful, almost holy. They exemplified a reverence for life, a reverence for excellence, curiosity, precision, knowledge—a way of engaging with the wonder and mystery of the world, a way of understanding the beauty and complexity of the universe and everything in it.

The living see what they want to see.

She could see it all laid out before her now — an infinite array of miracles, just waiting to be discovered by those with the eyes to see them — and she understood now what it was she had really lost: the opportunity to discover, to become an expert on something, to be excellent, to be passionate, fiery, and emotional. It didn't matter at what — star gazing, rock collecting, automobile engines, sports, toy poodles...anything. Everything. Life wasn't for passing time, for superficial and trivial engagement. It was for exploration, inquiry, amazement, puzzlement, and joy.

They turned into the cemetery and she almost had to turn back — here, too, were stories: life expectancy, wars and tragedies, burial rites, family structure, wealth and poverty. There were a hundred million things to discover, to know, to learn, to feel and think and believe and wonder at, and she hadn't experienced any of it.

Jonah had said once that he felt bad for her. Now she understood why. How sad he must think life for people, like her, who skated through the world never questioning, never examining, never understanding. His whole world must be full of such people — his parents, his sister, the status-obsessed kids at school. No wonder he sought to escape, even if it meant hanging out with the dead.

They parked a little way from the gravesite. Jonah, perhaps thinking the thought of seeing her casket and her tombstone saddened her, took her hand and led her gently through the neat rows of graves.

They were burying her near her parents' plot — not adjoining but across the narrow road. Irene hadn't been sure how to take the fact that her mother had settled on a simple graveside service rather than the traditional full service at the funeral home, but upon further reflection, she decided it was what she would have picked for herself, if she had to choose. Simple, touching, yet without the cringing discomfort of a long, emotional — or God forbid, religious — service.

The service was closed casket. Irene felt both relief and disappointment that she would not get to see her body one last time. She had wondered what she would feel. She had thought she would know when they found her body, when they pulled her from the river, but she hadn't felt a thing. She wondered if this was normal or if it meant that the world of the living had truly slipped beyond her grasp. She was ready to move on, but it still stung to know she couldn't go back, even if she wanted to.

Jonah was studying the crowd with interest. She guessed he was probably trying to figure out who each person was, so she began pointing them out.

"That's my mom, and that's Mrs. Boine and her daughter and grandkids." Irene had no idea how the old lady had arranged to hitch a ride to the cemetery, but she was impressed and touched that she had managed it. Mrs. Boine, seated on the other side of the casket from them, saw them looking at her and waved.

"It's a good turnout," she called to Irene.

"That's Jamaica. That's my Aunt Betty and Uncle Robert." It looked like most of their children — an assorted tribe of first cousins and their kids — were there as well. Since she'd be hard pressed to identify any of them by name she skipped over them.

"That's my friend LaRayne. She's the one I was out with...you know...when I..." Even now, she couldn't bring herself to say it. Irene scanned the attendees. She didn't see Alexia. She wasn't surprised, but she still felt a stab of disappointment.

Jonah was studying LaRayne with narrow, assessing eyes. If friends where a reflection of the person, then she wondered what it was that he saw.

"That's my boss, Donna. She was pretty cool. We got along really well." Donna was surreptitiously wiping her eyes with a tissue. Irene was surprised, but touched.

"Uh...oh, those four over there were my project team — they were a lot of fun to work with." Mai had just arrived and Jamal was hugging her in greeting. They both seemed to be fighting tears. As she looked again, Irene saw that quite a few of her coworkers had come, including Eddie — who looked sincerely grave and solemn.

"That's the guy who took over my office," she said, pointing him out to Jonah.

"Was he your boyfriend?" Jonah asked.

"No," she said emphatically. "Just my assistant." She scanned the crowd again — not a single ex-boyfriend there. She didn't really expect that there would be — none of her relationships had ever ended on a good note — but, once again, she felt a stab of disappointment. It would have been nice to think that at least one of them thought more of her than she believed they did.

"Let's see…that guy works in accounting. He was always staring at my chest instead of my face. The blonde works with him and is a bitch. I don't know why either of them is here. I don't know them all that well. Same with those three over there…I think they work at my company but I don't know. Apparently, they just wanted an excuse to get out of work this afternoon." She felt a stab of anger mingled with disappointment. "That's it, I guess. All the important people."

There was a truth here, in who had come and who had not, in her choice of friends, and in her choice of lovers. The same truth as had been in her realization that her life had been without passion. A truth she did not want to acknowledge. A commentary on her life, her choices, her capacity to love and be loved, her capacity to believe she deserved better. She looked away, unable to face it.

Jonah, astute as ever, was watching her intently. Now he touched her hand. "Maybe we should go," he said. "This just seems to be upsetting you."

Irene looked at him, expecting to see disgust or possibly even pity, but his pale eyes looked back without judgment.

She stood up, slinging the beach bag over her shoulder. "Yeah, maybe we should."

And that's how my life ends, she thought. *Not even with a whimper.*

Thirty-Four

The clock had run out—the three weeks were up.

There was nothing left to do, no longer any reason to stay. She had seen and done everything she had meant to, wrapped up all the loose ends, said all her goodbyes. There was no longer any reason to delay facing what was ahead.

Irene stared out the window, one hand curled around the bottle of vodka. Early dawn fingers of red and orange streaked the sky. Jonah was still asleep on the couch, Samyel was missing—he hadn't returned last night from his daytime adventures.

Yesterday, as he was leaving the room, she had told him, "I'm ready to go. You better be, too, when I see you next."

Irene hadn't seen him since.

She felt jittery, on edge. The funeral should have made things better, but it had only made them worse. She had thought it would give her closure, a sense of finality, but instead, it had simply reminded her of mistakes, lost opportunities, and all the things she'd never had and never done. She felt empty, bereft, as if she had lost something irreplaceable.

Now she stood at the window, having slipped out of bed in the pre-dawn hours, downing great, gasping swallows of vodka as she watched the sun rise, trying to drown the fraying, cracking, straining feeling that threatened to split her apart.

"What are you doing?"

She whirled around. Jonah was standing there, stockinged feet sticking out the bottom of his too-short pants.

"Jonah," she said wearily. "Could you please stop—"

"Why don't you give me the bottle?" His eyes flashed but his voice was calm and steady. He held out his hand.

Her voice was suddenly dangerous, low and full of warning. "You know, I'm sick of you trying to tell me what to do, and I'm sick of you acting like I'm a drunk and a whore."

His lips disappeared into a thin line and his chest heaved, as if it took a great effort to control himself. He didn't say anything, though, just stood there looking at her.

"If you've got something to say, then say it," she demanded. She screwed the cap back on and set the bottle down on the end table, challenging him. When he didn't speak, she said with deliberate cruelty, "Yeah, I thought not." She couldn't seem to stop herself. There was something in her now, clawing at her to push him, goad him, hurt him if she could, and words flew from her, reckless and wild.

Points of color flashed in his cheeks, and with a movement almost too fast to be seen, he grabbed the bottle and jumped back.

They stared at each other, poised on the edge of decision, hovering between two futures.

She felt something hot and hateful flash across her face. A muscle in his jaw twitched and then, his eyes telegraphing grim determination, he slammed the bottle to the floor. It hit the leg of the table and smashed, spraying apart. In an instant, the liquid was gone, swallowed by the carpet.

She let out a squeal of disbelief and outrage. The outline of her hand blazed on his cheek while the ringing sound of the slap hung in the air.

There was a moment of pin-dropping silence as they stared at each other, chests heaving.

"I suppose you're going to leave now," she said coldly.

"No," he said with quiet dignity, his eyes never leaving hers. "I'm not going to leave."

She couldn't breathe. Shame, despair, anger, and self-loathing swirled together in a suffocating mix. She couldn't stand how he was looking at her—direct and unwavering. She grabbed her bag off the bed and strode past him. "Fine. Then I will." She slammed the door behind her.

She ran down the stairs and out onto the street. She might be dead, her heart no longer actually beating, but her mind didn't seem to know that at the moment—her heart pounded, the blood throbbing in her ears. She walked, head down, the tears flowing freely now, obscuring the buildings around her, melting them into a blur of gray and brown as she passed.

She felt like she had one night, long ago, when she was sixteen. Her father had caught her sneaking into the house hours after her parents thought she had gone to bed. She remembered the look on his face. He had opened his mouth to yell, but then seemed to change his mind. Instead, he said, very quietly, "I guess you're one of those people who have to learn everything the hard way." Then he'd simply turned his back on her and gone upstairs, leaving her standing there—angry and confused. She had waited weeks for the other shoe to drop—for the punishment to come—but it never had. In fact, he never mentioned the incident again, never even told her mother about it. However, something had broken between them. Their relationship had never been the same. He had never had a word to say about any of her behavior after that—never tried to correct her, punish her, or rein her in. In fact, the worse she acted the less he said, and from then on, whenever he had looked at her, she thought she saw resigned disappointment lurking in his eyes.

Now Jonah would look at her the same way.

She leaned against a building and dug through her bag, only to remember that the bottle was gone. She swore. With grim determination, she pushed away from the wall and headed for the hotel, to the room at the end of the hall.

349

She didn't bother to knock. Somehow, she knew the door would be unlocked. She walked in and dropped her bag. Ernest was leaning over the desk, and he straightened up in surprise. She reached around and unzipped her dress, letting it drop to the floor.

"Contrary to what you might think, princess, I don't just sit around all day waiting to be of service."

"Fine," she said, slipping off her panties. "Send me away."

His lips twisted in a self-deprecating smile as his eyes raked over her and he began unbuttoning his shirt.

Ernest seemed to know she needed to ruthlessly, relentlessly drive away every thought, every feeling, or maybe he needed it, too; their lovemaking was mindless and determined, grim and unrelenting.

She stayed with him for two days. Then she got up and dressed, her back to him.

"I'm leaving," she said. "Tonight. Now. As soon as I get my stuff."

He blew a cloud of smoke and didn't say anything.

"Well, it's been nice knowing you!" she cried, stung by his lack of response. She didn't want to stay, but she wanted him to ask her anyway.

"What is it you modern girls say?" he asked sardonically. "Don't get your panties in a bunch? If you wait twenty minutes, I'll get some pants on and come with you."

She whirled around. "I mean I'm going through the tunnel."

He stubbed out his cigarette. "I know what you meant." He threw back the covers and stood up.

For a second, relief flooded through her. Then it faded. She shook her head. "Ernest, you can't…"

He was hunting for his clothes. "Don't worry about it, princess. I suspect if anyone tries to give me any grief you'll clonk them over the head with one of these clogs of yours." He tossed a shoe to her.

She shook her head again, even though he wasn't looking at her. "It's not that. It's just that...you and me..."

He straightened up quickly. "Don't be stupid," he said, but he sounded more alarmed than irate.

She shook her head for a third time. "This..." she waved a hand between them, "isn't anything. It's just..." She wanted to say "despair," but that sounded too unkind. However, she couldn't think of any other word to describe it so she let the sentence hang.

Ernest crossed the room and grabbed her by the shoulders, giving her a little shake, suddenly angry. "Whatever it is, it's *something*. I feel...and that has to mean something."

Disgust is a feeling, she thought. *So is self-loathing.*

Her face must have reflected these thoughts because he released her, his face grim. He appeared poised to argue and then seemed to sense that it was hopeless. He sighed and ran a hand through his hair. "Irene, I'm offering to do a brave and noble thing here. It's very unlike me. Are you sure you don't want to accept?"

She let out a brittle laugh. "What the hell good is brave and noble to someone like me? I eat people like that for breakfast."

He managed a rueful grin. She let out a laugh and it was a cross between a hiccup and a gasp. "Besides, the role of Jiminy Cricket is already taken."

"That kid—"

She silenced him with a slash of her hand. "Don't," she warned. "Leave him out of it."

Immediately, she felt a twinge of remorse for being severe. She rummaged in her bag and pulled out her car keys. She took his hand, held it open, and put the keys in his palm. Then she folded his fingers over the cold metal. "There's a car parked on Hancock Street with your name on it."

His eyes crinkled and he seemed to understand. She returned his smile then she stood on tiptoe and kissed his cheek. "Look me up sometime, if you ever make it to the other side." Then she left without looking back.

Thirty-Five

She took a deep breath as she entered the room, not sure what she'd say if Jonah was there and what she'd do if he wasn't.

He was there.

Jonah was reading on the couch, in the same position as the first time she had tried to slip in after a tryst with Ernest. This time, however, he stood up and faced her as soon as she crossed the threshold.

"I was starting to think you weren't going to come back," he said.

She turned and closed the door. When she turned back, he had come closer and was holding something out to her. It was a bottle of gin.

"I shouldn't have smashed it." His voice was quiet. Not angry. Not accusing. Not anything, in fact. It was carefully neutral.

She looked at the bottle, a taste like burning rubber in the back of her throat.

"Is Samyel back yet?" she asked, somehow squeezing the words out.

Jonah didn't answer. He just continued to silently hold the bottle out to her. She had no doubt he would stand there until the end of time, wordlessly challenging her to make a choice, to either take or refuse the hateful bottle.

"I hope this is okay. I couldn't find anything that was the same as the other one."

She couldn't bear to touch it, but he was watching her. Waiting to see what she'd do. She could see the challenge in his eyes. She lifted her chin and reached out, taking the bottle.

"Yes. Thank you. This is fine," she said, matching his dull tone.

His gaze was steady and unflinching. "Where have you been?"

"Does it matter where I've been?"

"I was worried."

"What do you want me to say?" she said, the careful veneer of calm instantly shattering. "That I've been with Ernest, and we've been humping like rabbits? Is that what you want to hear?"

He flinched but didn't look away.

The door opened and Samyel walked in.

"Where have you been?" she cried wildly, enraged and relieved by the interruption.

Samyel didn't answer; he just gave her the usual impassive look and continued past, walking around Jonah who hadn't moved a muscle.

"I'm going," she called to Samyel. "I'm sick of waiting for you. I'm going now, with or without you."

"One day more," Samyel said.

"No! NOW."

Samyel shrugged. "Then there is no choice."

"Good, then get your stuff! We're going!"

Jonah's expression turned pained. "Irene, please...don't go...not like this..."

Samyel impassively turned out the trench coat's pockets, indicating he didn't have anything to take.

"Fine!" she snapped. "Let's go."

"Irene..." Jonah said miserably.

"I'm not a saint, Jonah!" she cried, the words wrenched from deep inside. "When are you going to get that through your head? You have to stop expecting so much from me!"

"I don't think you're a saint."

She had enough presence of mind to realize Samyel was still standing there, listening to every word. She opened the door and ordered him into the hall. She closed the door after him and faced Jonah again.

"I don't think you're a saint," he repeated.

"But you want me to be. You want me to be something I'm not. You want—"

"No," he said. "I don't! I just want—"

"I was drinking," she cried wildly, unable to hold onto the secret any longer. "Did you know that? The night I died...I was drinking."

His eyes never left hers. "I know."

Her words were sharp and brittle, and she tried to drive them deep like knives, to make him see, to make him understand: she was no good—she never had been, never would be. She was bound to let him down, it's what she did. "I was drunk...and my friends let me go, and then I drove off the road—"

"I know," he repeated more firmly.

She stared at him, frozen with shock.

He'd known—he had always known—and he had stayed, anyway— stayed through the abuse, the cruelty, the lashing out, the wanton self-destruction. He had stayed. For some insane, incomprehensible reason, he had stayed.

This knowledge was too big, too overwhelming, and she began to shake. Now, when she really needed them, the tears wouldn't come. She stood there, dry-eyed and panting, the pain in her heart so great she couldn't breathe.

She wanted to speak, wanted to explain, to apologize. She wanted to promise to do better and then actually be better. Words, however, seemed too inadequate for what needed to be said. There was only one thing she could think to do. She reached into her bag, pulled out the bottle he had given her, and held it out to him. "I won't need this," she said, her mouth so dry she could barely get the words out.

He understood immediately. He stared at her, pain and grief etched deeply across his face as fat, silent tears rolled down his cheeks. Then she was crying, too—great wrenching sobs. She thought she would split apart, the pain was so great. She wanted to hug him but knew she couldn't, so instead, she began to unbuckle his watch. "This belongs to you," she managed to say.

He took a quick step toward her and laid a restraining hand over hers, just as he had at Madame Majicka's. "You keep it." He squeezed her wrist gently. She looked into his eyes and understood—he was going to try to find a way to come with her, to cross to the other side. He wanted her to keep the watch so he could find her. Her tears pressed close and hard once more, and she panted, trying to hold them in.

"Jonah, listen," she said urgently, willing him to listen, to hear her, willing herself to say the hard thing she should have said from the beginning but had never had the courage to. "I want you to promise me something—"

"Don't!" he cried fiercely, putting a hand over her mouth. His lower lip trembled and he suddenly looked younger and more vulnerable than she'd ever seen him.

She hesitated. She knew she should tell him not to look for her, to stop visiting the land of the dead, to live his life—grow up, get a job, get married, have kids, travel, do all the things that make a life. However, she couldn't do it. She couldn't throw his youth and inexperience in his face, couldn't pretend to be the wise, old adult and he the child, after all he'd done for her, so instead, she said, "Just...don't spend so much time in the land of the dead, okay?" Then she added, "And maybe wait until you're a little older to look me up."

Jonah smiled, relief flooding his face. For the briefest of instances, there was a very different look in his eyes, and it held a promise: it might take twenty, fifty, or even seventy years, but she would see him again.

He gave her wrist another squeeze and then let go, stepping back. "You better go," he said bravely, "the afterlife isn't going to wait forever, you know."

She laughed, because she had no more tears. Then she opened the door and called Samyel back in.

"Wait!" Jonah grabbed something off the table. He thrust a paper at her and she saw it was the map he had been working on. "Look for a river," he said urgently. "That's the first thing."

Samyel removed the shade from a nearby lamp and stood waiting beside the naked light. Irene held out her hand to him. "Ready?"

Jonah stood back, watching her, and though his face was stoic, pain, loss, anguish, and even a little fear filled his eyes. Her heart lurched. She couldn't bear it to end like this, for this to be her last memory of him. She caught his eye and smiled. "Fuck it," she said.

He laughed.

And there it was—the memory of him she'd take with her and hold onto forever. She turned to the light and stared into the bulb, relaxing her eyes and summoning the tunnel. As before, the light melted and ran, a golden vortex of dazzling brilliance. She stood before the portal, anticipation and anxiety mixing. After all the buildup, all the suspense, all the wondering and worry, she was going to finally find out. She was going to see behind the veil.

She took a deep breath and stepped into the tunnel.

As before, something pulled her forward, sucking her through the doorway, into the swirling, molten glow.

There was a moment of confusion. A feeling of falling, plummeting, and then a cushioning, a resistance. The air turned thick and clear, a glassy blue-green. Filtered rays of faraway light cut through the air, winking in and out.

This isn't so bad, she thought.

Her arm sliced through the air in front of her, waving languidly before her eyes and she realized she was floating.

I'm floating, she thought with amazement and the thought seemed to come from far away, traveling with slow and ponderous weight. Then thoughts came rushing in, punching through the fog.

Water.
This is water.
I'm in the water.
I'm drowning.
Drowning!

There was pain now, an icy, knifing pain, in her chest as she gulped in lungfuls of the beautiful, green-blue world. There was a sucking, howling, roaring sound — the noise of a subway train rushing into a station, a jet plane taking off, a thunderous crowd cheering the winning touchdown. It was the blood pounding in her ears. Her chest and head were going to explode.

She was kicking, flailing, splashing, twisting, trying to break free.

She wanted to pull back, to pull out of the tunnel and retreat to the safety of Jonah and the hotel, but there was no turning back now. She forced herself forward, throwing herself into the pain, willing it all to be over as quickly as possible. The terror of dying overwhelmed her, the wild shrieking commands of her mind tumbling over each other in a tangled confusion, a massive knotted jumble that circled in on itself, never reaching her body. Unaware of the orders to kick, push, swim, head for the surface, her body relaxed, the tension melting away, and miraculously, the noise and pain faded.

Now, all was quiet and still.

She could still see her arm floating in front of her.

That's my arm, she thought, and the thought seemed to drift alone in a vast, empty expanse. Somewhere inside a warm calm flowed through her. Then there were no other thoughts. Her mind was empty. Her arm no longer moved with purpose. It swayed gently, moved by the current. Her heart relaxed. The frantic pounding subsided, and then it stopped altogether. There was only calm now, silent and thick.

Now it was as if she was looking at her arm from a long way away, and now as if through the wrong end of a telescope, as the world shrank and narrowed to a quarter-sized circle of light—soft and gentle, warm and comforting, blue-green fading to black.

Then she saw it: a beautiful white glow in the far distance, welcoming and warm, beckoning her forward, guiding her home, to the place where all things were possible. Lakes of fire and three-headed dogs. Women on winged horses. Sun-bathed fields of wheat and wildflowers. Robes and harps. Her family. Her dog. Everything that ever was and everything that ever would be. Everything she had lost and everything she had gained.

Even forgiveness for her mistakes.

The pain and fear evaporated, replaced by certainty and hope.

She let go and entered the light.

EXTRAS

HEREAFTER Discussion Guide

1. Some readers have expressed a desire to know more about Jonah's background and to have a better understanding of his perspective in the story. How might the story be different if it had been told from his perspective, rather than Irene's?

2. Irene is not generally considered a sympathetic character. What makes her unsympathetic? In what ways might she have been depicted more sympathetically? How would that have changed the story?

3. Does Irene's reaction to being dead seem realistic? How do you think you would react in the same situation? What would it take to convince you that you were really dead? Do you agree with Irene's decision to cross over? Why? Which option would you choose — stay on earth as a ghost or cross over — if faced with the same choice?

4. Mrs. Boine and Amy are two very different people but both choose to remain on earth as a ghost. What is each woman's motivation for staying? In what ways are their motivations similar? In what ways are they different? Do you think their stated reason for staying is the real reason or is there something else behind each woman's decision? What about Scalper and Ernest? Why do they stay, and is each man's stated reason for staying the real reason?

5. How does Irene react to Ernest's declaration of love? Why do you think she reacts this way? Do you think Ernest is really in love with her? Do you think Irene believes he is? How does this understanding color your belief about why Irene reacts the way she does?

6. Overall, did you feel that *Hereafter* was a hopeful or a bleak story? Did it have a "happy" ending? Why or why not? What about *Hereafter*'s version of the afterlife—was that hopeful or bleak?

7. In what ways, if any, did *Hereafter*'s version of the afterlife match your own beliefs? In what ways did it differ? What did you find to be the most surprising about the version of the afterlife depicted in Hereafter? Were there any myths/beliefs that you were missing/not included?

8. Did you have any favorite quotes or scenes from the story? What made that quote or passage stand out to you?

9. Many reviewers have called *Hereafter* an uncomfortable read. What do you think they mean by this? Do you agree? In what way did the story make you uncomfortable? Did the story challenge any of your assumptions or change any of your views?

10. *Hereafter* is the first book in a series. What do you think will happen to the characters next? What do you wish would happen to the characters? How would you like to see the series progress? What, for you, would be a "happy" ending, given that Irene is dead?

Learn More About the Author

Keep up to date with all the latest news and sign up to be notified of new releases in the Afterlife Series at:

Website/Blog:
http://www.terribruce.net

Twitter:
http://www.twitter.com/@_TerriBruce

THEREAFTER (Afterlife #2)

When recently-deceased Irene Dunphy decided to "follow the light," she thought she'd end up in Heaven or Hell and her journey would be over.

Boy, was she wrong.

She soon finds that "the other side" isn't a final destination but a kind of purgatory where billions of spirits are stuck, with no way to move forward or back. Even worse, deranged phantoms known as "Hungry Ghosts" stalk the dead, intent on destroying them. The only way out is for Irene to forget her life on earth — including the boy who risked everything to help her cross over — which she's not about to do.

As Irene desperately searches for an alternative, help unexpectedly comes in the unlikeliest of forms: a twelfth-century Spanish knight and a nineteenth-century American cowboy. Even more surprising, one offers a chance for redemption; the other, love. Unfortunately, she won't be able to have either if she can't find a way to escape the hellish limbo where they're all trapped.

Coming May 1, 2014

6/15

31392057R00223

Made in the USA
Charleston, SC
15 July 2014